Natsume Sōseki, one of Japan's most distinguished writers, was born in Tokyo in 1867. At an early age he studied the Chinese classics, and later intended to become an architect. He changed his mind, however, and entered Tokyo Imperial University to take up literature. In 1900 he was sent to London by the Japanese Ministry of Education to study English literature for two years. He was not happy there, and returned to Japan in 1903 to succeed Lafcadio Hearn as lecturer in English at his old university. After publishing his first novel, *I Am a Cat* in 1905, Sōseki immediately rose to fame, and shortly after this he resigned his teaching post to become literary editor of the *Asahi Shimbun.* Many more novels followed, and Sōseki became the leading voice of the age, often ruthlessly criticizing his contemporary society for its acceptance of westernization. He died in 1916 at the age of forty-nine.

And Then

Natsume Sōseki's novel
SOREKARA

Translated from the Japanese
With an Afterword and Selected Bibliography
by Norma Moore Field

Charles E. Tuttle Company
RUTLAND · VERMONT TOKYO · JAPAN

Published by the Charles E. Tuttle Company, Inc., of
Rutland, Vermont and Tokyo, Japan with editorial offices at
Suido 1-chome, 2-6, Bunkyo-ku, Tokyo, Japan by special
arrangement with Louisiana State University Press.

UNESCO COLLECTION OF REPRESENTATIVE WORKS
JAPANESE SERIES

This book has been accepted in the Japanese Literature
Translation Series of the United Nations Educational,
Scientific, and Cultural Organization (UNESCO).

International Standard Book No. 0-8048-1537-2

First Tuttle edition, 1988

Printed in Japan

I would like to dedicate
this translation to
my mother and my grandmother.

And Then

To my respected professor
James Kulas
who loves animals
and loved by them

Feb. 1988.

Hitoshi Nakata

Note: Japanese names throughout this book are given in Japanese order, that is, surname followed by given name.

Chapter I

AS HURRIED FOOTSTEPS clattered past the gate, a pair of large clogs hung suspended from the sky. When the footsteps grew distant, the clogs slipped quietly away and vanished. Daisuke awoke.

Turning to the head of his bed, he noticed a single camellia blossom that had fallen to the floor. He was certain he had heard it drop during the night; the sound had resounded in his ears like a rubber ball bounced off the ceiling. Although he thought this might be explained by the silence of the night, just to make sure that all was well with him, he had placed his right hand over his heart. Then, feeling the blood pulsating correctly at the edge of his ribs, he had fallen asleep.

For some time, he gazed vacantly at the color of the large blossom, which was nearly as large as a baby's head. Then, as if he had just thought of it, he put his hand to his heart and once again began to study its beat. It had become a habit with him lately to listen to his heart's pulsation while lying in bed. As usual, the palpitation was calm and steady. With his hand still on his chest, he tried to imagine the warm, crimson blood flowing leisurely to this beat. This was life, he thought. Now, at this very moment, he held in his grasp the current of life as it flowed by. To his palm it felt like the ticking of a clock. But it was more, it was a kind of alarm that summoned him to death. If it were possible to live without hearing this bell—if only his heart did not measure out time as well as blood—then how carefree he would be! How thoroughly he would savor life! But—and here Daisuke shuddered involuntarily. He was a man so attached to life that he could scarcely bear to picture his heart calmly beating to the coursing of his blood. There were times when, lying in bed, he would place his hand just below his left breast and wonder, what if someone gave me one good blow with a hammer here. Although he lived in sound health, there were instances when his consciousness awakened to the indisputable fact of his being alive as a near-miracle of good fortune.

Lifting his hand from his heart, he picked up the newspaper beside his pillow. He reached from beneath the covers and with both hands spread out the paper. On the left was a picture of a man stabbing a woman. He quickly averted his gaze and turned to another page where the school dispute was written up in large print. Daisuke read the article for a while but soon let the paper slip from languid hands onto the covers. Drawing on a cigarette, he slid himself about six inches from the bed, picked up the camellia from the floor mat, and turning it over, drew it to the tip of his nose. His mouth, mustache, and nose were all but hidden in the flower. The smoke, mingling with the petals and stamens, curled out thickly. Then placing the flower on the white sheet, he got up and went to the bathroom.

He carefully brushed his teeth, taking pleasure, as always, in their regularity. He stripped and scrubbed his chest and back. There was a deep, fine luster to his skin. Whenever he moved his shoulders or lifted his arms, his flesh exuded a thin layer of oil, as if it had been massaged with balm that was then carefully wiped away. This, too, gave him satisfaction. Next, he parted his black hair, which, even without oil, was perfectly manageable. Like his hair, his mustache was fine and gave him an air of youthful freshness, elegantly defining the area above his mouth. Stroking his full cheeks two or three times with both hands, Daisuke peered into the mirror. His motions were precisely those of a woman powdering her face. And in fact, he took such pride in his body that had there been the need, he would not have hesitated to powder his face. More than anything he disliked the shriveled body and wizened features of a Buddhist holy man, and whenever he turned to the mirror, he was thankful that at least he had not been born with such a face. If people called him a dandy, he was not in the least disturbed. To this extent had he moved beyond the old Japan.

Some thirty minutes later he sat at the table. As he sipped his tea and buttered his toast, Kadono, the houseboy, brought in the newspapers, placing them, neatly folded, beside the cushion and beginning loudly, "It's really something, isn't it, Sensei, this business!" This houseboy always used the respectful term *Sensei** in addressing Daisuke. At first, Daisuke had protested with a wry smile, but Kadono had always answered, oh, yes, yes, but Sensei—and so Daisuke had been forced to leave the matter as it was; eventually, it had become a custom so that now, with Kadono alone, Daisuke felt no qualms about passing off as Sensei. It was only when he began to keep a houseboy that Daisuke realized there were no other appropriate forms of address to use toward a master like himself.

"I suppose you mean the school dispute?" Daisuke calmly continued to eat his toast.

"Well, don't you think it's awfully exciting?"

"You mean, trying to get rid of the principal?"

"Yes, that's it. He's going to have to resign." Kadono was gleeful.

"Do you stand to gain in any way if the principal resigns?"

"Oh, come on, Sensei, you shouldn't joke like that. A fellow doesn't get excited over something just because he might gain or lose."

Daisuke continued to eat. "Do they want to get rid of the principal because they really hate him, or is there a question of profit involved—do you know?"

---

* The title *Sensei* is generally applied to teachers of every variety and to doctors. It is also used for those who have in other ways gained distinction, for example, artists, critics,,or politicians.

"No, I don't know about that. How about you, Sensei, do you know?"

"No, I don't know either. I don't know, but there's no chance that people today would stir up all that trouble if they didn't think they were going to get something out of it. They're just making excuses."

"Is that right?" Kadono's face showed some concern. With this, Daisuke abruptly put an end to the conversation. Kadono could understand no more. Beyond a certain level, no matter what anyone said, Kadono would unabashedly cling to his favorite "Is that right?" It was impossible to tell whether one's words had registered with him or not. It was precisely this uncertainty, and the consequent absence of any need to stimulate the youth, that appealed to Daisuke and led him to keep Kadono as a houseboy. He neither went to school nor studied, but spent all his time loafing. Why not try his hand at a foreign language, Daisuke might ask. Kadono invariably answered, do you think so? or, is that right? Never would he actually say that he would try it; being as lazy as he was, he was incapable of giving a more definite reply. Daisuke, for his part, having better things to do than educate Kadono, had let the matter drop at a suitable point. Fortunately, Kadono's body, unlike his mind, functioned well, and Daisuke fully appreciated this point. Not only Daisuke, but also his old housekeeper was finding things much easier these days. Consequently, the old woman and the houseboy got along exceedingly well. They talked a great deal in the absence of their master.

"I wonder what on earth Sensei plans to do, eh, Auntie?"

"When you get as far as he has, you can do anything. No need to worry."

"I'm not worrying. It just seems like he ought to do something."

"Well, he's probably planning to find a bride first and then to take his time looking for a position."

"That's not a bad idea. I sure wish I could spend my days reading books and going to concerts like that."

"You?"

"Well, I don't care if I read or not. I just wish I could play around like that."

"You know all those things were decided in your previous life. Nothing you can do about it."

"Is that the way it is."

This was how their conversations ran. Two weeks before Kadono joined Daisuke's household, the following exchange took place between the young bachelor master and the idle youth:

"Are you going anywhere to school right now?"

"I was for a while. But I'm not any more."

"Where did you used to go?"

"Well, I went to all kinds of places. But I seemed to get tired of them right away."

"You mean you get fed up easily?"

"Well, yes, I guess that's it."

"So you don't have plans to do much in the way of studying?"

"No, not really. Besides, things aren't too good at home these days."

"The old woman at my place says she knows your mother?"

"Yes, she used to live right near here."

"Then, your mother doesn't . . . ?"

"That's right, she doesn't have much of a job either. She just takes in odd jobs to do at home. But business is bad everywhere these days, and things don't seem to be going too well."

"Don't *seem* to be going well? But don't you live in the same house?"

"Well, yes, we live together, but I've never really bothered to ask how she's doing. It's too much trouble. It seems like she's always complaining."

"How about your older brother?"

"He works at the post office."

"Is that all in your family?"

"I have a younger brother, too. He's at the bank—you might say he's a step above messenger boy."

"Then you're the only one who's sitting around, right?"

"Yes, I guess that's right."

"And what do you do when you're home?"

"Well, most of the time, I guess I sleep. Other times, I go out for walks."

"Isn't it a little embarrassing to sit around when everyone else is out earning money?"

"No, not really."

"Your family must get along extremely well."

"Strangely enough we never seem to fight much."

"I should think your mother and older brother would want you to get out on your own as soon as possible."

"You might have a point there."

"You seem to have an extraordinarily easygoing temperament. Is that how you really are?"

"Well, I don't see why I should lie about things."

"So you're a completely carefree sort?"

"Yes, I guess that's what you'd call me."

"How old is your older brother?"

"Hm . . . he must be going on twenty-six."

"Then he'll probably be looking for a wife, isn't that right? Do you plan to stay on like this even after he gets married?"

"I'll have to wait and see. When the time comes, I'm sure something will happen."

"You don't have any other relations?"

"There's an aunt. This one runs a freight business in Yokohama."

"Your aunt does?"

"Oh, it's not really my aunt who runs it; I guess it's my uncle."

"Couldn't you get them to give you a job? The freight business must need a lot of people."

"Well, I'm basically lazy, so I think they'd probably say no."

"It doesn't help if you look at yourself like that. You see, the point is, your mother has asked the old woman at my place if we could find something for you to do there."

"Yes, I've heard something like that."

"And how do you feel about it?"

"Well, yes, I'm planning on not being too lazy. . . ."

"You mean you'd rather come to my place?"

"Well, yes, that's right."

"But it won't do if you're just going to sleep and take walks."

"Oh, you don't have to worry about that. I'm strong at least. I'll fill the bathtub and things like that."

"We have running water so you won't need to carry water to the tub."

"Then maybe I can do the cleaning."

Such were the conditions under which Kadono became houseboy to Daisuke.

Daisuke finally finished his meal and began to smoke. Kadono, who had been sitting with his back propped up against the cupboard, his arms around his knees, decided enough time had passed for him to try another question. "Sensei, how's your heart this morning?" He had learned of Daisuke's habit a few days earlier, and his tone was slightly bantering.

"So far it's all right."

"You make it sound as if it might be in danger tomorrow. The way you worry over your body, Sensei, you're going to end up really sick someday."

"I am sick already."

Kadono only said "Oh," and stared at Daisuke's healthy complexion and the ample flesh about his shoulders, visible even through his clothes. After such conversations Daisuke invariably felt sorry for this youth. He could only think that Kadono's skull was crammed with the brains of a cow, for he could follow but half a block down the avenue of conversation that ordinary people walked. On the rare occasions when Daisuke so much as turned a corner, he was immediately lost. And of course, he could never set foot on even the bottom rung of a ladder upon which the foundations of logic were vertically laid. As for his sensitivity, it was a sorrier case still. He gave the impression that his nervous system was a network of coarse straw. Observing the state of Kadono's existence, Daisuke wondered to what end the youth ventured to breathe and subsist. But Kadono idled away unconcerned. Not only was he unconcerned, he tacitly understood that this very idling conferred upon him a claim to kinship with Daisuke and he was apt to behave more than a little triumphantly. Moreover, playing up his body's dogged strength, he would close in on the sensitive points of his master's high-strung nature. Daisuke, in turn, regarded his own nerves as the tax he had to pay for his uniquely keen speculative powers and acute sensibilities. It was the anguish that echoed from the achievement of a lofty education; it was the unwritten punishment dealt to natural aristocrats, those designated by heaven. It was precisely by submitting to these sacrifices that he had been able to become what he was. Indeed, there were times when he recognized the very meaning of life in these sacrifices. Kadono could not begin to understand this.

"Kadono, wasn't there any mail?"

"Mail? Oh yes. A postcard and a letter. I left them on your desk. Shall I get them?"

"I suppose I could go over there."

Given this uncertain response, Kadono got up and brought the postcard and letter. On the postcard was scribbled in light ink this exceedingly simple message: "Arrived in Tokyo yesterday; put up at above inn; would like to see you tomorrow morning." On the front, the names of an inn at Urajimbōchō and of the sender, Hiraoka Tsunejirō, had been dashed off as carelessly as the message.

"So he's here already. He must have come in yesterday," Daisuke murmured as if to himself as he picked up the envelope, which was addressed in his father's hand. His father first announced that he had returned two or three days before, that there was no particular hurry but that there were many things he wished to discuss and Daisuke was to come as soon as this letter reached him. Then the letter turned to such desultory matters as how it had been too early for the cherry blossoms in Kyoto, how crowded and uncomfortable the express train had been, etc., etc. Folding up the letter, Daisuke compared the two pieces of mail with a peculiar expression on his face. He then summoned Kadono.

"Kadono, will you go make a phone call? To my house."

"Yes, to your house. What should I say?"

"That I have an engagement today—I'm supposed to see someone so I can't come. I'll come tomorrow or the day after."

"I see. To whom?"

"The old man's come back from a trip and says he wants to talk to me. But you don't have to get him on the phone. Just give the message to whoever answers."

"Yes, I will."

Kadono went out noisily. Daisuke left the morning room and went through the living room to his study. He noticed that it had been nicely cleaned; the fallen camellia had been swept away. He went over to the bookshelves at the right of the vase and lifted a heavy photograph album from the top. Still standing, he undid the gold clasp and began flipping the pages until he came to the middle, where he suddenly rested his hand. There was a portrait of a woman about twenty years old. Daisuke gazed intently at her face.

DAISUKE WAS THINKING
of changing and going to Hiraoka's inn when Hiraoka made a
timely appearance. He casually rode the ricksha right up to
the gate. The voice that cried "Here it is, here it is," ordering
the driver to lower the shaft, had not changed in the three
years since the two had parted. No sooner had he seen the old
woman who met him at the door than he was explaining that
he had forgotten his wallet at the inn, that he needed to borrow some change; this, too, was the Hiraoka of their school
days. Daisuke went running to the door and all but dragged
his old friend in.

"How are things? Come in and relax."

"Oh, I see you've got chairs," Hiraoka observed and threw
his body heavily into the easy chair. To judge from the way he
handled himself, he set not a penny's value on his rather ample flesh. He leaned his shaven head against the back of the
chair and looked around the room for a moment.

"Not a bad house. Better than I expected," he praised.

Without answering, Daisuke opened a cigarette case. "So,
how have things been?"

"How? Why, you know—I'll tell you all about it by and
by."

"You used to write a lot, so I could tell how things were.
But lately you haven't written at all."

"I must owe letters to everyone I know." Hiraoka abruptly
removed his glasses and, pulling out a wrinkled handkerchief
from his breastpocket, began to wipe them, blinking rapidly

all the while. He had been nearsighted since their student days. Daisuke watched him intently.

"But how about you, how have you been?" he asked, pulling the slender bows over his ears and holding them there with his hands.

"There's nothing new with me."

"That's the way it should be. There's been too much new with me." Hiraoka knitted his brows and began to stare at the garden. Suddenly, in an altered tone, he said, "Look, there's a cherry tree over there. It's just begun to bloom, hasn't it. The climate's so different here."

The conversation had lost its touch of intimacy. Daisuke answered without interest, "It must be pretty warm over there."

With unexpected, almost excessive vigor, Hiraoka came back, "Yes, it's quite warm." It was as if he had been startled into a sudden awareness of his own presence. Daisuke looked at his face once more. Hiraoka lit a cigarette. The old woman finally appeared with the tea, putting a tray on the table and apologizing all the while that it had taken so long because she had put cold water into the kettle. While she chattered the two stared at the red sandalwood tray; then seeing that they ignored her, the old woman gave a little self-conscious laugh and left the room.

"What's that?"

"The maid I hired. I've got to eat, after all."

"Gracious, isn't she."

Daisuke curled his rosy lips and laughed depreciatingly. "She's never served in a place like this before; it can't be helped."

"Why didn't you bring someone over from home? There must be a good many of them there."

"Yes, but they're all young," answered Daisuke seriously.

At this, Hiraoka laughed heartily for the first time. "Why, so much the better if they're young!"

"Anyway, it's not good to have somebody from home."

"Is there anyone besides that old woman?"

"There's the houseboy."

Kadono had come back and was talking with the old woman in the kitchen.

"Is that all?"

"That's all. Why?"

"You haven't got a wife yet?"

The hint of a blush crossed Daisuke's face, but he quickly resumed his normal, nondescript manner: "You know I would have let you know if I'd gotten married. But how about you . . ." and he stopped abruptly.

Daisuke and Hiraoka had know each other since middle school. At one time they had been almost like brothers, especially during the year following their graduation. In those days their greatest pleasure had been to confide in each other absolutely and to offer each other words of encouragement. On more than a few occasions these words had been translated into action; hence, they firmly believed that the words they exchanged, far from being a mere source of pleasure, always held the possibility of some sort of sacrifice. As soon as one sacrificed, his pleasure immediately turned into anguish: but of this simple truth they went unaware.

At the end of that year Hiraoka got married and was transferred to a Kansai branch of the bank for which he worked. On the day of their departure Daisuke went to Shimbashi Station to see the young couple off. Clasping Hiraoka's hand, he cheerfully urged him to come back soon. Hiraoka said it couldn't be helped, that he had to put in his time. The words were tossed out carelessly, but from behind his glasses there gleamed an almost enviable pride. When he saw this, Daisuke suddenly found his friend odious. He went home and shut himself in his study and spent the rest of the day brooding. He was to have taken his sister-in-law to a concert, but he canceled the engagement, causing her not a little anxiety.

Hiraoka wrote regularly: a postcard announcing his safe arrival, news of setting up a household, and, when that was over, accounts of his job and hopes for the future. Daisuke responded conscientiously to each letter. Curiously enough, each time he wrote he experienced a certain uneasiness. At times, when he no longer wished to put up with the discomfort, he stopped in the middle. Only when Hiraoka expressed some gratitude for what Daisuke had done in the past did his brush flow easily, allowing him to compose a relatively fluent response.

In time, however, these exchanges became less frequent, dwindling from once a month to once every two, even three months, until finally, Daisuke did not write at all and began to feel apprehensive about that. Sometimes, just to rid himself of this tension, he moistened an envelope. But after six months had passed in this way, his mind and heart appeared to have undergone a change, so that it no longer mattered whether he wrote to Hiraoka or not. In fact, after establishing his own household he let a year go by before bothering to send his new address, and then he wrote only because it was the season for New Year's cards.

Nevertheless, for certain reasons, Daisuke was unable to forget Hiraoka. He remembered him from time to time and occasionally tried to imagine how he might be getting along. But he never went so far as to inquire after him, feeling neither the courage nor the urgency to worry to that extent. In any event, he had let the time slip by until suddenly, two weeks ago, he had received a letter from Hiraoka. In the letter, Hiraoka announced his intention of leaving the branch office soon and returning to Tokyo. He did not, however, want Daisuke to think of the move as one ordered by the office, implying promotion. He had other plans; he had decided to change jobs, and upon his arrival in Tokyo he might have need of Daisuke's good offices. It was unclear whether the last remark was intended in earnest or simply added as a matter of form, but it was apparent that some drastic change of fortune had befallen Hiraoka. When he realized this, Daisuke was startled.

Therefore, he was anxious to hear all the details as soon as he saw Hiraoka; unfortunately, their conversation, once derailed, obstinately refused to return. If Daisuke seized an opportune moment and raised the topic himself, Hiraoka would parry, saying he would talk about it at length some day; the talk went nowhere. Daisuke finally suggested, "It's been so long since we've seen each other. Why don't we get something to eat?" But Hiraoka still persisted with his "one of these days, when there's more time," until Daisuke simply dragged him to a Western-style restaurant nearby.

There, the two of them drank a good deal. When they agreed that as far as eating and drinking went they were the same as ever, the ice was broken at last. Daisuke began an animated account of an Easter celebration he had seen two or three days before at St. Nicholas'. The festival had begun at midnight, when all the world was asleep. After circling a long corridor the worshipers entered the sanctuary and were greeted with thousands of lighted candles. A procession of robed priests passed on the other side, their black shadows looming against the stark walls. Hiraoka listened with his cheeks resting on his palms, his eyelids red behind his glasses. That night, around two o'clock, Daisuke had walked alone along the wide avenue of Ōnari, over the tracks that ran straight through the midnight darkness until he arrived at the Ueno woods. There, he stepped into the midst of cherry blossoms lit by street lights.

"It's nice, you know, cherry blossoms at night without a soul around," he said.

Hiraoka emptied his glass without a word. Then he spoke, with a touch of pity. "It must be nice, though I've never seen it myself. As long as you can go around doing things like that, you're pretty lucky. Once you get out into the world, it's not so easy anymore." Hiraoka seemed to be looking down from above at his friend's inexperience. But for Daisuke it was not so much the content of the response, but the tone that was absurd. As far as he was concerned, that Easter night counted far more than any practical, worldly experience. So he answered, "I think there's nothing more worthless than this so-called worldly experience. All it can do is cause pain."

Hiraoka widened his drunken eyes just perceptibly. "It sounds like your thinking's changed quite a bit. . . . Wasn't it your idea that this pain becomes a good, if bitter medicine later on?"

"That's just a theory I had when I was young and stupid. I gave in to all those conventional proverbs and spouted off nonsense. I don't know how long ago I tossed that one out."

"But you're going to have to get out into the world soon, right? You won't get away with that kind of thinking then."

"I've been out in the world for some time now. It seems to me that especially since we went our separate ways, my world has grown much bigger. It's just a different kind of world from the one you went into."

"Oh, go ahead and brag. You'll have to give in sooner or later."

"Of course, if I find that I'm starving I'll give in right away. But why should a person who doesn't have any wants at the moment strain to taste these inferior experiences? It would be like an Indian buying an overcoat just to be ready for winter."

For an instant displeasure flickered at Hiraoka's brow. Gazing ahead with his reddened eyes, he puffed at his cigarette. Daisuke, thinking that he might have gone too far, resumed in a more measured tone: "There's a fellow I know who doesn't know the first thing about music. He's a schoolteacher, and he can't make it teaching at just one place so he moonlights at three, maybe four other places. You can't help feeling sorry for him. All he does is prepare a lesson, dash off to the classroom, then move his mouth mechanically. He doesn't have time for anything else. When Sunday comes around, he calls it a day of rest and sleeps the whole day away. So, even if there's a concert somewhere or a famous musician from abroad performs here, he can't go. In other words, he's going to die without ever having set foot in the beautiful world of music. For me, there's no inexperience more wretched than that. Experience that's tied to bread might be sincere, but it's bound to be inferior. If you don't have the kind of luxurious experience that's divorced from bread and water, there's no point in being human. You're probably thinking that I'm still a child, but in the luxurious world where I live, I'm your senior by years."

Tapping the ashes from his cigarette, Hiraoka said in a low, dark voice, "It's fine if you can stay in that kind of world forever." His heavy words seemed to drag behind them a curse upon plenty.

The two went outside, drunk. Because of the strange argument they had begun under the impetus of alcohol, they had gotten nowhere with the real business at hand—that is, Hiraoka's situation.

"Let's walk a little," Daisuke suggested. Hiraoka was apparently not as busy as he claimed, for with a few half-hearted protests, he strolled along with Daisuke. Daisuke tried to direct their steps toward the quiet side streets where they might talk more readily, and eventually, the conversation came around.

According to Hiraoka's account, he had tried working quite hard when he was first transferred. He had done considerable research on the economic conditions of the region in order to learn his new job well. In fact, he had even thought of doing—if given permission—a theoretical study of actual business practices. But his position was not high enough, and he had had to put away his plans and await a future opportu-

nity. Even so, he had tried presenting a number of suggestions to the branch manager, though they had always met
with cold indifference. If he so much as mentioned any sophisticated theory, the manager became peevish. His attitude
seemed to be, what could a greenhorn like Hiraoka possibly
understand? But the manager himself knew nothing. As Hiraoka saw it, his superior was unwilling to deal with him not
because he, Hiraoka, was unworthy, but because the manager was afraid. And this was the source of Hiraoka's cha-
grin. More than once they had verged on a clash.

As time passed, however, Hiraoka's annoyance began to
fade, and he increasingly felt comfortable in his surroundings. He made an effort to feel that way, and accordingly, the
branch manager's attitude toward him changed bit by bit.
There were even times when he took the initiative to ask Hiraoka's opinion. And since Hiraoka was no longer fresh out of
the university, he was careful to avoid complex issues that
would be incomprehensible, hence awkward, for the manager.

"But it's not as if I went out of my way to flatter him or
manipulate him," Hiraoka emphasized.

Daisuke answered solemnly, "No, of course not."

The branch manager began to show concern for Hiraoka's
future. He even promised, half jokingly, that since it was his
turn to return to the main office, Hiraoka should go with
him. By that time Hiraoka was quite experienced and had
gained considerable trust; his social circles had widened, and
he no longer had time for study. At that point, he had begun
to feel that study would only get in the way of practice anyway.

Just as the branch manager confided everything to him, so
Hiraoka had trusted in a subordinate named Seki and con-
sulted him on various matters. This Seki became involved
with a geisha and ended up embezzling company funds. When
this was exposed, there was no question of Seki's dismissal,
of course, but due to circumstances, it seemed that even the

manager might be placed in an awkward situation. Hiraoka had shouldered the responsibility and submitted his resignation.

This was the gist of Hiraoka's story. Daisuke thought that Hiraoka might have been urged by the manager to tender his resignation, to judge from his last words, "The higher you get in a company, the more you can get away with. If you think about it, it's really too bad that a fellow like Seki had to get fired for embezzling a piddling sum like that."

"So the branch manager's got the best deal of all?" Daisuke asked.

"I guess you could look at it that way." Hiraoka's response was slurred.

"What happened to the money that fellow took?"

"Oh, it didn't amount to much, so I paid it off."

"I'm surprised you had it. It looks as if you were getting a pretty good deal too."

Hiraoka's face turned bitter, and he darted a sharp glance at Daisuke. "Even if I was, it's all gone. Now I'm having a tough time just making ends meet. I borrowed that money."

"Oh." Daisuke's response was calm. He was a man who did not lose his normal tone of voice under any circumstances. And from this tone, subdued but no less apparent, there emerged a note of leisure.

"I borrowed from the manager to cover up that hole."

"I wonder why he didn't lend to this fellow Seki himself."

Hiraoka did not answer and Daisuke did not press the issue. The two walked on in silence.

Daisuke guessed that Hiraoka had not told all, but he knew he did not have the right to take another step forward in pursuit of the truth. Furthermore, he was too much an urbanite to have his curiosity aroused over something like this. Daisuke, who lived in twentieth-century Japan, Daisuke, who had barely reached the age of thirty, had already arrived at the province of *nil admirari*. His thinking was hardly so unsophisticated as to be shocked by an encounter with the darker side of man. His senses were hardly so wearied as to take pleasure in sniffing at the hackneyed secrets Hiraoka might harbor. Or, from another angle, one might say they were so fatigued that stimuli many times more pleasurable could not have satisfied them.

Thus had Daisuke evolved in his private, distinctive world, which bore almost no resemblance to Hiraoka's. (It is a regrettable phenomenon that behind every evolution, past and present, lies regression.) But Hiraoka knew nothing of Diasuke's development. He seemed to regard him as the same naïve youth of three years ago. If he were to bare his soul before this little master and confide to him all his weaknesses, it might be like a farmhand's tossing horse manure before the startled young lady of the house. Better not take such a risk and incur Daisuke's displeasure—this was how Daisuke read Hiraoka's thoughts. It seemed to him stupid that Hiraoka walked along without answering him. To the extent that Hiraoka regarded him as a child—perhaps even more so— Daisuke had begun to view Hiraoka in the same light. But when the two resumed their conversation some two or three blocks later, not a trace of this feeling showed.

"So, what are you planning to do from now on?"

"Well . . ."

"Maybe, with all the experience you've built up, it would be best to stay in the same business?"

"Well, that would depend on the circumstances. Actually, I've been meaning to talk it over with you. What do you think, is there a chance I could get something in your brother's company?"

"I'll ask him about it; I have to go home anyway in the next two or three days. But I wonder . . ."

"If there isn't anything in business, I'm thinking of trying the newspapers."

"That might not be bad either."

The two walked toward the streetcar stop. Hiraoka, who had been watching the top of the train approaching in the distance, suddenly announced that he was going to take it. Daisuke assented without attempting to detain him, but neither did he make any move to part. He walked on to the red pole marking the stop. There he asked, "How's Michiyo-san?"

"She's the same as ever, thanks. She sends her regards. I was going to bring her today, but the train ride must not have agreed with her; she was complaining of a headache so I left her at the inn."

The streetcar came to a halt before the two. Hiraoka started to hurry toward it, but stopped at Daisuke's warning. It was not his train.

"That was a shame about the baby."

"Yes, it was too bad. Thanks for your card. It might as well not have been born if it was going to die."

"And—since then?"

"No, nothing yet. There's probably no chance now. Her health isn't too good."

"Well, when you're moving around like this, it's probably easier not to have a kid."

"That's true, too. Maybe if I were single like you, it'd be even better—more relaxed."

"Well, why not become single?"

"Don't kid me. Anyway, my wife keeps wondering if you've gotten married yet."

The streetcar arrived.

Chapter III

DAISUKE'S FATHER, NAGAI TOKU, was old enough to have seen the battlefield during the Restoration, but he was still in robust health. After quitting the civil service he had entered the business world, and while trying his hand at this and that, money had seemed to accumulate naturally, until, in some fourteen or fifteen years' time, he had found himself a wealthy man.

Daisuke had an older brother named Seigo. After finishing school, he had gone straight into a company with which his father had ties, so that by now he held a position of considerable authority. He had a wife, Umeko, and two children. The older of these was a boy, Seitarō, now fifteen years of age. The girl, Nui, was three years younger.

Besides Seigo, there was an older sister, but she had married a diplomat and they now made their home in the West. There had been another brother between Seigo and this sister, and still another between her and Daisuke, but both of them had died young. Their mother was dead as well.

Such was the composition of Daisuke's family. The married sister and Daisuke, who had recently set up his own household, were gone, so that left five people, including the children, in the main house.

Once a month without fail, Daisuke went home for money. He lived on money that could be specified neither as his father's nor his brother's. When bored, he went more frequently. He would tease the children, play a game of go with the houseboy, or engage his sister-in-law in theater talk.

Daisuke was fond of his sister-in-law. Hers was a character in which Tempō mannerism and Meiji modernism were ruthlessly patched together. Once she had gone to the trouble of ordering an inordinately expensive piece of brocade with an unpronounceable name through her sister in France. She had cut it up with four or five other people to fashion into obi. Later, when it was discovered that the material had been exported from Japan, the family had a good laugh. It was Daisuke who had investigated the matter by checking the display cases of Mitsukoshi. Umeko also liked Western music and was easily persuaded to accompany Daisuke to his concerts. At the same time, she showed an unusual interest in fortune-telling, idolizing Sekiryūshi and a certain master Ojima. On two or three occasions Daisuke had tagged along in a ricksha to keep her company on her visits to these fortunetellers.

These days, Seitarō was completely absorbed in baseball and sometimes Daisuke would toss him a few pitches. He was a child with a peculiar ambition: every year, at the beginning of the summer when all the hot-potato venders converted into ice parlors, Seitarō liked to be the first to run over and buy ice cream, well before the first hint of perspiration. When there was no ice cream, he contented himself with ices and still came home triumphant. Lately, he was saying that he wanted to be the first person to enter the new sumō wrestling hall as soon as it was completed. Once he asked if Daisuke knew any wrestlers.

Nui was given to answering everything with "I'm warning you, you'd better watch out." She also changed her hair ribbon several times a day. She had recently begun violin lessons, and as soon as she got home, she would practice what she had learned, producing sawlike noises. But she would never play if someone was watching. Since she shut herself up in her room and squeaked away, her parents thought she must be quite good. Daisuke was the only one who would ever peek in on her, at which times she would scold, "You'd better watch out."

Daisuke's brother was often away from the house. When he was especially busy the only meal he took at home was breakfast. The children had no idea what he did with the rest of his day and Daisuke was equally ignorant on this point. In fact, he had decided that it was preferable not to know; as long as it was unnecessary, he did not probe into his brother's outside activities.

Daisuke was enormously popular with the children, reasonably so with his sister-in-law. With his brother, he could not tell. On the rare occasions when they met, they exchanged stories about their experiences with women. They talked perfectly nonchalantly, like men of the world trading common gossip.

Daisuke's biggest headache was his father, who, in spite of his age, kept a young mistress. Daisuke had no objections to this; indeed, he was rather in favor of it, for he thought that it was only those who lacked the means who attacked the practice. His father was quite a disciplinarian. As a child, there were times when this had sorely troubled Daisuke, but now that he was an adult, he saw no reason why he should let it disturb him. No, what bothered Daisuke was that his father confused his own youth with Daisuke's. Hence, he insisted that unless Daisuke adopted the same goals with which he himself had ventured into the world long ago, it would not do. Since Daisuke had never asked what would not do, the two had not quarreled. As a child, Daisuke was possessed of a violent temper and, at eighteen or nineteen, had even come to blows with his father once or twice. But time passed and soon after he finished school, his temper had suddenly subsided. Since then, he had never once been angry. His father believed this to be the consequence of the discipline he had imparted, and he secretly prided himself.

In actuality, this so-called discipline had succeeded only in slowly cooling the warm sentiments binding father and son. At least Daisuke thought so. His father had completely reversed this interpretation. No matter what happened, they were of the same flesh and blood. The sentiment that a child felt toward a parent was endowed by heaven and could not possibly be altered by the parent's treatment of the child. There might have been some excesses, but these had occurred in the name of discipline, and their results could not touch the bond of affection between father and son: so Daisuke's father, influenced by the teachings of Confucianism, firmly believed. Convinced that the simple fact of bestowing life upon Daisuke permanently guaranteed him grateful love in the face of any unpleasantness or pain, his father had pushed his way. And in the end, he had produced a son who was coldly indifferent to him. Admittedly, his attitudes had changed considerably since Daisuke finished school. He was even surprisingly lenient in some areas. Still, this was only part of the program designed at the moment Daisuke was delivered into this world, and it could not be construed as a response to whatever inner changes the father might have perceived in his son. To this day he was completely unaware of the negative results his plan of education had yielded.

His father was enormously proud of having gone to war. Given the slightest opportunity, he was apt to dismiss the likes of Daisuke with sweeping scorn; they were useless, those fellows, because they had never fought; they had no nerve. He spoke as if "nerve" were man's most glorious attribute. Daisuke felt an unpleasant taste in his mouth every time he had to listen to such speeches. Courage might well have been an important prerequisite to survival in the barbaric days of his father's youth, when life was taken right and left, but in this civilized day and age, Daisuke regarded it as a piece of equipment primitive as the bow and arrow. Indeed, it seemed plausible to him that many qualities incompatible with courage were to be valued far above it. After his father's last lecture Daisuke had laughed about it with his sister-in-law, saying that according to their father's theory, a stone statue would have to be admired above all else.

Needless to say, Daisuke was cowardly. He could feel no shame in this. There were even occasions when he proudly styled himself a coward. Once, as a child, at his father's instigation he had gone to the cemetery in Aoyama all by himself in the middle of the night. He had withstood the eeriness of the place for one hour, then, unable to endure it any longer, had come home pale as a sheet. At the time he himself was somewhat chagrined. The next morning, when his father laughed at him, he found the old man hateful. According to his father, it had been customary for the boys of his day, as part of their training, to get up in the middle of the night and set out all alone for Sword's Peak, some two and a half miles north of the castle, where they climbed to the top and waited in a small temple to greet the sunrise. "In those days we started out with a different understanding from young people nowadays," he observed.

The old man who had uttered such words, who even now might utter them again, cut a pitiful figure in Daisuke's eyes. Daisuke disliked earthquakes. There were times when, seated quietly in his study, he could feel their approach far in the distance. Then he would begin to think that everything—the cushion beneath him, the floor, and even the main pillar— was shaking. Daisuke believed that for him, this was the natural response. People like his father were either primitives with undeveloped nervous systems or fools who persisted in deceiving themselves.

Now Daisuke sat face to face with his father. The small room had extended eaves, so that as one looked out upon the garden while seated, the edge of the eaves seemed to cut off the view. At least, the sky did not look very wide from this room. But it was a quiet room, where one could settle down.

His father was smoking cut tobacco and had drawn a long-handled brazier close to him. From time to time he tapped off the ashes and the sound echoed pleasantly in the quiet garden. Daisuke arranged four or five gold cigarette holders in the hand brazier; he had tired of blowing the smoke through his nostrils, so he sat with folded arms, studying his father's face. For all the years, there was a considerable amount of flesh left to that face. Yet the cheeks were sunken and the skin on the eyes sagged beneath the heavy brows. The hair was yellow rather than snowy white. When he addressed someone, he had a habit of distributing his glances equally between the listener's face and his knees. These eye movements made the whites flash from time to time, producing a peculiar sensation in his listener.

The old man was holding forth: "Man must not think of himself alone. There's society. There's country. Without doing a few things for others, one doesn't feel right. Take you, for instance, you can't possibly feel very good just loafing around. Of course, it would be different with an uneducated, lower-class sort, but there's no reason why a man who has received the highest education should be able to enjoy doing nothing. What one has learned becomes interesting only when applied to actual practice."

"Yes, that's right," Daisuke had been answering. Being hard pressed to respond to his father's sermons, Daisuke had made it his practice to give vague, perfunctory answers. As far as he was concerned, his father's ideas were always but half thought out. Having resolved a given question to his liking, he would launch out from that point; thus there was not an ounce of significance to what he said. Furthermore, though he might seem to be arguing for altruism as the guiding principle one minute, he would switch to the protection of self-interest the next. His words flowed abundantly, with an air of great importance, but their content was worth hardly a moment of their listener's reflection. To attack his logic at its foundations and bring it tumbling down would have been an enormously difficult task, and what was more, an impossible one; Daisuke had concluded it was preferable to leave it untouched altogether. His father, however, starting from the premise that Daisuke belonged to his solar system, assumed that it was his right to determine every inch of his son's orbit. Hence, Daisuke had no choice but to revolve politely around the sun that was his father.

"If you don't like business, that's that. Making money is surely not the only way to serve Japan. I won't object if you don't earn any money. I can understand that you wouldn't take it well if I meddled in your affairs merely for the sake of money. As far as money is concerned, I will continue to support you as I always have. I don't know how many years are left me, and I can't take it with me when I die. Your monthly allowance is no problem. So stand up and do something. Do your duty as a citizen. You're thirty now, aren't you?"

"Yes."

"It is unseemly to be idle and unemployed at thirty." Daisuke had never considered himself idle. He simply regarded himself as one of those higher beings who disposed of a large number of hours unsullied by an occupation. Whenever his father started in this vein, Daisuke felt sorry for him. The crystallization of heightened intellectual and esthetic sentiments—the fruit of all those days and months spent in meaningful pursuits—none of this would register on his father's infantile mind. Since there was nothing else to be said, Daisuke answered seriously, "Yes, it is a problem." The old man could not for a moment cease to regard Daisuke as a child, and since in fact his responses invariably had a childlike air about them, being simple and unworldly, the old man was scornful, and complained that little gentlemen were useless even when they grew up. If, on the other hand, Daisuke's tone was cool, restrained, unabashed, and totally nonchalant, he became annoyed that perhaps this son had gone beyond his reach.

"You're in good health?"

"I haven't caught a cold in the past two or three years."

"You don't seem to be on the stupid side, either. Didn't you have a fairly strong record at school?"

"Well, yes."

"Then it's a shame to play around like this. What was his name—you know, the fellow who used to come over to talk with you? I saw him two or three times myself."

"Do you mean Hiraoka?"

"That's the one, Hiraoka. Now, he didn't have much, but didn't he go somewhere right after graduation?"

"But he blundered and came back."

The old man could not suppress a sardonic smile. "Why?"

"Why? Probably because he works to eat."

The old man could not understand Daisuke's meaning. "I wonder if he didn't do something unpleasant."

"He probably does the right thing for each particular set of circumstances, but the right thing, in the end, probably turns out to be a blunder."

"Oh," was the doubtful answer. Then, changing his tone, he launched out: "When young people 'blunder,' it's because they are lacking in sincerity and devotion. I've tried a lot of things over the years, and judging from all my experiences, success is impossible without these two qualities."

"Aren't there times when one fails because of sincerity and devotion?"

"No, never."

A frame enclosing the words "Sincerity is the way of Heaven" * hung conspicuously above the old man's head. He had had it done by the former lord of his clan and prized it greatly. Daisuke hated it ardently. First of all, he disliked the hand. Secondly, the sentiment did not suit him. After the words "Sincerity is the way of Heaven," he would like to have added, "and not the way of man."

* From the Chung Yung (the Doctrine of the Mean), one of the four books compiled during the Sung dynasty (960–1279), thought to embody the heart of Confucian teaching.

Long ago, when the clan finances had deteriorated beyond repair, it was Daisuke's father who had taken the responsibility of putting things in order. He had gathered two or three merchants who had close ties with the clan lord, and removing his sword and bowing to the ground, had begged for temporary loans. Since he had no way of knowing if they could be repaid, he had honestly admitted as much, and was successful on this account. It was then that he had asked his lord to write out these words. Since then, Nagai had hung the frame in his living room and gazed at it night and day. Daisuke could not count the number of times he had been made to listen to this story.

Then, fifteen or sixteen years ago, monthly expenditures began to accumulate in the old lord's household, threatening the finances so painstakingly revived. Once again, on the basis of proven ability, Nagai was entrusted with their restoration. This time he tried heating the bath himself and discovered a discrepancy between the amount he spent on firewood and the figure indicated in the books. Beginning with a thorough investigation of this point, he dedicated his soul night and day for an entire month to this problem until finally, he arrived at the perfect technique for heating the bathtub. Since then, the old lord had lived in relative comfort.

Given this past history, and given that he had not ventured to carry his thinking one step beyond this past, Nagai continued to proclaim the twin virtues of sincerity and devotion.

"I don't know why, but it seems that you are lacking in sincerity and devotion. That won't do. That's why you can't do anything."

"I am both sincere and devoted. It's just that I can't apply these qualities to human affairs."

"And why is that?"

Daisuke was again at a loss for a reply. Sincerity and devotion were not ready-made commodities that one kept stored in the heart. Like the sparks produced by rubbing iron and stone, they were phenomena that arose from a genuine encounter between two human beings. They were not so much qualities to be possessed as they were by-products of a spiritual exchange. Hence, without the right individuals, they could not come into being.

"Father, the words of the Analects or Wang Yang-ming are like gold plate, and you've swallowed them whole. That must be why you talk the way you do."

"Gold plate?"

Daisuke was silent for a moment. "The words are still gold plate when they come out of your mouth." Although his curiosity was aroused, Nagai would not venture to grapple with this bookish, eccentric, naïve youth's epigrammatic words.

Some forty minutes later, the old man changed into street clothes and took the ricksha somewhere. Daisuke saw him to the entranceway, then returned and opened the door to the living room. This room, a recent addition to the house, was Western in style, and many of its furnishings had been executed by professionals according to Daisuke's design. Of particular interest to Daisuke was the decorative painting around the transom, the result of lengthy discussion with a certain artist acquaintance. Daisuke stood up and examined the colors unfolding like a picture scroll, and was pained to discover that they were not nearly as pleasing as the last time he had seen the painting. Disturbed, he began to scrutinize each section when suddenly, his sister-in-law entered.

"Oh, here you are," she said, adding immediately, "Have you seen my comb anywhere?" It turned out to be at the foot of the sofa. She had loaned it the day before to Nuiko, who had misplaced it. As if supporting her head in both hands, she began to thrust the comb into her hair, which was done in Western style; meanwhile, she looked up at Daisuke and teased, "Standing around, looking blank as usual."

"I got another lecture from Father."

"Again? You do get scolded a lot. How tactless of him, to

get going as soon as he's home. But you haven't been very good either. You don't do a thing your father wants you to."

"I never argue with him. I always restrain myself and listen to everything."

"That's what makes it worse. Whenever he says something, you say yes, yes, but you don't do it."

Daisuke gave a wry smile and was silent. Umeko sat down facing him. She was a slender, dark-complexioned woman with clear eyebrows and thin lips. "Come, have a seat. I'll keep you company for a while."

But Daisuke remained standing, studying his sister-in-law's appearance. "That's a funny collar you're wearing today."

"This?" Umeko drew in her chin and knit her brows, trying to see her collar. "Oh, I bought this the other day."

"It's a nice color."

"Never mind that, just sit down."

Daisuke took a seat directly opposite hers. "I'm seated."

"What did you get a scolding about today?"

"I'm not really sure. But I was a little surprised by Father's 'service to society and country.' It seems that he's been serving without a moment's rest since he was eighteen."

"That's how he's gotten where he has."

"If serving society and country earns you as much money as it has Father, I wouldn't mind doing it either."

"So why don't you get serious and start doing something? You think you can make money lying down."

"I've never yet tried to make money."

"Even if you don't try to make money, you spend it, so I don't see the difference."

"Did my brother say something?"

"Your brother was shocked by your behavior long ago; he doesn't say anything anymore."

"That's pretty stiff. But anyway, I think he's more admirable than Father."

"Why? Oh, you awful thing, trying to flatter me. That's what's wrong with you. You put on a serious face and then make fun of people."

"Is that right?"

"Is that right, indeed! As if we were talking about someone else! You ought to do some thinking once in a while."

"Every time I come here, I end up feeling like Kadono."

"What's kadono?"

"Oh, the houseboy at my place. If you ask him anything, he always answers, 'Is that the way it is' or 'Is that right.'"

"He says that? He must be terribly strange."

Daisuke paused for a moment and looked over Umeko's shoulder between the curtains at the beautiful sky. Far in the distance there stood a tall tree. It had sprouted light brown shoots all over, and the soft tips of its branches melted into the sky, as if blurred by a drizzle. "The weather has turned nice, hasn't it. Shall we go cherry-blossom viewing somewhere?"

"Yes, let's. I'll go. So tell me."

"Tell you what?"

"What Father said."

"He said a lot of things, but I don't think I could repeat them so that they would make any sense; I'm not smart enough."

"There you go again, playing the fool. I know all about it."

"Then let me hear about it."

Umeko drew herself up a little primly. "You've become rather free with your tongue these days."

"Oh, it's nothing you can't handle. Anyway, it's terribly quiet here today. Where are the children?"

"The children are at school."

A young chambermaid, sixteen or seventeen years old, opened the door and poked her head in to deliver the message that the master was on the phone and wished to speak to the mistress. She stood waiting for an answer. Umeko got up immediately. Daisuke also got up. As he started to follow her out of the room, Umeko turned and said, "You stay here. I want to talk to you about something."

Daisuke was always amused when his sister-in-law assumed this commanding stance with him. "Please take your time," he said, and began to study the painting again. After some time, the colors no longer seemed to be painted upon the wall at all, but were leaping from his pupils and flying out to the wall, where they became glued. Soon, by controlling the colors that flew from his eyes, Daisuke was able to correct all the places that had displeased him, and finally, having achieved the most beautiful hues that his imagination could conjure, he sat in a state of rapture. Just then, Umeko came in and Daisuke was brought back to his usual self.

As he listened politely to what she had to say, Daisuke understood that she was raising the marriage issue again. Even before he had finished school, Daisuke had been presented with a variety of prospective brides, both through pictures and in person, thanks to Umeko's efforts. At first, he had made his escape in conventionally acceptable objections, but in the past two years or so, he had become brazen. His complaints were curious: this one's mouth was set at the wrong angle with her cheeks; that one's eyes were disproportionate to the width of her face; another had misplaced ears. Since they were never the normal excuses, Umeko herself began to wonder. She concluded that she had exerted herself too much, that that was why Daisuke had begun to abuse her kindness and behave so irresponsibly, and that the best thing would be to abandon him to his own resources until he came begging for help. Having settled upon this, Umeko did not utter a word about marriage. But Daisuke had not seemed troubled in the least and had remained an unfathomable entity.

But now their father had returned from his trip with a new candidate, whose family was deeply involved with the Nagais. Umeko had been told the story two or three days before and had therefore assumed that today's interview would concern this topic. Daisuke, however, had heard nothing of the matter. Perhaps the old man had indeed summoned him with the intention of discussing it, but observing Daisuke's attitude, had chosen silence as the wiser course for the day and deliberately avoided the topic.

Daisuke had a peculiar relationship with this candidate. He knew her family name but not her first name. He knew nothing of her age, looks, education, or character. As for why she had been selected, he knew only too well.

Daisuke's father had had one older brother, named Naoki. He was but one year older and was of smaller build than Daisuke's father, with similar features; people who did not know often took them for twins. Daisuke's father did not go by the name of Toku in those days, but rather by the childhood name of Seinoshin.

Just as Naoki and Seinoshin resembled each other in appearance, so were they brothers by temperament. As far as possible, they contrived to be in the same place doing the same thing. They came and went from their lessons at the same time. Indeed, at night, they read by the light of a single lamp.

It was the autumn of Naoki's eighteenth year. The two had been sent on an errand to Tōgakuji Temple on the outskirts of the castle town. Tōgakuji was the family temple of the lord of the clan. A priest there named Sōsui was a friend of the family, and the boys had been sent to deliver a letter to him. It was just an invitation to a game of go and required no answer, but Sōsui had kept the boys to talk about this and that, and by the time they left, it was only an hour before sunset.

There was a festival that day and the town was bustling. The two hurried through the crowds, but just as they were about to turn a corner, they ran into a fellow named Hōguri.

Hōguri and the brothers had never been on good terms. That evening Hōguri appeared to be quite drunk, and after shouting two or three words, lunged out at Naoki, sword in hand. Naoki had no choice but to draw his sword and stand up to him. His opponent had a formidable reputation for violence and was powerful in spite of his intoxicated condition. Left alone, Naoki was sure to lose. So the younger brother drew his sword, and together the two cut Hōguri to pieces.

In those days, the understanding was that if one samurai killed another, the aggressor had to commit seppuku. The brothers went home fully resigned to their fate. Their father, too, was prepared to line them up and assist in the rite. Unfortunately, however, their mother had been invited to an acquaintance's house for the festival and was away. Their father, out of the very human desire to let them see their mother just once more, sent for her immediately. While awaiting her return, he stalled for time by admonishing the boys and supervising their preparations of the room for the rite.

Now it happened that their mother was visiting a distant relation named Takagi. Takagi was a man of considerable influence, a convenience in those days when the world was just beginning to stir and the samurai code was not enforced as strictly as it had once been. Moreover, the victim was a villainous youth of ill repute. So Takagi returned with the boys' mother and persuaded their father to take no action until official instructions were handed down.

Takagi set out to exert his good offices. He won over the chief retainer, and through him, convinced the lord himself. The victim's father, unexpectedly enough, turned out to be a man of reason who not only deplored his son's misconduct, but once it was established that it was he who had dealt the first blow and created the disturbance, made no move to protest the lenient treatment being sought for the boys. The brothers closeted themselves in a single room for some time as a sign of penitence. Then they slipped away without anyone's notice.

Three years later the older brother was killed in Kyoto by a roaming samurai. On the fourth year after the incident, the Meiji Era dawned, and five or six years after that, Seinoshin brought his parents over to Tokyo. He found a wife and changed his name to the single character one of Toku. By then, Takagi, who had saved his life, was dead, and his adopted son-in-law headed the family. Nagai tried to persuade this man to come to Tokyo, perhaps to lecture on the procedures of government service, but he refused. The man had two children. The son went to Kyoto and entered Dōshisha University. Upon graduation, he had reportedly spent several years in America, but now he was in business in Kobe, a man of considerable means. The daughter had been married to a man who ranked among the largest taxpayers in the prefecture. It was their daughter who was now being considered for Daisuke.

"What a complicated story! I couldn't believe it," said Umeko to Daisuke.

"We've heard it so many times from Father."

"Well, there's never been any talk of marriage up to now so I didn't pay much attention."

"So Sagawa had a daughter. I didn't know at all."

"Why don't you accept her?"

"You're for it?"

"Of course I'm for it. It was fated."

"It might be easier to marry a girl fated by my own doings than one fated by my ancestors'."

"Is there such a thing?"

Daisuke smiled ironically and did not answer.

Chapter IV

DAISUKE SAT BLANK,
his head propped on both hands, the thin Western book he
had just finished still open on his desk. His head was brimming with the last scene. . . . Far in the distance, behind
trees that stood cold, two small square lamps swayed noiselessly. There the gallows had been erected. The condemned
men stood in the dark. One of them complained that he had
lost a shoe, that he was cold. Another asked, what? The first
repeated that he had lost a shoe and was cold. Someone asked
where M was. Another voice answered, here. Something
large, whitish, and flat showed from between the trees. A
damp wind came from its direction. It's the ocean, said G.
Presently, the lamps lit up the letter containing the sentence
and the white hand—an ungloved hand—that held it. You
don't have to read it out loud, do you, someone said. His voice
trembled. Soon the lamps went out. Now I'm all alone, said
K. He heaved a sigh. S was dead. W was dead. M was dead.
He was all alone. . . .

The sun came up from over the ocean. They piled the
bodies onto a cart. And began to pull. The stretched necks,
the popped eyes, the tongues dampened by a froth of blood
like a horrible flower—'they piled them on and went back to
the road. . . .

Daisuke mentally reviewed the last scene from Andreev's
The Seven That Were Hanged up to this point, then drew in
his shoulders and shuddered. At such times, he was overcome by intense anxiety as to what he should do if ever con-

fronted with such a situation. When he thought about it, he knew he could not die. But still, he would be killed against his will—how cruel that was! He imagined his tortured self, trapped between the cravings of life and the oppressions of death, and as he sat picturing the agony of his wandering from one to the other, he began to feel every hair on his back stir until it was unendurable.

His own father often told how, at the age of seventeen, he had killed a fellow clansman and had to resign himself to committing seppuku. His plan had been to serve as Daisuke's uncle's second and to ask Daisuke's grandfather to be his own second when his turn came. How could he have thought of going through with such a gruesome affair! Every time his father recounted the past, Daisuke found him more distasteful than admirable. Or else he thought of him as a liar. Somehow, it would seem much more appropriate if it should turn out that his father was a liar.

It was not just his father. There was a story like this about his grandfather also. When he was young, a fellow fencing pupil was so skilled that he had incurred someone's envy, and one night, as he made his way through the rice fields back to the castle town, he was cut down. Daisuke's grandfather was the first to rush to the scene, lantern in his left hand and drawn sword in his right, and beating the corpse with the sword, he was said to have shouted, Take courage, Gumpei, the wound is slight!

Daisuke's uncle had been killed in Kyoto when a hooded man had noisily broken into the inn where he was staying. The uncle had leaped from the second-story eaves but tripped and fell on a garden rock and was mercilessly cut down from above. The story went that his face had looked like a piece of sliced-up raw fish. Some days before he was killed, he had walked in the middle of the night from Shijō Avenue to Sanjō in high clogs, wearing a raincoat and shielding himself from the snow with an umbrella. About two hundred yards from his inn, a voice had suddenly called from behind, Master

Nagai Naoki. Daisuke's uncle had not so much as cast a glance behind, but with his umbrella held high, had continued walking to the inn door, where he opened the grating and stepped in. Then, the story continued, he slammed it shut and turned and announced, I am Nagai Naoki. What is your business?

Daisuke's immediate response to such stories was not admiration but terror. Before he could get around to appreciating the bravery, he was overcome by the raw smell of blood penetrating his nostrils.

Daisuke's current theory was that if it were possible for him to die at all, death would have to come at that instant marking the height of a paroxysmic seizure. But he was hardly the convulsive type. His hands trembled. His feet trembled. It was nothing out of the ordinary for his voice to tremble or his heart to skip a beat. But in recent years he never became agitated. Heightened agitation was a condition that naturally enabled one to approach death, and it was obvious to Daisuke that each time it occurred, it became that much easier to die. At times, out of curiosity, he wished he could at least advance to the neighborhood of that condition. Whenever he analyzed himself these days, Daisuke was startled to discover how changed he was from the self of five or six years before.

He turned the book over on his desk and got up. The glass doors on the verandah were slightly open and a warm wind blew in gaily. It made the red petals of the potted amanthus flutter gently. Sunlight fell on the large blossoms. Daisuke bent over and peered into the flowers, then took a little pollen from the wispy stamen and carried it to the pistil, where he carefully smeared it on.

"Did the ants get to it?" Kadono came in from the entrance-way. He had on his hakama.*

Daisuke continued to stoop and lifted only his face toward Kadono. "You've already been?"

"Yes, I have. Yes, they said they were going to move in to-

* A long, divided skirt, a standard part of formal wear for men.

morrow. He said he had just been thinking of coming over today."

"Who said? Hiraoka?"

"Yes. Yes, it looked like he was terribly busy with something. You're completely different, aren't you, Sensei. If it's ants, why don't you try pouring vegetable oil over them? Then, when they can't stand it and come out of their holes, you can kill them off one by one. I can do it if you want."

"It isn't ants. On nice days like today, if you take the pollen and smear it on the pistil, it'll bear fruit one of these days. I have the time, so I'm doing just as the man at the nursery said."

"Oh, I see. The world sure has become convenient, hasn't it. But bonsai are nice things to have around—they're pretty, and they give you something to look forward to."

Daisuke thought it too much trouble to answer him. Eventually he said, "Maybe I'll quit fooling around for now," and got up and sat down in the caned easy chair on the verandah. Kadono became bored and left for his own three-mat room at the side of the entrance. He was just about to open the shoji and go in when he was called back to the verandah. "Hiraoka said he was coming today?"

"Yes, it sounded like he might come."

"Then I'll wait for him."

Daisuke decided against going out. He had been rather concerned about Hiraoka since the other day.

When he had last visited, Hiraoka's situation was such that he could not afford to be leisurely. His story then was that there were two or three possibilities he planned to look into, but Daisuke had no idea what had become of them. He had gone twice himself to their inn in Jimbōchō. The first time Hiraoka had been out; the second time he was in, but he was standing on the threshold of the room, still in his Western clothes, scolding his wife hurriedly—or so it unmistakably seemed to Daisuke though he had caught but a glimpse when he went down the corridor unannounced and appeared before their room. Hiraoka had turned toward him slightly and said, "Oh, it's you." There was nothing hospitable in his face or in his manner. His wife's pale face had peered from the room, and recognizing Daisuke, had blushed. Daisuke somehow felt awkward about sitting down. He brushed aside the mechanical invitations to come in and insisted that he had no business in particular, that he had just come to see how they were doing. If Hiraoka was about to go out, they could leave together. With that, he had stepped out as if to lead the way.

Hiraoka said that he had wanted to find a house and settle down quickly, but he had been too busy to look for himself. Even when he would hear about a place through the inn, either the people had not moved out or the walls were being painted. He grumbled about everything all the way to the train, where they parted. Daisuke felt sorry for him and said, in that case, he would have his houseboy look for a place. Business was bad, there shouldn't be too much trouble finding a vacancy. With this assurance, he had left Hiraoka.

True to his promise, he had sent Kadono out to hunt. No sooner had he left than Kadono was back with a reasonable find. Daisuke had him show the couple the house, and they thought it would probably do; but since Daisuke felt an obligation to the landlord, and moreover, planned to have Kadono look further if this house did not suit them, he had sent Kadono back to get a definite answer. "I hope you went over to the landlord's to tell him they were taking it?"

"Yes, I stopped on the way back and told him they were moving in tomorrow."

Daisuke sat back in his chair and thought about the future of the couple who were setting up housekeeping for the second time in Tokyo. Hiraoka had changed considerably since they had parted at Shimbashi three years ago. His record was that of a man who had climbed but one or two rungs on the ladder of life before stumbling and falling. The only fortunate thing was that he had not climbed very far; but that meant only that there were no obvious wounds to be exposed to the eyes of society; his emotional state already betrayed signs of impairment.

This had been Daisuke's immediate impression the first time he saw Hiraoka. But when he considered the changes in himself over the past three years, he thought it possible that they had affected Hiraoka's reaction toward him, and he revised his assessment. Still, when he recalled Hiraoka's manner, his words and gestures that time Daisuke had gone to the inn and left so hurriedly with him without even going in, he was forced to return to his original conclusion. That day the center of Hiraoka's face had been a bundle of nerve endings. Whether it was the wind or a grain of sand, he had uninhibitedly twitched his brows, which looked as if they were subject to constant irritation. Everything he said, regardless of the content, sounded restless and pressured to Daisuke. Hiraoka's manner, in short, brought to mind a man with weak lungs who was struggling to swim through a mass of gelatin.

"He's in such a hurry," Daisuke had murmured to himself after seeing Hiraoka off at the streetcar stop. Then he had thought of the wife left behind at the inn.

Daisuke had never yet addressed Hiraoka's wife as "Oku-san." * He always called her "Michiyo-san," just as he had in the days before she was married. After leaving Hiraoka, he had toyed with the idea of going back to the inn—perhaps he would have a talk with Michiyo-san. But somehow, he could not go. He even stopped in his steps to think it over, and though he could find nothing wrong with his going, he still felt uneasy and could not go. If he mustered up his courage, he thought, he could do it. But for Daisuke to be so coura-

* A general term designating married women.

geous would be a painful effort. Once he got home, however, he was restless and somehow dissatisfied. So he went out to drink. Daisuke could drink enormous quantities and that night he drank especially heavily.

"Something must have come over me then." Leaning back in his chair, a comparatively detached Daisuke examined his own shadow.

"Did you want something?" Kadono came in again. He had taken off his hakama, so that his dumpling-like bare feet showed. Daisuke looked at his face without a word. Kadono, too, looked at Daisuke's face, and for a moment was left standing blankly.

"Didn't you call me? Well, well," he said and disappeared. Daisuke did not see anything amusing in this.

"He said he didn't call me, Auntie. I thought it was funny. I told you I didn't hear him clap or anything." These words came from the morning room, followed by laughter from Kadono and the old woman.

Just then, the much-awaited guest arrived. Kadono, who had gone to answer the door, came back with a somewhat peculiar expression on his face. He wore this expression all the way to Daisuke's side, where he said, almost in a whisper, "Sensei, it's Okusan." Daisuke left his chair without a word and went into the living room.

Hiraoka's wife had rather dark hair for a fair-complexioned woman. Her face was oval with clearly shaped brows. Glancing at her, one felt a vague loneliness, reminiscent of the old ukiyoe woodblock prints. Her complexion had noticeably lost its luster since their return to Tokyo. So much so that Daisuke had been a little startled the first time he saw her at the inn. Thinking she might not have recovered from the long, tiring train journey, he had asked if that was what was wrong, but was told no, she always looked like this these days. Then Daisuke had felt sorry for her.

————————————————————————————

Michiyo had given birth one year after leaving Tokyo. The baby had died soon after, and Michiyo's own heart seemed to have been damaged in childbirth. She had often been ill since. At first, she had just rested at home, but no matter what she did, she could not seem to make satisfactory progress. She had finally gone to a doctor; he said he could not tell for sure, but it might be a certain heart disease with a difficult name. If that was the case, then some of the blood pumped into the arteries was backing up; this was a chronic condition with little hope for a complete cure—a verdict that had alarmed Hiraoka. Perhaps because he exerted his utmost for her recovery, she regained a good deal of her spirits at the end of a year. There were many days when her complexion had its old, clear glow, and Michiyo herself was feeling quite encouraged when, about one month before their return to Tokyo, she suffered a setback. The doctor's story was that this time, her heart was not at fault. It would never be strong, but it had certainly not worsened. He could detect no impairment in the functioning of the valves for the time being—this was what Michiyo herself told Daisuke. Then Daisuke looked at Michiyo's face and wondered if her condition was caused by some sort of anxiety after all.

Michiyo's eyelids had two beautiful lines, one above the other, making a distinct fold. Her eyes were on the long and narrow side, but whenever she fixed her gaze, they somehow became extremely large. Daisuke attributed this effect to her irises. He had often observed this eye movement of hers in the days before she was married and he still remembered it well. Whenever he tried to picture her face in his mind, those black eyes, blurred as if they were misty, rose immediately, even before the outline of her face was complete.

Shown in to the living room from the hallway, Michiyo took a seat facing Daisuke. She placed her lovely hands one above the other upon her lap. The hand she placed underneath had a ring; the one she placed above also had a ring.

The latter was of modern design, a large pearl in a narrow gold setting—a gift from Daisuke three years ago in celebration of her wedding.

Michiyo lifted her face. Daisuke, instantly recognizing those eyes, blinked in spite of himself.

She had planned to come with Hiraoka the day after they arrived, but she had not felt well, and after that, she would have had to come by herself, so she had just not gone out at all; but today, she was just . . . So she began, then cut herself short. Then, as if she had suddenly remembered it, she apologized—the other day, when Daisuke came to see them, Hiraoka was about to go out, and they had been very rude. . . . "You should have stayed and waited," she added with feminine graciousness. But her tone was subdued. It was, nevertheless, her normal tone of voice, and it served all the more to remind Daisuke of the past.

"But he seemed to be terribly busy. . . ."

"Well, he is busy, as far as that goes—but it would have been all right. Even if you'd stayed. You're being so—formal."

Daisuke thought of asking if something had happened between them that day, but decided against it. Normally, he might have gone so far as to ask whether it wasn't true that she was being scolded then—her face was red, what had she done wrong? Their relationship was close enough to have permitted as much, but he felt that her present charming conversation was a painful effort to cover up an awkward situation, and he did not have the heart to joke.

Daisuke lit a cigarette, and dangling it from his lips, leaned back in his chair and relaxed. "It's been such a long time—shouldn't we get something to eat?" As he said this, he thought that his manner was in some small measure comforting to the woman.

"No thank you, not today. I can't stay," answered Michiyo, showing a glimpse of an old gold tooth.

"Oh, come now." Daisuke lifted his hands behind his head,

and knitting his fingers together, looked at her. She bent over and pulled out a small watch from her obi. When Daisuke gave her the pearl ring, Hiraoka had presented her with this watch. Daisuke remembered how, after buying their respective gifts at the same store, they had exchanged glances, then laughed as they went out.

"Oh, it's already after three. I thought it was only two. I'd stopped by places on the way over," she explained as if to herself.

"Are you in such a hurry?"

"Yes, I'd like to get back as soon as possible."

Daisuke took his hands from his head and tapped the cigarette ashes. "You've become awfully domestic in three years. I guess it can't be helped," he said laughingly. But there was something bitter in his tone.

"Oh, but we're moving tomorrow." Michiyo's voice was suddenly animated.

Daisuke had completely forgotten about their moving. But taken in by her cheerful tone, he followed up ingenuously, "Then you should come for a long visit when you're moved in."

"But," Michiyo started. She was at a loss for an answer, and her forehead betrayed her confusion. She bowed her head. Presently, she lifted her face; a faint crimson had spread over it. "You see, I really came to ask you for a little favor."

Daisuke's sharp intuition told him immediately what it was that Michiyo had come for. In fact, ever since Hiraoka had returned from Kyoto, Daisuke had subconsciously resigned himself to being faced with this problem one day.

"What is it, don't hesitate to ask."

"You couldn't lend us some money?"

Michiyo's words were as guileless as a child's but her cheeks were nonetheless red. Daisuke found Hiraoka's situation painful indeed, that he should have to force this woman to undergo so humiliating an experience.

Listening to her story, he discovered that it was not that they needed money for moving or for setting up a household. When they left the branch office, they had brought with them three debts; one of them had to be taken care of immediately. Hiraoka had given his word that he would pay the debt within one week of his arrival in Tokyo; for certain other reasons too, this debt could not be neglected like the others. So a worried Hiraoka had been running about since the day after their return, trying to put together the sum, but so far, it seemed, without success. That was why he had had no choice but to send Michiyo to Daisuke's for help.

"Is this what he borrowed from the branch manager?"

"No, that one can be put off forever, but if he doesn't do something about this one, it could even affect his plans here."

Daisuke thought that that could well be the case. When he asked the amount of the debt, it turned out to be only five hundred yen. What a trifle, he thought; yet actually, he himself had not a penny at his disposal. He realized that although it seemed as if he had never been inconvenienced for money, he was, in fact, quite restricted.

"But why did he get into debt like this?"

"It makes me miserable to think about it. Of course, I got sick, too, so you can say it was my fault, but . . ."

"So it was from the expenses when you were sick?"

"No. There's a limit to what you can spend on medicine." Michiyo did not explain further. Nor did Daisuke have the courage to ask further. Looking at Michiyo's pale face, he felt in it an undefined anxiety for the future.

Chapter V

EARLY THE NEXT MORNING
Kadono hired three carts and went to Shimbashi to pick up
Hiraoka's luggage. It had arrived long ago, but because the
couple had not found a place to live, it had been left at the
station. Counting the time needed to get back and forth and
to load and unload the carts, this was bound to be at least a
half-day job. Unless Kadono hurried, he wasn't going to make
it, Daisuke warned the minute he got out of bed. Kadono answered in his usual manner that there was nothing to it. He
was unhampered by a sense of time and so could give such
a breezy answer; but when Daisuke explained the circumstances to him, his face began to show a glimmer of understanding. When told that in addition to delivering the luggage, he was to stay and help until all the cleaning was done,
he readily assented, saying yes, he understood, everything
would be all right, and left.

After he left, Daisuke read until past eleven o'clock.
Then suddenly, he remembered a story about a man named
D'Annunzio who had furnished part of his house in blue and
part in red. D'Annunzio's reasoning seemed to be that these
two colors expressed the two principal moods of existence.
Accordingly, rooms where excitement was called for, such as
the study or the music room, should be painted in red as
much as possible. Bedrooms and the like, on the other hand,
where the spirit should repose, were to be done in bluish
tones. Thus the poet seemed to have satisfied his curiosity by
applying a psychologist's theory.

Daisuke was puzzled that a man so readily aroused as D'Annunzio should have required the presence of the color red, which could reasonably be deemed a potent excitant. Daisuke himself was not pleasantly affected by the brightly painted gates at shrines. Had it been possible, he would gladly have set his head adrift by itself to sleep peacefully in the deep green sea. At an exhibit the other day, someone named Aoki had a painting of a tall woman standing at the bottom of the ocean. Of all the entries, Daisuke had found this one alone to be pleasingly executed. This was because he himself wanted to be in such a submerged, tranquil mood.

Daisuke went out to the verandah and noticed the green that was growing rampant in the garden. The flowers had already fallen; now green shoots and leaves were in their first growth. Daisuke felt the brilliant green as if it had burst in his face. He was glad, though, that there was still a subdued tone somewhere beneath all the brightness that dazzled the eye. Wearing a cap and ordinary cotton clothes, he went out the gate.

When he came to Hiraoka's new residence, the gate was open and the house seemed deserted. The luggage did not seem to have arrived; nor, for that matter, was there any sign of the couple. A man who looked like a ricksha driver sat alone on the verandah, smoking.

To Daisuke's query, the man answered yes, they had come, but they had decided that at the rate things were going, it would be past noon before their luggage would arrive, and so they had left again.

"Did the master and mistress come together?"

"Yes, they were together."

"And did they leave together?"

"Yes, they left together."

"The luggage should be here soon too. Thanks for your trouble," Daisuke said and went back to the street.

He went to Kanda but did not feel like stopping at Hiraoka's inn. Somehow, though, the two weighed on his mind, so he dropped in. The couple were eating side by side. A maid with a tray in her hand sat at the threshold, her back to the corridor. Daisuke called to them from behind her back.

Hiraoka seemed startled when he saw Daisuke. His eyes were bloodshot. It was because he hadn't slept well in two or three days, he said. Michiyo said he was exaggerating and laughed. Daisuke felt sorry but was also relieved. He refused their invitations to stay and went out to eat, then got a haircut, went to Kudan, and on the way home stopped in once again at the new home. Head wrapped in a scarf, sleeves tied back, and a long, printed underkimono sweeping in view, Michiyo was supervising the unpacking. The maid who had waited on them at the inn was also there. Hiraoka was cutting the strings on a wicker trunk on the verandah, and seeing Daisuke, laughed and asked if he wouldn't help a little. Kadono had taken off his hakama, and with his kimono hoisted up, was carrying in a chest of drawers with the ricksha driver. Sensei, how do you like the way I look, he asked, and warned Daisuke not to laugh.

The next day, as Daisuke sat at the breakfast table drinking his customary tea, Kadono came in, his face just washed and shining. "When did you get home last night, Sensei? I was so tired I just dozed off, I didn't notice at all. Did you see me sleeping? That was pretty mean of you, Sensei. Anyway, about what time was it when you got back? Where were you until then?" As usual, he chattered effortlessly.

Looking serious, Daisuke asked, "I hope you stayed until it was all cleaned up?"

"Oh, yes, we got the whole place cleaned up. It sure was hard work, though. It's different from us moving, say, because there're so many things. Okusan stood in the middle of the room, sort of blank, just looking around at everything—it was pretty funny."

"Her health isn't very good."

"I guess not. I thought she looked a little pale. Completely different from Mr. Hiraoka. He's got a good build, doesn't he. I was pretty surprised when we went to the bath together last night."

Daisuke soon went into his study and wrote two or three letters. One was to a friend in Korea to thank him for a piece of pottery he had sent; another was to his brother-in-law in France, asking him to look for an inexpensive Tanagra figurine.

Past noon, as he was going out for a walk, he looked in on Kadono; he was sprawled out, fast asleep. Seeing his innocent nostrils, Daisuke became envious. As a matter of fact, he himself had had an enormously difficult time falling asleep the night before. The pocket watch he had put by his pillow, as was his custom, had made a tremendous noise. He had reached out and shoved it under the pillow. But the ticking still echoed in his head. Listening to this sound, he had finally dozed off. Even when most of his senses had slipped into the dark caverns of sleep, he was still conscious of a sewing machine that stitched through the night, its needle traveling ceaselessly through his head. Some time during the night, that sound had turned into the chirping of insects, coming deep from the lovely shrubbery at the side of the entrance. . . . When he had followed his dream this far, Daisuke felt as if he had discovered the thread that spanned the space between sleep and wakefulness.

Daisuke was the sort of man who, once he was disturbed by something, no matter what, could not let go of it until he had pursued it to the utmost. Moreover, having the capacity to assess the folly of any given obsession, he was forced to be doubly conscious of it. Three or four years ago he had tackled the question of the process whereby his waking mind entered the realm of dreams. At night, when he had gotten under the covers and begun to doze off nicely, he would think, this is it, this is how I fall asleep. No sooner had he thought this than he was wide awake. When he had managed to doze off again, he would immediately think, here it is. Night after night, he was plagued by his curiosity and would repeat the same procedure two or three times. In the end, he became disgusted in spite of himself. He wanted somehow to escape his agony. Moreover, he was thoroughly impressed by the extent of his folly. To appeal to his conscious mind in order to apprehend his unconscious, and to try to recollect both at the same time was, as James had put it, analogous to lighting a candle to examine the dark, or stopping a top in order to study its movements; at that rate, it stood to reason that he would never again be able to sleep. He knew all this, but when night came, he still thought, now . . .

In about a year's time, the problem faded away without his notice. When he compared his dream of the previous night with this old problem, Daisuke had a strange feeling. It occurred to him that it would be more graceful to cut loose a part of his conscious self and, without his own knowledge, surrender it just as it was to a dream in progress. At the same time, he asked himself if this process did not resemble the state of incipient insanity. Thus far, Daisuke had never believed he could become insane, for he never became impassioned.

During the next two or three days, neither Daisuke nor Kadono had any word from Hiraoka. In the afternoon of the fourth day, Daisuke went to Azabu to a garden party to which he had been invited. There were quite a number of guests, both men and women. The guests of honor were an immoderately tall Englishman—supposedly a member of Parliament or a businessman of some sort—and his wife, who wore pince-nez. The latter was quite a beauty, almost too beautiful to have come to a place like Japan. She proudly carried a Gifu-painted parasol, which she had no doubt acquired somewhere.

Admittedly, the weather was unusually fine that day. As he stood on the grass in his frock coat under the piercingly blue sky, the feeling that summer had already come spread from Daisuke's shoulders to his back. The English gentleman frowned and looked up at the sky and said it was beautiful. His wife immediately responded, lovely. Since this exchange was made emphatically in high-pitched tones, Daisuke felt that compliments delivered in English were remarkable indeed.

Even Daisuke had two or three words addressed to him by the wife. But before three minutes were up, he found it unbearable and beat a hasty retreat. After him, a young lady in kimono with her hair purposely done in traditional style, and a man who was said to have spent some years in New York on business, took over. The latter professed to be a genius at speaking English and never missed an English-language gathering. His greatest pleasure was to converse in English with Japanese, then to deliver a table speech in English. He had a habit of saying something, then laughing loudly as if it were highly amusing. From time to time the Englishman looked at him dubiously, and Daisuke thought he should at least refrain from doing that. The young lady was doing quite well, too. She was the daughter of a well-to-do man who had hired an American tutor, with whom she had practiced English. Daisuke, thinking that she excelled in language more than in looks, listened to her, utterly impressed.

It was not because he was personally acquainted with the host or the English couple that Daisuke had been invited. An invitation had found its way to him simply because he floated in the wake of his father's and brother's position in society. So he made his rounds to all the guests, bowing suitably to each of them, and when that was done, began to saunter about aimlessly. Eventually, he spotted his brother.

"Oh, you came," said Seigo, not even touching his hand to his hat.

"It's quite a nice day, isn't it."

"Yes, it's fine."

Daisuke was not on the short side, but his brother was

even taller. And on top of it, he had put on weight in the past five or six years, which made him look quite impressive.

"Why don't you go over there and chat with the foreigners for a while?"

"No, never," his brother said, grimacing. He began to toy with the gold chain hanging over his large stomach.

"Foreigners are quite smooth, aren't they. Too smooth. With so much flattery, even the weather's got to behave."

"They have that many good words for the weather, do they? It's a little too hot for me."

"For me, too," said Daisuke.

Then, as if they had timed it, Seigo and Daisuke pulled out their white handkerchiefs and wiped their brows. Both had on heavy silk hats.

The brothers walked to a shady spot at the edge of the lawn and stopped. No one was around. It seemed that some sort of entertainment was beginning on the other side. Seigo watched it with the same expression he always wore at home. Seeing this, Daisuke thought, if you get to be like my brother, it must not make much difference whether you're at home or visiting. There probably isn't anything to look forward to once you get that worldly—how dull it must be.

"What's Father doing today?"

"Father's at a poetry meeting."

Seigo answered without any change of expression, but Daisuke was somewhat amused.

"And Umeko?"

"Entertaining guests."

Thinking that his sister-in-law would complain to him later, Daisuke was again amused.

Daisuke knew that Seigo always seemed very busy. He also understood that over half his business consisted of attending such gatherings as this. Without a hint of distaste or a word of complaint, his brother wined and dined and chatted with women at all hours. Yet, his appearance never betrayed fatigue and his manner was always unruffled; with almost otherworldly composure, his flesh grew more ample each year. Daisuke could not but admire his capabilities.

That Seigo could go into geisha houses, accept luncheon invitations, drop in at the Club, see people off at Shimbashi, meet them at Yokohama, run out to Ōiso to humor the elders —that he could put in his appearance at large gatherings from morning to evening without seeming either triumphant or dejected—this must be because he was thoroughly accustomed to this kind of life, thought Daisuke; it was probably like the jellyfish's floating in the sea and not finding it salty.

Daisuke was thankful for this; that is to say, his brother, unlike his father, had never yet preached troublesome sermons to him. Such stiff words as *principle, doctrine*, or *philosophy of life* never found their way to his lips, and it was difficult to tell whether he even had such beliefs. On the other hand, he had never shown any inclination to attack those stiff notions of principle, doctrine, or philosophy of life. He was wonderfully ordinary.

But uninteresting. As a conversationalist, Daisuke far preferred his sister-in-law. Whenever Daisuke saw his brother, Seigo was sure to say, how are things; wasn't there an earthquake in Italy; the Emperor of Turkey was deposed. Or, the cherry blossoms at Mukōjima were no good any more; a large snake was found in the bottom of a foreign ship in Yokohama; someone was run over by a train. They were all things that had appeared in the newspapers. He carried around with him an infinite number of inoffensive topics. No matter how long one talked with him, he never seemed to run out.

There were also times when he would ask such peculiar questions as, was that man named Tolstoy dead yet; or, who was the greatest novelist in Japan nowadays. In other words, he was completely indifferent to the arts and therefore shockingly ignorant. But when he asked these questions so nonchalantly, he was so far beyond respect or contempt that Daisuke found it easy to answer him.

Sitting face to face with his brother, Daisuke was never stimulated; on the other hand, he found Seigo's straightforwardness agreeably relaxing. But since he was out from morning to night, Daisuke could seldom catch him. His sister-in-law, Seitarō, and Nuiko were all quite surprised if Seigo stayed at home and took his three meals with the family.

So, when he stood next to his brother in the shade, Daisuke thought he had found a good opportunity. "I'd like to see you about something. Would you be free some time?"

"Free," Seigo repeated, and without any explanation, began to laugh.

"How about tomorrow morning?"

"Tomorrow morning I have to go to Yokohama."

"From noon?"

"From noon, I'll be at the office, but there'll be a conference, so even if you came I wouldn't be able to stay for long."

"Then the evening would be all right?"

"In the evening, I'm off to the Imperial Hotel. I'm supposed to host that foreign couple tomorrow night."

Daisuke looked at his brother and pouted. Then the two burst out laughing.

"If you're in such a hurry, how about today? Today would be all right. Why don't we get something to eat—we haven't done it in a long time."

Daisuke agreed. He thought Seigo would propose the Club, but unexpectedly enough, he suggested an eel place.

"I've never gone to an eel place in a silk hat before," said Daisuke hesitantly.

"What difference does it make?"

The two left the garden party and took a ricksha to an eel shop at the foot of Kanesugibashi.

It was an old-fashioned house set amidst a flowing river

and weeping willows. Daisuke turned their silk hats upside down and set them on the shelf next to the blackened alcove pillar. Seeing them side by side, he said it looked strange. Yet, with just the two of them sitting cross-legged in the large, open, second-story room, it was actually more agreeable than being at the garden party.

The two drank pleasantly. Seigo acted as if all they had to do was eat, drink, and gossip. Daisuke himself was on the verge of forgetting his purpose in getting together. But after the maid brought in the third round, he got around to business; needless to say, it concerned Michiyo's request for a loan.

Daisuke had never yet asked Seigo for money. Of course, there was the time just after he finished school when he had overindulged in geisha and left his brother to clean up the mess. On that occasion, his brother, far from scolding, had just said, well, what a problem, don't say anything to Father —and through Daisuke's sister-in-law had completely paid off the debt. Because of this, Daisuke had always felt obliged to his brother. He had often been hard pressed for spending money since then, but he had managed by going to his sister-in-law. In effect, this was his first experience at bringing such a matter to his brother.

To Daisuke, Seigo seemed like a tea kettle without a handle; he did not know where to begin to get ahold of him. But this was also what intrigued him.

Daisuke began to unfold the Hiraoka couple's history as if it were another piece of gossip. Seigo showed no signs of impatience as he sipped his sake and now and again threw in a "hm" as if to keep time. When the story advanced to the point where Michiyo came asking for money, he still only said "hm." Daisuke had no choice but to say, "So, I felt sorry for them and said I'd see what I could do."

"Oh. Is that right."

"What do you think?"

"Can you raise the money?"

"I can't raise a penny. I'd have to borrow."

"Who from?"

Since this was the point he had been leading to all along, Daisuke said firmly, "I thought I'd borrow it from you." He looked at his brother's face again. It was still unchanged.

And he calmly answered, "I wouldn't do that."

Seigo's reasons had nothing to do with obligation or kindness, or even with the practical question of whether the money would be returned or not. It was simply that he had concluded that in such circumstances, things invariably took care of themselves if left alone.

Seigo gave a number of examples to support his conclusion. There was a man named Fujino who rented a tenement house on Seigo's property. This Fujino had been asked to keep the son of a distant relative. Soon thereafter, the boy was conscripted and had to return to his home province for a physical. But Fujino had used up the money sent for the boy's schooling and travel expenses, and he came to Seigo asking for a loan to cover the gap. Seigo, of course, had not seen the man personally, but had instructed his wife to refuse him. This notwithstanding, the son had gone home at the appointed time and undergone his physical without any great inconvenience. Then there was the time when a relative of Fujino's had used up the deposit on a house he rented, and when the renters were ready to move, he could not return the sum and came begging through Fujino. Seigo had made his wife refuse again. Still, the deposit was returned without any great difficulty. There were other examples, mostly in the same vein.

"There's no doubt about it, Umeko's giving it away behind your back. You're pretty gullible, aren't you," said Daisuke, laughing heartily.

"Of course not. Nothing of the sort is going on." Seigo looked the same as ever. He lifted the sake cup before him to his lips.

Chapter VI

THAT DAY SEIGO WOULD NOT readily agree to lending him the money. For his part, Daisuke avoided whining about how pitiable Michiyo was, or how touching her situation. Even if he himself had such feelings toward her, it would take no ordinary effort to lead his brother, who knew nothing, to that point. Besides, if he were to rashly mouth sentimental phrases, his brother would be scornful— as it was, Seigo seemed to find him a trifle ridiculous. So Daisuke went on in his usual aimless way, wandering from one point to another as he drank. And as he drank, he thought that this was what his father meant by his lack of zeal. But he prided himself on not being so vulgar as to attempt to persuade people with tears. If anything was offensive, it was affected tears, anguish, earnestness, or zeal. His brother also understood this. Hence, if Daisuke were to use such a ploy and fail, he would forever lower himself in his brother's eyes.

Daisuke gradually moved away from the issue of money. He touched upon such topics as would make them both feel that it was only because they were there, face to face, that they had been able to drink so pleasantly. But when it came time to have their rice and tea, Daisuke suddenly asked, as if he had just remembered it, if Seigo wouldn't find Hiraoka a position in his company even if he wouldn't lend him money.

"No, I don't want to have anything to do with people like that. Besides, business is bad. There's nothing I can do."

The next morning, Daisuke's first thought upon waking was that only a business colleague could persuade Seigo; it did no good to appeal to him as a brother.

After he had determined as much, however, it still did not occur to him to regard his brother as particularly unsympathetic. Indeed, he felt that Seigo had given the appropriate response. Strangely enough, this same brother had willingly paid off the money that Daisuke had dissipated. What if Daisuke were now to affix his seal beside Hiraoka's and go into joint debt? Would Seigo clean it up as he had before? Had his brother in fact been anticipating as much when he refused? Or was he confident that he, Daisuke, would never try such a thing and therefore had not lent him the money?

Judging from Daisuke's current tendencies, anyone would think it most unlikely for him to affix his seal for another person. Daisuke himself thought so. But if Seigo had seen through this and in refusing to lend his younger brother the money was gambling on Daisuke's acting in character, then Daisuke was not immune to the temptation of doing the unexpected and seeing how his brother would react. Having gotten this far, Daisuke himself found his thoughts rather ill natured and mentally gave himself a sarcastic smile.

But one thing was certain: sooner or later, Hiraoka would come, loan note in hand, seeking Daisuke's seal.

With these thoughts, Daisuke got out of bed. Kadono had been sitting cross-legged, reading the newspaper, but as soon as he saw Daisuke coming from the bath with wet hair, he sat up and folded the papers away beside the cushion. "It's really something, isn't it, what's happening in *Smoke*," he said loudly.

"Have you been reading it?"

"Yes. Every morning."

"Is it interesting?"

"Yes. It seems interesting, somehow."

"In what way?"

"In what way? I can't answer when you ask like that, Sensei, so formal and all. Well, you know, doesn't it seem like it really shows that modern anxiety?"

"And doesn't it smell of the flesh?"

"Yes, it does. A good deal."

Daisuke fell silent.

Teacup in hand, he went into the study and sat down. As he gazed vacantly at the garden, he noticed that young shoots were springing in profusion from the knobby, dead branches and roots of the pomegranate; their color was like a mixture of dark green and dark red. They flashed for an instant in his eyes, then immediately lost their effectiveness as a stimulus.

There was nothing concrete in Daisuke's head at the moment. It was just quietly at work, almost like the weather outside. But an infinite number of undefinable particles were pushing against each other in the back of his mind. No matter how much the particles of mold in a piece of cheese move about, the motion goes undetected so long as the cheese remains stationary. Similarly, Daisuke himself barely noticed the seismographic movements taking place in his head. It was just that each time they provoked a physiological response, he was forced to shift in his seat.

Daisuke seldom used such words as *modern* or *anxiety*, which were very much in fashion. This was because, first of all, he thought it went without saying that he was modern; secondly, he clung steadfastly to the belief that modernity did not necessarily cause anxiety.

Daisuke explained the anxiety depicted in Russian literature by the climate and the oppressive political system; he saw the anxiety in French literature as a product of the prevalence of adultery. The anxiety in Italian literature, as represented by D'Annunzio, he judged to be a sense of self-loss resulting from uninhibited decadence. Thus, when Japanese writers chose to depict society exclusively from the angle of anxiety, Daisuke regarded it as an importation.

In his school days, Daisuke had indeed had some experience with the kind of anxiety that follows upon intellectual doubt. But after developing to a certain point, this anxiety had come to an abrupt halt and then had begun to reverse itself. It was as if he had thrown a rock at heaven; he wished he hadn't done it in the first place. That "doubt of all things visible," so dear to the heart of Zen priests, belonged to a land in which he had yet to set foot. Daisuke was far too cleverly made to doubt everything with such sincere impetuosity.

Daisuke, too, had been reading the newspaper serial *Smoke* which Kadono had praised. Today, he put the newspaper beside his teacup; he did not even feel like opening it. All of D'Annunzio's heroes were men without money worries, so it was not unreasonable that their excesses should lead to folly; when it came to the hero of *Smoke*, there was no such leeway. That he should push so far, this notwithstanding, must mean that he was under the power of love; it would be impossible otherwise. Yet, neither this character, named Yōkichi, nor the woman, Tomoko, gave any indication of being forced outside society because of true love. When he tried to identify the inner force that was driving the two, Daisuke grew skeptical. The hero, who could act so resolutely in such circumstances, was probably not subject to anxiety. It would be much more reasonable to suppose that the seeds of anxiety resided in Daisuke, who would hesitate in such a situation. Daisuke had always regarded himself as an original. But he was forced to recognize that Yōkichi was far ahead of him in this respect. He had started reading *Smoke* out of curiosity, but lately, since he had begun to feel too great a distance between himself and Yōkichi, he had let many days go without even scanning the day's installment.

From time to time, Daisuke stirred in his chair. He thought that he was completely relaxed. He finished his tea and began to read as usual. For about two hours he read steadily, but when he came to the middle of a certain page, he stopped and rested his chin on his hands. He picked up the newspaper and read the day's installment of *Smoke*. As before, he was out of tune with it. Then he read various articles here and there. Count Ōkuma was vigorously supporting the dissident students in the Tokyo Higher Commercial School dispute. This was written up in fairly strong language. Whenever he read something like this, Daisuke was apt to interpret it as a maneuver by Count Ōkuma to draw students to his own Waseda University. Daisuke tossed the paper aside.

Past noon, he finally began to realize that he was not at ease. He felt as if a thousand tiny wrinkles were constantly moving and changing position and shape in his stomach. Daisuke was occasionally dominated by such sensations, but up to now, he had always treated this kind of experience as a purely physiological phenomenon. He somewhat regretted having eaten eel with his brother the day before. He thought he might take a walk and drop in on Hiraoka, but he could not tell whether his real goal was to take a walk or to see Hiraoka. He had the old woman get out a change of clothing and was just about to dress when his nephew Seitarō arrived. Cap in hand, he bowed his well-shaped round head before Daisuke and sat down.

"Is school out already? It's too early."

"It's not early at all," said Seitarō, laughing and watching Daisuke's face.

Daisuke clapped his hands to call the old woman and asked, "Seitarō, would you like some hot chocolate?"

"Yes."

Daisuke ordered two hot chocolates and began to tease Seitarō. "Seitarō, your hands have gotten awfully big these days from playing baseball all the time. They're bigger than your head!"

Seitarō grinned and rubbed his round head with his right hand. He really did have large hands.

"I hear Daddy treated you yesterday, Uncle."

"That's right, I had quite a feast. Thanks to him, my stomach isn't feeling well today."

"It's nerves again."

"It's not nerves, it's real. It's all his fault."

"That's what Daddy said."

"What did he say?"

"'Go to Daisuke's after school and get him to treat you to something.'"

"Oh—in return for yesterday?"

"That's right—'I treated him today, so it's his turn tomorrow,' he said."

"You came all the way just for that?"

"Yes."

"You're my brother's son all right, good and shrewd. That's why I'm giving you the hot chocolate. That'll do, won't it?"

"Hot chocolate?"

"You won't drink it?"

"Oh, I'll drink it all right, but . . ."

It turned out that what Seitarō wanted was to be taken to the Ekōin when the sumō tournament opened and to watch the matches from the best seats in the center section. Daisuke agreed readily.

Then Seitarō, looking happy, suddenly came out with, "Even though you loaf around, Uncle, they say you're really a great man."

Even Daisuke was a trifle taken aback by this. He lamely answered, "Well, you knew that all along."

"But I heard it for the first time last night from Father," protested Seitarō.

Evidently, from what Seitarō had to say, after Seigo had come home the night before, he and Umeko and their father had undertaken an evaluation of Daisuke. Because the account was that of a child, it was somewhat confused, but since Seitarō was quite intelligent, he remembered some of the precise words even if they were fragmentary. Daisuke's father's assessment apparently was that Daisuke had little promise. His brother had countered with yes, maybe that was so, but he still understood some things rather well. It would be best to leave him alone for a while. It would work out all right; there was no need to worry. He would probably do something one of these days. His sister-in-law had seconded this. She had been to a fortuneteller about a week ago, and his judgment was that Daisuke was a man who was sure to stand at the head of others. Therefore, he was bound to be all right.

Daisuke had been listening with interest to all the details, from time to time prompting Seitarō with "yes, and then," but when he came to the part about the fortuneteller, he was genuinely amused. Presently, he changed his clothes, and seeing Seitarō home, went over to Hiraoka's.

Hiraoka's house was a good illustration of the tightening squeeze exerted on the middle class by a decade of inflation. It was an exceedingly crude, unsightly construction. And Daisuke was especially sensitive to its esthetic shortcomings.

There were only about two yards between the gate and the entranceway and the same distance between the gate and the kitchen door. Next to this house, in every direction stood similarly cramped houses. They were the work of the smallest of financiers, who, taking advantage of Tokyo's pitiful swelling, schemed to multiply their own meager funds two and three times by putting up these shabby structures, mementos to the struggle for survival.

In today's Tokyo, particularly in the outskirts, such houses were to be found everywhere. Moreover, like flies in summer, they continued to multiply every day at an extraordinary rate. Daisuke had once termed it the advance of defeat. He regarded these structures as the most accurate symbols of modern Japan.

Some of them were covered with the bottoms of kerosene cans patched together, like square fish scales. Not one among their inhabitants was spared the sound of pillars cracking in the middle of the night. Their doors always had knotholes. Their sliding doors were sure to become warped. Those who stored their capital in their heads and tried to live off the monthly interest earned by their mental endeavors invariably burrowed in such places. Hiraoka was one of them.

As Daisuke passed by the fence, the first thing to catch his eye was the roof. The murky black of the tiles had a singular effect on him and it seemed that the lusterless slabs of dirt could suck in endless quantities of water. In front of the entrance, bits of sawdust from the unpacking still lay scattered about. When he went into the living room, Hiraoka was seated at a desk, in the midst of writing a long letter. Michiyo was in the next room, softly clattering the handles as she opened and closed drawers. A large wicker trunk lay open beside her, and the sleeve of a pretty underkimono showed halfway. Sorry, but would he wait a minute, Hiraoka asked; Daisuke watched the trunk and the underkimono and the slender hand that occasionally dipped into the trunk. But Michiyo's face was hidden from his view.

Eventually, Hiraoka threw his brush at the table and sat up. He had evidently been grappling with something quite involved, for his ears were red, as well as his eyes, for that matter.

"How are you? Thanks for everything the other day. I meant to come thank you but I haven't gotten around to it."

Hiraoka's words had more the air of a challenge than an apology. Although he was wearing neither an undershirt nor long drawers, he immediately crossed his legs. Since his collar was not properly drawn together, his chest hair showed a little.

"You must not be quite settled yet?" Daisuke asked.

"Settled? At this rate, I won't be settled for the rest of my life." With these words, he began to smoke hurriedly.

Daisuke understood very well why Hiraoka was greeting him in this way. He wasn't striking out at Daisuke, he was striking out at society; or rather, he was striking out at himself, Daisuke thought, and he even felt sorry for him. Still, the tone was jarring to nerves like his. He could not, however, be angered by it.

"How's the house? The rooms seem to be arranged well enough, don't they?"

"Well, yes. Even if they aren't there's nothing I can do about it. If I wanted to move into a house of my liking, I'd have to play the stock market or something. Don't they say that all the fine houses going up in Tokyo these days are built by stockbrokers?"

"Maybe so. But for every fine house that goes up, who knows how many have to come down?"

"That's why they're all the more comfortable to live in!"

Hiraoka laughed hard at his own words. At this point, Michiyo came in. She greeted Daisuke lightly, thanking him for the other day. She sat down and took the red flannel that she had rolled in her hands and placed it it front of her to show Daisuke.

"What do you have there?"

"It's the baby's kimono. I made it and just haven't gotten around to undoing it. I found it at the bottom of the trunk so I took it out." She undid the tie strings and opened the sleeves.

"Hey! What do you have something like that around for? Tear it up quick and make some cleaning rags out of it or something."

Michiyo did not answer, but sat with the baby's kimono on her lap, her eyes cast down.

"I made it just like yours," she said, and looked at her husband.

"You mean this?" Underneath his lined, printed kimono, next to his skin, Hiraoka wore a layer of flannel. "This is no good any more. It's too hot."

For the first time, Daisuke caught a flash of the old Hiraoka. "It's too hot now to wear flannel underneath a lined kimono. Why don't you wear an underkimono?"

"Yeah, I just keep wearing this because it's too much trouble to change."

"I tell him to take it off so I can wash it, but he won't."

"No, I'll take it off, I'm pretty sick of it myself."

The conversation had finally moved from the dead child. There was even a little more warmth in the air. Hiraoka said that they should have a drink, they hadn't done it in such a long while. Michiyo said she would make a few things too, so wouldn't Daisuke please make himself at home. Her invitation sounded like a plea. Watching her from behind as she left for the next room, Daisuke wished he could somehow raise the money.

"Have you found some place to work?" he asked.

"Well, yes, I have and I haven't. If there isn't anything, I'll play around for a while. If I take my time and look, something's bound to turn up."

His words were calm, but as Daisuke listened he could not help feeling that in fact, Hiraoka was in quite a hurry. Daisuke had been planning to report the exchange that had taken place with his brother the day before, but on hearing these words, he decided to put it off for the time being. It would seem as if he were deliberately wrecking the defense that Hiraoka had erected. Moreover, Hiraoka himself had not said a word about the money to him; therefore, there was no need to say anything explicit. Yet if he just remained silent, Hiraoka was sure to resent him inwardly as a heartless fellow. Daisuke, though, had almost become insensible to such charges, and he thought that in fact, he was not such a terribly passionate person. If he were to return to the Daisuke of three or four years ago and evaluate his present self, he might find that he had degenerated. Yet, when his present self looked back at the old Daisuke, it was evident that he had been exaggerating his own moral sense and flinging it about proudly. Rather than painfully contrive to pass off gold plating for solid gold, Daisuke now thought it easier to proffer brass as brass and bear the contempt appropriate to the inferior metal.

It was not as if Daisuke had come to content himself with brass because he had suddenly been swept into the eye of a raging storm and had undergone a drastic change of heart from the shock—no, there was no such melodrama behind the change. Simply by using the powers of reasoning and observation so characteristic of him, he had gradually stripped off the gold plating. Daisuke held that most of it had been coated on by his father. There was a time when his father had looked like gold to him. Many of his seniors had looked like gold. Anyone who had attained a certain high level of education had looked like gold. Therefore, his own gold plating had been all the more painful, and he had been impatient to become solid gold himself. But once his keen eyes penetrated directly to the inner layers of those other people, his efforts suddenly came to seem foolish.

Other thoughts crossed Daisuke's mind. If, over three or four years, he himself had changed this much, then during that same time, Hiraoka must also have changed within the limits of his own experience. The old Daisuke, wanting Hiraoka to think well of him, would have managed to do something in these circumstances, even if that had meant fighting with his brother or arguing with his father; and he would have come to Hiraoka to give a word-for-word account of how it had gone. But then again, it was only the old Hiraoka who would have expected this; now, he probably did not take friends that seriously.

So with only a word or two on the crucial subject, they passed the time in small talk until the sake arrived. Michiyo held the bottle by the bottom and served.

Hiraoka became increasingly talkative as he drank. Sometimes, no matter how drunk he was, his manner did not change at all; at other times, he would become enormously animated and his tone would be charged with pleasure. When this happened, he not only became more loquacious than most drinkers, but he would even raise comparatively serious issues and argue them happily with his partner. It was strange for Daisuke to realize that it was easiest to argue with Hiraoka when he fell into this state. Hiraoka used to say, shall we have a drink and show our true colors? The boundary between the two had moved far from where it had been in those days. And within themselves, each knew that having moved apart, it would be difficult to find a path that would bring them closer together. The day after Hiraoka's arrival in Tokyo, their first encounter in three years, each had discovered that the other had already left his side.

But today, there was something peculiar. The more he warmed up to his sake, the more the old Hiraoka came out. As the sake brought him around to a comfortable point, he seemed to numb himself completely to his present financial predicament, the life ahead of him, its agonies, his discontent, the turmoil at the bottom of his heart. In a single bound Hiraoka's talk leaped to a lofty plane.

"Yes, I failed. I failed, but I'm still working. And I plan to work in the future too. You look at my failure and you laugh —even if you say you don't, it comes down to the same thing, so it doesn't matter. So, you laugh. You laugh, but you don't do anything, see? You're a fellow who takes the world just as it's given. Put it another way—you're incapable of working your will. If you say you have no will to work, I won't believe you. You're human, after all. I'll bet you always feel as if you're missing something, which proves my point. I couldn't go on living without exerting my will upon the real world and getting some concrete evidence that this world had, to some extent, become a little more to my liking because I had willed it so. That's where I see the value in my existence. All you do is think. Because all you do is think, you've constructed two separate worlds—one inside your head and one outside. Just the fact that you tolerate this enormous dissonance—why, that's a great intangible failure already. Ask why. I've pushed the dissonance outside, whereas you've shoved it into your head—and just because I've pushed it out, the degree of actual failure may be smaller on my part. But you laugh at me. And I can't laugh at you. No, I'd like to, but society says I can't, right?"

"Go ahead and laugh. Even before you laugh at me, I've already laughed at myself."

"That's a lie. Isn't it, Michiyo?"

Michiyo had been sitting silently all this time, but on this sudden appeal from her husband, she smiled and looked at Daisuke.

"It's true, isn't it, Michiyo-san?" said Daisuke, raising his sake cup to be served.

"No, it's a lie. I don't care what my wife says to defend you, it's a lie. Though of course, whether you're laughing at other people or at yourself, you do it all in your head, so it's hard to tell whether you're lying or telling the truth."

"Oh, quit kidding."

"I'm not kidding, I'm completely serious. Of course, you didn't used to be like that. No, you didn't used to be like that at all, but you're quite a different man today. Right, Michiyo? Anyone can see that Nagai's proud."

"But to hear the way you've been talking, it sounds like you're the proud one."

Hiraoka laughed loudly. Michiyo took the sake-warming bottle into the next room.

Picking at the appetizers on the table with his chopsticks, Hiraoka munched noisily with his face down. Soon, he lifted bleary eyes and said, "This is the first time in a long while that I've gotten drunk so nicely. But look—you're not feeling that happy, are you. It's unpardonable. I've become the old Hiraoka Tsunejiro, but you won't become the old Nagai Daisuke, that's unpardonable. Come on, try. Drink. I'll drink more myself. So you drink more too."

Daisuke recognized in these words a sincere and naïve effort to take him back to his old self. And he was moved. But at the same time, he could not help feeling that he was being begged to give back the bread that he had eaten the day before.

"When you drink, even though your words sound drunk, your head's usually clear—so I'll go ahead and speak."

"That's right, that's the old Nagai."

Daisuke suddenly did not want to continue. "Are you sure your head's steady?" he asked.

"Of course it is. As long as yours is steady; mine's always steady," he said, and looked Daisuke straight in the eye. Indeed, it was as he said.

So Daisuke said, "You've been attacking me quite a bit for not working, and I haven't said anything. I don't say anything because, just as you charge, I don't intend to work."

"Why not?"

"Why not?—well, it's not my fault. That is to say, it's the world's fault. Or, to exaggerate a little, it's because the relationship between Japan and the West is no good that I won't work. First of all, there's no other country with such a bad case of beggar's twitch. When do you think all those debts can be paid off? Oh, the foreign currency bonds might get paid. But they aren't the only debts. The point is, Japan can't get along without borrowing from the West. But it poses as a first-class power. And it's straining to join the ranks of the first-class powers. That's why, in every direction, it puts up the façade of a first-class power and cheats on what's behind. It's like the frog that tried to outdo the cow—look, Japan's belly is bursting. And see, the consequences are reflected in each of us as individuals. A people so oppressed by the West have no mental leisure, they can't do anything worthwhile. They get an education that's stripped to the bare bone, and they're driven with their noses to the grindstone until they're dizzy—that's why they all end up with nervous breakdowns. Try talking to them—they're usually stupid. They haven't thought about a thing beyond themselves, that day, that very instant. They're too exhausted to think about anything else;

it's not their fault. Unfortunately, exhaustion of the spirit and deterioration of the body come hand-in-hand. And that's not all. The decline of morality has set in too. Look where you will in this country, you won't find one square inch of brightness. It's all pitch black. So what difference would it make, what I said or what I did, me standing all alone in the middle of it? I've always been a loafer. No, I was a loafer even when I was going around with you. In those days, I tried to look a little lively—that's probably why I seemed talented and promising to you. Of course, if Japanese society were in sound spiritual, moral, and physical health—if it were just in all-around good health, then I'd still be talented and promising, don't you see? Because then there would be plenty of incentive to shake me out of my inclination to just loaf. But as things are, it's no good. I'd rather be alone. As for your so-called world-as-it's-given, I'll take it as it is and content myself with having contact with just those things that are most suited to me. To go out and bring other people around to my way of thinking—that's something that can't be done. . . ."

Daisuke paused for an instant. Then he turned to Michiyo, who sat looking somewhat uncomfortable, and coaxed, "What do you think, Michiyo-san. About my idea. Isn't it nice and easygoing? Won't you be on my side?"

"In a way it sounds pessimistic, and in a way it sounds easygoing. It's strange. I don't understand very well. But it seems like you're cheating a little."

"Oh? Where?"

"Where?—well, don't you think . . .?" and Michiyo turned to her husband. Hiraoka had been sitting silently with his elbows on his thighs and his chin on his hands; without a word, he put his sake cup before Daisuke. Daisuke received it silently. Michiyo filled their cups again.

Touching the cup to his lips, Daisuke felt there was no need to say more. To begin with, he was not arguing for the sake of bringing Hiraoka around to his viewpoint; nor had he come to be lectured by Hiraoka. Since he realized from the start that the two were destined to stand apart, he had tried to tie up the argument at a reasonable point and bring the conversation around to more common social topics in which Michiyo could join.

But Hiraoka became stubborn when drunk. Thrusting out his chest, which was flushed to the roots of its hairs, he said, "That's interesting. Very interesting. People like me who tackle a part of reality and struggle with it don't have time to think up things like that. Japan might be poor, it might be weak—but I forget about that when I'm working. Society might be degenerating, but I don't notice it; I keep busy in the middle of it. Oh, I suppose that the poverty of Japan or the degeneracy of people like me might disturb a man of leisure like you; but that's the kind of thing that only a man who's got nothing to do with the rest of society, a spectator, can say. In other words, it's because you have the time to look at your own face in the mirror that you come up with things like that. People forget their faces when they're busy."

Hiraoka had naturally hit upon this metaphor as he talked, and feeling as if he had found a great ally, he paused triumphantly. Daisuke had no choice but to smile weakly. Hiraoka picked up immediately. "What's wrong with you is that you've never had to worry about money. You don't feel like working because you don't have to in order to make ends meet. In other words, you're still little Master Daisuke—that's why you keep on saying these nice, refined things. . . ."

At this point, Daisuke found Hiraoka a trifle provoking and cut him short: "It's fine to work, but as long as you're going to work, it ought to be for more than subsistence, else it won't be to your credit. All toil that is sacred transcends the realm of bread."

Hiraoka studied Daisuke's face with strangely unpleasant eyes. Then he asked, "Why?"

"Why? Because toil for the sake of subsistence is not toil for its own sake."

"I can't understand that—it sounds like a proposition from a logic textbook. Can't you put it in terms that a practical man can understand?"

"I mean that it's hard to work sincerely at a job that you're doing just to eat."

"I think just the opposite. It's because you're working to eat that you feel like working furiously."

"Maybe you can work furiously, but it's hard to work sincerely. If you're working in order to eat, which do you think is the main object—work or food?"

"Food, of course."

"See? If food's the object and work the means, then it stands to reason that you'll adjust your work to make it easier to eat. In that case, it won't matter what you do or how you do it as long as you can get bread—that's what it's bound to come down to. As long as the content and direction, or the procedure of a given endeavor are circumscribed by external conditions, then that endeavor is degenerate endeavor."

"That sounds pretty theoretical again. But why should that matter?"

"Then let me explain it to you with a very refined example. This may sound a little musty, but I remember reading it in a book. Oda Nobunaga once hired a famous cook. The first time he ate something prepared by the cook, he thought it tasted terrible, so he gave the cook a sound scolding. After that, the cook, who had been punished for serving his finest dishes, would only make second and third-rate dishes, and he was always praised. Now, take this cook—he might have been very shrewd as far as working for a living went, but as for working for his art, which was cooking, why, he was insincere; he was a degenerate cook."

"But if he hadn't done that, he would have been fired. He couldn't help it."

"That's why I'm saying, unless you're a man without worries about food and clothing, doing something on a whim as it were, it's impossible to do any serious work."

"So that means only a man in your position is capable of sacred toil. Then it's your duty all the more to do something. Right, Michiyo?"

"Yes, that's true."

"It seems that we're right back where we started. That's why arguments are no good," said Daisuke, scratching his head. The argument was over at last.

Chapter VII

DAISUKE WAS TAKING A BATH.

"How's the temperature, Sensei? Shall I heat it up a bit?" Kadono popped his head in at the door. He was quite attentive to these matters.

Soaking in the water, Daisuke remained motionless. "This is fine," he answered.

"Is it," Kadono said abruptly and returned to the morning room. Daisuke found Kadono's response terribly interesting and grinned broadly to himself. Daisuke had a sensibility that registered perceptions unknown to most people. He occasionally suffered agonizing experiences on account of it. Once, when a friend's father died, he had attended the funeral. He happened to glance at his friend in formal attire, following the coffin with a green bamboo stick; the sight struck him as so funny he did not know what to do. Another time, listening to his father lecture, he had unwittingly looked at the old man's face and was seized by an uncontrollable desire to burst out laughing. In the days before he had his own bath, he used to go to a neighborhood bathhouse, where there was one unusually muscular attendant. Whenever Daisuke went, this fellow would come dashing out from the back, crying "Let me wash you down," and proceed to rub his back. Each time he had his back scrubbed by this fellow, Daisuke felt as if it were being done by an Egyptian. Try as he would, he could not picture the man as a Japanese.

There were other strange things. The other day he had discovered in his readings that a physiologist named Weber could accelerate and decelerate his heartbeat at will; Dai-suke, who was in the habit of examining his heartbeat any-way, was tempted to try it, but when he was at the point of making two or three timid attempts a day, he began to feel that he was becoming like Weber. Startled by the thought, he abruptly halted his investigations.

Daisuke, who had been quietly soaking in the water, me-chanically lifted his right hand to his left breast; no sooner had he heard the throbbing of life two or three times than he remembered Weber and immediately got out of the tub. There, sitting cross-legged on the floor, he stared absently at his legs. They began to look strange. They no longer seemed to grow from his trunk at all, but rather, completely uncon-nected, they sprawled rudely before him. When he got this far, he realized something he had never noticed before—that his legs were unbearably hideous. With hair growing unevenly and blue streaks running rampant, they were terribly strange creatures.

Daisuke got into the tub again and wondered if, as Hira-oka had said, such thoughts came to him because he had en-tirely too much time on his hands. When he left the bath and looked at his form in the mirror, he recalled Hiraoka's words again. Now it was time to shave his cheeks with the broad Western razor; the sight of the sharp blade gleaming in the mirror aroused a ticklish sensation in him. Pressed by the knowledge that if the sensation became more acute he would feel as if he were looking down from a high tower, he finally managed to finish shaving.

Just as he was about to pass through the morning room, he heard the words, "Sensei's pretty crafty, somehow." It was Kadono talking to the old woman.

"What do you mean, crafty?" Daisuke stopped and looked at Kadono.

Kadono answered, "Oh, you're out already, Sensei. That was quick." Given this greeting, Daisuke could not very well repeat, what do you mean, crafty. So he went straight back to his study, sat in a chair, and rested.

As he rested, it occurred to him that it could not be good for his health to have his mind working in such odd ways; perhaps he should do a little traveling. For one thing, it would be a convenient way of avoiding the marriage issue that had reared its head again. But then, Hiraoka still weighed on his mind, and he quickly erased all thought of seeking a change of air. When he pursued the matter further, it became clear that it was Michiyo, not Hiraoka, who weighed on his mind. But even when he had pursued the issue this far, Daisuke did not feel the slightest qualms. On the contrary, he felt rather elated.

It was four or five years ago, when he was still a student, that Daisuke had become acquainted with Michiyo. In those days, because of the Nagai family's standing, Daisuke was familiar with a number of the names and faces of the young women who had risen to the surface of society. But Michiyo was not among them. One would have said that in appearance she was more sober, and in spirit, more subdued than they were. In those days, Daisuke had a schoolfriend named Suganuma, who was on friendly terms with both Daisuke and Hiraoka. Michiyo was his younger sister.

This Suganuma was from a neighboring prefecture, and in the spring of his second year at the university, he brought his sister out from the country to further her education. He immediately left his old boarding house, and the two set up housekeeping. At the time, his sister had just graduated from a girls' higher school. The story was that she was eighteen or thereabouts. She wore fine, bright collars and shoulder tucks. Soon, she began to commute to a girls' school.

Suganuma's house was in Shimizuchō in Yanaka. There was no garden, but instead, from the verandah, there was a view of the old cedars of Ueno forest. These had a singularly mysterious color, like rusted iron. One of them was half-dead and all but bare at the top; toward evening, many crows came to perch and cry. Next door, there lived a young artist. They were on a narrow side street where even rickshas seldom passed. It was an extremely quiet dwelling.

Daisuke went to visit often. The first time he met Michiyo, she retreated with just a bow. Daisuke appraised the view of Ueno forest and went home. The second and even the third times he went, all Michiyo did was to serve the tea. But it was a small house, and she could only have been in the next room. As he talked with Suganuma, Daisuke could not help being conscious that Michiyo was in the next room, listening to what he said.

Daisuke's memory had kept no record of the occasion that had led him to start talking to Michiyo. It must have been that trifling and ordinary an incident. For Daisuke, sated with poems and novels, this had made it all the more interesting. But once they began to talk, the two became friendly, just as in all the poems and novels.

Like Daisuke, Hiraoka had often gone to visit at Suganuma's. There were occasions when the two had set out together. And just about the same time as Daisuke, Hiraoka became acquainted with Michiyo. At times, Michiyo had tagged along when her brother and the two young men went for a walk to the edge of the pond.

The four passed slightly less than two years in this manner. In the spring of the year Suganuma was to graduate, his mother came out from the country and spent a few nights in Shimizuchō. It was the mother's custom to come to Tokyo once or twice a year and spend five or six days with her children; this time, however, she began running a fever the day before her departure and could not move. A week later, her case was diagnosed as typhus, and she was immediately taken to the university hospital. Michiyo moved in to take care of her. The patient's progress was satisfactory at first, but midway she suffered a setback and, in the end, died. That was not all. Michiyo's brother, who had visited his mother, also contracted typhus and died not long after. Only their father was left at home in the country.

Since he came out both when the mother died and when Suganuma died to make the necessary arrangements, the father became acquainted with the two young men who had been deeply involved with the deceased. When the time came for him to take Michiyo home, he took his daughter and called at their respective boarding houses to thank them and bid them farewell.

That fall, Hiraoka married Michiyo. It was Daisuke who had arranged everything between them. Officially, a senior alumnus from the home province was asked to fill the role of go-between at the ceremony, but it was Daisuke who had actually busied himself and made the necessary arrangements for Michiyo.

Shortly after the wedding, the couple left Tokyo. Unexpected circumstances at home forced Michiyo's father to leave, and he ended up going to Hokkaido. Michiyo had been placed in a somewhat forlorn situation. Daisuke wanted somehow to make it possible for her to settle down in Tokyo. He thought that perhaps he should try consulting with his sister-in-law again to devise some means of raising the money. He also thought of seeing Michiyo and asking her for more intimate details of the situation.

But even if he went over to Hiraoka's, Michiyo was not a woman to rashly wash her dirty linen before others; besides, even if he were able to obtain the details behind their present indebtedness, it would still be no easy matter to probe the depths of the couple's relationship—and that, Daisuke was forced to admit when he looked into his heart, was precisely the true focus of his interest. To be honest, therefore, he had already bypassed the need to learn why they wanted the money. It made no difference whether he knew such superficial details or not; he wanted to lend Michiyo the money and make her content. But he had not the slightest intention of raising the sum in order to win her favor. Daisuke could no longer afford to be so calculating with Michiyo.

Moreover, it would be difficult to chance upon a time when Hiraoka was absent and he could get a full account of their circumstances, even those particulars relating only to finances. It went without saying that as long as Hiraoka was at home, there could be no intimate discussion. Even if there were, Daisuke would of course not be able to accept all the details at face value. Hiraoka, prompted by various worldly motives, maintained a display of pride before Daisuke. Even where such display was unnecessary, he for some reason guarded his silence.

Daisuke decided that in any case, he would consult with his sister-in-law first. Yet he felt himself that the prospects were extremely dim. He had time and again harassed her with requests for trifling sums, but never before had he confronted her so brashly. But Umeko had some funds at her disposal, so it was not absolutely certain that nothing would come of the request. If that did not work, he might even go to a money lender, but he was not yet inclined to go that far. If, however, Hiraoka was sooner or later going to press him into a formal joint liability and he was to find himself unable to refuse, then it was far more pleasant to take the initiative himself and please Michiyo directly. This decision, reached without the help of reason, had already settled somewhere in Diasuke's head.

There was a warm, humid wind blowing on the day he chose to visit his sister-in-law. Sometime after four o'clock, as the cloudy weather hung lazily in the sky without any sign of clearing, Daisuke left his home and took the streetcar to his brother's house. Just before the Aoyama Palace, his father and brother passed on the left, hurrying their special speed rickshas. Since they passed too quickly even to exchange nods, the two of course had not noticed him. Daisuke got off at the next stop.

As he entered the gate to his brother's house, the sound of the piano came from the drawing room. Daisuke paused for an instant on the gravel, then immediately cut to the left and went around to the kitchen entrance. There, outside the grating, a large English dog named Hector lay asleep with a leather muzzle over his mouth. As soon as he heard Daisuke's footsteps, Hector shook his long-haired ears and sharply lifted his spotted face. Then he moved his tail.

Daisuke looked into the houseboy's room at the side of the entrance, said a few pleasantries from the threshold, and went straight to the Western room, where he opened the door to find his sister-in-law seated at the piano. At her side stood Nuiko, wearing a long-sleeved kimono, her hair hanging to the shoulders. Every time he saw her hair, Daisuke recalled the sight of Nuiko on a swing. Her black hair, light pink ribbon, and yellow crepe sash had caught the wind all at once and looked as if they floated in the air. . . . The image was carved vividly in his mind.

Mother and daughter turned around at once.

"Well."

Nuiko came running over without a word. She grabbed his hand and dragged him forward. Daisuke found himself beside the piano.

"I wondered who the great master was."

Without a word, Umeko, her brows knitted, smiled and waved her hands to cut him short. "Dai-san, you play this part and show us."

Daisuke silently took his sister-in-law's place. With his eyes on the notes, he skillfully worked his fingers for a while, then said, "That's about right, isn't it?" and quickly left the seat.

For some thirty minutes, mother and daughter took turns

at the instrument, reviewing the same passage. Finally, Umeko said, "Let's stop here. Why don't we go over there and eat. You come too, Uncle Daisuke," and stood up. It was already growing dark in the room. Daisuke, who had been listening to the music, watching the white hands of his sister-in-law and niece, and, from time to time, gazing at the transom painting, had all but forgotten about Michiyo and the money he wanted to borrow. Looking back as he left the room, he noticed that only the areas where the ultramarine waves broke and blew white sprays were clearly visible in the dark. Above these billows Daisuke pictured golden cloud peaks flung everywhere. As for the skyline, he completed it skillfully by making the peaks appear, on close inspection, to be giant nude females with streaming hair and leaping bodies, forming a furious, frenzied band. Daisuke had ordered this design with the intention of having the clouds suggest the Valkyries. In his mind he had fused together these enormous clusters, distinguishable neither as cloud peaks nor as giant female forms, and he secretly delighted in them. But once the painting was actually executed and fitted into the wall, it had fallen far short of his imagination. By the time he left the room with Umeko, the Valkyries were barely visible. The ultramarine waves, of course, were not visible at all. Only the large clumps of white foam glimmered palely.

The lights had already been lit in the living room. There Daisuke took his dinner with Umeko and the two children. Daisuke had Seitarō bring him a cheroot from his brother's room, and as he smoked, he made small talk. In time, the children, warned by their mother that they had to prepare their lessons for the next day, retired to their rooms, and Daisuke and Umeko were left face to face.

Daisuke thought it would be strange to launch directly into his request and so began his advance from various unrelated points. Where were his father and brother rushing off to in their rickshas? Seigo had treated him to lunch the other day. Why hadn't Umeko gone to the garden party at Azabu? Father's Chinese poetry was mostly empty talk. In the course of exchanging such questions and answers, Daisuke learned one new fact. It had to do precisely with what he had witnessed earlier. According to Umeko, his brother and father had been conspicuously busy during the past four or five days —so much so that they barely had time to sleep. What on earth was happening, Daisuke asked, his face composed as usual. His sister-in-law likewise responded in her normal manner, saying yes, she supposed something was going on; since neither his father nor his brother told her anything, she didn't know, but anyway, Dai-san, about a bride for you, she began, when the houseboy came in.

They were going to be late again; if such-and-such parties called, tell them to come to the _____ teahouse. The houseboy delivered this telephone message and left. Thinking it would be bothersome to have the conversation return to the marriage issue, Daisuke came straight out and said that as a matter of fact, he had come to ask a small favor.

Umeko listened to his story obediently. Daisuke took some ten minutes to recite everything. In conclusion he said, "So won't you take a chance and lend me the money?"

Then Umeko, looking serious, said "Yes, well, let me see. When do you plan to pay it back?" It was a completely unexpected question. Pinching his chin with his fingers, Daisuke silently studied his sister-in-law's manner. Umeko, looking increasingly serious, said, "I'm not being sarcastic. You mustn't get angry."

Daisuke was of course not angry. He simply had not expected a question like this from his sister-in-law. If, at this point, he were to elaborate and say yes, he planned to return it, or no, he had actually counted on being given it, things would become much too absurd; therefore, he tamely submitted to Umeko's offensive. Umeko felt as if she finally had this difficult younger brother in her grasp, and she found it easy to follow up with "Dai-san, you've always looked down on me, haven't you? No, I'm not trying to be disagreeable. It's the truth, it can't be helped. Isn't that right?"

"I don't know what to say when you interrogate me like this, so deadly serious."

"It's all right. You don't have to cover up. I know perfectly well. Why don't you come out and admit it honestly? Unless you do, I can't go on with the rest."

Daisuke sat grinning without a word.

"See? What did I say! But I take it for granted. It doesn't bother me at all. No matter how I strut about, of course I'm no match for you. You and I are satisfied with our relationship as it's always been, so I won't complain. That's that, but you also look down on your father, don't you."

Daisuke was taken by the sincerity of her manner. So he answered, "Yes, I do look down on him a little."

At this, Umeko laughed out loud as if terribly delighted. Then she said, "You also look down on your brother."

"My brother? I respect my brother tremendously."

"Don't lie. Go ahead and confess it all while you're at it."

"Well, I don't not look down on him in some ways."

"There! What did I say. You look down on every member of the family."

"I'm very sorry."

"You needn't bother with such apologies. As far as you're concerned, I'm sure we all deserve to be looked down upon."

"Why don't we call it quits? You're being awfully hard on me today."

"No, I mean it, it really doesn't matter. We aren't going to fight over this or anything. But anyway, why should a great man like you have to borrow money from someone like me? Isn't it funny? You're probably angry, thinking that I'm trying to trip you up in your own words. But that's not it at all. It just so happens that when you don't have money, even a great man like you has to come and bow before a person like me."

"That's why I've been bowing all this time."

"You're still not taking me seriously."

"But this is my way of being serious."

"Maybe it's also your way of being great. But what will you do if no one will lend you the money and you can't help your friends? No matter how great you are, it won't do any good. You're just the same as a ricksha driver as far as skills go."

Daisuke had never expected to receive such pointed criticism from his sister-in-law. But in fact, ever since he had thought of trying to raise the money, he had been dimly aware of this weakness himself. "You're right, I am no better than a ricksha driver. That's why I've come to ask your help."

"What shall we do with you! You're too great. You find the money yourself. I wouldn't mind considering it if you were a real ricksha driver, but I won't lend to you. You're a little too much, aren't you? Every month you come around to your father and brother for your keep, and now, on top of it, you've taken on other people's needs and offer to lend to them. Who would be willing to pay for that?"

Umeko's point was most reasonable. Daisuke had overstepped the reasonable without noticing it. Looking back, he saw his sister and brother and father huddled together. He felt that he, too, would have to retrace his steps and stand with the rest of society. Before he left his own house, he had worried that his sister might refuse him the money. But even so, he could never have resolved to work hard and raise the money himself. Daisuke did not take the matter that seriously.

Umeko, making the most of this opportunity, tried to rouse Daisuke on a score of points. But Daisuke understood very well what she was about. The more he understood, the less inclined he was to be roused. Eventually, the conversation left the topic of money and returned to that of marriage.

Since their earlier conversation, Daisuke had been twice harangued by his father on the latest prospect. His father's reasoning was, as always, old-fashioned and obligation-bound, but this time his tactics were not as high-handed as usual. It was a fine thing to cement ties with someone of the same blood as his very lifesaver, said his father; wouldn't Daisuke accept her? In that way, Nagai Toku could at least repay his obligations in a small way. As far as Daisuke was concerned, it was unclear as to what was so fine, or what constituted the repayment of a debt—it was all utterly illogical. Daisuke had no particular objection to the candidate herself. Given that the propriety of his father's reasoning lay beyond the pale of argument, Daisuke did not especially mind marrying the girl if it came to that. Just as he had made it his practice not to place too much weight on anything over the past two or three years, so he recognized no need to place undue emphasis on marriage. He only knew Sagawa's daughter from a photograph, but he felt that that was quite enough—admittedly, in the photograph she looked rather beautiful. So, if it came to marrying her, he had no intention of putting forth cumbersome conditions. It was just that he could not bring himself to actually say yes.

Such vacillation, his father would criticize, was the attitude of a blockhead who understood nothing. For his sister-in-law, who regarded marriage as the single crucial event lying between birth and death, to which all other events were to be subordinated, his attitude was appalling.

"Surely even you don't plan to stay single all your life? Why don't you quit acting like a spoiled child and make up your mind?" said Umeko, a trifle exasperated.

To stay single all his life, or to keep a mistress, or to have relations with geisha—Daisuke himself had no clear plans. The only certain thing was that unlike other single men, he could not get very interested in marriage. This could be traced to three factors: first, the quality of his disposition, which was such that he could not wholeheartedly concentrate on any one thing; second, the considerable keenness of his mind, which, given the conditions of contemporary Japan, had been primarily directed at dispelling illusions; and last, the opportunity that relatively unconstrained finances had given him to know quite a number of a certain type of woman. But Daisuke saw no need to take his analysis this far. While keeping a firm grip on the reality that was evident to him—that he was uninterested in marriage—he simply planned to let the future unfold naturally. Therefore, to set out with the premise that marriage was a necessity, and to struggle to realize it at some point, was to Daisuke unnatural, irrational, and moreover, tainted with vulgarity.

Of course, Daisuke did not intend to elaborate on this philosophy to his sister-in-law. But sometimes, driven into a corner, he would ask in despair, "But is it absolutely necessary that I get a wife?" Daisuke was of course perfectly serious in asking this, but his sister-in-law was aghast. She would end up interpreting it as Daisuke's making fun of her. That night, after going through the usual procedure with him, Umeko said, "It's strange, how much you don't want to get married—you say it's not that you don't want to, but if you won't get married it comes to the same thing as your not wanting to. In that case, there must be someone you like. Why don't you tell me her name?"

Of all the prospects thus far, Daisuke could not recall a single one whom he had mentally designated as a woman he liked. But now, confronted with Umeko's question, the name *Michiyo* came floating to his mind, and behind it, the words "that's why I'd like you to lend me the money" formed of their own accord. But Daisuke only smiled ironically and sat quietly before his sister.

Chapter VIII

THE NIGHT WAS LATE
by the time Daisuke left for home without having succeeded
with his sister-in-law. So late, in fact, that he barely managed to catch the last streetcar from Aoyama. Even so, all the
while he was talking, neither his father nor his brother came
home. Umeko was called to the telephone twice. Since there
was nothing unusual in her manner, Daisuke had not bothered to ask after them.

That night, the sky, which threatened rain, seemed to
have taken on the color of the earth. As he waited all alone by
the red pole marking the streetcar stop, a small ball of fire appeared in the distance. It struck him as terribly forlorn as it
flickered up and down, heading straight toward him. When
he got on, he found himself the only passenger. Sandwiched
between the black-garbed conductor and the driver, he moved
on, buried in a certain kind of sound, and saw that everything
was black outside the moving train. Seated all alone in the
spotlight, Daisuke felt as if he might ride on and on, and, in
the end, without having had the chance to get off, be dragged
along forever.

When he got off at Kagurazaka, the deserted road, hemmed
in by two-storied houses on either side, closed in long and
narrow before him. When he was halfway up, the road began
to reverberate. Daisuke thought that it must be the wind hit-
ting the ridges of the houses. He stopped and looked up at the
dark eaves. As he swept his eyes from the roofs to the sky, he
was suddenly overcome by a kind of terror. The rattling of

the doors, glass panels, and shoji became furious, and by the time he said to himself, it's an earthquake, his legs, though still standing, were bent double. At that instant he thought the two-storied houses would come toppling down from both sides and bury the hill. Just then, a small side door burst open and a man came out carrying a child, shouting, it's an earthquake, it's an earthquake, it's a huge earthquake! Hearing the man's voice, Daisuke felt reassured at last.

When he got home, the old woman and Kadono were full of talk about the earthquake. But Daisuke thought that neither of them could have felt it as he had. When he got into bed, he tried once more to think of how he should handle Michiyo's request. But he did not go so far as to tax his mind. He tried to guess what lay behind his father's and brother's recent extreme activity. He resolved to continue to vacillate on the marriage question. Finally, he fell asleep.

The next day, the so-called Japan Sugar Company Incident appeared in the newspapers for the first time. The report was that the executives of a sugar refinery had used company funds to bribe several members of the Diet. Kadono, as usual, found it "thrilling" that business executives and politicians were being taken into custody, but Daisuke could not find it all that thrilling. In two or three days, as the number of those under investigation increased, people began to clamor as if it were a major scandal. One paper even termed it a "roundup for England." The explanation went that the British ambassador had bought up Japan Sugar stock and lost on it; when he began to register his dissatisfaction, the Japanese government had embarked on this course to mollify him.

Shortly before the Japan Sugar Incident, a firm called the Oriental Steamship Company had reported a loss of eight hundred thousand yen in the six-month period following payment of a 12 percent dividend. Daisuke remembered this incident. He also remembered that at the time, the newspapers had questioned the credibility of the report.

Daisuke knew nothing about the firm with which his father and brother were associated. But he had always thought that something could happen any day. And he did not believe that his father and brother were blameless in every respect. He even wondered if, under strict scrutiny, they might not both qualify for investigation. Even if it did not go that far, he certainly would not affirm that their fortunes had been made with sheer skill and daring. In the early years of the Meiji Period, the government, in order to encourage immigration to the Yokohama area, had offered free land. There were people today who enjoyed considerable wealth because of the land they had received at that time. This belonged to the category of heaven-bestowed good fortune. But, men like his father and brother, thought Daisuke, built their own hothouses in which they could artificially, and moreover, calculatingly, go about creating the good fortune that would benefit only themselves.

With thoughts such as these, Daisuke was not particularly surprised by the newspaper reports. Nor was he so honest as to worry about his father's and brother's company. Only Michiyo weighed on his mind somewhat. But to go to her empty-handed was disagreeable; he resolved to do something in the near future, and then he spent four or five days immersed in his reading. Strangely enough, he heard not a word from either Hiraoka or from Michiyo about the money. In his heart, Daisuke thought that Michiyo might come alone to get his answer, and he waited expectantly. But the waiting was in vain.

In the end, he began to be beset by ennui. Wondering if there might not be some place where he could divert himself, he began to look through the entertainment guides and thought of going to a play. He took the Sotobori line from Kagurazaka, but by the time he got to Ochanomizu, he changed his mind and decided instead to visit an old classmate named Terao in Morikawachō. This fellow, upon graduation, had announced that since he did not want to teach, he was going to make literature his business. Heedless of the warnings of those around him, he had launched out on a risky venture. Three years had gone by, but he had yet to make his name. Gasping and panting, he continued to make his living by writing. Daisuke, pressed to write something—anything—for a magazine with which Terao was associated, had once sent in a humorous piece. For one month it had lain exposed to the elements in the stands at the front of magazine shops and then was doomed to disappear forever from the world of man. Since then, Daisuke had refused to pick up his brush. Every time he saw Daisuke, Terao urged him to write again, never failing to add, look at me. But report had it that he was actually on the verge of giving up. He was partial to Russian works, especially those by writers whom others had never heard of, and his vice was to spend his last penny on a newly published book. Once, when he had become too bombastic, Daisuke had teased that as long as writers were obsessed with Russia they would never get anywhere. It was impossible to talk with those who hadn't gotten beyond the Russo-Japanese War. Looking serious, Terao had answered that he was willing to do battle any time, but simply to ascend to paradise as postwar Japan had done was terribly dull. It might be cowardly, but it was still safer to be afflicted with a passion for Russia. Thus Terao persisted in championing Russian literature.

Going in from the entranceway, Daisuke found Terao seated at a lacquered desk in the middle of the room, a towel tied around his head (a headache, he said), sleeves rolled up, working on a manuscript for *Imperial Literature*. Daisuke offered to come another day if he was busy, but Terao answered no, there was no need to leave, he had already done (here he paused to calculate) five times five, two yen and fifty sen's worth of work since the morning. Presently, he took off the towel and began to talk, almost immediately commencing to rail—with a ferocity that all but took one's breath away—at contemporary Japanese writers and critics. Daisuke listened, entertained. But he secretly thought that Terao was engaging in mudslinging because no one would praise him. Why not publish some of those views, he urged; that wouldn't do, Terao laughed. Asked why not, he refused to answer. After a while, he came back with, of course, if he were in Daisuke's shoes and had an easy life, he would not hesitate to speak out; as it was, he had to eat after all. It wasn't a serious business anyway. That was all right, he should just do his best, encouraged Daisuke. It wasn't all right at all, answered Terao. He very much wanted to do something serious. How about it, didn't Daisuke feel like lending him a little money and making a serious fellow out of him? No, when the time came that Terao felt he was being serious doing just the kind of thing he was now doing, then he would lend him money, teased Daisuke. With these words he stepped outside.

He came out to the street in Hongō, but the feeling of ennui was the same as ever. No matter where he wandered, he felt unsatisfied, and he had lost the urge to visit.

Examining himself, he realized that his whole body felt as if it had turned into an enormous upset stomach. He caught the streetcar from Fourth Street and arrived at Dentsūinmae. Each time the train shook, he felt as if something rotten inside his five-foot-plus upset stomach were pulsating in waves. It was past three when he listlessly meandered home. Kadono met him at the door, saying "There was a messenger from your home. I left the letter on your desk in the study. I signed the receipt for it myself."

The letter was in an old-fashioned message case. Nothing, not even the addressee's name, was written on its red exterior; it was marked with black ink where the narrow folds had been sealed and pushed through a brass ring. Daisuke took one look at the top of his desk and knew the sender to be his sister-in-law. There was no mistaking Umeko's quaint tastes, which from time to time found unexpected expression.

Poking at the sealed folds with scissors, Daisuke thought she had gone to troublesome lengths.

But the letter within was just the opposite of its container. It was simple, colloquial, and to the point. She was sorry that she had been unable to comply with his request the other day when he had taken the trouble to come over. Looking back, she was disturbed that she had been so forward and rude. She hoped he would not think badly of her. But she was giving him the money. Though she couldn't quite manage the entire sum. She had put together just two hundred yen. He should take it to his friends right away. This was to be kept a secret from his brother, so he should bear that in mind. She had not forgotten the question about his wife, so he should think his answer over carefully.

Rolled inside the letter was a check for two hundred yen. As he looked at it, Daisuke began to feel apologetic toward Umeko. On his way out the other night, she had asked, didn't he need the money, then? When he had thrust the request at her, she had flung it back sharply, yet when he had given up and was about to leave, she had anxiously sought his reassurance. Daisuke saw in her behavior both the beauty and the frailty of women. And he lost the heart to take advantage of such a weakness, because he could not bear to trifle with such beautiful frailty. Saying no, he didn't need it, things would probably work out somehow, he had left. No doubt Umeko had thought that a cruel response. It must have been those cold words that had caught somewhere behind her normal resoluteness and led to this letter.

Daisuke answered immediately. He tried to express his gratitude as warmly as possible. Daisuke never felt such inclinations toward his brother. Nor toward his father. Nor, naturally, toward society at large. And lately, he had seldom felt this way even toward Umeko.

Daisuke thought of going to Michiyo's right away. But the fact was, two hundred yen was an odd sum. He even thought that as long as she was going to give him this much, she should have gone all the way and satisfied him completely by giving him what he had asked for to begin with. But this thought came to him only when his mind turned from Umeko to Michiyo. And for Daisuke, who believed that all women, even the most resolute, wavered when it came to matters of the heart, Umeko's action did not seem cause for complaint. Indeed, insofar as it was indicative of a more expansive sympathy, he found the attitude more agreeable than the intransigency of men. If it had been his father instead of Umeko who had sent the two hundred yen, Daisuke would have seen it as an instance of financial wavering and doubtless would have found it more disagreeable.

Daisuke went out without eating dinner. He followed the banks of the Edogawa River from Gokenchō, and by the time he crossed the river, the spiritual fatigue that had beset him during his afternoon walk had lifted. Climbing the hill and coming out at the side of the Dentsūin, he came upon a tall, narrow chimney, spewing dirty smoke from between the temples into the cloudy sky. The labored breathing of a puny industrial force struggling to survive was unsightly to Daisuke. He could not help half-consciously associating this chimney with Hiraoka, who lived nearby. At such times his esthetic sense always took precedence over his sympathy. Daisuke was so affected by the wretched coal smoke dispersing into the sky that for an instant, he all but forgot Michiyo.

In Hiraoka's doorway, a pair of women's sandals lay where they had been flung off. When Daisuke opened the grating, Michiyo came out from the back, letting her hem rustle softly. It was already dark in the cramped vestibule. Michiyo sat down and greeted him from the midst of the darkness. At first, she could not seem to tell who it was, but as soon as she heard Daisuke's voice, she said, rather low, that she had wondered who it was. Daisuke gazed at Michiyo's indistinct form and found it more beautiful than usual.

Hiraoka was absent. When he heard this, Daisuke found it at once easier and harder to go on talking; it was a peculiar feeling. But Michiyo, for her part, was as composed as ever. The two sat together without even lighting a lamp or opening up the dark room. Michiyo said the maid was also out. She herself had been out to do an errand and had just finished her dinner. Eventually, Hiraoka's name was mentioned.

As Daisuke had anticipated, Hiraoka was still running about busily. But in the past week or so, he had begun not to go out very much. He said he was tired and often stayed home to sleep. Or else he drank. If anyone came to visit, he drank still more. And he scolded a good deal. He railed all the time. This was Michiyo's story.

"I don't know what to do, he's become so violent, so different from the way he used to be," said Michiyo, as if tacitly seeking sympathy. Daisuke was silent. The maid had returned and was rattling the kitchen door. Presently, she brought in a lamp with a spotted bamboo base. As she went out, she stole a glance at Daisuke's face.

Daisuke took the check from his kimono. He placed it as it was, folded in two, before Michiyo and said, Okusan. It was the first time he had ever called her "Okusan."

"The money that you asked for the other day . . ."

Michiyo said nothing. She only lifted her eyes and looked at Daisuke.

"I meant to bring it right away, but I couldn't quite arrange it, so it's late—but how about it, have you managed to settle that affair?" he asked.

Then Michiyo's voice suddenly became low and forlorn. She sounded bitter as she said, "No, not yet. There's no reason why we should be able to clear it up." With these words, she continued to gaze steadily at Daisuke.

Daisuke opened the folded check and said, "This much wouldn't do?"

Michiyo extended her hand to take the check.

"Thank you. Hiraoka will be glad." She quietly placed the check on the tatami.

Daisuke briefly explained how he had obtained the money, and added, as if to excuse himself, that carefree as his situation seemed, whenever he attempted to do anything for someone else, he became quite incompetent; he hoped she would not think badly of him on that account.

"Of course, I know that perfectly well, too. But I just didn't know what to do, that's why I made such an unreasonable request." Michiyo's apology was sympathetic.

Daisuke wanted to be sure. "Will that be enough to settle the affair? If, not, I'll try something else."

"Something else?"

"I'll put my seal down and get a high-interest loan."

"No, not that!" said Michiyo immediately, as if to erase the thought. "That would really be terrible, you know."

Daisuke learned that Hiraoka's woes had all begun when he borrowed from usurers; those loans had bounced around and were still plaguing him. When they first went to Kansai, Hiraoka had the reputation of being a diligent worker, but after Michiyo's pregnancy, when she began to suffer from heart trouble, he had started to play around. At first it had not been terribly excessive, and Michiyo had resigned herself, thinking it was out of social obligation; in the end it had exceeded all bounds and Michiyo had worried. If she tried to improve matters, her health would deteriorate. If her health deteriorated, his debauchery would be aggravated. It wasn't that he was unkind. It was her fault, Michiyo protested. But looking lonely again, she confessed that there were times when she thought that if only the child had lived, things might have been much better.

Daisuke felt that he could guess at the substance of the marital relations hidden behind the financial problems and refrained from asking too many questions. On his way out, he tried to encourage her, saying "You mustn't get so down-hearted. Try to be cheerful, the way you used to be. And come over and visit sometimes."

"Yes, you're right," Michiyo smiled. Each saw the past in the other's face. Hiraoka had not come home after all.

Three days later, Hiraoka came without warning. That day, a dry wind fanned the cheerful blue sky, and the weather was hotter than usual. The morning papers carried iris-viewing reports. The large potted clivia that Daisuke had bought had finally shed its petals on the verandah. In their place, the green leaves, almost as wide as a broad sword, were pushing through the stems and growing long. The old, now blackened leaves lingered to glisten in the sun. One of them had by chance been folded in two and drooped sharply about six inches from where it left the stem. It was unsightly to Daisuke. He went out to the verandah with the scissors, cut the leaf just before the fold, and threw it away. The thick edge seemed to ooze, and as Daisuke watched, a drop sounded on the verandah floor. A thick, heavy green fluid had gathered at the cut edge. Wanting to smell it, Daisuke poked his nose into the tangled leaves. He left the drip on the verandah just as it was. Then he stood, and pulling a handkerchief from his sleeve, was beginning to wipe the blades of the scissors when Kadono came in to announce that Mr. Hiraoka was here. At that moment, neither Hiraoka nor Michiyo had any part of Daisuke's thoughts. He was under the spell of the strange green fluid, moving in an atmosphere quite apart from the outside world. The moment he heard Hiraoka's name, the feeling was dispelled. And he somehow did not feel like seeing him.

"Shall I show him in this way?" Prompted by Kadono, Daisuke only said "Hm" and stepped inside. Hiraoka, who was shown in after him, was already wearing a summer suit. Not only were his white shirt and collar new, but he also had on a

kind of knit tie that was much in vogue. He was so fashion-
ably put together that no one would have guessed he was unemployed.

After some talk, it became clear that Hiraoka's situation
had not progressed at all. Lately, it was useless even to try;
that was why he played around like this every day. Or else he
stayed at home and slept, he said, making a point of laughing
loudly. Daisuke said that was probably good, too. After that
they passed the time in innocuous gossip. But since it was not
so much gossip that came up naturally as gossip designed to
skirt a particular problem, they both felt a certain tension at
the bottom of their stomachs.

Hiraoka would bring up neither the money nor Michiyo.
Consequently, he also said nothing about the visit Daisuke
had made in his absence three days before. At first, Daisuke
had also deliberately avoided the topic and tried to appear
nonchalant, but as Hiraoka persisted in maintaining his distance, Daisuke became uneasy.

"By the way, I went over to your place two or three days
ago, but you weren't there," he began.

"Hm. So I heard. I have to thank you for that. Thanks to
you . . . oh well, we could have managed without bothering
you, but she worried so much, we ended up inconveniencing
you." Hiraoka offered his chilly thanks. "I guess, in a way,
I've come today to thank you, but she'll probably come herself
one of these days," he added, quite as if Michiyo were an en-
tirely separate entity from himself.

Daisuke simply answered, "There's no need to go to such
trouble." There the conversation came to a halt. Then again
it slid into areas common to both but of no great interest to
either, until Hiraoka said suddenly, "There's a chance I may
quit business altogether. The more I learn about the inside
workings of the business world, the more I get sick of it. Besides, I've made a few stabs at it since I got here and I've lost
all my nerve." It sounded like a confession from the heart.

Daisuke only said, "Of course."

Hiraoka seemed startled by the extreme coolness of the response, but he continued, "As I mentioned a while back, I'm thinking of going into the newspaper business."

"Is there an opening somewhere?" Daisuke asked.

"There's one right now. It looks like I can get it."

When he first came in, Hiraoka had said that he was playing around because it wasn't worth trying to find a job at the moment; now, he was saying there was an opening in the newspaper business that he was considering taking; it was a bit inconsistent, but Daisuke thought it would be too troublesome to press the matter and confined himself to expressing approval with, "That should be interesting."

After seeing Hiraoka to the door, Daisuke remained standing on the threshold for a while, drawing close to the shoji.

As if to keep him company, Kadono also stayed to watch Hiraoka's retreating figure. Soon he opened his mouth. "Mr. Hiraoka is more fashionable than I thought. He almost puts us to shame, looking like that."

"Oh, not really. Nowadays, everybody looks pretty much like that," answered Daisuke, straightening himself.

"Well, you sure can't tell by looks any more, can you. You might be wondering who some gentleman is, then he walks into a shack."

Daisuke did not bother to answer and returned to his study. The fluid that had dripped from the clivia had begun to cake. Daisuke deliberately closed the study off from the next room and shut himself in. It was his habit to seclude himself after receiving guests. On a day like today, when he was thrown off balance, the need for this was particularly acute.

Hiraoka had finally moved away from him. Every time Diasuke saw him, he felt as if he were meeting him from a distance. But in fact, it was not just Hiraoka. He felt like this no matter whom he saw. Modern society was nothing more than an aggregate of isolated individuals. The earth stretched boundlessly, but the instant houses were built upon it, it became fragmented. The people inside the houses became fragmented, too. Civilization took the collective *we* and transformed it into isolated individuals. This was Daisuke's interpretation.

The Hiraoka who had been close to Daisuke had enjoyed having people weep for him. Maybe he was still like that. But since he never gave any indication of it, it was hard to tell. No, in fact, he made a point of behaving so as to repel sympathy. Either he had decided to rely on himself and show that he could get through the world alone, or he had realized that isolation was the true condition of modern society.

The Daisuke who had been close to Hiraoka had enjoyed weeping for others. Gradually, he had become unable to weep. It was not that it was more modern not to weep. In fact, he would rather assert that he was modern precisely because he did not weep. Daisuke had yet to meet the individual who, as he stood groaning beneath the oppression of Occidental civilization in the seething arena of the struggle for survival, was still able to shed genuine tears for another.

It was less estrangement than aversion that Daisuke felt for the new Hiraoka. He judged that Hiraoka was developing the same feelings. There had been times when the old Daisuke was surprised to recognize such shadows in his own heart and was extremely saddened. But now that sadness had all but rubbed off. All he did was to stare at the dark shadows. This was the way it really was, he thought. It could not be helped, he thought. That was all.

Having fallen to the depths of such isolation, Daisuke's mind was far too lucid to agonize over it. He believed that these were the conditions destined for modern man. Accordingly, when he now considered his estrangement from Hiraoka, he concluded it was nothing more than the result of their having proceeded along the normal course of all men to a particular point. At the same time, he could not help recognizing that they had arrived at this point more quickly than most because of certain circumstances that lay between them. These had to do with Michiyo's marriage. It was he, Daisuke, who had counseled Hiraoka to marry Michiyo. He was not so weak of will as to have regretted it at the time. Even now, when he looked back, his act appeared as an honorable one that lit up his past. But in the course of the three years since then, nature had thrust upon the two men consequences peculiar to nature. And the two had had to shed their satisfaction and their glory and bow their heads before this force. Hiraoka came to have fleeting moments of wondering why he had taken Michiyo. Daisuke heard a voice from somewhere asking why he had urged his friend to take her.

Closeted in his study, Daisuke spent the entire day buried in his thoughts.

At dinner time, Kadono called, "You've been studying all day today, Sensei. How about going for a little walk? Today's the festival of the tiger, and some Chinese student's supposed to perform at the auditorium. Why don't you go see what he has to show? Those Chinese aren't shy at all, they'll do anything. It should be fun." He chattered on by himself.

Chapter IX

DAISUKE WAS SUMMONED
by his father again. He could guess quite well what he wanted.
Daisuke had always tried to avoid seeing his father. These
days, he was more careful than ever to steer clear of the inner
quarters of the house, because no matter how politely he addressed his father, inside, he was full of contempt for him.

Contemporary society, in which no human being could
have contact with another without feeling contemptuous, constituted what Daisuke called the decadence of the twentieth
century. The life appetites, which had suddenly swollen of
late, exerted extreme pressure on the instinct for morality
and threatened its collapse. Daisuke regarded this phenomenon as a clash between the old and new appetites. And finally,
he understood that the striking growth of the life appetites
was, in effect, a tidal wave that had swept from European
shores.

These two forces would have to come to an equilibrium at
some point. But Daisuke believed that until the day came
when feeble Japan could stand shoulder to shoulder finan-
cially with the greatest powers of Europe, that balance would
not be achieved. And he was resigned to the likelihood that
the sun would never shine upon such a day. Thus, most of
the Japanese gentry, confronted with this predicament, had
every day to commit crimes that fell just short of running into
the law—or failing that, they had to commit crimes in their
heads. Among themselves, they had to silently acknowledge
each other's crimes and make them the subject of friendly

banter. As a member of the human race, Daisuke could neither bear to receive nor to inflict such insults.

Daisuke's father was a complicated case because his reaction to this dilemma was rather unique. He had received the
morality-centered education peculiar to the pre-Restoration
warrior class. This education was an unreasonable affair that
placed the standard of emotional conduct at some distant
point beyond the self and refused to eye the truths borne out
by immediate facts. Nevertheless, his father remained the
captive of habit and clung tenaciously to this education. At
the same time, he was engaged in business—that activity so
prone to attack by the life appetites. And in fact, over the
years his father had been corroded by these appetites. It stood
to reason that there should be a vast gulf between his present
and past selves. But he would not admit this to himself. He
persisted in declaring that he was the same as ever, that he
had built his business to its present state with the same attitudes he had always held. But Daisuke thought it impossible
to satisfy modern appetites without first limiting the influence of an education valid only in feudal times. Any individual who would dare appease both masters would of necessity
suffer great anguish from the ensuing contradictions. One
who experienced such anguish and failed to recognize its
source was a dim-witted, primitive creature. Each time he
faced his father, Daisuke could not help feeling that either
the man was a dissimulating hypocrite or a fool deficient in
judgment. And Daisuke hated feeling this way.

Even so, his own cleverness was of no avail before his father. And Daisuke knew it well. That was why he had never
yet pushed his father to the limits of his own contradictions.

It was Daisuke's conviction that all morality traced its origins to social realities. He believed there could be no greater
confusion of cause and effect than to attempt to conform social reality to a rigidly predetermined notion of morality. Accordingly, he found the ethical education conducted by lec-

ture in Japanese schools utterly meaningless. In the schools, students were either instructed in the old morality or crammed with a morality suited to the average European. For an unfortunate people beset by the fierce appetites of life, this amounted to nothing more than vain, empty talk. When the recipients of this education saw society before their eyes, they would recall those lectures and burst out laughing. Or else they would feel that they had been made fools of. In Daisuke's case it was not just school; he had received the most rigorous and least functional education from his father. Thanks to this, he had at one time experienced acute anguish stemming from contradictions. Daisuke even felt bitter over it.

When he had gone home to thank Umeko, she had warned him that he had better go to the back and pay his respects. Daisuke had laughed and played the innocent, asking if Father was home. Even when given the unequivocal answer that he was, he said he was in a hurry that day and left.

Today, however, since he had come for the express purpose of seeing his father, he had no choice. When he went around from the inner vestibule to the living room, he found, to his surprise, Seigo sitting cross-legged and drinking. Umeko was at his side. Seeing Daisuke, Seigo said, "How about a drink?" and grabbed the wine bottle in front of him, waving it at Daisuke. There was still quite a bit left. Umeko clapped her hands and sent for a glass.

"Guess how old it is," she said as she poured.

"Daisuke would never know," said Seigo, watching his brother's lips. After one sip, Daisuke put down his glass. Instead of appetizers there were thin wafers on a cake dish.

"It's good," he said.

"That's why I told you to guess how old it is."

"Does it have an age? You've really got something here. I'll take one with me when I go."

"Sorry, this is all there is. It was a gift." Umeko got up and went to the verandah, where she brushed the wafer crumbs from her lap.

"What happened today? You seem very relaxed," Daisuke asked Seigo.

"Today is a day of rest. I've been so busy lately, I had to take a break." Seigo put a cigar that had just gone out into his mouth. Daisuke found a match beside him and lit it for his brother.

"Dai-san, you're the one who's relaxed," said Umeko as she returned from the verandah.

"Have you been to the Kabukiza yet? If you haven't, you should go, it's interesting."

"You've been already? I'm surprised. You really are lazy, aren't you."

"I wouldn't call it lazy. It's just that my studies lie in a different direction."

"You always talk so big. You don't understand how others feel." Umeko turned toward Seigo. Seigo sat with reddened eyelids, blankly blowing the smoke from his cigar.

"Isn't that right?" Umeko prompted.

Transferring his cigar to his fingers with an annoyed look, Seigo answered, "Isn't it better to have him study hard now so that one of these days, when we're poor, he'll be able to save us?"

"Dai-san, could you become an actor?" asked Umeko.

Without answering, Daisuke put his glass before his sister-in-law. Umeko was also silent as she lifted the wine bottle.

"I hear you were terribly busy recently." Daisuke took the conversation back to the beginning.

"Oh, it was too much'." Seigo sprawled out on the floor.

"Did it have anything to do with the Japan Sugar Refinery Incident?"

"It didn't have anything to do with Japan Sugar, but I've been busy, that's for sure."

Seigo's answers were never much clearer than this. He probably did not care to be any clearer just now, but to Daisuke's ears it sounded no different from his habitual laziness in speech. Thus Daisuke had always found it easy to plunge into the heart of his brother's answers.

"Japan Sugar's in a mess, but wasn't there anything they could have done before things came to that?"

"Well, maybe. Actually, you never can tell what might happen in this world. Ume, you have to tell Naoki to take Hector out today so he gets some exercise. It's not good for him to eat like this and sleep all day." Seigo repeatedly rubbed his drooping eyelids.

"I guess it's about time to go to the back and get a scolding from Father," said Daisuke, putting his glass before his sister-in-law. Umeko laughed and poured the wine.

"About a wife?" asked Seigo.

"Yes, I suppose so."

"Go ahead and take her. Shouldn't make an old man worry so much," he said, then continued more decisively, "You'd better watch out. There's been a low pressure front out these days."

Daisuke, who had been about to rise, paused to check, "I hope it's not a low caused by all this recent activity."

His brother, still sprawled out, answered, "Can't say. Even if we look solid like this, there's no telling when we might be dragged off like those Japan Sugar executives."

"Don't talk so foolishly," reproved Umeko.

"It's probably a low brought on by my loafing." Daisuke got up laughing.

He followed the verandah past the inner garden to his father's quarters, where he found the old man seated before a Chinese desk reading a Chinese book. His father was fond of poetry, and whenever he had the time would read collections of Chinese poetry. At times, however, this was an indication of his worst moods. On such occasions even Daisuke's imperturbable brother avoided him at all cost. If an encounter was absolutely necessary, he took the precaution of dragging Seitarō or Nuiko along with him. Daisuke remembered this when he got as far as the verandah, but thinking that he needn't go to quite such extremes, he passed by one room and entered his father's sitting room.

His father first removed his glasses. He placed them on the book he was reading, then turned to face Daisuke. He simply said, "You're here." One might almost have said his tone was milder than usual. Placing his hands on his knees, Daisuke wondered if his brother had not been pulling his leg. As usual, he was forced to drink some bitter tea and spend a little time in small talk: the peonies were out early this year; it was the season for dozing off to tea-picking songs; at some place there was wisteria with clusters over four feet long. . . . The conversation went far afield. Since this was very much to his advantage, Daisuke did his best to prolong it by adding to whatever his father said. Finally, the old man seemed to sense that things had gotten out of hand and launched out with a by the way, Daisuke, I had you come out today because . . .

After that Daisuke did not utter a word. He listened respectfully to what the old man had to say. With Daisuke adopting this posture, his father had no choice but to continue at length by himself, as if he were giving a lecture. Over half of what he said was a repetition of previous deliveries, but Daisuke listened as attentively as if he were hearing it for the first time.

He even spotted two or three new points in his father's lengthy sermon. One of them was a serious query as to what he, Daisuke, planned to do from now on. This was a familiar demand that Daisuke was accustomed to sidestepping with equivocations. But when the question was put so solemnly, he could not blurt out the first thing that came to mind. One reckless word and he would ignite his father's wrath. Yet, if he were to be honest, he would have to spend two or three years educating his father's mind before he could make himself understood. Moreover, he had no clear declaration to make about his future in response to such a solemn question. He felt that this was only reasonable for him. But to tell his father that and bring him around to the point of saying "I see" would require an enormous expenditure of time. There was also the possibility that he would never understand. All Daisuke had to do to please him was to say something about serving the country or serving the world—something grand that could not be linked to marriage. But no matter how inclined he was to self-ridicule, this was simply too stupid; he did not have the courage to let such words fall from his lips. So he had no choice but to reply that in fact, he had a number of ideas, but he planned to sort them out first and then consult his father. After delivering this reply, he found it terribly comical, but there was nothing to be done.

Daisuke was then asked if he did not want an income sufficient to make him independent. Daisuke answered that of course he did. His father then proposed that in this case, he should marry Sagawa's daughter. It remained exceedingly unclear as to whether Sagawa's daughter was bringing the money with her or whether his father was going to give it to him. Daisuke tried to find out, but could confirm nothing. He quit, thinking that there really was no need to investigate the point.

Next, he was asked if he would not just as soon go abroad. Daisuke agreed that that would not be bad. But again, marriage seemed to be the prerequisite.

"Is there really such a pressing need for me to marry Sagawa's daughter?" Daisuke ended up asking. His father's face reddened.

Daisuke had not the slightest intention of angering his father. His current philosophy was that to quarrel with others constituted a species of human degeneracy. To anger another human being, which was one aspect of quarreling, was not so much damaging in itself, but insofar as the angered party's countenance presented an unappealing spectacle to one's own eyes, it was clearly an injury to the precious moments of one's own existence. Daisuke also had his own views about sin. But he did not for a moment believe that because of this he would escape punishment so long as he acted in accordance with his nature. He firmly believed that the punishment dealt one who had killed another human being was contained in the blood that flowed from the dead man's flesh. This stemmed from his conviction that no one could look upon the color of blood spurting forth without experiencing violent turmoil in the sanctum of his heart. Daisuke's nerves were sensitive to this degree. Therefore, when he saw his father redden in the face, he found it singularly unpleasant. But he had no intention of doubly atoning for his sin by doing as his father wanted. This was because, in certain ways, Daisuke paid enormous respect to his own mental faculties.

Meanwhile, his father was heatedly explaining that he was growing old, that his son's future weighed on his mind, that it was a parent's duty to provide a son with a bride, that a parent paid far more scrupulous attention to such matters as the bride's qualifications than the groom himself possibly could, that parental kindness might seem like unwanted interference at the time, but the day was sure to come when he would long for such meddlesome advice. Daisuke listened seriously. But when his father's words ceased their flow, he still showed no signs of assenting. Then his father said in a deliberately restrained tone, "Then don't take Sagawa. Go ahead and marry whomever you like. Is there someone you want?"

This was the same question that Umeko had posed. Daisuke could not put his father off with the ironic smile he had used with her. "There's no one in particular I want to marry," he answered clearly.

Then his father, in a fit of passion, burst out, "In that case, why can't you think a little about my position instead of thinking about yourself all the time?"

Daisuke was surprised that his father had suddenly jumped from his son to the question of his own interests. But the surprise was only over the illogicality and the abruptness of the shift.

"If it is so convenient for you, then let me think it over once more," he answered.

His father's humor only worsened. There were times when, in his dealings with others, Daisuke was incapable of abandoning his sense of logic. Because of this, people often felt that he was deliberately trying to corner them. Actually, there were few who disliked cornering others more than Daisuke.

"I'm not saying that you should marry just for my convenience," his father revised. "If you're going to be so argumentative, let me say, just for the record, that you are thirty, are you not? You can guess pretty well what society thinks of a man who won't get married even when he reaches the age of thirty. Oh, of course, nowadays it's up to the individual if he wants to stay single, but what do you plan to do if your father and brother are embarrassed on account of it, or if, in the end, something happens that could even touch upon your own honor?"

Daisuke looked at his father's face blankly. He could not tell where the old man thought he had stabbed him. Eventually, he said, "I do have my vices, of course, but . . ."

His father cut him short. "That's not what I'm talking about."

After that, the two were silent for some time. His father believed the silence to be a result of the blow he had delivered. Presently, softening his words, he said, "You think it over carefully." Daisuke said he would and retired from his father's room. He went to the living room to look for his brother, but he was not there. When he asked where Umeko was, a maid told him that she was in the parlor, so he went there and opened the door to find that Nuiko's piano teacher had come. After greeting the teacher briefly, Daisuke called Umeko to the door. "Are you sure you didn't say something to Father behind my back?"

Umeko laughed out loud. "Why don't you come in? You've come at a good time," she said, and pulled him over to the piano.

Chapter X

IT WAS THE SEASON
for ants to crawl indoors. Daisuke poured water into a large
bowl and filled it with snowy white lilies-of-the-valley, their
stems still uncut. The delicate, swarming flowers hid the
rim's dark pattern. They spilled over at the slightest motion.
Daisuke placed the bowl on top of a large dictionary. Then he
put his pillow beside it and fell on his back, his black head
lying just in the shadow of the bowl, so that the scent from
the flowers traveled easily to his nostrils. He dozed off smell-
ing the fragrance.

At times, the ordinary physical world affected Daisuke
with inordinate severity. In extreme cases, he could not even
tolerate the sunlight on a clear day. When this happened, he
tried to reduce his contacts with society to a minimum and to
sleep, whether it was morning or noon. He often employed a
faint, lightly sweet floral scent as a part of this stratagem. If
he lay still with his eyelids shut to block out the light, breathing quietly through his nose, the flowers beside his pillow
would gradually lure his restless consciousness into the world
of dreams. When this tactic succeeded, Daisuke's nerves were
renewed, and it became easier than before to maintain his
contacts with society.

For two or three days after his father's summons, Daisuke had been bothered by the red roses in a corner of his garden; whenever he noticed them, they seemed to prick him in
the eye. At such times, he always turned to the leaves of the
stone leek flowers at the side of the washbasin. Each of those

leaves contained three or four white streaks that meandered indulgently. Every time Daisuke looked at them, the leaves seemed to have grown longer, the white streaks growing unhampered with them. The flowers of the pomegranate were gaudier and even more oppressive than the roses. Their color was so strong that they seemed to glitter through the green. And they, too, were unsuited to Daisuke's present mood.

His present mood, as sometimes happened, had taken on an overall tone of darkness. Consequently, when he was exposed to overly bright objects, he found the dissonance difficult to endure. Even the stone leek leaves repelled him if he looked at them long enough.

Moreover, Daisuke began to be beset by a kind of anxiety peculiar to modern Japan. This anxiety was a primitive phenomenon arising from lack of faith between individuals. Thanks to this psychological phenomenon, Daisuke experienced severe discomposure. He was a man who disliked putting his faith in gods, and, as an intellectual, was by nature incapable of doing so. He believed that if people had faith in one another, there was no need to rely on gods. Gods acquired the right to exist only when they became necessary to deliver men from the anguish of mutual suspicion. Accordingly, he concluded that in those countries where gods existed, the people were liars. But he discovered that present-day Japan was a country having faith neither in gods nor men. He attributed it all to Japan's economic situation.

Four or five days ago, he had read in the newspaper about policemen who colluded with pickpockets to commit thefts. It was not a question of one or two cases, either. According to other papers, if the matter were pursued to the bottom, Tokyo risked becoming unpoliced. Reading the article, Daisuke had only smiled cynically. It stood to reason, he thought, that the meagerly paid police, who had to contend with the hardships of existence, should turn to petty crime.

Daisuke had had a similar cynical feeling about his father's

marriage proposal. But that was no more than a misgiving—
an unfortunate one for Daisuke—which arose from lack of
faith in his father. Daisuke could not feel it dishonorable to
harbor such repugnant thoughts, because he fully intended,
should his misgivings be borne out by fact, to support his father's behavior as only reasonable.

Daisuke had similar thoughts about Hiraoka. But in Hiraoka's case, he allowed that such behavior was the only natural one. He simply could not bring himself to like Hiraoka.
Daisuke loved his brother. Yet, he could not have faith in
him either. His sister-in-law was a sincere woman. But Daisuke thought that it was easier to be close to her than to his
brother only to the extent that she did not have to face the
vicissitudes of existence.

Thus Daisuke had always dismissed society lightly. And
thus, in spite of his extreme sensitivity, he was seldom seized
by anxiety. He was himself fully aware of this. Now, for
some reason, anxiety had been set in motion. Daisuke guessed
that it resulted from physiological changes. That was why he
had undone the bouquet of lilies-of-the-valley someone had
brought him from Hokkaido, immersed them in water, and
fallen asleep beneath them.

One hour later, Daisuke opened his large, black eyes. For
some time, those eyes were fixed upon one spot. Neither his
hands nor his feet had stirred from their position in sleep. He
looked for all the world like a corpse. At that moment, a black
ant threaded its way up his flannel collar and fell on his throat.
Wrinkling his forehead, he pinched the small animal between
his fingers and brought it above his nose for inspection. The
ant was already dead; Daisuke flicked the black thing from
his index finger with his thumb. Then he sat up.

There were still three or four others crawling about his
knees; he beat them to death with a thin ivory paper knife.
Then he clapped his hands.

"Are you awake?" said Kadono as he came in. "Shall I serve tea?"

Tugging his clothes over his bare chest, Daisuke asked quietly, "Didn't someone come in while I was asleep?"

"Yes, as a matter of fact. Mr. Hiraoka's wife. How did you know?" Kadono's tone was matter-of-fact.

"Why didn't you wake me?"

"You were sleeping so soundly."

"But if it's a guest, it can't be helped." Daisuke's tone had become more emphatic.

"Yes, but since it was Mr. Hiraoka's wife herself who said it was better not to wake you . . ."

"And did Mr. Hiraoka's wife leave?"

"No, it's not really that she left. She had a little shopping to do in Kagurazaka, so she said she'd take care of that, then come back."

"Then she's coming again?"

"Yes. Actually, she even came into this room thinking she'd wait till you woke up, but when she saw your face—the way you were sound asleep, she must've thought you'd never wake up."

"So she went out again?"

"Yes, that's about the way it was."

Daisuke laughed and patted his freshly awakened face with his hands. Then he went to the bathroom to wash it. When he came out to the verandah with his head streaming and looked out at the garden, he found that he felt considerably refreshed. The sight of two swallows flying in the cloudy sky struck him as immensely cheerful.

Ever since Hiraoka's visit the other day, Daisuke had been waiting expectantly for a visit from Michiyo. But Hiraoka's words had failed to materialize. Daisuke did not know whether Michiyo had particular reasons for not coming or if Hiraoka was just being conventionally polite when he said that she would come; in any case, he had been feeling an emptiness somewhere in his heart. He had simply viewed this emptiness as one experience among others in his daily life and made no attempt to do anything about its cause. This was because he thought that if he peered deep into the experience itself, he might find dark shadows flitting about.

Therefore he had avoided taking the initiative to visit Hiraoka. On his walks, his steps had often turned in the direction of the Edogawa River. When the cherry blossoms began to fall, he had crossed the four bridges, blown by the evening wind, then crossed back and threaded his way along the long bank. Now the cherry blossoms were long since gone, and it was the season for shady trees. At times, Daisuke would stand in the middle of one of the bridges, leaning his elbows on the parapet, his face cupped in his hands, and gaze into the light of the water that flowed straight through the thick leaves. Then he would look in the distance where the light narrowed and the woods of Mejirodai loomed high. But he would come home without crossing the bridge and climbing the hill of Koishikawa. Once, at Ōmagari, he recognized Hiraoka's form about sixty yards ahead of him. He was getting off a streetcar. Daisuke was sure it was Hiraoka. And he immediately turned away toward the wharf.

Daisuke cared about Hiraoka's welfare. He was probably still in the uneasy position of eating without working. Daisuke tried to imagine that Hiraoka might have discovered the key to opening a path for his future. But he did not feel like running after him to find out. He had come to anticipate an inexplicable sort of unpleasantness from his encounters with Hiraoka. Nevertheless, he did not hate him so much that he worried about his situation only for Michiyo's sake. There was still something in his heart that prayed for Hiraoka's success for his own sake.

So Daisuke had come upon this day, still carrying that

empty spot in one corner of his heart. It was but a few hours ago that he had asked Kadono to bring him a pillow, and he had ravenously partaken of sleep. If it were possible, he would have submerged his head—which could no longer tolerate the stimuli emitted by a universe brimming with life—deep into a blue pool. Daisuke was too acutely conscious of life. At the time he rested his hot head on the pillow, Hiraoka and Michiyo had barely existed for him. Fortunately, he had been able to sleep pleasantly. But in the middle of that peaceful sleep, he had felt as if someone had noiselessly slipped into the room and as noiselessly slipped out. The feeling lingered even after he had awakened and sat up, and he could not erase it from his mind. That was why he had called Kadono.

With his hands at his forehead, Daisuke had been standing on the verandah following the movement of the swallows as they swooped gaily through the faraway sky. After a while it became dizzying and Daisuke went inside. But the expectation that Michiyo would soon come had already broken his composure, and he could neither think nor read. In the end, he brought down an art book from the bookshelf and began flipping the pages on his lap. But this, too, was just a matter of his fingertips turning one page after another. He could not even halfway appreciate a single painting. He came to Brangwyn. Daisuke had always had great interest in this decorative painter, and for a moment, his eyes acquired their usual light as they rested on the painting. It was a representation of a harbor somewhere. In the background ships and masts and sails were depicted on a large scale, and the remaining spaces were filled in with clouds in a brilliant sky and bluish-black water. In the foreground were four or five naked laborers. As he looked at those men, their muscles swelling like mountains, with mounds of flesh between shoulder and back that dipped and met to form eddy-like valleys, Daisuke experienced some pleasure in the power of the flesh; but soon, with the volume still open, his eyes left the page and his ears pricked up. The old woman's voice sounded from the direction of the kitchen. The milkman went out with hurried footsteps, rattling his empty bottles. With the house as quiet as it was, the noise echoed painfully on Daisuke's sensitive auditory nerves.

Daisuke stared blankly at the wall. He thought of calling Kadono again to ask if Michiyo had said when she would be back, but that seemed so foolish that he hesitated. It was not only foolish, there was no point in being so eager for a visit from another man's wife. If he was going to be so eager, he should have gone over himself to have a talk. Daisuke could not help feeling ashamed of his lapse in logic. He half rose from his chair. He was also well aware, however, of the various factors underlying his illogic, and he thought that for his present self, this condition of illogic was the only reality; there was nothing to be done about it. Therefore, logic that clashed with this reality was but a patchwork of propositions which had nothing to do with him, which insulted his very essence, which was nothing more than mere formality. With these thoughts, he once again settled in his chair.

After that, Daisuke hardly knew how he passed the time until Michiyo's arrival. When a woman's voice sounded outside, he felt a single throb in his heart. Daisuke, whose powers of reasoning were formidable, was terribly weak in matters of the heart. It was because of his head that in recent years he had been unable to become angry; his intellect would not allow such an act of self-abasement as anger. But in other situations, he was more than most the unwilling subject of emotions. By the time Kadono, who had answered the door, arrived noisily at the entrance to the study, Daisuke's rosy cheeks had lost a shade of their luster.

Kadono asked simply, "Will this be all right?" He must have abbreviated his question because it was too much trouble to ask whether he should show Michiyo in to the study or whether Daisuke would see her in the living room. Daisuke said yes, and as if to drive Kadono away as he stood waiting in the doorway for an answer, stood and stuck his head out toward the verandah. Michiyo stood where the entranceway joined the verandah, looking hesitantly in his direction.

Her face was rather more pale than the last time he had seen her. Daisuke signaled with his eyes and chin for her to come forward, and she approached the door to the study. He noticed that she was breathing hard. "Is something the matter?" he asked.

Without answering, Michiyo came into the room. She was wearing an unlined serge kimono over an underkimono. In her hand she held three large, white lilies. Without warning, she tossed them on the table and sank into the chair beside it. Heedless of her newly coiffed hair, she pushed her head against the back of the chair and said, "I was so uncomfortable." She looked at Daisuke and smiled. Daisuke was about to clap and send for water when Michiyo silently pointed to the top of the Western-style desk. There was a glass that Daisuke used for rinsing his mouth after meals. About two sips were left.

"It's clean, isn't it?" asked Michiyo.

"I drank from it a little while ago, so . . ." he said, picking it up and hesitating. If he tried to empty it from where he sat, one of the glass panels outside the shoji would get in the way. Kadono had a habit of leaving one or two panels shut every day. Daisuke got up and went to the verandah, where he emptied the glass in the garden and called Kadono. Kadono, who had just been there, was now nowhere to be seen. Feeling somewhat confused, Daisuke came back to Michiyo and said, "I'll get you some water right away." He went out to the kitchen, leaving behind the glass he had just now taken the trouble to empty. As he passed the morning room, he found Kadono clumsily struggling with the canister of the best tea.

Seeing Daisuke, Kadono explained, "I'll be there right away, Sensei."

"The tea can wait. I need some water," said Daisuke and went to the kitchen himself.

"Oh, is that right? She's going to have water?" Kadono abandoned the canister and followed after him. Together they searched for a glass but could not readily find one. Daisuke asked where the old woman was; it turned out that she had gone to buy sweets for the guest.

"If we're out of sweets, why didn't she get them sooner?" said Daisuke as he turned on the faucet and filled a teacup to the brim.

"Well, it just slipped my mind to tell her we were having company." Kadono scratched his head sympathetically.

"Then you should have gone," lashed out Daisuke as he left the kitchen.

But Kadono had more to say. "Well, she said she had a lot of other shopping to do. Her legs aren't good and the weather's bad, so she shouldn't have gone, but . . ."

Without even looking back, Daisuke returned to the study. He looked at Michiyo as soon as he crossed the threshold; in her lap she held with both hands the glass Daisuke had left behind. There was as much water in it as Daisuke had tossed into the garden. Teacup in hand, Daisuke stood dumbly before Michiyo. "What happened?" he asked.

Michiyo answered in her usual composed manner. "Thank you, I've had plenty. I drank some of that. It was so beautiful," she said, looking back at the bowl with the lilies-of-the-valley. Daisuke had filled the large bowl almost to the top. From amidst the toothpick-thin, light green stems aligned in the water, the design of the porcelain floated up faintly.

"Why did you drink that?" Daisuke was aghast.

"It won't hurt, will it?" Michiyo held the glass out to Daisuke so that he could see through it.

"It might not hurt, but what if the water had been standing for two or three days?"

"No, when I was here before, I put my face right up to it

and smelled. Then that person told me it had just been poured from the pail. It's all right. Such a nice scent, isn't it."

Daisuke sat down without a word. He did not have the courage to find out whether she had drunk the water in the bowl for poetry's sake or from physical necessity. Even supposing it was the former, she clearly had not affected an imitation of poetry or novels. So he only asked, "Are you feeling better?"

The color had finally returned to her cheeks. Taking a handkerchief from her sleeve, she wiped her mouth and began to talk—usually, she took the streetcar from Dentsūinmae to Hongō to do her shopping, but she had heard the prices were a good 10 to 20 percent higher in Hongō than in Kagurazaka, so she had tried coming out here once or twice. She had planned to drop in the last time, too, but she was late and had to hurry home. Today she had set out early on purpose. But, Daisuke was asleep so she had decided to go out and finish her shopping first, then stop on the way home. But the weather had turned bad and just as she was going up Waradana, it had begun to sprinkle. She hadn't brought an umbrella so she had hurried, not wanting to get too wet. But this immediately hurt her; she didn't know what to do, it was so hard to breathe—"But I'm used to it, so it didn't surprise me,"she said, and gave Daisuke a lonely smile.

"Your heart isn't completely well yet?"Daisuke's face was full of sympathy.

"It won't ever be completely well—not for the rest of my life." Michiyo's words did not sound as subdued as the despair in their meaning might have warranted. She tilted a slender finger and glanced at the ring she was wearing. Then she rolled up her handkerchief and put it back in her sleeve. Daisuke gazed at the woman's lowered forehead where it joined her hair.

Then, as if she had just remembered it, Michiyo thanked him for the check. Her cheeks seemed to become faintly red as she spoke. Daisuke's keen vision did not miss it. He interpreted it only as shame over her indebtedness and therefore quickly shifted the conversation.

The lilies Michiyo had brought were still lying on the table. A sweet, strong aroma permeated the space between the two. Daisuke could not bear to keep the oppressively heavy smell right under his nose. But he could not be so free with Michiyo as to remove the flowers without first asking her. "Where did you get these flowers? Did you buy them?" he asked.

Michiyo nodded silently. Then she said, "Isn't it a nice scent?" She took her nose right up to the petals and sniffed to show him.

Daisuke involuntarily planted his feet and tilted his body back. "You musn't smell so close up."

"Oh, why not?"

"Why not? There's no reason, but you just shouldn't." Daisuke knitted his brows a little.

Michiyo lifted her face to its former position. "You don't like these flowers?"

Daisuke was still leaning back in his chair, and without answering, he smiled.

"Then I shouldn't have bought them. It wasn't worth it —I even went out of my way. And on top of it, I ran out of breath trying not to get drenched."

The rain began to fall in earnest. The drops collected in the gutter, then flowed out with a rushing sound. Daisuke got up from his chair. He picked up the bunch of lilies and tore away at the wet straw that bound them together. "If you're giving them to me, let's arrange them right away." As he spoke, he tossed them into the big bowl. The stems were long, and their ends spattered water, looking as if they would jump out. Daisuke lifted the dripping stems from the bowl again. Taking a pair of Western scissors from the desk drawer, he snipped them to half their length. Then he let the large flowers float among the clustering lilies-of-the-valley. "Now, that's good." He put the scissors on top of the desk.

Michiyo, who had been gazing at the lilies arranged in this oddly careless fashion, suddenly asked a peculiar question: "When did you start disliking these flowers?"

Once, long ago, when Michiyo's brother was still alive, Daisuke had bought some long-stemmed lilies and visited the house in Yanaka. On that occasion, he had directed Michiyo to clean a vase, which she had done with unsteady hands, and then he had painstakingly arranged the lilies himself. When this was done, he had made Michiyo and her brother turn to face the alcove and admire the flowers properly. Michiyo had remembered the incident. "You put your nose to them too," she said. Daisuke thought it likely that something of the sort had happened and had no choice but to smile ruefully.

The rain fell in thick sheets. A distant sound muffled the house. Kadono came in, saying it seemed a little chilly, shouldn't he close the glass doors? While he pulled the panels together, the two sat with their faces turned to the garden. Every one of the green leaves was wet, and a silent dampness blew in through the doors to Daisuke's head. All the floating things in the world seemed to have settled to the earth. For the first time in a long while, Daisuke felt as if he had come to himself. "It's a nice rain," he said.

"It's not nice at all, I only wore my sandals." Michiyo's face was more resentful than anything as she watched the raindrops fall from the gutter.

"It's all right, I'll get a ricksha for you when you go home. You can relax."

Michiyo did not look as if she could relax for too long. She looked straight at Daisuke and chided, "You're still as carefree as ever, aren't you?" But the trace of a smile hovered at the edge of her eye.

Hiraoka's face, which up to now had been hidden in a blur in Michiyo's shadow, suddenly projected itself clearly on Daisuke's mind's eye. He felt as if he had been stabbed in the dark. Michiyo was, after all, a woman who walked with a dark shadow dragging behing her—a shadow that could not easily be shed.

"How is Hiraoka?" he asked, deliberately nonchalant.

Michiyo's lips tightened a bit. "As usual."

"He hasn't found anything yet?"

"That part seems to be taken care of now. It looks like there's going to be an opening in a newspaper office starting next month."

"That's good. I had no idea. Then that should do for a while."

"Yes, I'm quite thankful." Michiyo's voice was low and serious.

Just then Daisuke found Michiyo very sweet. He continued, "And the other business—it doesn't look like you'll be pressed on that score for the time being?"

"The other business?" Michiyo hesitated for an instant, then suddenly blushed. "To tell you the truth, I came here today to apologize about that." As she spoke, she lifted the face she had just turned away.

Daisuke could not bear to show the slightest sign of displeasure that would further distress her gentle woman's heart. At the same time, he avoided saying anything that might anticipate her meaning and force her to become even more apologetic. So he quietly listened to what she had to say.

The two hundred yen was to have gone toward the debt as soon as Daisuke gave it to her. But setting up a new household had entailed expenses, and it all began when she used a part of that money for 'the house. But the rest . . . she had thought. Then she began to be hounded by daily expenses; though she had not felt good about it, she had had no choice; she had used the remainder as the need arose, and now, the money was all but gone. Of course, if she hadn't done that, the couple would not have survived to this day. Still, looking back, if the money hadn't been there at all, she probably would have managed somehow—but because it was right there, she had used it out of desperation to tide them through emergencies. So the debt, which was the main concern, remained just as it was. Hiraoka was not really to blame. It was all her fault. "I know I did a very bad thing, and I'm regretting it. But please forgive me, I had no intention of lying and misleading you when I borrowed the money." Michiyo sounded terribly distressed.

"I gave the money to you, so however you spend it, no one's going to say anything. If it served your needs, then that's fine," consoled Daisuke. And he put particular emphasis on the *you*, letting it linger softly.

"Then I can feel a little easier at last," was all Michiyo said.

Since the rain persisted, when it came time for her to leave Daisuke hired a ricksha as he had promised. Because it was cold, he tried to put a man's serge wrap over her, but Michiyo laughed and would not wear it.

Chapter XI

ALL OF A SUDDEN,
people were walking the streets in silk gauze kimonos. Daisuke, who had spent two or three days doing research at home
without looking any further than his own garden, suddenly
felt the heat when he stepped out wearing a winter hat. Just
as he was thinking that he too should put away his serge, he
passed two people in the space of ten or twelve blocks who
were still wearing lined kimonos. On the other hand, there
were students gathered in a newly opened ice parlor, glasses
in hand, drinking something cold. Daisuke thought of Seitarō.

These days, Daisuke had grown fonder than ever of Seitarō. When he talked to other people, he felt as if he were
talking to their shells, and he found it terribly irksome. But
when he looked at himself, he had to admit that he of all people must be irksome to others. When he thought that this
was yet another consequence of prolonged exposure to the
misfortunes of the struggle for survival, he did not feel very
grateful.

These days, Seitarō was forever wanting to practice bal-
ancing on a ball. This was because Daisuke had taken him to
the amusement quarters of Asakusa the other day. His single-
mindedness was something he had inherited from Daisuke's
sister-in-law. But being his brother's child as well, there
was something generous and unpressing about his single-
mindedness. It was a pleasure for Daisuke to keep him company, for his soul poured into Daisuke's without any reserve.
Daisuke was finding it painful to be surrounded by spirits
that refused to shed their armor whether it was night or day.

This spring Seitarō had begun middle school. He seemed to have shot up suddenly. In another year or two his voice would change. There was no way of knowing what path he would take from there, but in order to survive as a human being, he was sure to arrive at the fate of having to incur the dislike of other human beings. When that time came, he would probably clothe himself inconspicuously, so as not to attract attention, and beggarlike, linger about the market places of man, in search of something.

Daisuke went out by the moat. Just the other day, mounds of azaleas had stamped a pattern in red and white upon the green of the other bank, but now there was no trace of them; on the steep slope where the grass grew rampant, pine tree after pine tree stood as far as the eye could see. The sky was beautifully clear. Daisuke thought of taking the streetcar home, teasing his sister-in-law and playing with Seitarō, but he suddenly lost the desire and decided to look at the pines and follow the bank of the moat until he became tired.

When he came to Shinmitsuke, the streetcars going to and fro became irritating, so he crossed the moat and cut out from the Shōkonsha toward Banchō. There, as he circled about, it suddenly struck him as foolish to wander aimlessly. Normally, he believed that only the lowly walked with a purpose, but in this particular instance, he felt that the lowly might be more admirable. He realized that he had been seized with ennui again and began walking home. In Kagurazaka, he came upon a shop that had a blaring phonograph out front. The sound was terribly metallic and pierced his head.

When he entered his own gate, he encountered Kadono, who, taking advantage of his master's absence, was singing biwa* songs at the top of his lungs. When he heard Daisuke's footsteps, he stopped instantly. "Well, that was mighty quick, Sensei," he said, coming to the door.

---

* Musical instrument somewhat comparable to the lute.

Without a word, Daisuke hung up his hat and went from the verandah to the study. There, he deliberately closed the shoji. Kadono, who had followed, teacup in hand, asked, "Should I leave it closed? Isn't it hot?"

Daisuke took a handkerchief from his sleeve and wiped his brow, but still ordered, "Keep it closed." Kadono shut the shoji with a puzzled expression and left. Daisuke sat blankly in the dark room for some ten minutes.

Daisuke had skin that glowed in a way that made others envious, and muscles so supple that it would have been hard to find their like in a laborer. He was so blessed with health that since birth he had not experienced what could be called a major illness. Since he believed that this was the only way that life was worth living, health was at least twice as valuable to him as it was to most people. His head was as sound as his body. Of course, he was constantly plagued by his sense of logic. There were also times when the center of his head felt like a longbow target—a series of two or three concentric rings. Since that morning, he had suffered more than usual from this feeling.

At such times Daisuke would silently ponder to what end he had been born into this world. He had often grappled with this problem and held it before his eyes. Sometimes he was motivated by simple philosophical curiosity; at other times, the social forces surrounding him pressed to imbue his brain with their all too complex hues, or, like today, the thoughts came as a result of ennui. Each time, however, he came to the same conclusion. But this conclusion was not a solution to the problem; in fact, it amounted to a denial of it. According to his thinking, man was not born for a particular purpose. Quite the opposite: a purpose developed only with the birth of an individual. To objectively fabricate a purpose at the outset and to apply it to a human being was to rob him at birth of freedom of action. Hence, purpose was something that the individual who came into this world had to make for himself. But no one, no matter who, could freely create a purpose. This was because the purpose of one's existence was as good as announced to the universe by the course of that existence itself.

Starting from this premise, Daisuke held that one's natural activities constituted one's natural purposes. A man walked because he wanted to. Then walking became his purpose. He thought because he wanted to. Then, thinking became his purpose. Just as to walk or to think for a particular purpose meant the degradation of walking and thinking, so to establish an external purpose and to act to fulfill it meant the degradation of action. Accordingly, those who used the sum of their actions as a means to an end were in effect destroying the purpose of their own existence.

Therefore, Daisuke had lived to this day making it his purpose to actualize whatever fancies and desires entered his mind. It was the same when two incompatible desires or fancies battled in his heart. He viewed it merely as the consumption of a purpose that had arisen from contradiction. What this boiled down to was that Daisuke had always conducted himself with so-called purposeless acts as his purpose. And he understood that insofar as it deceived no one, it was the most ethical form of conduct.

Daisuke, who lived to actualize this principle as much as possible, was at times unwittingly beset by the question he had long ago rejected: he would begin to ask why he was doing what he was doing. This was precisely what had happened as he strolled through Banchō and wondered why he was strolling. . . .

In such instances Daisuke noticed the undernourished state of his vitality. A starved act contained neither sufficient courage nor interest to be executed in one blow; that was why he found himself questioning its significance midway. This he labeled ennui. He believed that his bouts of confusion in logic were brought on when he was beset by a case of ennui. For him to stop in the middle of an act to inquire its purpose —putting the cart before the horse—could only be the work of ennui.

Inside the closed room, he clasped his head in his hands and tried shaking it once or twice. He could not bear to drag out and ponder once again the meaningless doubt that countless thinkers had repeatedly experienced throughout the ages. When its form flickered before his eyes, he thought, not again, and shut it out immediately. At the same time, he felt acutely the inadequacy of his vital energies. He did not have enough interest to peacefully execute an act for its own sake. He stood alone in the midst of a wilderness. He was at his wits' end.

Daisuke ardently desired the satisfaction of his highly refined life appetites. And in some ways, he also tried to buy the satisfaction of the demands posed by morality. He expected that there would come a point when the two would clash and set off sparks. He therefore maintained his life appetites at a low level and tried to rest content. His room was an ordinary Japanese-style room. There was nothing of note in its furnishings. As far as he was concerned, there was not even a single decent frame. All that was beautiful enough to catch the eye in the way of color was concentrated in the Western books arranged in the bookcase. He now sat vacantly amidst those books. It was no small thing that had lured his consciousness into such heavy torpor, he thought, and to rouse it to its full sharpness, he would have to do something about his surroundings. His eyes traveled all around the room. Then, they again stared vacantly at the wall. In the end, he thought that only one thing could save him from this diluted existence. And he said to himself, "I must see Michiyo-san after all."

He regretted having set out walking in a direction where his feet were reluctant to carry him. He was just thinking of leaving again and going to Hiraoka's when Terao came from Morikawachō. He was wearing a new straw hat and a modest summer cloak and complained repeatedly about the heat as he rubbed his red face.

"What did you come here for now?" Daisuke greeted him inhospitably. He had always conducted his relationship with Terao on such terms.

"Right now is about the best time for visiting you, isn't it? You were taking a nap again, weren't you. People who don't work just get too lazy. I wonder what on earth you were born for," he said, fanning his chest with the straw hat. Since the weather was not yet that hot, his exaggerated gesture was rather amusing.

"What I was born for is no business of yours. What did you come here for, anyway? Is it another case of 'Just for ten days or so'? If it's got anything to do with money, I don't want to hear about it," refused Daisuke bluntly in anticipation.

"You really don't have any manners, do you," was the only reply Terao could make. But he showed no sign of being offended. Actually, words like these could never sound rude in Terao's ears. Daisuke watched his face silently. The face made no more impression on him than on a blank wall.

Terao pulled out a dirty, roughly stitched-together book from his kimono. "I have to translate this," he said. Daisuke was still silent. "Don't look so lazy just because you don't have to worry about your next meal. Wake up, will you? It's a matter of life and death for me." With these words he twice slapped the small book against the corner of his chair.

"By when?"

Terao rustled the pages back and forth. "Two weeks," he announced firmly. "If I don't get this cleared away one way or the other by then, I can't eat. So there's no two ways about it."

"Such ambition." Daisuke was sarcastic.

"That's why I came running all the way over from Hongō. Oh, you don't have to lend me any money—though it'd be even better if you did—but anyway, there're some places I don't understand so I came to ask your opinion."

"What a bother. My head doesn't feel right today, I can't sit around doing that. Just go ahead and fudge it—what difference does it make? They're paying you by the page anyway, right?"

"Look, even I can't be that irresponsible. It'll mean a lot of trouble if people point out mistranslations."

"You're such a pain." Daisuke was still being lazy.

"Look here," said Terao. "It's no joke. You've got to do something once in a while. A guy like you who's always loafing around must get so bored that he doesn't know what to do with himself. Now, if I'd wanted to find someone who could really read this stuff, I wouldn't have bothered to come all the way over here. But such people aren't like you, they're all busy." Terao was utterly nonplussed.

Daisuke made up his mind that he either had to have a fight or give in. Although he was capable by temperament of being contemptuous of a person like Terao, he was not capable of working himself up to anger. "Then keep it as short as possible," he warned, and turned only to the marked passages. He did not even dare ask for a synopsis of the story. And he could not resolve many ambiguous points in the passages Terao asked about. Eventually, Terao said "Thanks" and turned the book over.

"What are you going to do about the places we didn't understand?" asked Daisuke.

"Oh, I'll do something—no matter who I ask, there's probably no one who would understand it completely. And anyway, there's no time, so it can't be helped." Terao took it for granted that his livelihood was a far more important concern than any mistranslation.

The consultation being over, Terao, as usual, launched into literary topics. A dramatic change took place now that he was no longer talking about his own translation, and he became his usual impassioned self. Daisuke thought that among the works bearing the names of leading writers of the day, there must be many that had the same significance for their authors as Terao's translations had for him, and he smiled to himself at this contradiction in Terao. But because it was too much trouble, he did not say anything.

Thanks to Terao, Daisuke never got to Hiraoka's that day.

At dinner time, a small package arrived from Maruzen. Daisuke put down his chopsticks and opened it to find two or three books that he had ordered from abroad quite some time ago. He put them under his arm and went to his study. One by one he picked them up and, although it was dark, flipped through two or three pages; but there was nothing to draw his attention in any of them. He had even forgotten the title of the last book. Thinking he would read them eventually, he left them bundled together and got up to put them on top of the bookcase. When he peered out from the verandah, he discovered a beautiful sky on the verge of losing its brilliant colors; above the paulownia next door, now conspicuously dark, a pale moon had risen.

Then Kadono came in carrying a large lamp. It had a green shade with vertical markings like crinkled silk. Kadono placed it on the table and went out to the verandah, remarking on his way out, "It's getting to be about the time for fireflies, isn't it?"

Daisuke looked puzzled and answered, "They wouldn't be out yet."

"Is that right?" Kadono asked, then immediately continued in a serious vein, "Fireflies used to be quite a thing, but the literary gentlemen these days don't seem to make much of a fuss over them, do they? I wonder why. Nowadays, you hardly even see things like fireflies and crows."

"That's true. I wonder why." Daisuke, playing it straight, was equally solemn.

"It's probably because they've been overwhelmed by the

electric lights; they've begun to retreat," said Kadono, and with a ha, ha, ha, as the finishing touch to his own joke, he went back to his room. Daisuke followed to the entranceway. Kadono looked back. "Would you be going out again? Fine, I'll watch out for the lamp—the old woman's been lying down for a while; she says her stomach aches. It's probably nothing serious. Please enjoy yourself."

Daisuke went out the gate. When he got to the Edogawa, the river's waters were already dark. Needless to say, he intended to visit Hiraoka. Therefore he did not follow the bank as usual but crossed the bridge directly and went up Kongō-jizaka.

As a matter of fact, Daisuke had recently seen both Hiraoka and Michiyo two or three times. The first time was after he had received a comparatively long letter from Hiraoka. The letter first expressed thanks for Daisuke's help since Hiraoka's return to Tokyo. This was followed by something to the effect that he had received invaluable assistance from many friends and superiors, but recently, thanks to the good offices of an acquaintance, he had been urged to become the head reporter in the financial section of a certain newspaper. He himself felt that he would like to try it. But since he had also asked Daisuke for his help in this matter shortly after arriving in Tokyo, he did not think it right to proceed without asking his leave, and he was therefore writing for advice. Daisuke had done nothing more about Hiraoka's request to recommend him for a position in his brother's firm; he had simply let the matter go, not even refusing. Therefore he took this letter as Hiraoka's way of pressing him. He decided it would be much too cold to refuse by mail, so he visited Hiraoka on the following day, and, carefully explaining the situation in his brother's company, asked him to give up on that idea for the time being. Hiraoka said that he himself had been thinking that something of the sort was probably the case, then turned to Michiyo with an odd look in his eyes.

On another occasion, he had received a postcard from Hiraoka saying that the newspaper job was final at last, he would like to relax and drink with him some night, would Daisuke come on such and such a date? Daisuke stopped by on a walk to tell him that unfortunately, something else had come up and he would not be able to make it. Hiraoka was sprawled out on his back in the middle of the room, asleep. He had gone to a gathering the night before and had too much to drink, he said, repeatedly rubbing his red eyes. Then he looked at Daisuke and suddenly declared that human beings had to be single, like Daisuke, in order to do any work. He complained loudly about the inconveniences of marriage, claiming that he would go anywhere—Manchuria, America —if only he were single. Michiyo was working stealthily in the next room.

The third time, Daisuke had visited while Hiraoka was away at work. That time, he had not gone on any business. He spent about half an hour there, sitting on the verandah talking.

Between that time and this evening, he had tried to avoid going in the direction of Koishikawa. Daisuke went to Take-hayachō, cut through, and two or three hundred yards later, came out right in front of a door lamp bearing the name Hiraoka. When he called from outside the grating, the maid came out with a lamp. Both husband and wife were out. Daisuke left immediately without even asking their whereabouts and, catching the streetcar, rode to Hongō, changed for Kanda, got off, went to a certain beer hall, and gulped down some beer.

When he awoke the next morning, he still felt as if rings with unequal radii partitioned his brain into two layers. Whenever this happened, Daisuke could not but think that his brain was a piece of patchwork whose inner and outer surfaces were of different material. He would often shake it, trying to mix the two together. Now, with his head against the pillow, he curled his right hand into a fist and hit above his ear two or three times.

Daisuke had never attributed this dysfunction to excessive indulgence in alcohol. Since childhood he had always been able to hold his liquor. No matter how much he drank, he never departed noticeably from his normal behavior. Moreover, once he had slept soundly, his body showed no signs of impairment. Once, he had somehow gotten into a drinking bout with his brother and managed to put down thirteen three-cup bottles. The next day he had gone to school looking just as usual. His brother complained of a headache and looked wretched for two days. Seigo had said it was a question of age.

Compared to that occasion, the beer he had drunk the night before was trifling, thought Daisuke as he hit himself on the head. Fortunately, even when his head felt layered like this, his brain continued to function normally. True, he did become reluctant at times to use his head. But he was confident that if he but made the effort, he was equal to any complex task. Therefore, there were no grounds for worry that changes in his brain tissue might bring about mental disorders. The first time he had experienced this sensation, he was surprised. The second time, he rather welcomed it as a novel experience. These days, this experience most often seemed to accompany a decline in mental vigor. It had become a symptom of those periods when he ventured to persist in substanceless acts. This was the sore point for Daisuke.

Sitting up in bed, he shook his head once more. At breakfast, Kadono had tried to talk to him about the story in the morning paper recounting the battle of the serpent and the eagle, but he had not responded. Kadono, thinking one of those periods had begun again, left the morning room. He went to the kitchen and said solicitously to the old woman, "It's not good for you to work so hard, Auntie. I'll clear off

Sensei's tray, so go over there and rest." Daisuke remembered for the first time the old woman's indisposition. He was on the verge of saying something kind, but decided it was too much trouble and stopped.

As soon as he put down his knife, he picked up his teacup and went into the study. It was already past nine when he looked at the clock. For a while he sat gazing at the garden as he slowly sipped his tea. Then Kadono came in and announced, "Someone from your home has come to fetch you." Daisuke did not recall that anyone was to have been sent for him from home. When he asked about it, Kadono would only mumble something about the ricksha driver, so Daisuke got up and went to the entranceway, shaking his head all the while. There he found a man named Katsu, who pulled his brother's ricksha. He pulled the rubber-wheeled vehicle sideways to the door and bowed politely.

When he asked, "Katsu, what's this about sending you to fetch me?" Katsu answered apologetically, "The mistress said I was to take the ricksha and bring you back."

"Is it something urgent?"

Katsu of course knew nothing. He simply said, "She said you would understand when you got there—" and would not finish his sentence.

Daisuke went back into the house. He was about to call the old woman and have her get out a change of clothing, but not wanting to use her when she had a stomachache, he scurried through the drawers himself and dressed hurriedly, then stepped into Katsu's ricksha.

There was a strong wind blowing that day. Katsu's movements were labored as he bowed forward and ran. Inside, Daisuke was so windblown that the two layers of his brain spun around and around. But it was pleasant to feel his numbed self, still in a state of half sleep, be lifted into space by the wheels that spun beautifully, without sound or echo. By the time he arrived in Aoyama, he felt considerably more refreshed than when he got up.

Wondering if something had happened, he popped his head into the houseboy's room on his way in. There he found Naoki, the houseboy, and Seitarō sitting alone, eating strawberries sprinkled with white sugar.

When he said, "Well, that looks good," Naoki righted himself immediately and greeted him. Seitarō, his lips still wet, suddenly asked, "When are you going to get married, Uncle?" Naoki grinned.

Daisuke felt a little trapped. So he said to Seitarō, half-teasingly, half-scoldingly, "Why aren't you in school today? Eating strawberries at this hour of the day!"

"But it's Sunday today," answered Seitarō seriously.

"Oh, so it is." Daisuke showed surprise. Naoki looked at Daisuke's face and in the end burst out laughing. Daisuke also laughed and went out to the drawing room. There was no one there. A round, carved sandalwood tray lay on the freshly changed floor mats. On it was a teacup with a design by Asai Mokugo of Kyoto baked into it. From the garden the morning green streamed into the wide, empty room and made everything look still. It seemed that the wind outside had suddenly died down.

As he crossed the drawing room and walked toward his brother's room, he saw someone's shadow. "Oh, that's too much," he heard his sister-in-law say. Daisuke stepped into the room. Inside stood his brother and sister-in-law and Nuiko. His brother stood facing in his direction, wearing a man's stiff obi with a gold chain wrapped around and a cloak of a peculiar silk currently in fashion. Seeing Daisuke, Seigo said to Umeko, "See, there he is. So have him take you."

Daisuke of course had no idea what he meant. Then Umeko turned to him and said, "Dai-san, you're of course free today?"

"Well, yes, I'm free," answered Daisuke.

"Then please go to the Kabukiza with me."

As he listened to his sister-in-law's words, a certain sense of comedy rose swiftly in Daisuke's head. But today he lacked the daring to tease her as usual. To avoid any complications, he put on a casual expression and said good-humoredly, "Fine, let's go."

Then Umeko asked back, "But you said you've already seen it once."

"Once, twice, it makes no difference. Let's go." Daisuke smiled at Umeko.

"You really are dissolute, aren't you?" observed Umeko. Daisuke felt the comedy mount.

Saying that he had business to attend to, his brother went out. Apparently, he had promised to come around to the theater about four o'clock, after he had finished his work. It would seem that Umeko and Nuiko could very well have watched by themselves until then, but Umeko had said she did not want to. Seigo had said that in that case, she should take Naoki, but Naoki had sat stiffly in his navy-blue printed kimono and hakama and announced that he would not go. So they had sent for Daisuke as a last resort. This was the explanation Seigo gave on his way out. Daisuke thought it did not make much sense, but he only said, is that so. He concluded that his sister-in-law had gone to the trouble of sending for him because she wanted someone to talk to between acts and to run errands.

Umeko and Nuiko spent a great deal of time on their toilet. Daisuke stood by, a patient director of their preparations. From time to time he made lighthearted fun of them, drawing two or three protests from Nuiko that Uncle Daisuke was too unkind.

Daisuke's father had gone out early that morning and was not home. His sister-in-law said she did not know where he had gone. Daisuke did not particularly want to know. He was only grateful that he was out. Since their last interview, he had not crossed his father's path more than twice, and then only for ten or fifteen minutes. When the conversation showed signs of becoming involved, he had bowed politely and left. As a result his father had come into the living room and complained that lately, Daisuke could never seem to sit down; no sooner did he see his father's face than he was preparing his escape. This was what Umeko had to say as she stood before the mirror, patting the back of her summer obi.

"I really have lost credit, haven't I?" said Daisuke, and with his sister-in-law's and Nuiko's parasols in hand, he stepped out ahead of them to the entranceway. There, three rickshas were lined up.

Fearing the wind, Daisuke had worn a hunting cap. But the wind had died at last, and from between the clouds the sun beat down upon their heads. Umeko and Nuiko, who went ahead, put up their parasols. From time to time, Daisuke shaded his eyes with the back of his hand.

At the theater, Umeko and Nuiko were both attentive viewers. But Daisuke, partly because it was his second time, and partly because of the state of his mind these past three or four days, failed to be totally distracted by the stage. He was relentlessly aware of an oppressive heat that weighed heavily on his spirits, and he frequently picked up his fan to send air from his collar to his head.

Between acts, Nuiko would turn to Daisuke and ask him strange questions. Questions which, in fact, were usually unanswerable. Why was the man drinking sake from a wash tub? Or, how could a priest become a general? Umeko laughed every time she heard Nuiko. Daisuke suddenly remembered a review he had seen in the paper two or three days ago by a certain literary figure. According to the article, Japanese plays so abounded in fantastic plots that they were difficult for the audience to follow. When he read this, Daisuke had thought that if he were an actor, he would not care to have people like that come to see him. He said to Kadono that to scold the actor for what the playwright had done was as foolish as wanting to hear Kojirō's jōruri* recitation in order to know Chikamatsu's works. Kadono, as usual, had said oh, is that right.

Daisuke, who had been accustomed to watching traditional Japanese theater from childhood, was, like Umeko, a pure and simple appreciator of the art form. For him, the "meaning" of the art performed on the stage was to be construed narrowly as applying only to the actor's skill. Therefore, he and Umeko got along famously. They exchanged glances from time to time, adding commentary that sounded quite professional, and they were mutually impressed. But in general, Daisuke had already begun to lose interest in the stage. Even while the curtain was up, he would look this way and that through his opera glasses. Far in the corner of his field of vision, there were many geisha. Some of them had turned their own glasses toward him.

To Daisuke's right was a man of about the same age who had brought along his beautiful wife. Her hair was done up in the married woman's style. Looking at the wife's profile, Daisuke thought she bore a strong resemblance to a certain geisha of his acquaintance. To his left was a male party of about four. They were all academics and Daisuke remembered each of their faces. Next to them, two people had taken over a wide area just for themselves. One of them seemed to be about his brother's age and was dressed correctly in a suit. He wore gold-rimmed glasses, and whenever he wanted to say something, he had a habit of sticking his chin out and turning it slightly upward. When he saw this man, Daisuke thought that he somehow looked familiar. But in the end he did not even try to recall who it was. His companion was a young woman. Daisuke decided that she was not yet twenty. She had come without a cloak, and she let her pompadour hang forward more than most; much of the time she sat with her chin pressed against her collar.

* Ballad-drama

Out of discomfort Daisuke got up a number of times and went to the rear corridor, where he looked out upon a narrow sky. He was quite ready to hand over Nuiko and his sister-in-law as soon as his brother arrived and to leave early himself. Once he took Nuiko with him and walked all around to stretch his legs. In the end, he even thought of sending for a little sake.

His brother came just at dusk. When Daisuke told him he was terribly late, his brother pulled a gold watch from his obi and showed it to Daisuke. It turned out to be only a little after six. As usual, his brother sat calmly, looking all round. But when the time came to eat, he went out to the corridor and did not return for a long time. After a while, Daisuke happened to look over and found him talking in the stall of the man with the gold-rimmed glasses. From time to time he seemed to address a few words to the young woman as well. But the woman would only show a slight smile, then turn earnestly to the stage. Daisuke thought of asking his sister-in-law the man's name. But his brother was a man whose social circles were so wide, who in fact looked upon society as his own home, that wherever people were gathered, he easily made way into any group as he was doing now. Thus Daisuke did not give it a second thought and remained silent.

Then, toward the end of the act, his brother came to their entrance and called to Daisuke to come for just a minute. He took him over to the man with the gold-rimmed glasses and introduced him as his younger brother. Then he told Daisuke that this was Mr. Takagi of Kobe. The gold-rimmed gentleman looked back at the young woman and said this was his niece. The woman bowed gracefully. Daisuke's brother added that she was Mr. Sagawa's daughter. When he heard the woman's name, Daisuke realized how neatly he had been trapped. But he pretended to know nothing and chatted about this and that. His sister-in-law turned toward him for an instant.

After five or six minutes, Daisuke returned to his seat with his brother. Until Sagawa's daughter had been presented to him, he had planned to escape as soon as his brother appeared, but he could not get away with that any more. He sensed that if he were to appear too selfish now, it would backfire later, so he sat on, enduring his discomfort. His brother did not seem to have any interest in the program either, but he sat poised in his usual easygoing manner, puffing heavily on his cigar. If he made any comments at all, they were on the level of, isn't that a pretty scene, Nuiko? Unlike her usual curious self, Umeko did not ask a single question or offer any observations on Takagi or Sagawa's daughter. Her prim manner struck Daisuke as comical. In the past he had from time to time been trapped by his sister-in-law's stratagems, but never once had he gotten angry. If he were his usual self, he might even have laughed off today's farce as a welcome diversion from his boredom. That was not all. If he had had any intentions of marrying, he might have turned this farce to advantage and used his ingenuity to create a comedy with a happy ending. He would have been content for the rest of his life laughing at himself. But now, when he thought that even his sister-in-law was colluding with his father and brother to lure him into a pitfall, he could not stand back and watch it as a comic act. As he wondered how his sister-in-law intended to develop the incident further, Daisuke became a trifle anxious. Of all his family, it was Umeko who most enjoyed such intrigues. Somewhere in Daisuke's mind lurked the fear that if she pressed in on him on the marriage issue, then the closer she pressed, the further he would have to remove himself from his family.

It was nearly eleven o'clock when the performance ended. When they stepped outside, they found that the wind had completely died, but there was neither moon nor stars, and only a few lamps shed light on the quiet night. Since the hour was late, there was hardly any time to linger and chat in the teahouse. There were men to meet the other three, but Daisuke had carelessly neglected to order a ricksha for himself. Thinking it would be troublesome, he pushed aside his sister-in-law's invitations and took a streetcar from in front of the teahouse. As he waited to change in the middle of a dark road in Sukiyabashi, a woman carrying a child on her back moved wearily toward him. Two or three trains passed on the other side. Between Daisuke and the tracks, there was a high, bank-like mound of piled dirt or rock. Daisuke realized for the first time that he was standing in the wrong place.

"If you're waiting to catch the streetcar, you can't get it here. It's the other side," he called to the woman as he began walking. The woman thanked him and followed from behind. Daisuke walked uncertainly in the dark, almost as if he were groping. When he had gone some thirty yards to the left, guided by the border of the moat, he finally found the pole marking the stop. There, the woman got in the train going toward Kandabashi. Daisuke alone got on the Akasaka train on the opposite side.

In the train, Daisuke felt sleepy yet unable to sleep. Even as he was tossed about, he anticipated the trouble he would have falling asleep that night. Although he was often exhausted and overcome with listlessness toward everything offered by daylight, some unknown excitement would beset him and prevent him from passing a quiet night as he would have liked. In his mind the colors that had left their mark by turn during the day flickered all at once without regard for chronology or shape. And he could not tell exactly what colors or what activities they were. With his eyes shut, he resolved that when he got home he would again seek the aid of whiskey.

This disorderly, brilliant flow of colors inevitably brought in its wake a reflection—the reflection of Michiyo. And there Daisuke felt as if he had come upon a haven. But this haven would not project itself clearly on his eye. He perceived it only with the rhythm of his heart. It amounted to no more than a discovery that Michiyo's face, her manner, her words, her relationship with her husband, her illness—in short, her entire situation constituted an entity exactly suited to his liking.

The next day, Daisuke received a long letter from a friend in Tajima. This friend had returned to his home province right after graduation and had not been back to Tokyo since. Of course, he had not intended to live in the middle of the mountains, but parental orders had confined him to his hometown. Still, for about one year he had continued to write, to the point of becoming a nuisance, that he would prevail over his father yet and return to Tokyo. Lately, he seemed to have resigned himself at last and sent no more fretful complaints. His family was an old one in the area, and the principal business apparently consisted of cutting trees in the ancestral forest. In this latest letter, he described in detail his daily life. Then he jokingly announced in deadly serious language that he had been elected mayor a month ago and had attained the status of receiving an annual salary of three hundred yen. A middle school teacher straight from the university would earn at least three times as much, he wrote, comparing himself to some of their friends.

About one year after his return home, this friend had married the daughter of a wealthy man from the outskirts of Kyoto. Needless to say, this was in accordance with parental instructions. Soon afterward, a child was born. He never wrote a word about his wife after the wedding, but did seem to take an interest in the child's development and from time to time, sent reports that made Daisuke smile. Every time he read one of them, Daisuke imagined the life of this friend, who was deriving satisfaction from his child. He wondered to what extent his feelings for his wife had changed since the wedding because of this child.

From time to time the friend sent him dried fresh-water

trout or dried persimmons. In return, Daisuke had usually
sent recently published works of Western literature. In the
friend's response, there was sure to be some comment indi-
cating that he had read the books with interest. But this had
not lasted for long. In the end, his friend had not even ac-
knowledged the arrival of the books. When Daisuke finally
inquired about them, his friend wrote that he had indeed
gratefully received the books. He had thought to send his
thanks after reading them, but time had somehow slipped
away. In fact, he still had not read them. To tell the truth, it
was not so much that he did not have the time, but that he
did not feel like reading them. To put it even more bluntly,
he could no longer understand them even if he read them.
After that, Daisuke decided not to send any more books but to
buy toys instead.

As he put the letter back in the envelope, Daisuke felt
keenly the fact that this old friend, with whom he had once
shared the same inclinations, was now playing a different
tune, governed by thoughts and actions that were nearly the
precise opposite of those of the past. And he carefully compared the two sets of notes that sounded from the vibrations
of the chord of life.

As a theorizer, Daisuke accepted his friend's marriage.
He understood that it was a principle of nature that a man
living in the mountains with only trees and valleys for com-
panions would want to ensure his security by taking a wife
chosen by his parents. By the same reasoning, he concluded
that for city dwellers, all marriage was bound to bring misfor-
tune. This was because the city was nothing more than a
showcase of human beings. To arrive at this conclusion from
his premise, Daisuke had traced the following course:

He held that spiritual beauty and physical beauty were
two distinct categories, and that it was the right of urbanites
to expose themselves to every kind of beauty. He concluded
that anyone who did not avail himself of this opportunity,

thus transferring his affections from A to B, then moving from B to C, was an insensitive brute who did not properly appreciate life. He believed that on the strength of his own experiences, this was irrefutable fact. From this he arrived at the conclusion that all men and women who lived in the city were subject to unpredictable changes, according to circumstance, in their attractions for each other. As a corollary, it followed that the parties to a marriage, threatened by what was popularly called infidelity, were perpetually subject to misfortunes begotten in the past. Daisuke chose the geisha as the outstanding urbanites because of their heightened sensibilities and broad-ranging freedom of contact. Who knew how often in the course of a lifetime some among them would change lovers? Were not all urbanites geisha, only to a lesser degree? Anyone who sang the praises of undying love in this day and age belonged to the first rank of hypocrites in Daisuke's estimate.

When he had carried his thoughts this far, Michiyo's form suddenly drifted into his head. Then he wondered if he had not omitted some factor from his calculations. But try as he would, he could not discover what it might be. In that case, according to his own reasoning, the sentiments he held toward Michiyo were no more than a passing fancy. His mind duly recognized this. But his heart did not have the courage to accept it as a certainty.

Chapter XII

DAISUKE FEARED HIS
sister-in-law's pressures. He also feared Michiyo's magnetic
powers. It was still too early for summering. He lost interest
in every form of diversion. Even when he read, he could no
longer recognize his own form in the black print. If he tried
to settle down and think calmly, thoughts would come to him
as thread off a spool; but once he put them together, they
were all such as to be fearful to man. In order to stir up his
pale brain, as one would a milkshake, Daisuke decided that
he should travel for a while. At first he planned to go to his
father's villa. But insofar as he would still be vulnerable to attack from Tokyo, it would not be very different from staying
in Ushigome. Daisuke bought a travel guide and began to research where he should go. He felt as if no ideal place existed
on the face of the earth. Still, he tried to force himself to
go somewhere. He decided that this did not call for exten-
sive preparations. Daisuke got on a streetcar and arrived in
Ginza. It was an afternoon when a cheerful wind blew over
the streets. Daisuke walked all around the bazaar in Shimbashi then strolled down the wide avenue toward Kyōbashi.
The houses on the other side looked flat, as if they were part
of a stage backdrop. The blue sky was painted right above the
roofs.

Daisuke stopped at two or three haberdashers, equipping
himself with a few necessities. Among them was a comparatively expensive bottle of perfume. When he tried to buy tooth-
paste at the Shiseidō, a young clerk kept pressing a home-

made product on him in spite of his protests. Daisuke finally left the store frowning. Carrying the paper packages under his arm, he walked to the periphery of Ginza, and from there went around to Daikongashi, where he crossed the Kajibashi Bridge in the direction of Marunouchi. As he walked aimlessly westward, he ended up thinking that even this could be called a simple trip. He became tired and looked for a ricksha, but none was to be found, and he finally had to take the streetcar home.

When he got back, he found shoes that looked like Seitarō's neatly arranged in the entranceway. He asked Kadono about it and Kadono answered yes, that was right, Seitarō had been waiting for some time. Daisuke went immediately to the study. Seitarō had settled himself in Daisuke's big chair and was reading an account of Alaskan explorations. Some buckwheat cakes and a tea tray had been placed side by side on the Western table.

"What's this, Seitarō, coming over when I'm out and feasting yourself, eh?" Seitarō laughed and stuffed the Alaskan explorations in his pocket, then left the seat.

"If you want to stay there, go ahead." But Seitarō would not listen.

As usual, Daisuke began teasing him. Seitarō knew the number of times Daisuke had yawned at the Kabukiza the other day. And he posed the same question as before: "When are you going to get married, Uncle?"

Seitarō had come on an errand for his father. The message was for him to come by eleven o'clock on the following morning. Daisuke found it annoying to be at his father's and brother's beck and call. He turned to Seitarō and said, halfangrily, "What is this! It's terrible, just calling a person over without even telling him what it's about." Seitarō continued to grin. Daisuke shifted the conversation in another direction. Their principal topic was the results of the previous day's sumō matches listed in the newspaper.

Daisuke urged Seitarō to stay for dinner but he declined, saying he had to prepare for school, and went home. Before he left, he asked, "Then you're not coming tomorrow, Uncle?"

Pressed for an answer, Daisuke said, "Hm, I don't know. Would you tell them at home that your uncle might be going on a trip?"

When Seitarō asked "When?" Daisuke answered, today or tomorrow. Seitarō accepted this and went to the entrance-way, but as he stopped to put on his shoes, he looked up at Daisuke and asked, "Where are you going, Uncle?"

"Where? How would I know? I'll just go somewhere." Seitarō grinned and stepped out.

Daisuke intended to set out that very night and had Kadono bring out his Gladstone bag. He stuffed it with a few personal things. Kadono, who had been eyeing the bag with more than a little curiosity, said, still standing, "Shall I help with anything?"

"No, this is nothing," he declined, and pulling out the bottle of perfume he had already packed away, he tore off the wrappings, removed the stopper, and put it to his nose.

Kadono stalked back to his own room. In two or three minutes he came back with, "Should I be ordering the ricksha then, Sensei?"

Daisuke put the Gladstone bag before him and looked up. "Well, why don't you wait a while."

When he looked at the garden, he saw that daylight still hovered faintly over the Chinese hawthorn hedge. As he peered out, Daisuke thought that in thirty minutes he would have chosen a destination. He intended to take the first train that left at a convenient hour, get off wherever it took him, and make that place his home until the following day. There he would wait for a new fate to sweep him off. His travel funds were, of course, inadequate. If he were to stay at places suited to his style, they would last no more than a week. But Daisuke was unmindful of such details. If worse came to

worst, he would send home for money. Besides, since his original purpose was to get a change of air, he was determined
not to place the emphasis on luxury. If the mood seized him,
he was even prepared to hire a baggage carrier and walk all
day.

He opened the travel guide again and began to pour labo-
riously over the fine print, but before he could come any closer
to a decision, his mind slipped off to Michiyo. It occurred to
him that he might see how she was once more before leaving
Tokyo. He decided that he could take care of packing the bag
that night—as long as the plans could be carried out the next
day, it would be all right. He hurried out to the entrance.
Hearing his footsteps, Kadono came dashing out. Daisuke,
still in his ordinary clothes, was taking his hat from the hook.

"Are you going out again? Is it shopping? I'd be glad to do it
if I can," said Kadono, surprised.

Daisuke simply declared, "The trip's off for tonight," and
went out. It was already dark. The stars seemed to add their
light one by one to the beautiful sky. A pleasant wind blew at
his sleeve. But Daisuke, who had strode swiftly on his long
legs, had not gone two or three hundred yards before he felt
sweat at his brow. He took his hat off and let the night dew
fall on his black head, from time to time swinging his hat as
he walked.

When he came to Hiraoka's neighborhood, dark, human
shadows flitted about softly like bats. Lamplight filtered
through a crack in the shabby wooden wall onto the street.
Michiyo was reading a newspaper by the light. Asked if she
always read the paper at that hour, she answered that it was
her second time.

"You have that much time on your hands?" Daisuke moved
his cushion to the threshold, and with his body half hanging
over the verandah, leaned against the shoji.

Hiraoka was absent. Michiyo said she had just come from
the bath and had a fan beside her. With a slight tinge of color

in her usually pale cheeks, she said he should be back soon, so wouldn't Daisuke stay, and went to the morning room to prepare tea. Her hair was done in Western style.

Hiraoka did not come soon as Michiyo had said. Asked if he was always this late, she smiled and said it was about like this. Daisuke detected a hint of sadness in her smile and redirected his intent gaze on her face. Michiyo suddenly picked up the fan and began fanning at her sleeve.

Daisuke was concerned about Hiraoka's finances. He tried asking straightfowardly, they must no longer be troubled for living expenses these days? Michiyo said, well, and smiled as she had before. Since Daisuke did not respond immediately, she asked in turn, "Does it look that way to you?" Then she tossed the fan aside and spread her beautiful, slender, freshly bathed fingers to show Daisuke. The fingers wore neither the ring Daisuke had given her nor any other ring. Daisuke, who had always kept the image of his keepsake in his heart, understood her meaning. As she withdrew her hands, Michiyo's face became flushed. "It can't be helped, so please forgive me," she said. Daisuke felt mournful.

That night Daisuke left Hiraoka's house about nine o'clock. Before he left, he took what was in his wallet and handed it to Michiyo. That had taken some quick calculating on his part. First, he had casually opened the wallet in the folds of his kimono, and without even counting the bills inside, thrust them carelessly in front of Michiyo with the words that he was giving them to her and she was to use them.

Michiyo said in a low voice, as if from concern over the maid, "Oh, no, you mustn't," and put both hands against her body. But Daisuke would not withdraw his hand.

"If you could accept the ring, then you can accept this. It amounts to the same thing. Think of it as a paper ring and take it."

Daisuke said these words with a smile. But Michiyo still hesitated, saying it was too much. Daisuke asked if Hiraoka

would scold if he found out. Michiyo did not know if he would
scold or approve, so she continued to hesitate. Daisuke advised that if there was a chance that he would scold, then
she should say nothing to him. Still, Michiyo would not put
out her hand. Daisuke of course could not withdraw what
he had extended. Finally, he had no choice but to lean over
slightly and reach his palm toward Michiyo's bosom. At the
same time, he brought his face to within a foot of hers and
said in a low, firm tone, "It's all right, go ahead and take it."
Michiyo drew back, almost burying her chin in her collar,
and without a word, put out her right hand. The bills fell
onto it. At that moment, Michiyo beat her long lashes together two or three times. Then she slipped into her obi what
her hand had caught.

"I'll come again. Give my regards to Hiraoka," said Daisuke and went outside. When he had crossed the block and
entered a small lane, it had turned quite dark. He cut through
the dark night feeling as if he had seen a beautiful dream. In
less than thirty minutes he arrived at his own gate. But he
did not feel like going in. Crowned by the stars high above, he
wandered through the quiet residential neighborhood. He felt
that he would not tire even if he walked like this until early
morning. Eventually, he came back to his own gate. All was
quiet inside. Kadono and the old woman seemed to have been
gossiping in the morning room.

"It's quite late, Sensei. What train will you be taking tomorrow?" The question came as soon as he was in the entranceway.

Smiling, Daisuke answered, "It's off for tomorrow, too,"
and went into his room. His bed had already been laid out.
Daisuke took the perfume he had opened earlier and put one
drop on his stuffed pillow. Not satisfied with that, he went to
the four corners of the room, bottle in hand, and sprinkled
one or two drops in each spot. Having thus indulged himself,
he changed into a white cotton kimono and peacefully re-

clined his limbs beneath a light, new comforter. He fell into a rose-scented sleep.

When he awoke, the sun had climbed high and was sending golden vibrations onto the verandah. At his pillow were two neatly folded newspapers. Daisuke had no idea when Kadono had opened the shutters or brought in the newspapers. With one long stretch, he sat up. While he was scrubbing in the bath, Kadono came in, looking somewhat disconcerted. "Your brother has come from Aoyama." Daisuke answered to the effect that he would be with him shortly, and dried himself with care. The living room would scarcely have been cleaned, but Daisuke saw no point in his running out, so he took his time and parted his hair and shaved as usual before sauntering into the morning room. Once there, however, he could not bring himself to linger over the breakfast table. He sipped a cup of tea on his feet, rubbed a towel over his mustache, flung it away, and went into the parlor, where he greeted his brother. As usual, his brother had between his fingers a dark cigar that had gone out; he was calmly reading one of Daisuke's newspapers. As soon as he saw Daisuke's face, he asked, "It smells awfully good in this room. Is it your head?"

"It was like this before my head came in, wasn't it?" he answered, and told him about last night's perfume.

"You're getting pretty stylish, aren't you," his brother said calmly.

Seigo seldom came to Daisuke's. On the rare occasions when he did, it was always because some business had brought him. As soon as that was settled, he left. Daisuke was sure that something had come up today, too. He imagined that it was because he had sent Seitarō away with careless excuses the night before. After five or six minutes of small talk, his brother finally came out and said, "Last night Seitarō came home and said you were going on a trip today—that's why I came over."

"Yes, I was planning to leave around six this morning."

Daisuke delivered what amounted to a lie with perfect composure.

His brother, also looking serious, said, "If you were the sort who could get up early enough to leave at six, I wouldn't have come running all the way over from Aoyama at this hour." As Daisuke had anticipated, Seigo's business turned out to be nothing more than a part of the campaign now being launched against him. That is to say, plans had been made to invite Takagi and Sagawa's daughter to a luncheon that day, and it was their father's orders that Daisuke attend. From what his brother had to say, their father had been mightily displeased when he heard Seitarō's story last night. A worried Umeko had said she would go see Daisuke before he left and make him postpone his trip. Seigo, however, had restrained her by saying, "You don't think that fellow would set out tonight! He's probably sitting in front of his bag right now thinking. Wait till tomorrow, he's sure to come over even if we leave him alone—that's how I reassured her." Seigo was as calm as ever.

Daisuke became a little provoked and said, "Then why didn't you leave me alone and wait and see?"

"Women are such impatient creatures—the minute she got up this morning, she started nagging me, saying we were responsible to Father." Seigo did not look amused. In fact, he was staring somewhat resentfully at Daisuke. Daisuke would not say definitely whether or not he would go. But he did not have the courage to send his brother off with the same vague excuses he had used on Seitarō. Besides, even if he were to refuse to attend the luncheon and set out on a trip instead, he could no longer count on his own purse. He was now in a corner from which he could not stir without appealing to his brother or his sister-in-law or even his father—in short, one of the opposition. So he launched into a noncommittal appraisal of Takagi and Sagawa's daughter. He had only seen Takagi once before, about ten years ago, but strangely enough, he somehow seemed familiar, and when he spotted him at the Kabukiza the other day, he had tried to think who it was. On the other hand, he had only recently held a photograph of Sagawa's daughter in his hand, but even with the actual person before him, he had made no connection. Photographs were curious things; if one knew the person and then saw a photograph, it was easy to tell who it was, but the opposite—to guess the person from a photograph—was quite difficult. To put it philosophically, it came down to the impossibility of producing life from death, although for life to turn into death was only a natural progression. "That's what I thought," said Daisuke.

His brother agreed but did not seem particularly impressed. He carelessly shifted his cigar in his mouth; it had grown so short that it was on the verge of lighting his mustache. Then he asked, "You don't necessarily have to go on a trip today, do you?"

Daisuke had no choice but to answer that he did not.

"Then you can come and eat with us today, can't you?"

Again, Daisuke could not help assenting.

"In that case, I have to stop by a few places now, so you be sure to come, all right?" He seemed to be in as much of a hurry as ever. Now that he had resigned himself, Daisuke felt that he did not care what happened and so answered as his brother would have wanted.

"How about it, anyway? Don't you feel like marrying that girl? It wouldn't hurt to take her. It's funny, if you're going to put so much weight on a wife that you have to go around picking and choosing, you'll look like one of those Genroku* dandies. I thought everybody in those days, both men and women, had terribly uncomfortable affairs—isn't that true?

* A period (1688–1704) marked by the stability of the feudal government and the increasing prosperity of the merchant class, accompanied by displays of lavishness.

Well, however that may be, try not to make an old man angry, all right?" With these words Seigo left.

Daisuke went back to his room and chewed on his brother's warning. He was forced to admit that in fact, he and his
brother shared the same views on marriage. Therefore, Seigo,
who would urge marriage upon him, should in fact leave him
alone; Daisuke thus came to the opposite conclusion from his
brother, a conclusion suited to his own convenience.

According to his brother, Sagawa's daughter had been
brought by her uncle on a rare visit to Tokyo, combining business with sightseeing. Once the uncle's business was settled, she would be taken home again. Whether his father was
taking advantage of this occasion to cement their interests
permanently, or whether, during his recent trip, he had
taken the initiative to create this opportunity, seemed imma-
terial to Daisuke. As long as he sat at the same table with
those people and ate his food as if he enjoyed it, he would
have fulfilled his social obligations. He decided that if further
steps became necessary, he would have to look for a solution
then—that was the only course open to him.

Daisuke called the old woman and had her get out his
clothes. Although it was bothersome, out of respect he put on
a cloak with the family crest. Since he did not have an unlined hakama, he decided to get into one of his father's or
brother's when he got home. For all his sensitivity, Daisuke
did not particularly mind social functions because he was accustomed to them from childhood. If there was a banquet, reception, or a farewell party, he usually arranged his schedule
so that he could attend. He was therefore familiar with quite
a number of the faces well known in certain circles. Some
among them were aristocrats, on the order of counts and vis-
counts. Daisuke did not feel that he derived either gain or
loss from associating with such people. His speech and manner were the same regardless of where he went. Superficially,

he resembled his brother quite closely in this respect. As a result, those who knew them but slightly believed the brothers to be similar in temperament as well.

It was five minutes to eleven when Daisuke arrived in Aoyama. The guests had not yet arrived. His brother was not home either. Only his sister-in-law was sitting in the living room, fully prepared. As soon as she saw Daisuke, she attacked: "You're outrageous, trying to outwit me like that and go off on a trip!" On certain occasions Umeko was incapable of being logical. In this instance she seemed completely oblivious of the fact that it was she who had outwitted Daisuke. Daisuke found it charming. So he sat down and immediately began to appraise her appearance. He learned that his father was in his room, but he refused to go back. Pressed to do so, he said, "When the guests arrive, I'll go announce it to him. I can pay my respects then, won't that do?" As usual, he gave free reign to his tongue. But he would not utter a single word on Sagawa's daughter, though Umeko struggled her utmost to bring the conversation to this subject. This was only too apparent to Daisuke. It made him play the innocent all the more and take his revenge on her.

Presently, the awaited guests arrived, and just as he had promised, Daisuke went to inform his father. Sure enough, his father only said, "All right" and immediately got up. He had no time to scold. Daisuke went back to put on a hakama and then proceeded to the parlor. Hosts and guests were all facing one another. His father and Takagi opened the conversation. Umeko concentrated on Sagawa's daughter. Soon his brother ambled in, still wearing what he had worn earlier that morning. He turned to the guests and said, "Excuse me for being late," then took his seat and, turning to Daisuke, said in a low voice, "They're early, aren't they."

The room next to the parlor had been prepared as the dining room. Through the crack in the door Daisuke caught a glimpse of the corner of a conspicuously white tablecloth, and understood that the meal would be Western style. Umeko left her seat for a moment and looked in the door. This was to signal their father that the luncheon preparations were complete.

"Please come this way." Their father stood up. Takagi bowed and also stood. Sagawa's daughter followed her uncle's example and stood. Daisuke discovered then that the woman's body was comparatively long and slender from the hips down. At the table, his father and Takagi sat face-to-face at the center. Umeko sat at Takagi's right and the daughter took her place at their father's left. Just as the women now sat facing each other, so Seigo and Daisuke sat opposite each other. It worked out so that Daisuke could look at the young lady's face from a slight angle over the cruet stand. He thought that the flesh and color of her cheeks, which caught the sun's vigorous rays from the window behind, cast too dark a shadow on the edge of her nose. On the other hand, the area bordering her ear was clearly a light pink. Her conspicuously small ears looked delicate enough to admit the light. In contrast to her skin, her large eyes were a dark brown-black. The young lady's face, whose chief merit consisted of the colorfulness of this contrast, was on the whole rather round.

Given the number of people present, the table was not on the large side. Compared to the size of the room, it was even too small, but with freshly cut flowers to frame the snowy white cloth, the knives and forks stood out nicely.

Conversation at the table generally consisted of ordinary small talk. At first, even that failed to provoke much interest. In such situations, Daisuke's father normally introduced his favorite topics of paintings, books, and antiques. And if the mood seized him, he would bring out any number of them from storage and arrange them before his guest. Thanks to him, Daisuke had acquired some discrimination in these matters. His brother likewise knew at least the names of a few artists. However, this meant no more than his standing in front of a scroll and saying, oh, this is a Kyūei, isn't it, or oh, this is an Ōkyo, isn't it. Since he never changed his expression at all, he did not seem in the least interested. Neither Seigo nor Daisuke ever brandished magnifying glasses in an effort to ascertain the authenticity of a work. Nor, whatever the painting in question, did they ever apply the sort of criticism their father was wont to pronounce—the old masters never painted waves like that, those waves contradicted the teaching.

To add life to the withering conversation, their father eventually tried touching upon his favorite areas. But after two or three words, it became apparent that Takagi was totally indifferent to those subjects. Veteran that he was, Daisuke's father immediately retreated. But once the conversation returned to territory that was safe for both, neither felt any interest in it. Finally, Daisuke's father asked Takagi what his hobbies were. Takagi answered to the effect that he had no hobbies in particular. The old man, apparently deciding that all was lost, handed Takagi over to his sons and for some time remained outside the circle of conversation. Seigo effortlessly cultivated topics ranging from an inn in Kobe to Nankō Jinja Shrine—anything that came to mind. And he also created a natural opening for Sagawa's daughter. The daughter would punctuate the conversation with the necessary words, then retreat immediately. Daisuke and Takagi first took up Dōshisha University, then turned to the state of American universities. In the end, the names of Emerson and Hawthorne came up. But Daisuke merely ascertained that Takagi possessed knowledge of this sort and did not pursue the matter any further. The literary conversation thus came to an end after the names of two or three authors and works had been raised and failed to develop at all.

Umeko, of course, had been chattering ceaselessly from the start. The principal object of her efforts, was, naturally, to break through the reserve and silence of the young lady seated before her. Out of politeness if nothing else, the latter could not but respond to Umeko's uninterrupted flow of questions. But there was hardly a trace of her having taken the initiative to win Umeko's heart. Whenever she spoke, she had a habit of crooking her neck slightly. This, however, failed to strike Daisuke as coquettish.

The young lady had been educated in Kyoto. In music, she had begun with lessons on the koto but had later changed to piano. She had practiced the violin as well, but because the fingering was difficult, she might as well not have touched the instrument. She seldom went to the theater.

When Umeko asked, "What did you think of the Kabuki the other day?" Sagawa's daughter did not answer. Daisuke took this less as a sign of not understanding drama than as an expression of contempt for it. Still, Umeko persisted with the topic, saying that actor A was such and such whereas actor B was thus and so. Daisuke saw that his sister-in-law was again overstepping the bounds of good judgment and had no choice but to cut in from the side, "Even if you don't care for theater, you must read novels?" thus putting an end to the theater talk.

Then, for the first time, the young lady looked straight at Daisuke for an instant. Her answer was unexpectedly distinct: "No, not even novels."

At this, the company, who had all been awaiting her answer expectantly, burst out laughing. Takagi took it upon himself to explain for his niece. Under the influence of Miss So-and-So who had been in charge of the young lady's education, she had in some respects been trained almost as a Puritan. Accordingly, she was very much behind the times, he added, offering his own view of the matter. Naturally, no one laughed this time.

Daisuke's father, who was not very favorably disposed toward Christianity, praised, "That's very fine."

Umeko failed to see any merit in such an education. Still she said, "Yes, that's true"—an ambiguous observation hardly in keeping with her nature.

Seigo, not wanting Umeko's words to weigh unduly heavily upon the other party, immediately changed the subject. "Then your English must be quite good?"

The young lady smiled and said no.

The meal being over, guests and hosts returned to the drawing room and began talking. But the flame of conversation would not light on to new subjects as from one candle to another. Umeko stood and opened the piano and looked back at the young lady. "Won't you give us a piece?" she asked. The young lady, of course, did not stir. "Then Dai-san, why don't you start us off?"

Daisuke knew that he was not skilled enough to play before others. But if he were to make such excuses, matters would only become complicated, so he simply said, "Why don't you just leave it open. I'll get to it later," and continued to talk about unrelated subjects.

The guests left in another hour. The four went out together to the entranceway. On his way back, the old man said, "Daisuke isn't leaving yet, is he?" Daisuke, one step behind the others, stretched so that he could nearly touch the lintel with both hands. Then he wandered around the deserted drawing room and dining room for a short while and returned to the living room to find his brother and sister-in-law sitting face-to-face discussing something.

"Hey, you can't go home yet. Father says he wants to see you. Go on to the back," said his brother in an exaggeratedly serious tone. Umeko betrayed a faint smile. Daisuke scratched his head in silence.

He did not have the courage to enter his father's room alone. He tried every possible means to drag his brother and sister-in-law along. When his efforts met with failure, he simply sat down on the spot. Then a chambermaid came in to say, "If the young master would please come to the back for a moment."

"Hm, I'll be there right away,"Daisuke answered and pro-

ceeded to advance the following argument to his brother and
sister-in-law: given their father's disposition and his own in-
discreet character, he might well end up angering the old
man if he were to go by himself. Should that happen, his
brother and sister-in-law would have to step in and mediate.
That would be far more troublesome for them in the end, so
they might as well go now rather than try to spare themselves
a little effort.

Seigo, who disliked arguments, wore an expression that
all but said, how stupid! "Then let's go," he said, and got up.
Umeko also got up, laughing. The three crossed the corridor
to their father's room and seated themselves innocently.

Umeko adroitly maneuvered the conversation so that their
father's scoldings would not touch upon Daisuke's past history. She directed the flow of conversation as much as possible
toward an evaluation of the guests who had just left. She
praised Sagawa's daughter as a very quiet, nice girl. Their
father and Seigo and Daisuke all expressed agreement with
this. But his brother raised the question that if she was indeed educated by an American Miss, then shouldn't she be a
little more direct in the Western manner? Daisuke thought
the question a valid one. His father and sister-in-law were
silent. Then Daisuke offered the explanation that her quiet-
ness came from shyness and therefore was quite separate
from the Miss's training; it probably had to do with the
standards of male-female social intercourse in Japan. His
father thought that that was quite true. Umeko guessed that
the place of the young lady's education, Kyoto, might have
something to do with it as well. His brother said that even in
Tokyo, not all women were like Umeko. At this, their father
tapped his ash receptacle and adopted an expression of severe
neutrality. Then Umeko said her looks were better than average, too. Neither their father nor Seigo had any objections
to this. Daisuke also admitted his agreement. The four then
moved on to an assessment of Takagi. This was easily settled

with the view that he had a good, stable character. Unfortunately, no one knew the young lady's parents. But their father gave his word that they were modest, trustworthy people. He had had a member of the House of Peers from the same prefecture check into their background. Lastly, they launched into the topic of the Sagawa family fortunes. Their father said that people like them were more stable than ordinary businessmen because they rested on a solid foundation.

With the young lady's eligibility thus largely established, his father turned to Daisuke and asked, "You can't have any serious objections?" Neither his tone nor words could be taken to mean, well, what do you think of it?

"Well, no." Daisuke was still inconclusive. His father was watching Daisuke intently, but his wrinkled brow clouded increasingly. Then his brother, feeling pressed to say something, said, "Well, why don't you think it over carefully?" and created a little breathing space for Daisuke.

Chapter XIII

SOME FOUR DAYS LATER,
Daisuke went on his father's orders to see Takagi off at Shimbashi Station. Perhaps it was because he had been roused
early that morning after too little sleep and then had let the
wind toss his sleepy head—but by the time he arrived at the
station, he felt that he might have caught a cold. No sooner
had he stepped into the waiting room than Umeko advised him
that he looked unwell. Daisuke removed his hat without answering and clasped his wet head from time to time. In the
end, his hair, so neatly parted in the morning, became completely rumpled.

On the platform, Takagi suddenly turned to Daisuke and
said, "How about it—why not take this train and come for a
visit to Kobe?" Daisuke only answered, thank you. Just as the
train was about to leave, Umeko made a point of approaching
the window and, calling Sagawa's daughter by name, said "Do
be sure to come again soon." From the other side of the window, the young lady bowed politely, but on this side of the
glass no words could be discerned. When the train had gone,
the four left the ticket area and went their separate ways.
Umeko tried to take Daisuke back to Aoyama, but Daisuke
clasped his head and refused.

He took a richsha straight to Ushigome and, as soon as he
arrived, went directly into his study and fell on his back. Kadono came out to check on him, but knowing Daisuke's ways,
said nothing and left after picking up the cloak flung over a
chair.

As he lay, Daisuke wondered what would happen in his immediate future. If he left things as they were, he would end up having to accept this match. He had refused quite a number of them already. If he rejected this one in addition to all the others, it seemed likely that the family would either give up on him in disgust, or become seriously angry. If they were to give up pressing a wife on him, nothing could be better, but to have them get seriously angry with him would be highly inconvenient. On the other hand, it seemed stupid for a modern man to accept something he did not want. Daisuke wandered in the midst of this dilemma.

Unlike his father, Daisuke was not the old-fashioned sort who began with a plan and then tried to force nature to conform to it. This was because he believed nature to be greater than any plan fabricated by man. For his father to force him to run counter to his own nature and do his bidding was the same as an abandoned wife's waving the letter of divorce as proof of her married state. But Daisuke had not the slightest intention of confronting his father with such an argument. To attack his father with logic was the most difficult of undertakings. Furthermore, even if he were to risk the difficulty, he stood to gain nothing. The result would only be to invite his father's displeasure and would be no different from rejecting the match without giving a reason.

Of his father, brother, and sister-in-law, Daisuke had the greatest doubts about his father's character. He went so far as to guess that even in the case of the current match, the marriage itself was not his father's sole objective. But of course, he had not been afforded an opportunity to determine precisely where his father's motives lay. He did not think it immoral that he, a son, should speculate in this way on his father's intentions. Nor did he for a moment consider himself particularly unfortunate as a son. It was just that he found it disagreeable that the gulf between them was likely to widen more than ever on account of this.

At one extreme of their rift lay the possibility of disinheritance. Daisuke tried to imagine that situation. He recognized that some anguish would attend upon it, but not so much as to be unbearable. He was rather more fearful of the cessation of funds that would ensue.

Daisuke had always maintained that man was finished when potatoes became more important to him than diamonds. If he brought his father's wrath upon himself, and if the worst came true and their financial ties were broken, then he would have to abandon the diamond and gnaw at the potato. All that would be left in compensation was a love that came naturally to him. And the object of that love was another man's wife.

He thought and thought as he lay. But no matter how much time elapsed, his mind would not arrive at anything. Just as he did not have the right to determine his life span, so he could not determine his future. But just as he could make certain estimates about his life span, so he could also perceive certain shadows in his future. He dallied at trying to capture these shadows.

At moments like this Daisuke's brain only flitted with fantasies like bats that startle the night. As he lay chasing the light of their beating wings, his head seemed to lift from the floor, becoming buoyant. Before he knew it, he fell into a light sleep.

Suddenly, someone sounded a bell in his ear. Daisuke awoke even before the thought of fire crossed his mind. However, he did not spring up; he simply continued to lie. It was almost normal for such sounds to appear in his dreams. At times, the echoing persisted even after he was awake. Five or six nights ago, his sleep had been shattered by the awareness that the house was shaking violently. At the time, his shoulders, hips, and part of his back had clearly felt the floor move. It also happened frequently that the throbbing of his heart, which he had felt in a dream, would carry over into wakefulness. On such occasions he would place his hand on his chest and saintlike, lie with his gaze turned to the ceiling.

Daisuke lay waiting for the bell to finish buzzing deep in his ear. Then he got up. When he went into the morning room, he found that his tray had been covered and left next to the brazier. The clock pointed past twelve. The old woman must have finished her meal; she was in the maid's room, nodding away with her elbow leaning on the rice pot. Kadono was nowhere to be seen.

Daisuke went to the bathroom, wet his head, then returned to his tray. He finished a lonely meal and went back to his study. That day, for the first time in a long while, he felt like looking at some of his books.

He opened at the bookmarker a Western book he had once begun, and he discovered that he could make no connection with what had come before. Such a lapse of memory was rather unusual for Daisuke. Since his student days, he had been something of a reader. Now he prided himself on his situation which, free from the cares of food and shelter, allowed him, even after graduation, to reap as he pleased the benefits of various subscriptions. If he let one day pass without glancing at a single page, habit led him to feel a vague sense of decay. Therefore, in the face of most intrusions, he tried to arrange it so that he could stay in touch with the printed word. There were moments when he felt that books constituted his only legitimate province.

Daisuke puffed absently on his cigarette and flipped back two or three pages that he had already read. He had to struggle somewhat to focus his mind on the arguments and the sequence in which they were being presented. The effort required for this was not as trifling as that for moving from a barge onto the wharf. It was more like puzzling over a piece of a block that would not fit and being forced to move on to another piece with the first still out of place. Even so, Daisuke persevered and kept his eyes on the pages for some two hours. Finally, he could stand it no longer. True, as a collection of print the words projected a certain meaning on his mind. But they showed no sign of circulating to his flesh and blood. He felt as unsatisfied as if he had bit into ice from outside the ice bag.

He turned the book face down. He decided that it was impossible to read under such circumstances. He also felt that he could no longer rest peacefully. His anguish was not the usual ennui. It was not that he was too listless to do anything; his mind was now in a state in which he could not bear not to do something.

He went to the morning room and threw on the cloak that had been folded. Then he put on the clogs that he had kicked off in the entranceway and all but ran out the gate. It was about four o'clock. He went down Kagurazaka and with no destination in mind took the first streetcar he saw. Asked by the conductor where he was going, he blurted out whatever came to mind. When he opened his billfold, he discovered, buried deep in the fold, what was left of the travel money he had given to Michiyo. Daisuke bought his ticket and counted the bills that remained.

He passed that night in a certain teahouse in Akasaka. There he heard an interesting story. A young and beautiful woman had relations with a certain man and came to harbor the consequences. When it was time for the birth, she shed sorrowful tears. Later, when asked why, she replied that at her age she felt miserable at having to bear a child. The period of love's supremacy had been all too brief, and in the mercilessness with which parenthood had fallen on her young head, the woman had caught a glimpse of life's transiency. She was, needless to say, not a respectable woman. Daisuke found the story extremely interesting for the insight it provided into the psychology of a woman who had dedicated herself exclusively to beauty of the flesh and love of the soul without reflecting upon anything else.

The next day, Daisuke finally went to see Michiyo. He

was going because he was worried about whether Michiyo had told Hiraoka about the money of the other day, and if so, what effect this had had on the couple: this, at least, was the excuse he made to himself. He decided that it was this worry that had harried him and kept him from enjoying a moment's peace, and now, having dragged him to the ends of the earth, was blowing him right against Michiyo.

Before leaving the house, Daisuke freshened his spirits by changing from the underwear and unlined kimono he had worn the night before. Outside, it was that time of the year when the mercury climbed higher with each passing day. As he walked, the sun shone so brightly that he actually longed for the damp rainy season. Daisuke, as a reaction to the previous night, was oppressed by his own black shadow falling in the cheerful air. From beneath his broad-brimmed summer hat, he wished that the rainy season would begin quickly. It was only two or three days away. His head, as if to forecast its coming, was dull and heavy.

When he finally stood before Hiraoka's house, his hair, which formed a thick covering for his cloudy head, was hot and damp. Daisuke removed his hat before going in. The grating was locked. Hearing noises, he followed them to the back, where he found Michiyo fulling cloth with the maid. Still bent over, she leaned her slender neck from the middle of the fulling board, which was propped against the side of the storage shed, and resting the hand that had been painstakingly stretching the wrinkled cloth, looked at Daisuke. At first she did not say anything. Daisuke also stood silent for a moment. Finally, when he said, "I've come again," Michiyo shook her wet hands and went in by the kitchen door almost in a run. At the same time she signaled to him with her eyes to come around to the front. She came out to the stepping stone to open the lock and explained, "Because it's unsafe." Her pale cheeks were flushed from working in the clear sunny air. The color faded into her usual pallor toward the hairline, where a thin layer of sweat gleamed. Daisuke watched Michiyo's almost transparent skin and waited quietly for the door to open.

"I'm sorry to keep you waiting," Michiyo said, and as if to draw him in, moved aside one step. Daisuke almost brushed against her as he went in. Inside, he found a purple cushion placed properly before Hiraoka's desk. Seeing it, Daisuke felt a tinge of distaste. In the garden, where the unworked earth gleamed yellow, long, unsightly grass was growing.

As he offered some commonplace apology about disturbing her again when she was busy, Daisuke stared at the tasteless garden. Then the thought came to him that it was unkind to leave Michiyo in such a house. Michiyo folded her hands on her lap; the fingertips were slightly swollen from working in water. She said she had been fulling cloth because she was bored. By being bored Michiyo meant that with her husband out all the time, the tedious hours of housekeeping hung heavy on her hands.

Daisuke deliberately teased, "What a fine position!"

But Michiyo was not evoking the dreariness in her heart to appeal to him. Silently, she stood and went into the next room. She rattled the handles of the Western-style chest of drawers and came out with a red velvet-covered box. She sat before Daisuke and opened it. Inside was the ring Daisuke had given her long ago. "It's all right, isn't it?" she said, as if in apology, then got up and went back into the next room. There, as if in deference to society, she furtively returned the keepsake to its place and came back to her seat.

Daisuke said nothing about the ring. Looking at the garden, he said, "If you've got so much time on your hands, why don't you weed the garden?" It was Michiyo's turn to fall silent.

When this had lasted some minutes, Daisuke asked again, "Did you tell Hiraoka about it?"

In a low voice, Michiyo answered, "No."

"Then he doesn't know yet?" he asked back.

Michiyo's explanation was that she had meant to tell him, but Hiraoka was never home long enough these days, and she had just let the time slip by without letting him know. Daisuke of course did not question the truth of her explanation. But it was something that would have required only five minutes to tell. He could not help feeling that for Michiyo to have let the matter go so long, there was something weighing on her mind that made it difficult for her to tell Hiraoka. And he thought that he had made Michiyo a guilty woman before Hiraoka. But this did not wound Daisuke's conscience all too deeply. For he also felt that whatever the verdict of the law, Hiraoka would clearly share in the censure dealt by nature.

Daisuke tried to sound out Michiyo on Hiraoka's recent behavior. As usual, Michiyo was reluctant to say much. But it was clear that Hiraoka's conduct toward his wife had changed since their marriage. Daisuke had already seen as much when the couple returned from Kyoto. Since then, he had never explicitly asked the two about their feelings, but it seemed indisputable that each day their relationship deteriorated with increasing speed. If this estrangement had come about because he, a third person, had come between the couple, then Daisuke might have been more careful in his conduct. But when he appealed to his reason, he could not believe that this was the case. Daisuke traced part of the current state of affairs to Michiyo's illness, judging that the change in their physical relationship had had an emotional effect upon the husband. He traced yet another part to the death of their child. Other factors were Hiraoka's dissipations and his failure as a company employee. And finally, Daisuke traced the last part to the financial situation resulting from Hiraoka's dissipations. When all was summarized, he concluded that Hiraoka had taken a wife he should not have taken and Michiyo had married a man she should not have married. Daisuke sorely regretted having responded to Hiraoka's request and interceded on his behalf. But he simply could not think that it was because he, Daisuke, had stirred his wife's heart that Hiraoka was drifting from her.

At the same time, he could not deny outright that the couple's present relationship constituted a necessary condition for the growth of his love for Michiyo. Leaving aside for a moment the question of the extent to which their relationship had developed before Michiyo was married to Hiraoka, Daisuke was certainly incapable of remaining indifferent to her now. He found the Michiyo who had been stricken with illness more piteous than the old Michiyo. He found the Michiyo who had lost her child more piteous than the old Michiyo. He found the Michiyo who suffered from the difficulties of eking out an existence more piteous than the old Michiyo. But Daisuke was not so bold as to make a direct attempt to sever for good the bond between the couple. His love was not that blind.

Michiyo's immediate suffering stemmed from financial difficulties. Her intimations made it clear that Hiraoka was not giving her what he could for household expenses. Daisuke thought that as a start, he should at least do something about that. So he said, "I'll get together with Hiraoka and see if I can't talk to him." Michiyo turned to him with a lonely expression on her face. Knowing all too well that it would be fine if things went well, but that if he failed, it would only be worse for Michiyo, Daisuke did not press the point. Michiyo got up again and brought a letter from the next room. The letter was in a pale blue envelope. It had been addressed to Michiyo by her father in Hokkaido. Michiyo pulled the long letter from the envelope and handed it to Daisuke.

The letter described in detail the unsatisfactory conditions there, the high prices that made life difficult, the uncertainty of being without family or relations, and his desire to come to Tokyo if something could be arranged; everything in it was plaintive. Daisuke rolled the letter carefully and handed it to Michiyo. She was holding back her tears.

Michiyo's father had once owned enough fields and rice paddies to be known as something of a wealthy man. At the time of the Russo-Japanese War, he had followed the urgings of a friend and dabbled in the stock market. He failed completely, manfully sold all the property inherited from his ancestors, and went to Hokkaido. This was the first news Daisuke had had of him since then. As for their relations, Michiyo's dead brother had often told Daisuke that they might as well not exist. In effect, Michiyo could count only on her father and Hiraoka.

"I envy you," she said blinking. Daisuke lacked the courage to deny her words. After a pause, she asked, "Why haven't you found a wife yet?" Daisuke could not respond to this question either.

As he silently gazed at Michiyo's face, the blood slowly drained from her cheeks until they were even more pale than usual. Then for the first time, Daisuke realized the danger of remaining yet another minute before her. Their words, flowing from a natural sympathy, had driven them on and it was only a matter of two or three minutes before they would be pushed beyond the bounds fixed by society. Daisuke was of course equipped with conversation that, even if they went further, would allow him to retreat as if nothing had happened. He had always wondered at the conversations recorded in Western novels, for to him they were too bald, too self-indulgent, and moreover, too unsubtly rich. However they read in the original, he thought they reflected a taste that could not be translated into Japanese. Therefore, he had not the slightest intention of using imported phrases to develop his relationship with Michiyo. Between the two of them at least, ordinary words sufficed perfectly well. But the danger was of slipping from point A to point B without realizing it. Daisuke managed to stand his ground only by a hair's breadth. When he left, Michiyo saw him to the entranceway and said, "Do come again, please? It's so lonely." In the back the maid was still fulling cloth.

Once outside, Daisuke walked unsteadily for about a hundred yards. He should have been relieved at having left just in time, but his heart knew no such satisfaction. Nor, on the other hand, did he regret not having stayed with Michiyo and said all that nature commanded. He remembered that whether he broke off then or five or ten minutes later amounted to the same thing in the end. He remembered that his present relationship was already established the last time he saw her. No, it was even before then. . . . As Daisuke retraced their past, there was no point at which he could not see the flaming torch of their love. Michiyo was in effect married to him when she married Hiraoka. When he had pushed his thoughts this far, Daisuke felt as if something unbearably heavy had been thrown into his heart. His feet faltered under the weight. When he got home, Kadono asked, "You look very pale. Is something the matter?" Daisuke went to the bathroom and wiped the sweat from his pale brow. Then he soaked his overgrown hair in the cold water.

For some two days after that Daisuke did not leave the house at all. In the afternoon of the third day, he got on the streetcar and visited Hiraoka at the newspaper office. He had resolved to see him and have a thorough talk with him on Michiyo's behalf. He gave his card to the office boy. While he waited in the dusty reception area, he frequently took his handkerchief from his sleeve and covered his nose. Presently, he was shown to a drawing room on the second floor. It was a stuffy, hot, gloomy, cramped room. Daisuke had a cigarette. A door marked "Editorial" swung open and shut to admit a steady stream of people. It was from this door that Hiraoka presently emerged. He was wearing the same summer suit that he had worn the last time; as usual, his collar and cuffs were impeccable.

"Well, haven't seen you in a while." He sounded hurried as he stood before Daisuke. Daisuke also felt compelled to stand. The two spoke briefly. Daisuke had come just at a time when there was a good deal of editing to be done, and it was impossible for Hiraoka to get away for any length of time. Daisuke asked when it would be more convenient for him. Hiraoka took his watch from his pocket and said, "Sorry— but would you mind coming back in another hour?" Daisuke took his hat and went down the dark, dusty stairs once more. Outside there was at least a cool breeze.

Daisuke wandered aimlessly about the neighborhood. He mulled over how he should broach his subject once he was with Hiraoka. His objective was to gain immediate peace of mind for Michiyo, however little it might amount to. But he was afraid he would end up irritating Hiraoka instead. He even anticipated the explosion that could occur as the worst possible consequence. Yet he had no plan for saving Michiyo in case of such an outcome. He lacked the courage to let their relationship develop further with their mutual acknowledgment. At the same time, he could not bear not doing anything for her. Today's meeting, therefore, was not so much a prudent stratagem developed by his reason as an adventure spun out of the whirlwinds of emotion. This was something new to Daisuke, something of which he himself was still unaware. One hour later he stood again before the door marked "Editorial." With Hiraoka, he went out the gates of the newspaper office.

When they had gone three or four blocks down a side street, Hiraoka stepped ahead and entered a certain house. A wreath of hare's foot fern hung from the eaves of the room, and the narrow garden glistened with sprinkled water. Hiraoka took off his jacket and immediately crossed his legs. Dai-

suke did not think it was that hot. For him it sufficed to have
a fan in his hand.

Their conversation began with a description of the internal conditions of the newspaper office. Hiraoka said that it
seemed busy, and yet it was a good job, quite relaxing. His
tone did not suggest that he was simply trying to conceal a
sense of failure. Daisuke teased that Hiraoka liked the job because it was an irresponsible business. Hiraoka became serious and began to defend the profession. He explained that
there was no other business today that was as competitive or
demanded as much shrewdness.

"True, it's probably not enough just to be a good writer."
Daisuke showed no sign of being especially impressed.

"I'm only in charge of the financial section, but even there,
interesting things come up. Maybe I'll do a little story on the
inside facts of your family's company."

Given his long-standing observations, Daisuke was not to
be caught off guard with such a remark. "It might be interesting to do that. Only keep it fair, will you?"

"Naturally, I don't intend to print lies."

"No, I mean that your muckraking should be directed im-
partially at everyone, not just my brother's company."

Hiraoka laughed maliciously. "It's no fun just to stop with
that Japan Sugar Incident, you know," he said pointedly. Daisuke drank his sake silently. Their conversation seemed to be
losing momentum. Then suddenly, on some impulse, Hiraoka launched into an anecdote which he seemed to think was
related to the state of affairs in the business world. It was
about an incident that had occured in the Ōkuma Company
during the Sino-Japanése War. The Ōkuma Company had
been charged with the delivery of more than several hundred
head of cattle to the army in Hiroshima. Every day they delivered a certain number and by night stole a few back. On
the next day, they would redeliver the same cattle. The offi-
cials were buying the same cows every day. Finally, they re-

alized what was happening and branded the cows they had bought. The company unknowingly brought back the same cows on the following day and thus was exposed at last.

When he heard this story, Daisuke thought that insofar as it dealt with actual society, it afforded a taste of modern comedy. Hiraoka went on to tell of how the government feared a socialist named Kōtoku Shōsui. Two or three policemen stood on guard at his house night and day. At one point they even put up a tent and watched him from there. When Shōsui went out, the police followed him. If they ever lost sight of him, it was a major event. He's showed up in Hongō, now he's in Kanda—the telephones rang all over Tokyo, and the commotion was enormous. The police station in Shinjuku spent one hundred yen a month on Shōsui alone. When one of his group, a candy maker, sat on the street making his candy, the white-clad policemen kept getting in his way.

This story also failed to strike a serious note in Daisuke's ear.

"It's just another example of modern comedy, is it?" Hiraoka repeated Daisuke's last assessment to challenge him. Daisuke said it was, and laughed. Not only was he uninterested in such stories, but today, he had not come to exchange small talk as usual. So he let the topic of socialism slide. For the same reason, when Hiraoka had wanted to call a geisha, he had restrained him, though with difficulty.

"To tell you the truth, I wanted to talk with you about something," Daisuke said at last.

Hiraoka's manner changed suddenly, and with uneasy eyes on Daisuke, he came out with the unexpected words, "I've been meaning to do something about it for a long time, but as things are now, there's nothing I can do. Just wait a little more. In exchange, you see I haven't written about your brother and father."

Daisuke was taken aback. He did not find the response silly so much as odious. "You've changed quite a bit, haven't you," he said coldly.

"I've changed as much as you have. What can you do, I'm jaded. Anyway, just wait a little more." Hiraoka laughed unnaturally.

Daisuke decided that regardless of Hiraoka's words, he himself would say what he had come to say. If he were to explain that he hadn't come to press him on the matter of the loan, Hiraoka was sure to try to get the upper hand again; Daisuke found the prospect irritating and so let the misunderstanding lie. Instead, he prepared to launch his campaign. But there was an immediate stumbling block: if he started out by saying he had learned of Michiyo's budgetary problems from her, then she would be inconvenienced. Yet, if the discussion failed to touch on that point, all his warnings and suggestions would be quite useless. Daisuke chose to detour. "You must be getting quite familiar with places like this—everyone here seems to know you."

"My wallet isn't as fat as yours, so it's nothing grand. I can't help it—have to keep up my social ties after all." Hiraoka dextrously lifted his sake cup to his lips.

"This may be none of my business, but with all this, can you manage to make ends meet at home?" It was a determined thrust on Daisuke's part.

"Oh, I manage one way or another." Hiraoka had suddenly dropped his tone; his answer was half-hearted.

Daisuke could make no further inroads. He ended up asking,"You must normally be home by now? You seemed to be quite late that night I visited."

Still evasive, Hiraoka said, "Sometimes I am and sometimes I'm not. I can't help it. It's in the nature of the job." His ambiguity seemed to be half in self-defense.

"Michiyo-san must be lonely."

"No, she's all right. She's changed a lot." With these words, Hiraoka looked at Daisuke.

Daisuke sensed a strange fear in those eyes. Perhaps the couple's relationship was already beyond repair, he thought. If they were to be split asunder by nature's ax, then fate held an ineluctable future before his own eyes. The wider the rift between the two became, the closer he and Michiyo would be forced together. Daisuke blurted out as if on impulse, "That can't be true! Oh, even if she's changed, it's only that she's older. Try to get home regularly so that Michiyo-san'll feel a little easier."

"Is that what you think?" Hiraoka took a swig.

"Is that what I think? But anyone would think so." Daisuke was saying whatever came to mind.

"Do you think Michiyo's the same Michiyo as three years ago? She's changed quite a lot. Yes, quite a lot." Hiraoka took another swig.

Daisuke felt his heart throb in spite of himself. "She's the same. As far as I can tell, she's exactly the same. She hasn't changed one bit."

"But even when I do go home, it's not especially pleasant, so what can I do?"

"That can't be!"

Hiraoka looked wide-eyed at Daisuke. Daisuke's breathing became a little constricted. But he did not in the least feel like a sinner struck by lightning. He was saying illogical things on impulse, unlike his usual self. But he never doubted for a moment that he was doing this for the sake of the man seated before him. Half-consciously, he was making a last attempt to restore the Hiraoka couple to what they had been three years ago, and on the strength of that, to fling himself forever from Michiyo. He never once thought of it as a deceptive maneuver to blind Hiraoka to his relationship with Michiyo. Daisuke regarded himself too highly to behave in such a dubious manner.

Presently, he returned to his normal tone. "But if you're always out like this, it's natural that you'd need money. Then the family budget gets tight, and things get less and less pleasant at home."

Hiraoka rolled his white shirt sleeves midway up his arms

and said,"Home. Home isn't much to be thankful for. It seems that the only people who take home seriously are bachelors like you."

At these words, Daisuke found Hiraoka hateful. If he were to have spoken his mind candidly, he would have said outright, if you hate home so much, go ahead and hate it; but I'm going to take your wife. But there was still considerable ground to be covered before their exchange could go that far. Daisuke tried once more to reach Hiraoka from the outside. "When you first came back to Tokyo, I got a lecture from you, right, that I should do something."

"Right. And I was told your negative philosophy and was shocked."

Daisuke thought it was probably true that Hiraoka had been shocked. At that time Hiraoka was like a feverish man driven by a thirst for action. What did he crave as a result of that action? Was it wealth? Fame? Power? If not these, was he seeking action for its own sake? Daisuke could not tell.

"People like me who are spiritual bankrupts can't help having negative ideas like that. Anyway, it's not as if ideas exist first and people conform to them second. First comes the individual, then the ideas suited to him. So my theory applies only to me. I didn't intend it to cover your fate at all. I admired your spirit then. You're a man of action, just as you said. I hope you'll really do something."

"Of course, I intend to," was Hiraoka's only response.

Daisuke inwardly shook his head. "You intend to do it in the newspaper business?"

Hiraoka hesitated for an instant. Then he firmly declared, "As long as I'm in the newspaper business, that's where I intend to do it."

"That certainly makes sense. I'm not asking you about your whole life, so that's a perfectly good answer. But I wonder, can you really do anything interesting in the newspaper business?"

"I'm planning on it," replied Hiraoka tersely.

So far, their conversation had only advanced on an abstract plane. True, Daisuke had understood the meaning of Hiraoka's words, but he had yet to get to the heart of the man. He felt as if he were talking to a high government official or perhaps a lawyer. At this point, he resorted to calculated flattery. The example of war hero Lieutenant Colonel Hirose figured prominently in it. When Lieutenant Colonel Hirose fell during a blockade in the Russo-Japanese War, the people of the time idolized and even revered him as a war hero. But now, some four or five years hence, the name of Lieutenant Colonel Hirose scarcely found its way to people's lips. Thus was the rise and fall of heroes meteoric. This was because in many cases, the term *hero* designated one who was of sizable importance to a given age; although the word itself sounded glorious, it actually indicated something extremely practical. Consequently, once the period of importance was over, society set about stripping the hero of his medals. In the midst of war with Russia, the blockade troops might have been important enough; but with the restoration of peace, a hundred Lieutenant Colonel Hiroses made no more difference than a like number of common mortals. Just as people were fickle toward their neighbors, so they were with their heroes. Thus, even among idols, there was a continuous metabolic process, an ongoing struggle for survival. Daisuke had not the slightest yearning to join the ranks of heroes. But if there were an ambitious, energetic young man somewhere, he would be far better off rejecting the momentary power of the sword for the eternal power of the pen, for that would bring him a more durable fame. The newspapers were a leading contributor to this end.

Daisuke tried expounding this much; but the fact that it was all flattery to begin with, and that his words sounded so terribly youthful, made him lose interest—so much so that it seemed slightly comical to him.

Hiraoka's only response was "Well, thanks." He did not seem particularly annoyed, but on the other hand, it was evident from his answer that he was in no way moved.

Daisuke was embarrassed to have somewhat underestimated him. It had been his design to appeal to his heart and once that was done, to shift and slide into the original topic of his household. But Daisuke had stumbled not far from the starting point of this circuitous and difficult course.

That night Daisuke ended up parting from Hiraoka without having gotten any further. To judge from the results of the meeting, he himself could not tell why he had called on Hiraoka at the newspaper office. It was even more puzzling from Hiraoka's viewpoint. He never managed to press Daisuke for the reason he had come to the office.

Alone in his study the next day, Daisuke went over and over in his mind the proceedings of the previous evening. In the two hours they had spent talking together, the only time Daisuke had been relatively sincere with Hiraoka was when he was defending Michiyo. Even that was only a sincerity of motivation; the words he had actually used were arbitrary. Strictly speaking, they might as well be called lies. Even the motivation, which he had believed to be sincere, was after all but a means to save his own future. Hiraoka would certainly not have regarded it as forthright. As for the rest of their conversation—well, it was from the start a calculated program in which Daisuke had set out to lead Hiraoka from his original position into a trap designed to serve his, Daisuke's, purposes. Consequently, he had been unable to do anything with Hiraoka.

If he had been bold, if he had attacked his subject head on, without reserve, alluding directly to Michiyo—then he could have said stronger things. He could have shaken Hiraoka more. He could have penetrated further into his heart. No doubt. But if he had failed, it would have meant troubling Michiyo. It would have meant fighting with Hiraoka. Perhaps.

Daisuke found it cowardly of himself that he had unconsciously adopted a safe but ineffectual course with Hiraoka. If it was true that he had been dealing with Hiraoka from such a position, though all the while unable to trust him for even one minute with Michiyo's fate—then in that case, he was guilty of a flagrant contradiction inadmissible by the rules of reason.

Daisuke envied the men of old: though they were actually motivated by self-interest, the muddiness of their reasoning enabled them to weep, to feel, to agitate, all the while convinced that it was for the sake of others, and in the end, to effect what they had originally desired. If only his head were as muddy. He might have put on a greater show of emotion last night and reaped more gratifying results. People—especially his father—said that Daisuke was a man without ardor. But according to his own analysis, the truth was as follows: human beings were not so consistently lofty, sincere, and pure of motive and deed as to be worthy of ardor. Indeed, they were far more lowly creatures. To meet their lowly motives and deeds with ardor was the behavior of one who possessed an indiscriminating, infantile mind, or a charlatan who feigned ardor in order to elevate his own position. Hence, Daisuke's coldness, even if it could not be considered another step in human evolution, was at least the result of an improved analysis of man. Because he was accustomed to scrutinizing his own motives and deeds and discovering in them such craftiness, such insincerity, and, in general, such deceitfulness, he could never bring himself to pursue them with ardor. This was what he firmly believed.

Here he came upon a certain dilemma: was he to allow his relationship with Michiyo to develop in a straight line, as nature commanded, or, on the contrary, ought he to return to the innocent past? Unless he chose one or the other, his existence would as good as lose all meaning, he thought. All other intermediate courses began in fraud and would inevitably end in fraud. They were safe as far as society was concerned, and ineffectual as far as he was concerned. So he thought.

To let his relationship with Michiyo ripen as heaven willed —he could only think of it as the will of heaven—was a socially dangerous course, as he was well aware. A love that obeyed the will of heaven but violated the laws of man was customarily accepted by society only upon the death of its subjects. Daisuke tried to picture the ultimate tragedy befalling the two—and shuddered in spite of himself.

He also tried, on the other hand, to imagine eternal separation from Michiyo. In that event, he would have no choice but to become a martyr to his own will rather than to heaven's. As a means to this end, he thought of the marriage being urged upon him by his father and sister-in-law. And he thought that in acceding to that marriage, he would be giving a new start to all his relationships.

Chapter XIV

TO BECOME A CHILD
of nature or a man of will: Daisuke was at a loss. As a matter of principle, he loathed the absurdity of shackling himself like a machine—he who responded instantly even to heat and cold—to a rigid, inflexible policy. At the same time, he was acutely aware that he had arrived at a juncture where he risked having to make a crucial decision.

He had been told to give careful thought to the marriage issue, but he had still not taken the time to consider it in earnest. Once he got home, he had been thankful to have escaped the lion's den once again and had left the matter at that. His father had not pressed him yet, but he had a feeling that he would be called to Aoyama within two or three days. Daisuke of course did not plan to do any thinking until he was actually summoned. Once there, he could study his father's countenance and compose a suitable answer on the spot. Daisuke did not necessarily mean to be contemptuous of his father. All responses, he thought, should flow spontaneously from a consideration of oneself and the other party to the discussion.

If he had not felt that his attitude toward Michiyo had been pushed to the brink, Daisuke would undoubtedly have adopted this course with his father. But now, regardless of his father's countenance, Daisuke would have to cast the die in his hand. Whether the face turned out to be inconvenient to Hiraoka or disagreeable to his father, as long as he was going to cast the die, he had no choice but to obey the laws of

heaven. As long as he was going to hold the die in his hand,
and as long as he had been fashioned so as to be able to cast
the die, then it had to be he and he alone who would determine the die's face. Daisuke decided in his heart that the final
authority rested with him. Neither his father nor his brother
nor his sister-in-law nor Hiraoka appeared on the horizon of
decision.

He was a coward only where his own fate was concerned.
He spent four or five days gazing at the die on his palm. It
was still in his grasp today. He wished that fate would rush in
from the outside and tap his hand lightly. Yet on the other
hand, the realization that he could continue to hold it in his
hand gladdened him enormously.

From time to time Kadono came into the study. Each time
he entered Daisuke was sitting still at his desk. Once or twice
he said, "How about going for a walk? It's not good for your
health to study like this all the time." True, his color was not
good. As it had turned summerlike, Kadono drew a bath for
him every day. Whenever he entered the bathroom, he spent
a long time gazing in the mirror. His beard was heavy, and
even the slightest neglect made it appear terribly unsightly to
him. When he touched and felt the roughness, it was even
more unpleasant.

He continued to take his meals as usual. But the insuffi-
cient exercise, irregular sleep, and mental strain produced
some disorder in his eliminatory functions. Daisuke thought
nothing of it. He scarcely had time to consider physical disorders, so preoccupied was he with one thing, circling it again
and again in his mind. Once this became habitual, it was
easier to spin around it forever than to make the effort to
break loose.

In the end, Daisuke came to abhor himself for his in-
decision. Since it was inevitable, why not refuse the match
with Sagawa's daughter in order to force his relationship with
Michiyo to develop? When he came this far in his thinking,

he was startled in spite of himself. But the idea of acceding to the match as a means of severing his ties with Michiyo never once appeared in the course of his mental revolutions.

As for refusing the match itself, he could resolve on that any number of times. But once he refused, that inexorable force which could be appeased only by throwing himself upon Michiyo was sure to set in as a reaction—and Daisuke became fearful again.

Daisuke waited expectantly for his father to press him. But there was no word from him. He thought of going to see Michiyo again but he did not have that much courage either.

Finally, he began to think that although marriage might sever his ties with Michiyo insofar as the conventions of morality were concerned, it would in no way influence them as far as the substance of morality went. If the relationship was able to develop with Michiyo already married to Hiraoka, why should the added circumstance of his being married signify its end? To see it as not continuing was but the public view; yet conventions, which were powerless to fetter the heart, could only increase in painfulness if multiplied. So Daisuke reasoned. He had no choice but to reject the match.

The day after the decision was made, Daisuke had his hair trimmed and his beard shaved for the first time in many days. During the first two or three days of the rainy season, it had rained in torrents, so that now, all that was dustlike had settled quietly on the earth and on the branches of trees. The sun's color was paler than it had been. The rays that fell from the rifts in the clouds were softened, as if they had lost half their reflective power because of the dampness of the earth. Looking at himself in the barbershop mirror, Daisuke stroked his cheeks, as plump as ever, and thought that today, he was embarking on a positive existence at last.

When he arrived in Aoyama, he found two rickshas parked at the entrance. One driver, waiting for his mate, had fallen asleep leaning against the running board and did not notice

Daisuke as he went by. In the living room Umeko sat with a newspaper in her lap, staring absently at the crowded green in the garden. She too seemed drowsy. Daisuke abruptly sat down in front of her.

"Is Father home?"

Before she would reply, Umeko studied Daisuke's appearance with the air of an inspector. "Dai-san, haven't you lost a little weight?"

"No, I don't think so," he replied.

"But your color isn't good." Umeko drew her eyes together and peered into Daisuke's face.

"It's because of the garden. I'm just getting the reflection from all the green." He looked out at the thick growth in the garden and added, "That's why you look pale, too."

"I haven't been feeling well for the past two or three days."

"No wonder you look so blank. Is something the matter? Do you have a cold?"

"I don't know what it is but I keep yawning all the time."

With these words Umeko let the newspaper slide from her lap and clapped for the maid. Daisuke inquired once more as to his father's whereabouts. Umeko had already forgotten the question. It turned out that the rickshas at the entrance had brought their father guests. Daisuke thought he would wait until they had left if it would not be too long. His sister-in-law got up, saying she wanted to splash water on her face to clear her head. The maid brought in a deep dish of fragrant arrowroot rolls. Daisuke dangled one of the sweets by the tail and sniffed at it.

When Umeko returned, looking refreshed, Daisuke was swinging the roll like a pendulum. This time, he asked, "How has Seigo been?"

Umeko, as if she felt unobliged to answer such a trite question immediately, stood for some time on the verandah gazing at the garden; then she observed, "See how the color of the moss has come out with the rain." With this uncharacteristic remark, she returned to her original seat and shot back, "What about your brother?"

When Daisuke repeated his question, she answered quite carelessly, "How is he? Well, he is as he always is, of course."

"Does he still stay out all the time?"

"Yes, yes, day and night, he's hardly ever home."

"Don't you get lonely then?"

"Why should you bother to ask a thing like that now?" Umeko began to laugh. Whether it was because she thought Daisuke was teasing her, or that it was all much too childish, Umeko hardly took notice of him. Daisuke, for his part, when he reflected on his usual self, was rather surprised that he had put such a question seriously. For all the years he had been witnessing his brother's and sister-in-law's relationship, he had never noticed this point. Nor had Umeko ever behaved so as to suggest to Daisuke that she found anything wanting.

"I wonder if that's how most couples get along," he said as if to himself; since he did not particularly expect an answer from Umeko, he did not even look at her but let his eye fall to the newspaper on the floor.

Then Umeko responded sharply, "What did you say?"

When Daisuke's eyes, startled by her voice, directed themselves at her, she said, "So, when you have a wife, why don't you stay home all the time and lavish affection on her?"

Then Daisuke realized for the first time that he was with Umeko and that he was not his usual self. He made an effort to assume his normal manner.

But his mind continued to dwell on the refusal of the proposed match and the relationship with Michiyo that was sure to ensue. Therefore, in spite of his resolve to return to his normal self and chat with Umeko, strange notes, unexpected to her, kept straying into the conversation without his notice.

Finally, Umeko said, "Dai-san, something's wrong with you today." Daisuke had on hand any number of ways to deflect his sister-in-law's words so as to avoid having to give a direct response. Today, however, he was reluctant to employ them—they seemed both hypocritical and bothersome. So instead, he implored rather earnestly that she tell him in what way he was strange. His question was so silly that Umeko gave him an odd look. But Daisuke only grew more insistent, so with the preface that in that case, she would, she began listing examples of the ways in which he was strange. Daisuke assumed that Umeko was deliberately pretending to be serious.

Eventually, she came out with, "And when you say things like 'with my brother out all the time, you must be lonely'— well, that's too thoughtful."

There Daisuke interposed, "No, you see, there's a woman I know who is in that position, and she seems so unhappy that I just felt like asking another woman how she felt. I didn't mean to make fun of you in any way."

"Is that true? Who is this person?"

"I can't really tell you her name."

"Then why don't you talk to her husband and tell him to pay more attention to her."

Daisuke smiled. "You think so too?"

"Why, of course."

"What if the husband won't listen to me?"

"Well, then that can't be helped."

"You'd just leave them alone?"

"What else is there to do?"

"Does that woman still have to fulfill her wifely duties?"

"You really try to push with logic, don't you. Well, I suppose that would also depend on the degree of the husband's unkindness."

"What if there's someone the wife likes?"

"I don't know. How foolish. If there's someone she likes, why doesn't she go there in the first place."

Daisuke fell into silent thought. Presently, he said,

"Umeko-san." Startled by the depth of his tone, Umeko looked at his face anew. Daisuke continued in the same tone. "I'm going to refuse this match."

The hand that held the cigarette trembled slightly. Umeko, on the other hand, heard his words with a face drained of expression. Daisuke proceeded, unmindful of her manner. "I've caused you a great deal of trouble over this business of marriage, and now I'm making you worry over this match. As you say, I am thirty now and should be willing to go along with your recommendations at a reasonable point. But I have some thoughts on the matter, and I would like to refuse this match as well. I am sorry about my father and brother, but it can't be helped. It isn't that the woman in question doesn't suit me, but I'm going to refuse. The other day, Father told me to think it over carefully and I have, but it still seems better to refuse, so that's why I'm going to say no. To tell you the truth, that's why I came over today, to see Father about this, but he seems to be busy with company. I shouldn't say incidentally, but I've taken advantage of this opportunity to tell you about it too."

Because Daisuke's manner was serious, Umeko heard him out without her usual frivolous interruptions, but when he was finished, she expressed her own views. Her words were extremely simple, brief, and to the point. "But Father will be troubled."

"I will tell Father myself so you don't have to worry."

"But the talks have come so far."

"No matter how far they may have come, I've never once said that I would marry her."

"But you've never clearly said you wouldn't."

"That's what I came here for today."

Then Daisuke and Umeko, sitting face to face, fell silent.

Daisuke felt that he had said all that needed to be said to Umeko. Umeko had many things to say and many to ask, but her lips could not form the words to logically connect these thoughts with what had preceded.

Finally, she said, "I don't know myself how far the talks have advanced without your knowledge, but no one expects you to refuse so flatly at this point."

"Why is that?" Daisuke's tone was coldly composed.

Umeko frowned. "Why? But it isn't a question of logic."

"It doesn't matter if it isn't logical; please tell me why."

"If you're going to refuse as many times as you have, it doesn't make any difference in the end, does it?" she explained. But her meaning was not immediately clear to Daisuke. He lifted uncomprehending eyes at her.

Umeko began to expand on her true meaning. "In other words, even you plan to get married some day, don't you? Even if you don't want to, it can't be helped. If you keep on being so selfish, it just causes Father problems. And so, well, no matter whom we find, she wouldn't suit you, so what I want to say is that it really doesn't make any difference whom you marry. No matter whom we show you, it doesn't do any good. There's not a single person alive in this world who would suit you. That's why you should just accept that a wife isn't meant to be pleasing in the first place, and get married— what other choice is there? If you'd just quietly marry the one we think is best, then everything would be nicely settled— true, maybe Father isn't consulting you on everything this time. But from his point of view, that's only natural. If he didn't do it this way, he'd never live to see your bride's face."

Daisuke listened patiently to his sister-in-law's words. Even when they came to an end, he would not open his mouth readily. He thought that if he were to refute her statements, things would only become more complicated, and his meaning would never penetrate Umeko's ear. Still, he had no intention of agreeing with her argument. He believed that practically speaking, to do so would only put both of them in a difficult situation. So he turned to his sister-in-law and said, "I understand your point, but I have my thoughts, too, so please leave me alone." His tone naturally betrayed the feeling that he found Umeko's interference bothersome.

But Umeko would not stay silent. "Of course, Dai-san, since you aren't a child, it's only natural that you should have some serious ideas of your own. I'm sure that unasked for advice from someone like me is only a nuisance to you, so I won't say any more. But try putting yourself in Father's place. Every month he gives you as much as you say you need, so that means you're even more of a dependent than in your student days. You're willing to take his help just as before, but now that you're grown up, you're not willing to listen to him —how can you expect anyone to accept that?"

Umeko's tone was becoming heated and she was about to pour out more words when Daisuke cut in, "But if I had a wife, I'd have to depend on Father even more, wouldn't I."

"But that's fine, since Father says he'd like it that way."

"Then Father's determined to have me get married, even if it's to a woman who doesn't suit me at all?"

"It'd be one thing if there were a woman to your liking, but we couldn't find one like that if we walked all over Japan."

"How do you know?"

Umeko turned a steadfast gaze upon Daisuke. Then she said, "You talk like a lawyer, don't you."

Daisuke drew his pale forehead toward his sister-in-law. "Umeko-san, there is a woman I like," he said in a low voice.

There were many times in the past when Daisuke had made such confessions in jest to Umeko. At first, Umeko had taken him seriously. There had even been comical instances when she had gone behind his back to probe into the matter. Once she had learned the truth, Daisuke's woman-that-I-like had no effect on her whatsoever. If Daisuke tried to use it, Umeko would take no notice. Or else she would tease him. Daisuke had been perfectly satisfied with that. But this case was unlike all the others. His facial expression, his eyes, the power concentrated in the depths of his low voice, everything that had preceded and brought him to this point—all of these things could not but startle Umeko. Daisuke's few words fell on her like a gleaming dagger.

Daisuke took his watch from his obi. His father's guests seemed unlikely to leave soon. The sky was beginning to cloud over again. He thought it would be wiser to withdraw for now and come back another time to settle the matter. He started to rise, saying "I'll come again. I think it would be better to see Father another time." In that space of time Umeko recovered herself. Being of a nature that sincerely insisted upon taking care of others to the end, she was not a woman to abandon things midstream. She all but held Daisuke back and asked the woman's name. Daisuke of course would not answer. Umeko insisted. Daisuke still would not accede. Then Umeko began to ask why he didn't marry the woman. Daisuke replied simply that he didn't because he couldn't. In the end, Umeko began to weep. He had thwarted her efforts to help him, she accused. Why hadn't he confided in her from the start, she reproached. Then all of a sudden, she became sympathetic—she felt sorry for him, she said. Still Daisuke would say nothing about Michiyo. Umeko finally gave in. As he was leaving, Umeko asked, "Then you're going to tell Father about it yourself? I suppose it would be better if I said nothing?"

Daisuke himself could not tell whether it would be better for her to be silent or for her to say something on his behalf. "Well," he hesitated, then continued, "I'm going to say no anyway, so . . ." and looked at his sister-in-law's face.

"Then if it seems better to say something, I'll speak to him. But if it doesn't look promising, I won't say anything and you can tell him everything from the beginning, that would be better," said Umeko kindly.

"I'll leave it to your judgment," Daisuke said and stepped

outside. When he came to the corner, he took the Shiochō streetcar on purpose, thinking he would walk from Yotsuya. As he passed the military parade grounds, the heavy clouds in the west parted and the setting sun—an unusual sight in the rainy season—cast scarlet rays over the wide field. They fell on the wheels of a ricksha moving in the distance, so that each time the wheels turned, they gleamed like steel. The ricksha looked small in the middle of the distant field; the field was wide enough to make it look small. The sun's rays were garish, like blood. As he watched the scene from an angle, Daisuke was swept away by the train that tore through the air. His heavy head felt giddy. By the time he got to the terminal, whether it was because his mind had attacked his body, or because his body had attacked his mind, he felt an unpleasant sensation that made him anxious to get off as quickly as possible. The umbrella he had carried in case of rain now served as a cane as he dragged it along.

As he walked, he murmured inwardly that today, he had of his own accord as good as destroyed half his life. Up to now, with his father and sister-in-law, he had gently pushed his way at moderate intervals. This time, he would have to reveal his true self or not get his way at all. At the same time, there was little hope of gaining the satisfactory results he had attained before. There was, however, still room for him to retreat. But to do that he would unquestionably have to deceive his father. Daisuke inwardly sneered at his past. He wanted desperately to recognize that with today's confession he had destroyed half his life, and on the strength of that shock, to throw himself before Michiyo and appeal to her with all his passion.

He wanted to prepare his own position so that the next time he saw his father, he would not be able to take a single step back. Therefore, he was deeply fearful of being called before he could have another meeting with Michiyo. He regretted having told his sister-in-law to use her discretion in conveying his intentions to his father. If she should tell him tonight, he might even be called tomorrow morning. In that case he would have to see Michiyo tonight and declare himself. But since it was night he decided it would be inconvenient.

When he came to the bottom of Tsunokami, the sun was about to set. From the military academy he walked straight toward the moat, and after two or three blocks, when he should have turned to Sadaharachō, Daisuke deliberately followed the streetcar tracks. He could not bear to go home as usual and pass the night idly in his study. Across the moat, upon the high banks, the pine trees formed a black line as far as the eye could reach, and at their base the streetcars passed to and fro. Daisuke derived a measure of gaiety from seeing the rapidity with which the small, light boxes slid effortlessly over the rails, to and fro. On the other hand, the Outer-moat Line that ran relentlessly along the same tracks he was following seemed noisier and more hateful than usual. By the time he arrived at Ushigomemitsuke, he could detect a few flickering lights in the distant woods of Koishikawa. Without a thought of eating dinner, Daisuke began walking in Michiyo's direction.

Some twenty minutes later, he climbed Andōzaka and came out before the burnt ruins of Dentsūin. He went beneath the tall trees that spread their branches on either side and turned left to come out by Hiraoka's house. A light glimmered through the wooden wall as usual. Daisuke pressed himself against the wall and strained his ears. For a while, there was not a single sound; all was quiet within the house. Daisuke thought of entering the gate and calling from outside the grating. But just at that moment, someone slapped his shins near the verandah. Then that person seemed to get up and walk inside. Presently, people could be heard talking. It was hard to make out what they said, but the voices were unmistakably those of Hiraoka and Michiyo. The conversation died out in a while. Then footsteps approached the verandah again and with a resounding thump, someone sat down. Daisuke withdrew from the wall. He began to walk in the opposite direction from which he had just come.

At first he was in a daze, not knowing where or how he walked. The scene he had just witnessed danced furiously in his mind as if it would burn itself in. When that had subsided somewhat, he felt unspeakable humiliation over his own conduct. He asked himself why he had engaged in such a vulgar act and then fled as if surprised in the midst of it. He stood in the dark lane and rejoiced to himself that the world was about to be conquered by night. The heavy air of early summer closed in on him, and with every step he took, he felt as if he would suffocate. When he came to the top of Kagurazaka, his eyes were suddenly blinded. Countless human forms enveloped his body and countless lights burned his head without mercy. Daisuke went up Waradana as if he were fleeing.

When he got home, Kadono met him with his usual aimless look and asked, "It's pretty late, Sensei. Have you had dinner yet?"

Since he did not want to eat, Daisuke replied that he had and shut Kadono out as if to drive him away. But before two or three minutes were up, he clapped his hands and called him back. "There wasn't a messenger from home?"

"No."

"Then that's fine," was all he said.

Kadono continued to stand in the doorway as if vaguely dissatisfied. "Sensei, does that mean you didn't go home?"

"Why?" Daisuke's face was ill-humored.

"Why, you said something like that as you were leaving."

Daisuke found it tiresome to keep talking to Kadono. "I did go home—if they haven't sent a messenger that's fine, isn't it?"

Kadono answered noncommittally, "Is that right?" and went out. Daisuke, knowing that his father was more impetuous where he was concerned than with anything else in the world, had questioned Kadono because he was afraid the old man might have sent a messenger on his heels. When Kadono had retired to the houseboy's room, he decided that he had to see Michiyo the next day.

As he lay that night Daisuke pondered the way in which he should arrange his meeting with Michiyo. If he sent a letter by a ricksha driver to fetch her, she would probably come, but given the discussion he had just had with his sister-in-law, there was no guarantee that he would not be visited even the next day by his brother or sister-in-law. On the other hand, the thought of seeing Michiyo at Hiraoka's house was painful to him. He decided that there was no choice but to meet at a place unrelated to them both.

In the middle of the night it began raining hard. The muffled roar that enveloped the house made the mosquito netting look cold and out of place. Daisuke lay in the midst of the noise, waiting for the night to end.

The rain did not clear until the next day. From the damp verandah, Daisuke stared up at the dark sky and once again changed the plans he had made the night before. It was distasteful for him to call Michiyo to a common teahouse to talk to her. For want of anything better, he had even thought of meeting her under the blue sky, but given the weather, there was little hope for that. From the start, he was disinclined to go to Hiraoka's house himself. He concluded that the only choice left was to bring Michiyo to his own house. Kadono would be something of a nuisance, but he thought they could manage so that their conversation would not carry into the houseboy's room.

Until shortly before noon, he sat gazing absently at the rain. As soon as he had finished his lunch, he flung on a rubber raincoat and went out. He walked in the rain to the bottom of Kagurazaka and there called his home in Aoyama. He took the initiative to announce that he planned to come over on the following day. It was his sister-in-law who came to the telephone. She had not yet told Father anything, so wouldn't Daisuke think it over carefully again? With his thanks Daisuke pushed the button and hung up. Next he rang the number of Hiraoka's newspaper office to find out if Hiraoka had reported to work that day. He received the answer that he had indeed. Daisuke made his way once more up the hill in the rain. He entered a flowershop and bought a good many large, white lilies, and with these in hand, went home. He divided the still dripping flowers and placed them in two vases. Then he filled the same large bowl he had used before, cut the stems short on the remaining lilies, and tossed them in. When that was done he sat at his desk and wrote Michiyo a letter. His message was exceedingly brief. He only said that since there was something he urgently wished to talk to her about, would she please come.

Daisuke clapped and called Kadono. Kadono appeared sniffing loudly. As he took the letter he said, "It smells awfully good in here, doesn't it."

"You're to take a ricksha and bring her back, all right?" Daisuke emphasized.

Gazing at the white lilies, Daisuke abandoned himself to the powerful scent that enveloped the room. In this scent he distinctly recognized Michiyo's past. And inseparable from that past, the shadow of his own past lay coiled like smoke. Presently, he said in his heart, "Today, for the first time, I am returning to the past, which belonged to nature." When he was able to say this, he felt a peace pervade his entire being such as he had not known in recent years. Why could he not have returned sooner, he thought. Why had he tried to resist nature at all, he thought. In the rain, in the lilies, in the now revived past, he saw a life of pure, unadulterated peace. There was no selfishness in this life, either on its face or on its back. No gain or loss. No oppressive morality. Only the free-floating clouds and nature flowing like water. All was blissful. And all was beautiful.

Presently, he awoke from his dream. Daisuke was suddenly seized by the eternal anguish spawned by that instant of bliss. His lips lost their color. He gazed at himself in silence. The blood flowing beneath his fingernails seemed to quiver violently. He stood and walked over to the lilies. He drew his face close so that his lips all but touched the petals, and he drew in the scent until he was dizzy. He wanted to move his lips from flower to flower and smother himself in the sweet scent until he fainted and fell to the floor in the middle of the room. Presently, he folded his arms and paced back and forth between the study and the living room. His heart throbbed without ceasing. From time to time he came to the corner of a chair or the front of his desk and stopped. And then began walking again. The agitation of his mind would not allow him to rest for long in one spot. At the same time, he had to stop at random points in order to deliberate.

The time gradually wore on. Daisuke never lost sight of the hands of the clock. Occasionally he peered out at the rain from beneath the eaves. It was still falling straight from the sky, which had become somewhat darker than before. Most of the clouds had gathered in one place, swirled in an eddy, and looked suspiciously ready to descend upon the earth. At that moment they sucked through the gate a ricksha glistening with rain. When the sound of the wheels, overwhelming the rain, echoed in Daisuke's ear, his pale cheeks betrayed a smile and he put his right hand to his heart.

Michiyo followed Kadono from the entranceway along the verandah. In her navy-blue and white cotton print kimono with an arabesque obi, she looked so different from the last time that Daisuke at first glance felt something new. Her color, as usual, was not good, but when she came to the doorway and stood face to face with Daisuke, her eyes, brows, and mouth ceased all their activity and became rigid. As she stood on the threshold, she gave the impression that even her legs were rooted. From the moment she had seen the letter, Michiyo had of course anticipated something. In that anticipation were mingled fear and joy and anxiety. In the space of time between stepping from the ricksha and being shown to the living room, Michiyo's face had overflowed with the colors of that anticipation. Then, her expressions had come to an abrupt halt. Daisuke's manner was so intense that it had jolted her.

Daisuke pointed to one of the chairs. Michiyo sat as she was told and Daisuke took the seat opposite hers. The two sat facing each other for the first time. But for some time neither uttered a word.

"You wanted to see me about something?" Michiyo asked presently.

Daisuke only said "Yes." With that, the two fell back to listening to the sound of the rain.

"Is it something urgent?" Michiyo asked again.

Daisuke said again, "Yes." The two could not talk lightly as they usually did. Daisuke was ashamed of the self that required the help of alcohol in order to declare itself. He had already resolved that when he bared his heart to Michiyo, he would have to be his own natural self. But now, seated formally opposite her, he found himself longing for a drop of alcohol. He thought of going to the next room where he could stealthily pour himself a glass of his customary whiskey, but in the end, he could not bear to come to that decision. Unless he could stand in the open air and broad daylight and make his declaration in his normal condition, he would not be his own true self. To erect a wall· of drunkenness and become bold from its heights was, he could not help feeling, cowardly, cruel, and insulting. He had come to be unable to adopt moral postures toward the practices of society; but in its place, he intended that there be not a shred of immorality in his intentions toward Michiyo. Indeed, he could not have stooped to base, vulgar acts, there was not the room for it, so deeply did he love her. Still, asked what he wanted, he could not come forth immediately. Asked a second time, he still hesitated.

The third time, he had no choice but to say, "Well, I'll get to it by and by," and lit a cigarette. Michiyo's face became increasingly pale each time the answer was postponed.

The rain continued, long and thick, falling noisily. Because of the rain, because of the sound of the rain, the two were cut off from the world. They were even cut off from Kadono and the old woman, who lived in the same house. Alone, the two were sealed in the scent of the white lilies.

"I went out and bought those flowers." Daisuke turned and looked around. Michiyo's face followed his and traveled once around the room. Then she took a deep breath with her nose.

"I wanted to recall the days when you and your brother were in Shimizuchō, so I bought as many as I could," said Daisuke.

"What a lovely scent." Michiyo had been gazing at the large petals, wide open as if in flight, but when she turned her eyes to Daisuke, her cheeks were faintly flushed. "When I think of those days," she began, and stopped.

"Do you remember?"

"I remember."

"You wore bright collars and did your hair in the butterfly style."

"But that was just after I came to Tokyo. I quit doing it right away."

"Weren't you wearing your hair like that when you brought the lilies the other day?"

"Oh, you noticed? That was the only time."

"You wanted to wear your hair like that then?"

"Yes, it was just a fancy."

"When I saw your hair, it reminded me of those days."

"Oh," said Michiyo bashfully.

When Michiyo was in Shimizuchō—it was after she and Daisuke had begun to talk easily—Daisuke had once complimented her on the hairstyle she had worn when she first came from the country. At the time, Michiyo had smiled, but even when she had heard those words, she would never do her hair in the butterfly style again. The two remembered the incident well. But they did not raise it to their lips.

Michiyo's brother had been generous and easygoing by nature, and the warmth of his companionship had endeared him to his friends. Daisuke had been especially close to him. The brother's own easygoing nature had made him particularly fond of his quiet, submissive sister. When he brought her out from the country, it was not at all from a sense of duty to educate his younger sister, but out of sympathetic concern for her future and, moreover, the desire to keep her at his side for the present. Even before he sent for Michiyo, he had confided as much to Daisuke. At the time, Daisuke, like any youth, had responded to these plans with considerable curiosity.

After Michiyo came, Daisuke and her brother had become even closer. As to which of them had advanced the pace of their friendship, Daisuke himself could not tell. Since the brother's death, whenever Daisuke looked back upon that period, he could not but recognize a certain significance in their intimacy. The brother failed to shed any light upon it before his death. Daisuke himself never ventured to disclose anything. And thus their thoughts remained secret and were buried away. If the brother had privately revealed his intentions to Michiyo during his lifetime, Daisuke was ignorant of it. It was only that he derived a special feeling from Michiyo's bearing and her speech.

Even in those days, Daisuke presented himself to Michiyo's brother as a man of taste. Michiyo's brother did not have more than an average sensitivity. Whenever their conversation turned to deeper subjects, he frankly confessed that he did not understand and avoided needless argument. He once found the phrase "arbiter elegantiarum" somewhere and abused it by using it as a second name for Daisuke. Michiyo would sit in the next room, listening silently to her brother's and Daisuke's conversation. She thus learned the term "arbiter elegantiarum" and once startled her brother by asking its meaning.

Her brother had as good as completely delegated the education of Michiyo's taste to Daisuke. For the sake of his sister's mind, which turned to Daisuke's for enlightenment, he endeavored to make their opportunities for contact as frequent as possible. Daisuke did not refuse. Looking back, he even detected traces of his having assumed the responsibility voluntarily. Michiyo, of course, received his instruction gladly. In this way, the three spun together from month to month like three spokes in a wheel. Knowingly or unknowingly, the spokes drew closer and closer as the wheel turned. Just as they were about to merge into one ring, one of them disappeared, and the remaining two lost their equilibrium.

Daisuke and Michiyo began to talk without reserve about their past of five years ago. As they talked, their present selves receded into the background and they slowly returned to their student days. The distance between them shrank to what it had once been.

"If my brother hadn't died then and were still alive and well, I wonder what I'd be doing now." Michiyo seemed to be longing for the past.

"Do you mean that you'd be a different person if your brother were alive?"

"I wouldn't be a different person. How about you?"

"It's the same with me."

Then Michiyo said, almost reprovingly, "Oh, that's not true."

Looking intently at her, Daisuke answered, "I have never changed, then or now." He did not remove his gaze from her for some time.

Michiyo averted her eyes immediately and said, almost as if to herself, "But you were already changed then."

Her voice was much too low to pass for an exchange in an

ordinary conversation. Daisuke, as if stepping on a fleeting shadow, caught the tail end of her words: "I haven't changed at all. It just seems that way to you. It can't be helped if it seems that way, but it's a misunderstanding."

For his part, Daisuke spoke more earnestly and clearly than usual, as if in self-defense.

"Misunderstanding or whatever, it doesn't matter."

Without a word, Daisuke studied Michiyo's manner. Her eyes had been cast down from the beginning. Daisuke could easily see the trembling of her long lashes. "You are necessary to my existence. Absolutely necessary. It was because I wanted to tell you this that I had you come all the way over."

Daisuke's words were unadorned by the sweet turns of an ordinary lover's speech. His tone, like his words, was plain and simple. It even verged on the severe. His using the pretext of urgent business to call Michiyo was all that smacked of childish poetry. But of course, Michiyo was a woman who could understand urgent business apart from its vulgar sense. Moreover, she had little interest in the adolescent phrases that appeared in popular novels. It was true that Daisuke's words did not offer anything dazzling to Michiyo's senses. It was also true that Michiyo did not thirst in that way. Daisuke's words bypassed her senses and penetrated her heart. The tears flowed from her trembling lashes down her cheeks.

"I want you to consent to this. Please."

Michiyo wept still more. She was utterly unable to respond to Daisuke. She took a handkerchief from her sleeve and put it to her face. Only a part of her dark brows and forehead and hairline was visible to Daisuke. Daisuke dragged his chair closer to Michiyo. "You will consent, won't you?" he said next to her ear.

Michiyo still kept her face covered. Between the sobs, a voice sounded from the handkerchief, "It's too much."

The words ran through Daisuke like an electric current.

From the bottom of his heart he felt that his confession had come too late. If he was going to declare himself, he should have done it before Michiyo was married to Hiraoka. He could not bear to hear these few words of Michiyo's which trickled alternately with her tears. "I should have confessed this to you three or four years ago," he said glumly and pressed his lips together.

Michiyo immediately removed the handkerchief from her face. She lifted her eyes from beneath their reddened lids and looked straight at Daisuke and began, "You didn't have to do that, but why . . ." and hesitated, but continued decisively, "why did you let me go?" No sooner had she said this than she put the handkerchief to her face again and wept.

"It was wrong of me. Please forgive me."

Daisuke grasped Michiyo's wrist and tried to take the handkerchief from her face. Michiyo did not even try to resist. The handkerchief fell to her lap. Still looking at her lap, she said faintly, "It's cruel." The flesh on her small mouth quivered.

"If you say that I'm cruel, there's nothing I can say to that. But I've been punished accordingly."

Michiyo lifted wondering eyes to his face. "How?"

"It's more than three years since you got married, but I'm still single."

"But that's of your own choosing."

"No, it's not of my choosing. Even if I think of marrying, I can't. I don't know how many times I've been pressed by my family to get married. But I've refused them all. I've just refused another match. As a result, I don't know what will happen between my father and me. But I don't care what happens, I'm going to refuse. As long as you're taking revenge on me, I have to refuse."

"Revenge?" said Michiyo. Her eyes moved as if in fear of the word. "In spite of everything, there hasn't been a single day since I got married that I haven't hoped that you would get married as soon as possible," came her somewhat formal words.

But Daisuke would not heed them. "No, I want you to take revenge on me as much as possible. That's what I truly want. Calling you over like this today, and baring my heart to you—I can only think of this as part of your revenge, too. Now, I've as good as committed a crime in the eyes of society. But this is the way I was born, so it's more natural for me that I should commit this crime. Even if society brands me a criminal, if I can do penance to you, then that's enough. I can think of nothing that could make me happier."

For the first time, Michiyo smiled through her tears. Still, not a word came to her lips. Daisuke gained more time to unbosom himself: "I know that it's cruel of me to tell you these things after all these years. But it can't be helped, the more cruel I sound to you, the more it means I've succeeded with you—that's what it amounts to. Besides, I have come to the point where I can't go on living without revealing these cruel facts. In other words, it's selfishness. That's why I'm apologizing."

"It's not cruel. So please don't apologize any more." Michiyo's tone had suddenly become clear. It was still subdued, but compared to before, it was very calm. After a pause, she began, "If you had only spoken a little sooner"—and tears gathered in her eyes.

"Would you have been happier if I had said nothing the rest of my life?"

"No, that's not it," Michiyo denied forcefully. "If you hadn't spoken, I don't know if I could have gone on living either."

It was Daisuke's turn to smile. "Then it doesn't matter."

"It's not just that it doesn't matter, I'm grateful. Only . . ."

"Only, it's wrong to Hiraoka—is that what you want to say?"

Michiyo nodded uneasily.

Daisuke asked, "Michiyo-san, tell me honestly. Do you love Hiraoka?"

Michiyo did not answer. The color drained visibly from her face. Her eyes and mouth became fixed. Everything about her communicated anguish.

Daisuke asked next, "Then does Hiraoka love you?"

Michiyo's eyes were still cast down. Daisuke, trying to supply a decisive conclusion to his own question, had already formed the words in his mouth when Michiyo suddenly lifted her face. The uncertainty of just a moment ago had almost vanished from her face. Even the tears were nearly dry. Her cheeks were pale as usual, but her lips were firm and showed no signs of trembling. From their midst came these low, heavy words, one by one as if they would not link together. "We have no choice. Let's make up our minds."

Daisuke shuddered as if someone had showered him with cold water from behind. They sat facing each other, the two who were sure to be driven from society, and gazed into each other's souls as if they would bore into them.

Presently, Michiyo, as if she had suddenly been seized by something, put her hands to her face and began to weep. Daisuke, unable to bear the sight of her weeping, leaned on his elbow and hid his forehead behind his five fingers. There they sat, immobile, a veritable sculpture of love.

While they were still, they felt a tension of spirit as if they had seen fifty years compressed before their eyes. And together with the tension, they did not lose sight of the realization that they existed side by side. Together they received the punishment and blessing of love, and together they savored each.

Presently, Michiyo took her handkerchief and carefully wiped her tears away. Then she said quietly, "I'll be going home now."

Daisuke answered, "Yes, go."

The rain had become light, but Daisuke of course did not want to send her home alone. He deliberately did not hire a ricksha but saw her back himself. Whereas he normally would have accompanied her all the way to Hiraoka's house, he now parted from her at the Edogawa Bridge. He stood on the bridge and followed her with his eyes until she had turned the corner. Then, slowly walking back, he pronounced to himself, "It's all over."

The rain lifted toward evening and when night came, the clouds raced through the sky. The moon rose pure and white as if it had been washed. For a long time, Daisuke gazed from the verandah at the moistened leaves in the garden flooded by moonlight, and in the end, he put on his clogs and stepped down. The garden, not a spacious one to begin with, had a surprising number of trees, leaving little room for Daisuke to walk. He stood in the middle and looked up at the vast sky. Then he got the lilies he had bought during the day and strewed them all around himself. The scattered white petals, bathed in the moonlight, became luminous. Some of them glimmered in the dark at the foot of the trees. For some time Daisuke stayed in their midst, huddled over.

He went in only when it was time to sleep. The scent of the flowers had not completely left the room.

Chapter XV

AFTER HE HAD SEEN
Michiyo and said to her the things that had to be said, Daisuke found it considerably easier to experience something resembling peace of mind, at least as compared with before. But this was only as he had expected and was in no way a particularly surprising result.

The day after their meeting, he rose with the conviction of a man who had decisively cast the die he had long held in his hand. He recognized that since the previous day, he had become obligated to bear a certain responsibility for his and Michiyo's fate. Moreover, it was a responsibility that he himself had taken the initiative to assume. Consequently, he could not find the burden painful. He even felt that pushed by its weight, his feet moved forward more naturally. Bearing the slice of fate he had carved out for himself on his head, he prepared to do final battle with his father. Behind his father stood his brother. And his sister-in-law. After he had fought them, there would be Hiraoka. Even if he made his way through them, there would still be all of society. There would be that machine-like society that would not for one moment make allowances for individual freedoms and private circumstances. That society now appeared to Daisuke as a total darkness. He resolved to fight everything.

He was surprised at his own bravery and daring. Until this day he had viewed himself as a perfect gentleman—disliking passion, incapable of risks, avoiding games of chance, cautious, peaceful. Morally speaking, he had never committed a cowardly act in any significant sense, but he still found it difficult to remove from his mind the impression that he was fainthearted.

He subscribed to a certain popular foreign magazine. In one number he had come across an article entitled "Mountain Accidents" and had been alarmed. The article recounted the injuries and mishaps that befell those adventurers who crawled up high mountains. There was a story of a climber lost in an avalanche whose bones appeared forty years later on the tip of a glacier; another described the plight of four adventurers who, about to pass a flat, vertical rock that stood halfway up the side of a peak, had piled one on top of the other like monkeys; but just as the highest was about to reach for the tip of the rock, it had crumbled, the rope had broken, and the three, doubled one upon the other, had plunged headlong past the fourth into the distance. In the midst of these accounts were inserted several illustrations of human beings glued like bats to a mountainside as sheer as a brick wall. Daisuke, imagining the wide sky and distant valleys that lay beyond the white space beside the precipitous cliffs, could not help reexperiencing the dizziness brought on by terror.

He discovered that in the world of morality, he stood on the same ground as those climbers. But now that he stood there himself, he had not the slightest intention of recoiling. It would have been infinitely more painful for him to recoil and gain a reprieve.

He wanted to see his father and talk to him as soon as possible. Fearing that he might be engaged and unable to see him, the day after Michiyo came he called to ask for a convenient time. He was told that his father was out. When he called again the following day, he was refused on the grounds of a prior engagement. The next time, he was told there was no need for him to come until such time as he should be called. Daisuke waited as he was ordered. In the meantime, there was not a single letter from either his sister-in-law or his brother. At first, Daisuke speculated that the family had plotted to allow him as much time as possible to reflect and reconsider, so he remained nonchalant. He took his meals heartily. At night he dreamt in relative peace. Once or twice, in the intervals of clear sky, he took Kadono for a walk. Still there was neither a message nor a letter from home. Daisuke became uneasy, thinking that the respite granted him midway up the precipice had lasted too long. In the end he made up his mind to go to Aoyama himself. His brother was out as usual. His sister-in-law gave him a pitying look when she saw him. But she would say nothing about the matter at hand. When she heard what had brought him, she said she would go to the back and ask Father if it was convenient for him to see Daisuke. Umeko's manner suggested that she was protecting Daisuke from his father's wrath. It could also have been interpreted as an attempt to estrange him. Daisuke waited, agonizing over which it might be. As he waited, he repeated over and over to himself that no matter what happened, he was prepared for it.

It was some time before Umeko emerged from the back. She looked at Daisuke and said, again with pity, that it was not convenient for Father to see him that day. Daisuke had no choice but to ask when he should come again. His former spirit had faded and the query sounded dejected. Umeko, in a tone that suggested that his manner had aroused her sympathy, promised to take it upon herself to let him know of a suitable time within two or three days, and urged him to go home for that day. As Daisuke stepped from the inner entrance, Umeko, who had deliberately come to see him off, warned "You'd really better think it over this time." Daisuke went out the gate without even answering.

On his way home he felt terribly annoyed. As he walked, the feeling mounted in him that the peace he had discovered since his meeting with Michiyo had been to some extent destroyed by his father's and sister-in-law's behavior. He would have told his father everything just as he felt it, his father would have expressed his thoughts without reserve, and whatever the outcome, Daisuke would have accepted it manfully. This was what Daisuke had anticipated. His father's tactics were unpleasant beyond expectation. And insofar as they reflected his father's character, Daisuke found them even more disagreeable.

On the way, Daisuke tried to recall why he had gone to the trouble of hastening the interview with his father. Since it was no more than an effort to respond to his father's demands in the first place, it should have been advantageous to his father, who was waiting for his answer. If his father was going to avoid him in this studied fashion and postpone their meeting, then it could only result in delaying a solution to his own problems. As far as Daisuke was concerned, he had already taken care of the important aspect relating to his own future. He decided that until his father specified a time and summoned him, he would do nothing more about his family.

Daisuke came home. Only a faintly dark shadow of annoyance with his father lingered in him. But this shadow was such that it was sure to become more somber in the near future. Other than that, he perceived two currents of fate lying before him. One pointed to the direction in which he and Michiyo would be swept along. The other was a threatening force that seemed determined to swallow both him and Hiraoka. Since his meeting with Michiyo the other day, he had done nothing about Hiraoka. Even if he were to see Michiyo now—and he had no intention of allowing a long period of time to elapse without seeing her again—he was unprepared to take a definite course of action and move beyond their present situation. On this point, Daisuke himself had simply not designed a lucid plan. As for the future that was sure to sweep him along with Hiraoka, all that he had was a readiness to face anything at any time. Of course, he intended to wait for an opportune moment to seize the initiative and appeal to

Hiraoka. But he had prepared nothing concrete. The one thing he had promised himself that he would not fail to do under any circumstances was to disclose everything to Hiraoka. Hence, the current of fate that would unite him with Hiraoka was a black and fearful thing. One of his worries was the problem of how he should save Michiyo from this terrifying storm.

Last of all, Daisuke had not ordered his thoughts toward the society that surrounded him with a mass of human beings. In point of fact, society possessed the right to sanction him. But, he believed, the right to his deeds and his motives issued strictly from his own natural endowments and from nothing else. He intended to proceed on the assumption that on this point, there were no grounds for debate between himself and society.

From his position at the center of his small world, Daisuke regarded the situation thus, and having surveyed once again its constituent relationships and their hierarchy, he said "This should do," and left the house. He walked one or two blocks to his customary ricksha landing, where he selected a particularly handsome and speedy-looking vehicle and leaped in. With no destination in mind, he named an arbitrary section of town and rode around and around for about two hours before going home.

The next day, once again in his study, he stood at the center of his world just as he had the day before and looked everywhere, to his left, to his right, in front, and behind, then said "Very well" and went out, this time to roam wherever his feet carried him, again without a goal, and then came back.

He repeated the same procedure on the third day. But as soon as he stepped out, he crossed the Edogawa River and went to Michiyo's place. "Why haven't you come since?" she asked, quite as if nothing had taken place between them.

Daisuke was rather taken aback by her utter composure.

Michiyo deliberately took the cushion from Hiraoka's desk and thrust it toward Daisuke. "Why are you so restless?" she asked, and made him sit on it.

As they talked for an hour or thereabouts, Daisuke's head gradually became calm. It occurred to him that rather than ride aimlessly in a ricksha, he should have come sooner, even if only for thirty minutes. On his way out, Daisuke said, "I'll come again. It'll be all right, don't worry," as if to reassure Michiyo. Michiyo only smiled.

That evening there was at last a message from his father. When it came, Daisuke was dining with the old woman in attendance. He put his bowl down to take the letter from Kadono and read the message that he was to come by a certain time on the following day. "Sounds like a government office, doesn't it?" he said, and showed the postcard to Kadono.

"Is it from your home in Aoyama?" asked Kadono, looking at it politely. Not having anything to say, he turned it over and resorted to flattery, saying, "Well, one thing's for sure, you have to admit those old people have a good hand," and went out. The old woman had been chattering about almanacs. The older brother of the sign of water and the younger brother of gold, the harvest festival, the sportless day, the nail-trimming day, the building day*—it was all terribly bothersome. Daisuke, of course, was only giving half an ear to what she said. She asked again for a job for Kadono. Even if it was only for twenty-five yen, couldn't he be placed somewhere? Daisuke paid so little attention that he hardly knew how he answered her. But to himself, he thought that it was no time to worry about Kadono; he himself was in danger.

Just as he finished his meal, Terao came from Hongō. Daisuke looked at Kadono's face and thought for a while. "Shall I say no?" asked Kadono carelessly. Since the other day, Daisuke had missed an appointment or two, which was rare for

* Terms used by the practitioners of Onmyōdō (Yin-yang and Taoistic magic).

him. When he thought he could get away with it, he had also refused to receive visitors, which had happened about twice.

Daisuke decided to go ahead and see Terao. As usual, Terao was desperately trying to get something. Seeing this, Daisuke did not feel like leveling his usual barrage of sarcasm at him. Whether it was translation or adaptation, Terao was determined to struggle through as long as he was alive, and in this respect he was more a faithful child of society than Daisuke was. If he were to stumble and find himself in Terao's position, what kind of work would he be able to withstand? When he thought about this, Daisuke felt sorry for himself. Resigned as he was to the not-so-distant, almost certain prospect of falling even harder than Terao, Daisuke could not look upon him with contempt.

Terao had managed to finish the translation by the end of the month; but the publisher had begun talking about unfavorable circumstances and said he would have to postpone publication until the fall. Unable to convert his labors directly into cash, Terao had turned to Daisuke as a last resort. Had he agreed to the work without a written contract? That did not seem to be quite the case either. But he would not say that the bookseller had disregarded an agreement between them. In other words, Terao was vague. The only sure thing seemed to be that he was in difficulty. But Terao, accustomed as he was to such slips, did not seem to be reproaching anyone for breach of faith. Outrageous, unpardonable, he might say, but that was only with his lips, and his real concerns seemed to be centered on rice and meat.

Daisuke felt sorry for him and gave him something to help with his immediate finances. Terao thanked him and went home. Before he left, he confessed that he had actually received a small advance from the publisher, but he had used it up long ago. After Terao left, Daisuke thought that this man too showed a certain strength of character. It was not something one could achieve just by living comfortably from day to day, as he himself did. Maybe the literary circles of the day were languishing under such deplorable conditions that they had seen a need for such a type and given birth to him naturally, Daisuke thought, as he stared into space.

That night the future weighed heavily on him. He wondered if, should his father withdraw his material support, he would have the resolve to become a second Terao. If he couldn't pick up a brush and at least imitate him, it was clear that he would starve. If he didn't pick up his brush, what could he do?

From time to time he opened his eyes and gazed at the lamp placed outside the mosquito netting. In the middle of the night, he struck a match and had a cigarette. He tossed and turned. The night was not so hot as to hinder sleep. The rain began to fall noisily again. Daisuke thought he might fall asleep to the sound of the rain, but he also woke up to it from time to time. The night passed in a fitful alternation of sleep and wakefulness.

Daisuke left at the appointed time. He got into the street-car with his rain clogs and umbrella, but with all the windows on one side closed and the large number of people hanging from the leather straps, his stomach soon became queasy and his head heavy. Thinking that he was probably suffering from the effects of sleeplessness, he struggled to reach and open the window directly behind him. The rain beat in mercilessly on his collar and hat. Two or three minutes later, he noticed the annoyed looks on the faces of his neighbors and pushed the glass in its place again. On the outer surface of the glass, crushed raindrops clustered together and warped the view of the street. Daisuke twisted his neck to look outside and rubbed his eyes several times. But no matter how he rubbed, he did not get the impression that the world had changed at all. This was particularly true when he looked at an angle through the glass into the distance.

Once he changed streetcars at Benkeibashi, the crowds thinned and the rain became light. Now he could comfortably turn his head toward the moistened world. But his father's ill-humored face with its variety of expressions assaulted his brain. He even heard the echo of an imaginary conversation in his ears.

As usual, before he passed from the entranceway to the inner quarters, he stopped to see his sister-in-law. "Isn't this disagreeable weather that we've been having?" she said, and hospitably poured him tea herself.

Daisuke did not feel like drinking it. "Father should be waiting, so I think I'll go see him," he said, and started to rise.

His sister-in-law looked uneasy and said, "Dai-san, if it's at all possible, don't make an old man worry. Father doesn't have that much time left him." It was the first time Daisuke had heard such gloomy words fall from Umeko's lips. He felt as if he had suddenly fallen into a dark pit.

His father sat with the tobacco tray before him, his head bowed. Even when he heard Daisuke's footsteps, he did not lift his head. Daisuke went before him and bowed politely. Where he had expected a stern scrutiny, Daisuke was surprised to find that his father's manner was mild, even solicitous. "It must have been troublesome coming in the rain."

Then he noticed for the first time that his father's face had hollowed markedly. Since it had been on the fleshy side to begin with, the change was all the more apparent to Daisuke. Almost involuntarily, he asked, "Is something the matter?"

For a moment, a paternal expression stirred on his father's face, but he did not seem to take Daisuke's concern particularly seriously. After a few exchanges, however, he said, "I've gotten quite old too." His tone was so altered that Daisuke had growing cause to take his sister-in-law's words seriously.

His father intimated that he wished to retire from the

business world soon on the grounds of failing health. However, he proceeded to explain carefully, the tide had turned since the commercial expansion following the Russo-Japanese War, and with the enterprise under his control in a state of decline, he would inevitably be charged with irresponsibility if he were to retreat before they had cleared this impasse. He therefore had no choice but to stay on for some time longer. Daisuke found his father's words most reasonable.

His father expounded on the dangers, difficulties, and pressures of ordinary businesses, and the fearful anguish and tension attendant upon their managers. In conclusion, he observed that whereas the great provincial landowners seemed more modest by comparison, they actually rested on a far more solid foundation than men like himself. With this comparison as his basis, he endeavored once more to bring about the realization of the proposed match. "It would be most useful to have at least one relation like that, and in this situation, it is almost imperative, don't you think?" he said. For his father, this was rather too bald a proposal of a marriage of convenience, but Daisuke had never overrated him so highly as to be surprised by it. Indeed, he found it rather pleasant that for their last meeting, his father had finally shed his old mask. Daisuke knew that he himself was not above making such a marriage without a moment's hesitation.

Beyond this, he felt a sympathy for his father such as he had never experienced before. His face, his voice, his efforts to persuade Daisuke—everything about him attested to the misery of old age. Daisuke could not interpret this as a part of his father's stratagems. He wanted to say that he did not care what happened to him,' he would like his father to decide as suited him best.

But now, with that last meeting with Michiyo behind him, Daisuke was not in a position to engage in such a spontaneous act of filial piety as would satisfy his father's will. He had always been a middle-of-the-road sort. He had never submitted word for word to anyone's command, but neither had he passionately rebelled against anyone's advice. Depending upon the interpretation, this was the posture of a schemer or the strategy of a born vacillator. If he himself had been confronted with either of these charges, he could not have avoided wondering if they might not be true. But in large part, this was to be attributed neither to artifice nor to vacillation but rather to the flexibility of his vision, which allowed him to look in both directions at once. To this day, it was precisely this capacity that had always dampened his determination to advance singlemindedly toward a particular goal. It was not unusual for him to stand paralyzed in the midst of a situation. His posture of upholding the status quo was not the result of poverty of thought, but the product of lucid judgment; but he had never understood this truth himself until he acted upon his beliefs with inviolable courage. The situation with Michiyo was precisely a case in point.

He had opened his heart to Michiyo, and it did not occur to him to wipe the slate clean before his father. At the same time, he was sincerely sorry for his father. It was obvious what course of action the usual Daisuke would have adopted under these circumstances. Without going through the inconvenience of renouncing his relationship with Michiyo, he would have acceded to the marriage in order to satisfy his father. Thus he could have balanced both parties. It was easy to stand in the middle, not adhering to either side, advancing without being consumed. However, he was now a man of different inclinations from the usual Daisuke. The hour was past for him to shake hands with other human beings with half his body standing beyond the pale of society. He took his responsibility toward Michiyo that deeply and that seriously. His conviction stemmed in part from an assessment of his mind, in part from the longings of his heart. The two overwhelmed him in an enormous wave. Thus he stood before his father, a man reborn.

Like the usual Daisuke, he waited, trying to say as little as possible. From his father's viewpoint, there was nothing different about him from the usual Daisuke. It was Daisuke who was startled by the change in his father. He had guessed that the real reason he had been refused a meeting these past few days was that his father, fearing Daisuke would disobey him, had deliberately postponed it. Daisuke had resigned himself to being met with a grim face. He had thought that he might even be scolded bitterly. This rather suited Daisuke's purposes. In fact, one third of him had secretly prepared to make psychological use of the reaction his father's outburst would provoke in him, enabling him to refuse outright. Daisuke was discomfited to discover that contrary to his expectations, his father's manner, his choice of words, his principal objective, all tended to blunt his resolve. But Daisuke had come armed with a resolve that could overcome even this discomfiture.

At last he said, "Everything that you say is most reasonable, but since I do not have the courage to consent to marriage, I have no choice but to refuse this match."

All his father did was to stare at his face. Presently, he tossed his pipe onto the floor mat and said, "Do you need courage?"

Daisuke stared at his knees and was silent.

His father asked again, "The woman doesn't suit you?"

Daisuke still did not answer. He had never confided so much as a quarter of his thoughts to his father. It was because of this that he had been able to maintain peaceful relations with him for a short while. But from the start, he had never intended to hide the matter with Michiyo. He disliked the cowardliness of scheming to escape consequences that were his due. Only, he felt that the time for confession had not yet come. For that reason Michiyo's name did not come to his lips.

Finally, his father said, "Then do as you please." His look was bitter.

Daisuke did not find it pleasant either. Still, having no alternative, he bowed and prepared to retire. Then his father stopped and said, "For my part, I don't intend to look after you any more."

When he returned to the living room, Umeko asked expectantly, "What happened?" Daisuke did not know how to answer her.

Chapter XVI

THE NEXT MORNING,
even after he awoke, his father's last words rang in Daisuke's
ears. Given the circumstances in which they had been uttered, he was forced to attach greater weight to their meaning
than might normally have been the case. At least, as far as he
was concerned, he would have to resign himself to the fact
that material assistance from his father would no longer be
forthcoming. In order to return to his father's good graces,
even if he rejected the current match he could not reject
all prospective matches. Even if he rejected all prospective
matches, he would have to give reasons sufficient to convince
his father. For Daisuke, neither alternative was available.
Still more impossible was deceiving his father on a matter
that touched upon the roots of his personal philosphy of life.
When he looked back at the previous day's interview, Daisuke could only think that things had proceeded as they had
been intended. Yet he was fearful. Daisuke felt that he was
furthering a destiny natural to himself; in the process, with
the weight of this destiny upon his back, he had been pushed
to the edge of a precipice.

Daisuke thought that as a first step, he should seek an occupation. But in his mind there was only the word *occupation*,
and it failed to appear in its fleshly reality. Since he had never
before been interested in any occupation, regardless of what
he tried to imagine, his mind would only slide over its surface
and refused to break in to consider the internal reality. Society appeared to him like a flat surface partitioned according to

a complex color scheme. And he could only think that he himself had no color whatsoever.

After he had surveyed the entire realm of occupations, his eye came to the vagabond and rested. He clearly perceived his own shadow in the crowd of beggars that roamed between man and beast. What pained him most about an existence of degradation was that it destroyed freedom of the spirit. When his body was besmirched with every kind of filth, how far his heart and mind would sink! Daisuke shuddered.

He would have to drag Michiyo to the depths of this degradation. Michiyo was no longer Hiraoka's possession in spirit. Daisuke intended to shoulder to his death the responsibility for this woman. Even so, it now seemed to him that between the falseness of a man of stature and the kindness of a man in the dregs of ruin, there was ultimately little difference. To say that he would shoulder the responsibility for Michiyo until he died meant only that he had such an intention, and it could never equal the fact of shouldering the responsibility. Like a man who had been struck by blindness, Daisuke fell into a vacant stupor.

He visited Michiyo again. She was quiet and composed, just as she had been the other day. The spring wind brushed her brow generously. Daisuke understood that she trusted him with her entire being. When he saw proof of this with his own eyes, he was overcome with uncontainable feelings of tender love and pity. And he berated himself for being a scoundrel. He failed to say any of the things he had intended. As he was leaving, he said, "Won't you arrange to come to my house again?"

Michiyo nodded yes, and smiled. Daisuke felt a pang.

Since the other day, unpleasant though it was, Daisuke had been obliged to choose times for his visits when Hiraoka would be absent. At first he had not thought much of it, but lately, it had become more than disagreeable; it was becoming daily more difficult for him to go. Besides, if he appeared too often in Hiraoka's absence, there was the risk of arousing the maid's suspicion. Even now, whether or not it was just his fancy, he could not help feeling that she regarded him with distrustful eyes when she served the tea. But Michiyo was completely unconcerned. At least on the surface, she seemed to think nothing of it.

Of her relationship with Hiraoka, there was of course no opportunity to inquire in detail. On the rare occasions when he phrased a question or two indirectly, Michiyo would not respond. Her natural inclination, whenever she saw Daisuke, seemed to be to drown in the happiness of the moment. However she felt privately, once before Daisuke, she showed not a shadow of the fear that the dark clouds surrounding them might descend at any moment. Michiyo was by nature a nervous woman. When he considered that her recent behavior exceeded her normal performance, Daisuke was forced to interpret it not so much as evidence that her situation was not yet critical, but as an indication that his own responsibility was that much weightier.

In the two days prior to Michiyo's visit, Daisuke's mind failed to break any new ground. The letters spelling *occupation* were burned squarely into his mind. If he shoved them away, the reality that he was without material support took their place and danced furiously. When that vanished, the vision of Michiyo's future appeared as a raging storm. The whirlwind of anxiety blew into Daisuke's head. These three concerns, like the points of a pinwheel, spun without a moment's pause. As a result, everything in his surroundings began to spin. He was like a person on board a ship. In the midst of a spinning head and a spinning world, he continued to remain calm.

There was no word from the house in Aoyama. Daisuke of course did not expect to hear anything. He made an effort to absorb himself in small talk with Kadono. Kadono, being the sort of idle creature with so little to do that he hardly knew what to do with himself in the heat, proudly chattered on just as Daisuke wished. When ever he tired of talking, he would propose, "Sensei, how about a game of shōgi?" * Toward evening they would water the garden. They walked barefoot, each with a pail in hand, carelessly splashing water everywhere. Kadono said he would prove that he could hit the top of the paulownia tree next door, and just as he flung his pail, he slipped and fell on his seat. The four o'clocks next to the fence began to blossom. The leaves of the begonia growing beneath the water basin grew strikingly large. The rainy season cleared at last, and daytime brought a world of cloud peaks. It was that time of year when the powerful sun burned until the sky was transparent, gathering all the heat of the atmosphere to direct upon the earth.

When night came, all Daisuke did was to gaze at the stars above his head. The mornings he spent in the study. There were two or three days when the cry of cicadas sounded steadily from morning on. He often went to the bathroom to cool his head. Then Kadono, thinking it was about time, would come in and say, "It's unusually hot today, isn't it." Daisuke passed about two days in this state of oblivion. On the third day, toward noon, he gazed from his study at the color of the glittering sky; when he smelled the flaming breath emitted from above, he was frightened. He thought his mind would be permanently affected by the fierce weather.

Michiyo braved the heat to keep the promise she had made previously. When he caught the sound of a woman's voice, Daisuke himself flew out to the entranceway. Michiyo stood outside the grating, her parasol closed and a bundle in her arms. She apparently had come out in her ordinary clothes: she was just taking a handkerchief from the sleeve of a modest white cotton summer kimono. At first sight of her, Daisuke felt as if fate had cut out Michiyo's future and thrust it cruelly before his eyes. But he smiled in spite of himself and said, "You look as if you're going to elope."

* Japanese chess

Michiyo answered calmly, "But if I didn't stop by on a shopping trip, I couldn't come in comfortably." With these earnest words, she followed Daisuke in. Daisuke immediately offered her a fan. Exposure to the sun had brought a pleasant glow to Michiyo's cheeks. The usual tired look was nowhere to be seen. Even in her eyes a youthful luster hovered. Daisuke allowed his senses to drown in the vitality of her beauty and for a while forgot all else. But presently, when he thought that it was he who was invisibly chipping away at this beauty, who would finally cause its collapse, he became sad. After all, even today, he had called her to cloud over yet another part of this beauty.

Daisuke hesitated several times before he could unburden his heart. For Daisuke, simply to ruffle this happy young woman's brow with anxiety constituted the greatest immorality. If not for the fact that a powerful sense of duty toward Michiyo was operating in his heart, he probably would not have revealed to her the circumstances that awaited them in the future, but instead, would have repeated in the same room his confession of the other day and abandoned everything to the simple bliss of love.

At last Daisuke made up his mind. "There hasn't been any particular change in your relationship with Hiraoka?"

Even when faced with this question, Michiyo continued to be happy. "Even if there were, it wouldn't matter."

"You trust me that much?"

"I couldn't go on like this if I didn't."

Daisuke's eyes turned to the burning mirror in the distant sky and were dazzled. "I don't think I deserve to have that much trust placed in me," he answered with an ironic smile, but the inside of his head was roasting like a kiln.

The remark did not seem to weigh on Michiyo's mind, and she did not even ask, why not? She simply said, "Oh," pretending to be surprised.

"I ought to confess to you, I'm a much less reliable fellow

than Hiraoka. I don't want you to overrate me, so I'll tell you everything. . . ." With this preface, he proceeded to recount the details of his relationship with his father up to the present. Finally, he said, "I don't know what my position will be from now on. At the very least, I won't become an independent, self-sufficient individual for quite some time. I won't even be half sufficient. So . . ."

"So, what will you do?"

"So, I'm worried that I might not be able to fulfill my responsibilities to you as I would like."

"Responsibilities? What responsibilities? I can't understand if you don't speak more clearly."

As a result of his habitual emphasis on material well-being, Daisuke knew only that the hardships of poverty were hardly suited to winning a lover's satisfaction. Thus he had concluded that wealth was one of his responsibilities toward Michiyo and had formulated no other clear conceptions. "It's not moral responsibility, I mean material responsibility."

"I'm not interested in any such thing."

"Even if you say you aren't, it's sure to become crucial. Whatever new relationship we move on to in the future, material resources will be half the answer to everything."

"Maybe so, but it's useless to worry about it at this point."

"You say so now, but when it comes right down to it, it's only obvious that it's going to worry us."

Michiyo's color changed slightly. "From what you have just been telling me about your father, it should have been clear from the start that things would turn out like this. I think that you yourself must have realized as much a long time ago."

Daisuke could not answer. He held his head and mumbled as if to himself, "Something's wrong with my head."

Tears came to Michiyo's eyes. "If this bothers you, don't worry about me, make peace with your father and go back to your old relationship."

Daisuke suddenly seized Michiyo's wrist and all but shook it to emphasize his words: "If I planned to do something like that I wouldn't worry in the first place. It's just that I feel sorry for you, that's why I'm apologizing."

"Apologize!" Michiyo cut him off with a trembling voice. "How can I let you apologize when all this is happening to you because of me." She began to weep out loud.

Daisuke, as if to soothe her, said "Then you'll put up with it?"

"It won't be putting up. It's what I expect."

"There'll be other things, too, in the future."

"I know. I don't care what happens. Since the other day— I—since the other day, I've been prepared to die if worse comes to worst."

Daisuke shuddered in horror. "Don't you have any wishes about how we should go on from here?" he asked.

"Wishes? No, I don't have any wishes. I'll do whatever you say."

"To wander . . ."

"I can face it. If you say die, I'll die."

Daisuke shuddered again. "But the way we are now . . ."

"I don't care if we go on like this."

"Hiraoka doesn't seem to have noticed anything?"

"Maybe he has. But I've already made up my mind, so it's all right. I don't care when I get killed."

"You shouldn't talk so cheaply about dying and getting killed."

"But even if nothing happened, my health isn't so good that I can live a long life."

Paralyzed with fear, Daisuke stiffened and stared at Michiyo. Michiyo gave herself up to weeping, as if seized by an outburst of hysteria.

In a short while, the outburst began to subside. Then she became once more the quiet, graceful, deep, beautiful woman she usually was. Her brow was especially clear.

Daisuke asked, "Would it be all right if I saw Hiraoka and tried to settle the matter?"

"Can you do that?" Michiyo seemed surprised.

"I believe that I can," answered Daisuke firmly.

"Then, however you see fit," said Michiyo.

"Then let's do it that way. It doesn't seem right for the two of us to do anything while deceiving Hiraoka. Of course, I intend to talk to him so that he'll understand the facts well. And where I'm wrong, I'm prepared to apologize. It may not turn out as I want. But no matter how badly it goes, I intend to work it so that nothing outrageous can come of it. If we leave things half done like this, it's painful for us, and it's not right to Hiraoka either. It's just that if I go ahead and do this, then you won't be able to stand up to Hiraoka—I can't help thinking about that. That's where I feel sorry for you. Though as far as that goes, I'm in disgrace too. If it's proper to bear moral responsibility for one's deeds, no matter how humiliating it is, then I ought to tell Hiraoka about what has happened between us even if it yields no other benefits. Besides, in this situation, it's a confession we have to make in order to resolve things for the future, so I think it's all the more necessary."

"I understand. Anyway, if it goes badly, I'm prepared to die."

"Die—all right, even supposing death is the solution, how much time is there—besides, if there were any danger of that, why would I take the initiative to tell Hiraoka?"

Michiyo began to weep again.

Daisuke waited for the sun to decline to send Michiyo back. But he did not see her off as he had the last time. He passed about one hour in his study, listening to the cicadas. He felt relieved, having seen Michiyo and cleared his chest about the future. He picked up his brush to write Hiraoka and ask for a suitable time for a meeting, but he was suddenly overcome by the enormity of his responsibility and lost the courage to continue beyond the salutation. Then he abruptly stripped to his shirt and dashed out barefoot into the garden. Kadono, who had been lost to the world in deep sleep while Michiyo was there, now appeared on the verandah, holding his shaven head between his hands. "It's too early, isn't it? The sun's still out." Without bothering to answer, Daisuke burrowed into a corner of the garden and swept out the fallen bamboo leaves. Kadono reluctantly took off his clothes and joined him.

Although it was a cramped garden, the dryness of the soil made it quite a task to moisten adequately. Halfway through, Daisuke said his arms hurt and wiped his feet and went inside. He sat down on the verandah with a cigarette. Seeing this, Kadono teased from below, "Sensei, is your heartbeat a little irregular or something?"

That evening he took Kadono to a fair in Kagurazaka and brought home two or three pots of autumn grasses which he arranged beneath the eaves where they would catch the dew. The night was deep and the sky distant. The color of the stars shone dark and dense.

That night Daisuke went to bed, having deliberately omitted drawing the shutters. It never crossed his mind that it could be unsafe. He put out the lamp and lay by himself inside the mosquito netting, peering from the dark into the sky. Inside his head the events of the day flashed vividly. In another two or three days, the final outcome would be clear, he thought, and his heart leaped for joy. Then, before he knew it, he was drawn into a big sky and bigger dreams.

The next morning he made up his mind and wrote to Hiraoka. He said that he wanted to see him privately about something and wished to know when would be convenient for him; he himself would be free at any time. This was all he wrote, but he still placed the message in an envelope.

When he had moistened the gum and affixed the red stamp, he felt as if he had finally given official recognition to crisis. He called Kadono and had him toss the fateful letter into the mailbox. When he handed the letter over, his hand had trembled slightly, but once that was done he became blank and fell into a stupor. When he recalled that three years ago he had stood between Michiyo and Hiraoka and worked toward their marriage, it seemed like a dream.

He spent the next day in anticipation of Hiraoka's reply. The following day as well he stayed at home, counting on its arrival. Three, four days went by. Still there was no letter from Hiraoka. Then the day came when he normally would have gone to Aoyama to get his money. Daisuke's purse had become exceedingly light. Since that day when he saw his father, Daisuke had resigned himself to the likelihood that he would no longer receive assistance from home. He could not think at this point of casually dropping in as if nothing had happened. Why, he could get along for two or three months just selling his books and clothes, he told himself, making light of it. He also thought, in a commonsensical vein, that once things settled down, he could take his time and look for a job. Daisuke had already begun to believe—prior to any actual experience—the words that people liked to repeat almost as a proverb, that it was quite difficult to starve to death, one always managed somehow.

On the fifth day, he braved the heat and took a streetcar to Hiraoka's office, where he found that Hiraoka had been absent from work for two or three days. Daisuke went outside, and as he looked up at the dirty windows of the editorial office, he thought that he should have telephoned before venturing out. It was even questionable whether Hiraoka had received the letter. Daisuke had deliberately addressed it to the newspaper office. On his way home he stopped at a second-hand bookstore in Kanda which he frequented and asked them to come and look over some books he no longer needed and wished to sell.

That night he did not even have the heart to water the

garden. He stared absently at Kadono's form, clad in a white net shirt.

"Are you tired tonight, Sensei?" asked Kadono, clanging his pail. Daisuke, his heart weighted with anxiety, could not answer coherently. At dinner, his food had virtually no taste for him. He pushed it past his throat as if he were drinking, then threw down his chopsticks. He called Kadono and said, "Would you go over to Hiraoka's and find out whether he received my letter of a few days ago, and if he has, ask if you might have an answer, and wait for it." Still worried that Kadono had not really understood, he further explained that he had sent a letter saying such and such addressed to the newspaper office the other day.

After he had sent Kadono on his way, Daisuke went out to the verandah and settled in a chair. When Kadono came back, he had blown out the lamp and was sitting still in the dark.

"I've been to the Hiraoka's," called Kadono in the dark. "Mr. Hiraoka was at home. He said he had seen your letter. He said he would come over tomorrow morning."

"Oh? Thank you," Daisuke answered.

"He said he had meant to come sooner, but there was sickness in the family, so he was delayed. He sent his regards."

"Sickness?" repeated Daisuke involuntarily.

"Yes. It seems that his wife isn't well." Kadono's cotton summer kimono with its white background was the only thing that loomed dimly in Daisuke's field of vision. The light left to the night was much too faint to illuminate their faces.

Daisuke grasped the arms of his cane chair with both hands. "Is she very unwell?" he asked sharply.

"Well, I really couldn't say. But it didn't sound like it was on the light side. But if Mr. Hiraoka can come over tomorrow, it can't be that serious."

Daisuke was somewhat reassured. "What is it? What's wrong with her?"

"Oh, I forgot to ask."

Here their exchange came to an end. Kadono retraced his steps along the dark verandah and went into his room. As he sat listening quietly, Daisuke soon heard the sound of a lamp shade knocking against the chimney. Kadono must have lit a light.

Daisuke remained motionless in the night. Even as he was still, his heart trembled. The arms of his chair gleamed with perspiration. Daisuke clapped his hands and called Kadono. The dim white of Kadono's kimono appeared once more at the end of the verandah.

"Oh, you're still sitting in the dark. Shall I light the lamp?" Daisuke declined and asked again about Michiyo's illness. He asked every question he could think of—whether they had engaged a nurse, how Hiraoka was taking it—even whether Hiraoka had taken time off from work on account of his wife's illness. But after all, Kadono could only repeat what he had already said, and anything he added was mere conjecture. Even so, questioning him was more tolerable for Daisuke than sitting silently by himself.

Before he went to bed, Kadono brought a letter from the night mailbox. Daisuke took it from him in the dark and made no attempt to look at it. Kadono, almost as if to prompt him, said "It looks like it's from your home. Shall I bring a lamp?"

Daisuke finally consented to having a lamp brought into his study and by its light opened the envelope. The letter was addressed to him by Umeko and was quite long:

I'm sure you've been quite annoyed over this matter concerning a wife for you. For our part, your father and brother and I have also been very worried. But all our efforts notwithstanding, you refused Father outright the last time you were here. It was terribly disappointing, but now I have resigned myself. I found out later that Father had gotten angry with you and told you he would not be bothered about you any more and that you were to be prepared accordingly. I wonder if that is why you have not come since. I thought that perhaps, on the day of your allowance—but you still did not come, and I am worried. Father says to leave you alone. Your brother is as easygoing as ever. He says that you'll come over once you're hard up, that we can make you apologize properly to Father then. If it doesn't look as though you're going to come, he says he'll go over and talk to you. But as far as the match goes, all three of us have given up, so I don't think there is any reason why you should be troubled further on that score. Although Father does seem to be angry still. As I see it, it is going to be difficult to return to your old relationship for some time to come. And maybe, given the circumstances, it is best that you stay away. But I am still worried about the money we give you every month. Knowing you, I think it would not immediately occur to you to provide for yourself, and I can see only too clearly the difficulties you will be faced with right away; it makes me terribly sorry for you. I am arranging to send you the usual sum, so when you receive it, try to make it last until next month. Some day Father will be in a better humor. I will have your brother put in a word for you. If there is a chance, I will apologize for you too. Until then, it would be best for you to keep your distance as you have been. . . .

Umeko had written much more, but being a woman, she had repeated herself a good deal. Daisuke pulled out the enclosed check and reread the letter from beginning to end. Then he carefully rolled it back and thanked his sister-in-law wordlessly. The hand that had signed "From Umeko" was rather clumsy. The colloquial style* of the body was as Daisuke had recommended to her in the past.

Daisuke gazed intently at the envelope in front of the lamp. His old life had been extended for another month. His sister-in-law's kindness was certainly welcome, but for Daisuke, who sooner or later had to make a fresh start, it was nevertheless poisonous. Still, since he did not intend to begin working for a livelihood until things were settled with Hiraoka, his sister-in-law's timely gift came as precious sustenance to him.

* It was only in the early years of the Meiji Era (1868–1912) that a few writers experimented with the use of the spoken language in their works. Until then, written (literary) and spoken Japanese had been strictly distinguished. The practice of writing as one spoke in informal contexts gradually became popular.

That night too he blew out the lamp before going under the mosquito netting. Kadono had come to draw the outer doors, and he had let him go about it without objecting. Since they were glass, he could still see the sky. It was darker than the night before. Wondering if it had clouded over, he even got up and went to the verandah to look up through the glass toward the eaves. A shiny streak flowed diagonally across the sky. Daisuke lifted the netting again and went in. He could not fall asleep and flapped his fan back and forth.

The situation with his own family did not weigh too heavily on him. As for jobs, he braced himself to accept whatever happened. It was Michiyo's illness, its cause, its outcome, that sorely troubled his mind. He also tried to imagine the various forms his meeting with Hiraoka might take. That agitated his brain more than a little. The message was that Hiraoka would come the next morning around nine o'clock, before it became too hot. Needless to say, Daisuke was not the sort to prepare conventional remarks with which he might open his conversation. What had to be said was clear from the start, and the order in which these things were said would depend on the circumstances. That part, therefore, did not bother him; but he was concerned about making himself understood in as peaceful a manner as possible. That was why he had shunned excessive excitement and hoped fervently for a night of repose. He shut his eyelids with the desire for sound sleep fixed firmly in his mind, but as luck would have it, his head was clear and he found it even more difficult to fall asleep than the previous night. The summer night began to lighten faintly. Unable to withstand it any longer, Daisuke sprang up. Barefoot, he leaped into the garden and passionately trod on the dew. Then he went back to the cane chair on the verandah, where he dozed off while waiting for the sunrise.

When Kadono came to open the doors, rubbing his sleepy eyes, Daisuke came to with a start. Half the earth's surface was already bathed in red sunlight.

"Why Sensei, you sure are early," said a startled Kadono. Daisuke went straight to the bathroom and splashed water on himself. He would not eat any breakfast but had a cup of tea. He looked at the newspaper but barely understood what was written. As he read, the words he had just read swarmed and faded away.

Only the hands of the clock concerned him. There were still over two hours before Hiraoka would arrive. Daisuke wondered how he should pass the time until then. He could not stay still. But whatever he tried failed to absorb him. He wished that he could at least sleep through the two hours and wake up to find Hiraoka before him.

In the end he tried to think of a task for himself. By chance his eyes fell on the envelope from Umeko lying on his desk. That was it, he thought, and forced himself to sit at the desk and compose a letter of thanks to his sister-in-law. He intended to write it with as much care as possible, but when he had put it in the envelope and addressed it, he looked at the clock and found that only fifteen minutes had gone by. Still seated, Daisuke turned uneasy eyes to the sky; he seemed to be mentally searching for something. Suddenly, he got up.

"If Hiraoka comes, tell him I'll be back right away and have him wait," he told Kadono and went out. The sun hit him full in the face with a force that all but toppled him. Daisuke blinked and squinted constantly as he walked. From Ushigomemitsuke he passed through Iidamachi and came out below Kudanzaka, where he went to the secondhand bookstore he had visited the day before and said, "Yesterday, I asked you to come over for some books I didn't want any more, but I've decided to put it off for a while, so . . ." On the way back, it was so hot that he took the streetcar to Iidabashi and went out toward Bishamonmae, across from the wharf.

A ricksha was parked in front of the house. A pair of shoes was neatly arranged in the entranceway. Daisuke knew without being told by Kadono that Hiraoka had come. He wiped the sweat, changed to a freshly washed cotton kimono, and went out to the living room.

"Oh, you've been on an errand," said Hiraoka. He was wearing a suit again and waved his fan as if he were being steamed.

"Thanks for coming in the heat." Daisuke also was forced to turn to formal phrases.

For a few minutes, the two talked about the weather. Daisuke wanted to ask about Michiyo right away. But for some reason, it was difficult for him to come out with it. Eventually, the usual exchanges came to an end. The burden now fell on him who had arranged the meeting.

"I hear that Michiyo-san is ill?"

"Yes. I've had to take two or three days off from the office on account of it. I completely forgot about answering your letter, too."

"That doesn't matter at all, but is Michiyo-san's condition that serious?"

Hiraoka could not give a clear yes or no answer. He explained briefly that while there seemed to be no immediate danger, it was definitely not a light case.

The morning after that hot day when she had stopped to visit Daisuke on her shopping trip to Kagurazaka, Michiyo was helping her husband get ready for work when she suddenly fainted, still holding his tie in her hands. Hiraoka was startled and had put aside his own things to tend to her recovery. Ten minutes later, Michiyo had said that she was all right and asked him to go to work. There was even the shadow of a smile on her lips. She was still lying down, but there seemed to be no particular reason to worry, so he had gone to work, leaving instructions to send for the doctor if she felt unwell or to call him at the office if necessary. That night, he had come home late. Michiyo had already gone to bed, saying she felt unwell. When he asked her how she was, she would not give a clear answer. The next morning when he got up, her color was very poor. Hiraoka, quite surprised, had called the doctor. The doctor had examined Michiyo's heart and knit his brows. The fainting, he had said, was from anemia. He warned that she was suffering from acute nervous exhaustion. After that, Hiraoka had taken off from work. Michiyo herself insisted that she was all right and almost begged him to go to work, but he had not listened. His second night of nursing her, Michiyo had wept and said there was something she had to apologize to him for and told him to go to Daisuke's for an explanation. The first time he heard this, Hiraoka had not believed her words. Thinking that her heart was giving her trouble, he had said yes, yes, just to put her mind at rest. On the third day, the same request was repeated. It was then that Hiraoka had finally recognized some sort of significance to Michiyo's words. And then the same evening, Kadono had come all the way to Koishikawa to get his answer to Daisuke's letter.

"Is there some connection between what you called me over for and what Michiyo was talking about?" Hiraoka looked wonderingly at Daisuke's face.

Hiraoka's words had affected Daisuke deeply, but when he was suddenly confronted with this unforeseen question, he was stopped for an answer. With its unexpectedness and its innocence, Hiraoka's question hit home sharply. Daisuke blushed slightly—an unusual thing for him—and looked down. But when he raised his head again, he had recovered his usual quiet manner, in which there was not a trace of fear.

"There's probably a good deal of connection between what Michiyo-san wants to apologize to you for and what I want to talk to you about. They might even be one and the same thing. I must tell you about it at any cost. I'm going to tell you because I have a duty to tell you, so for the sake of our friendship in the past, I hope you'll consent to letting me fulfill my duty."

"What is this? You're being so formal." Hiraoka's brow acquired an air of seriousness for the first time.

"Well, I would prefer to do without these preliminaries, which make it seem as if I'm making excuses, and talk to you candidly instead, but considering the rather serious nature of the matter, and the fact that it involves social taboos, it would be extremely distressing if you became agitated halfway through. I really would like to have you hear me out to the end. . . ."

"Well, what is it, this thing that you have to tell me about?"

In addition to reflecting intense curiosity, Hiraoka's face was becoming increasingly serious.

"But in return, when I've said everything I have to say, I'll listen quietly to whatever you might have to say about me."

Hiraoka did not say anything. From behind his glasses he fixed wide eyes upon Daisuke. Outside, the sun glared piercingly and even penetrated the verandah, but the two had all but dismissed the heat from their awareness.

Daisuke lowered his voice one pitch. He began to recount in detail the changes his relationship with Michiyo had undergone since the couple's return from Kyoto. Hiraoka listened with his lips tightly shut to Daisuke's every word and every syllable. Daisuke took a little over an hour to tell everything. During that time Hiraoka interrupted him approximately four times to ask exceedingly simple questions.

"And this is roughly the course of it," Daisuke concluded. Hiraoka's only response was a sigh so deep that it sounded like a moan.

Daisuke was enormously pained. "From your position, it must seem that I betrayed you. You must think me an unpardonable friend. There's nothing I can say to that. There's no way I can apologize for what has happened."

"Then you think that what you did was wrong?"

"Of course."

"So you kept on, knowing that it was wrong?" Hiraoka

emphasized. His tone had become rather more urgent than before.

"That's right. That's why I'm ready to accept manfully any punishment you might want to mete out to us. I just gave you the facts as they are to furnish you with material for your sentence."

Hiraoka did not answer. Then he drew his face close to Daisuke and said, "Do you mean to say that you think there is some way in this world of restoring my honor when it's been so disgraced?"

This time it was Daisuke who did not answer.

"The sanctions of the law and of society are of no use to me," continued Hiraoka.

"So you're asking if there's a way to restore your honor just with the parties concerned?"

"That's right."

"If I could make Michiyo-san undergo a complete change of heart, if I made her love you more than twice as much as before, and moreover, if I made her hate me like a monster, then that would be some measure of penance."

"Are you capable of doing that?"

"No," said Daisuke firmly.

"Then in effect you have pushed ahead to this day with something you considered to be wrong and now, still considering it to be wrong, you intend to push it through to the end, isn't that it?"

"It may seem like a contradiction. But it's a contradiction that comes from a situation in which a husband-wife relationship established as an institution of society happens not to coincide with a husband-wife relationship that has emerged as a fact of nature, so there's nothing to be done about it. I apologize to you as Michiyo-san's husband according to the social institution. But as far as my act itself is concerned, I don't feel guilty of a contradiction or of anything else."

"Then," Hiraoka raised his voice slightly. "Then, you are

of the view that my wife and I can't establish a husband-wife relationship that would satisfy the requirements of a social institution, is that right?"

Daisuke turned sympathetic, pitying eyes upon Hiraoka. Hiraoka's rugged brow softened slightly.

"Hiraoka. As far as society is concerned, this is a big scandal that touches upon a man's honor. In order to uphold your rights—even if you don't intentionally try to uphold them, it's only natural that the instinct should be there, and it can't be helped that you should become agitated—but anyway, won't you try to go back to the self you were during our schooldays, before all this happened, and listen to what I have to say once more?"

Hiraoka said nothing. Daisuke also held back for a moment. He took one puff on his cigarette, then without hesitation, said quietly, "You didn't love Michiyo-san."

"Well, but that's . . ."

"That may be none of my business, but I have to say it. Because I think that's probably the answer to all the questions behind this problem."

"Then you don't have any responsibility?"

"I love Michiyo-san."

"Do you have the right to love another man's wife?"

"It can't be helped. Legally, Michiyo-san belongs to you. But she's a human being, not a thing, so no one can own her heart. No one, no matter who, can give orders about the direction or quantity of love. The rights of a husband don't go that far. In fact, it's a husband's duty to keep his wife's love from straying, isn't it?"

"All right, even supposing it's true that I didn't love Michiyo as you might have hoped. . . ." Hiraoka seemed to be struggling to contain himself. Daisuke waited for his words to come to an end.

"You remember about three years ago, don't you?" Hiraoka had changed his approach again.

"Three years ago you and Michiyo-san got married."

"That's right. Do you still remember that time?"

Daisuke's mind suddenly flew back over the space of those three years. The memory of those days shone like a torch whirling in the darkness.

"It was you who said you'd work on my behalf to get Michiyo."

"It was you who confided to me that you wanted to marry her."

"Of course, I haven't forgotten that. I'm grateful for your kindness to this day."

With these words, Hiraoka was lost in thought for a minute.

"We went through Ueno at night and were going down to Yanaka. It had just rained, and the road was bad under Yanaka. We'd started talking in front of the museum, and when we got to the bridge, you wept for me."

Daisuke was silent.

"I've never been so thankful for a friend as I was then. I was so happy that I couldn't sleep at all that night. It was a night when the moon was out, so I stayed up until it disappeared."

"I was happy that night, too," said Daisuke, as if in a dream.

But Hiraoka broke him off sharply. "Why did you weep for me then? Why did you swear that you would help me get Michiyo? If you were going to do something like this, why didn't you just say to me, 'Oh, is that right?' and leave me alone? I don't remember ever having done anything so horrible that would make you take revenge on me like this." Hiraoka's voice trembled.

Beads of perspiration gathered on Daisuke's pale forehead. Then he said imploringly, "Hiraoka, I loved Michiyo-san before you did."

Hiraoka looked on blankly at Daisuke's suffering.

"I was not the person then that I am now. When I heard your story, I thought that even if it meant sacrificing my own future, it was my duty as a friend to try to help you fulfill your wishes. That's where I was wrong. If only my mind had been as ripe as it is now, there might have been another solution, but unfortunately, I was young, and so I was much too scornful of nature. Thinking back to that time, I've been overwhelmed with regret. Not just for myself. I'm regretful for you, too. What I apologize to you for from the bottom of my heart is not so much what's happened now but for my thoughtless chivalry of three years ago. Please, Hiraoka, forgive me. As you can see, nature has taken its revenge on me and I bow my head before you in apology."

Tears fell upon Daisuke's knees. Hiraoka's glasses clouded.

"It's fate, there's nothing we can do about it."

Hiraoka let out a low moan. For a while, the two gazed into each other's faces.

"If you have any thoughts on how to settle this, I'll hear them."

"I'm the one who's apologizing to you. I don't have the right to bring up anything like that. It's only proper that I listen to your thoughts first," said Daisuke.

"I don't have any." Hiraoka clasped his head.

"Then let me speak. Won't you give me Michiyo-san?" Daisuke's tone was determined.

Hiraoka took his hands from his head and let his arms fall like two sticks upon the table. At the same time, he said, "All right, I will." Then, before Daisuke could respond, he repeated, "I will. I'll give her to you, but I can't do it now. Maybe, as you've guessed, I haven't loved Michiyo all that much. But I haven't hated her either. Michiyo is sick now. And it's not a light case. I don't want to hand over a bedridden person to you. If I can't give her to you until she's well, then until that time, I'm her husband, and as her husband, it's my responsibility to nurse her."

"I've apologized to you. Michiyo-san is apologizing to you too. As far as you're concerned, we must be scandalous creatures. Maybe we can never justify ourselves, no matter how much we apologize. But after all, she is sick in bed."

"I know that. You probably think I'm going to take advantage of her being sick and be cruel to her out of spite—but really, even for me, that would be . . ."

Daisuke believed Hiraoka's words. And thanked him inwardly.

Next Hiraoka said, "Given this situation, since I am Michiyo's husband in the eyes of society, I can't associate with you any more. I want you to understand that from this day, I'm breaking all ties with you."

"I suppose it can't be helped," said Daisuke, hanging his head.

"Michiyo's illness, as I've said, isn't light. There's no telling what could happen. I know you must be worried too. But once we've broken ties with each other, there's no choice. Whether I'm there or not, I want you to refrain from entering my house."

"I understand," said Daisuke falteringly. His cheeks grew increasingly pale. Hiraoka rose. "Please stay just another five minutes," pleaded Daisuke. Hiraoka sat down and remained wordless.

"Is there any chance of sudden danger with Michiyo-san's illness?"

"Well."

"Won't you tell me that much?"

"Well, you probably don't have to worry that much."

Hiraoka's answer was pronounced in a dark tone; it seemed as if he were cursing the earth.

"If—if, by any chance, it looks like the worst could happen, then would you let me see her just once? I promise I won't ask anything else. Just that. Please agree to just that much."

Hiraoka's lips were closed; he would not readily give an

answer. Daisuke, with no outlet for his anguish, rubbed his palms together until the grime appeared.

"Well, that'll depend on the circumstances at the time," answered Hiraoka heavily.

"Then from time to time may I send to find out how she is?"

"No, that won't do. You and I don't have any ties any more. If there's to be any exchange with you in future, that'll only be when I hand Michiyo over to you."

Daisuke jumped from his chair as if an electric current had shot through him. "Oh! I know! You're planning just to show me Michiyo-san's dead body. That's terrible! That's cruel!"

Daisuke went around the edge of the table and came up to Hiraoka. With his right hand he grabbed Hiraoka's suit collar and shook him back and forth, saying, "That's terrible, that's terrible."

Hiraoka saw in Daisuke's eyes a crazed, frightening light. He stood up with Daisuke still shaking his shoulders. "Nothing of the sort will happen," he said, and held Daisuke's hand. The two looked at each other with faces that were possessed.

"You've got to calm down," said Hiraoka.

"I am calm," answered Daisuke. The words escaped painfully from between his gasps.

Presently, the reaction to the outburst set in. Like a man who had exhausted the power to support himself, Daisuke sank to his chair. He covered his face with both hands.

Chapter XVII

THAT NIGHT, PAST TEN O'CLOCK,
Daisuke crept out of the house. To a surprised Kadono who
asked, "Where would you be going at this hour, Sensei?" he
had answered vaguely, "Oh, nowhere," and then had gone to
Teramachi. Now that it was hot, the night had only begun. A
stream of people in cotton kimonos passed alongside Daisuke.
To him they appeared only as moving objects. The shops
on either side were brightly lit. Daisuke's eyes were dazzled,
and he turned off to a side street with fewer lights. When he
came out to the edge of the Edogawa River, a dark wind was
blowing just perceptibly, faintly stirring the black leaves of
the cherry trees. Two figures stood on the bridge, looking
down over the railing. He did not run into anyone from Kon-
gōjizaka either. The Iwasakis' high stone wall sealed the narrow hilly road on either side.

The section where Hiraoka lived was even more quiet. No
light glimmered from most of the houses. The wheels of an
empty ricksha coming from the distance rattled and startled
the heart. Daisuke went as far as Hiraoka's wall and stopped.
He drew himself close and tried to look in. Everything was
dark. Above the barred gate, a dim lantern lit the name plate
unsuccessfully. A gecko cast its shadow diagonally on the lantern glass.

Daisuke came here again in the morning. At noon, too, he
roamed the streets of the neighborhood. He thought of catching the maid on her way shopping and asking her about Michiyo's condition. But the maid never came out. There was no

sign of Hiraoka either. Even when he pressed himself to the wall and strained his ears, he could hear no voices. He thought of confronting the doctor and pressing him for details of Michiyo's condition, but nothing that looked like a doctor's ricksha stopped before Hiraoka's gate. After a while, his head, roasted by the powerful sun, began to move like the sea. If he stood still, he felt that he would topple over. If he walked, the earth swayed in enormous waves. Daisuke endured his agony and made his way home, almost crawling. Without eating his dinner, he lay where he had fallen and did not stir. Then the terrible sun sank at last and the night slowly deepened the color of the stars. In the darkness and coolness Daisuke came to life at last. And letting the dew moisten his head, he went once again to the place where Michiyo lay.

Daisuke went back and forth two or three times in front of Michiyo's gate. Every time he got to the lantern, he stopped and strained his ear. He would stand there for five or ten minutes. But he could tell nothing of what was going on inside the house. All was still.

Each time Daisuke came to the lantern, the gecko was still there, its body glued flat upon the glass. Its black shadow, still slanted, never moved.

Each time Daisuke noticed the gecko, he had an unpleasant sensation. Its unmoving form was peculiarly disturbing. His mind fell into the supersititiousness that comes from hyperacuity of the spirit. He imagined that Michiyo was in danger. He imagined that Michiyo was in agony at that very instant. He imagined that Michiyo, out of longing to see him once more, lingered on, unable to die, stealing every breath. Daisuke came to the point where he could no longer restrain himself from hardening his fists and pounding on Hiraoka's gates as if to shatter them. Immediately, he realized that he had not the right to so much as lay a finger on what belonged to Hiraoka. Stricken with fear, he began to run. On the quiet little street, only his footsteps echoed loudly. As he ran, Daisuke became even more fearful. When he finally slowed his steps, his breathing was extremely painful.

At the side of the road were several stone steps. Daisuke sat down upon them half in a daze; he covered his forehead with his hands and became immobile. After a while, he opened his eyes to find a large black gate. From above the gate towering pine trees extended their branches beyond the hedge. Daisuke had been resting at the gateway to a temple.

He got up. He began walking again, stupefied. In a little while, he came once again to Hiraoka's little street. He stood before the lantern as if in a dream. The gecko still cast its shadow in the same spot. Daisuke let escape a deep sigh and finally descended Koishikawa to the south.

That night his head spun ceaselessly in the middle of a vortex as red and hot as fire. Daisuke fought desperately to escape from it. But his head would no longer obey his commands. Like a falling leaf, it spun around and around, unresisting in the wind of flames.

The next day, the burning sun climbed high into the sky. Outside, everything began to reel in the violent light. Daisuke struggled to endure it and finally got up past eight o'clock. No sooner was he up than his eyes were dizzy. He splashed himself with water as usual, then went into the study and cowered.

Kadono came upon this scene to announce a visitor; no sooner had he spoken than he stopped and looked at Daisuke in amazement. It cost Daisuke an enormous effort just to answer. Without asking who it was, he turned his face halfway to Kadono, still supporting it in his hands. Just then the visitor's footsteps sounded on the verandah, and without waiting to be announced, his brother Seigo came in.

"Please, over there." It was all Daisuke could do to motion him to a seat. As soon as he sat down, Seigo took out his fan and fanned so vigorously that it parted his fine linen collar.

The heat must have been uncomfortable for his bulky frame, as his breathing was heavy. "It's so hot," he said.

"I hope that everything is all right at home?" Daisuke's manner was that of an utterly exhausted person.

For a while the two chatted as usual. Needless to say, Daisuke's tone and manner were not what they usually were. But his brother would not ask if anything was the matter. When the conversation came to a pause, Seigo reached in his kimono with the words, "Actually, today I . . ." and brought out a letter.

"Actually, I came because I wanted to ask you a few things," he said, and turning the back of the envelope toward Daisuke, he asked, "Do you know this fellow?" Hiraoka's name and address were written in his hand.

"Yes, I do," Daisuke answered almost mechanically.

"He says he was a classmate of yours; is that true?"

"Yes."

"You know this fellow's wife too?"

"Yes, I do."

His brother picked up his fan again and flapped it two or three times. Then, he leaned forward slightly and dropped his voice. "Is there some sort of connection between you and this fellow's wife?"

From the start Daisuke had had no intention of concealing anything. But when the question was put so simply, he wondered how he could begin to reduce the complicated developments into a yes or no answer, and he could not open his mouth readily. His brother took the letter from the envelope. He rolled it back four or five inches and handed it over to Daisuke with the words, "The fact of the matter is, this person named Hiraoka sent this letter to Father—do you want to read it?" Daisuke took the letter silently and began reading. His brother sat still, gazing intently at Daisuke's forehead.

The letter was written in a small hand. As Daisuke read,

one line after another dangled from his hand. Even when it had grown to nearly two feet, the letter showed no sign of coming to an end. Daisuke's eyes began to see spots. His head was leaden. He thought that even if he had to force himself, he should read on to the end. His whole body was under an indescribable pressure, and the sweat poured from his armpits. When he finally came to the end, he did not even have the heart to re-roll the letter. It lay sprawling across the table.

"Is it true, what he says there?" asked his brother in a low voice.

"It's true," he answered.

Like a man who had received a shock, his brother stopped his fan for an instant. For a while neither of them could speak. Finally, his brother asked, "What on earth made you do such a stupid thing?" His voice was dumbfounded. Daisuke still would not open his mouth.

"You could have married any woman you pleased, if you'd wanted," his brother continued. Daisuke was still silent.

The third time, his brother said, "It's not as if you haven't had your share of dissipations up to now. If you were going to pull a blunder like this, what was the use of giving you all that money?"

By this time, Daisuke lacked the courage to try to explain his position to his brother. Only a little while ago, he had been of exactly the same opinion himself.

"Your sister's been crying," said Seigo.

"Has she?" Daisuke answered as if in a dream.

"Father's angry."

Daisuke did not answer. He only gazed at his brother as if he were looking at some faraway place.

"You've always been a fellow who didn't understand things. But I went along with it until today because I thought that some day, there would come a time when you would understand. But this time, I've finally given up—you really are a fellow who doesn't understand anything at all. There's nothing more dangerous in the world than a person who doesn't understand. You can't feel safe about what he might do, what he's thinking. That might suit you perfectly well, but think about Father's or my position in society. Even you must have some notion of family honor."

His brother's words grazed Daisuke's ear and spilled outside. Throughout his body, all he felt was pain. But he was not so shaken as to suffer pangs of conscience toward his brother. Needless to say, he had not the slightest inclination to go through the motions of putting a plausible face on things in order to gain the sympathy of this worldly brother. In his own mind he was confident that he had taken the path that was right for him. He was content with that. Only Michiyo could understand this contentment. Beyond Michiyo, father, brother, sister-in-law, society, human beings—all were his enemies. They would all surround the two with roaring flames and burn them to death. It was Daisuke's deepest desire to stand in a silent embrace with Michiyo and be consumed as quickly as possible in this wind of flames. He made no reply to his brother. Supporting his heavy head, he sat as motionless as stone.

"Daisuke," his brother called. "I came today on an errand from Father. You haven't come near the house since the other day. Normally, Father would have called you and questioned you himself, but today he said he didn't want to see your face and so he sent me over to find out the truth. And, if you had some explanations to make, I was to hear them; if not, if everything Hiraoka says is based on fact, then this is what Father says to tell you: I will not see Daisuke for the rest of my life. He can go where he pleases, do what he pleases. In exchange, I will not treat him as a child of my own, and he is not to think of me as his father. That's only reasonable. And from what you say, there's not a single falsehood in Hiraoka's letter, so there's no choice. And on top of it, you don't seem to have any regrets, you don't seem penitent at all. So there's no way I can go home and try to plead with Father. All I can do is tell you exactly what Father said and leave. Is that clear? Do you understand what Father is saying?"

"I understand very well," Daisuke answered simply.

"You're a fool," his brother said loudly. Daisuke did not raise his head.

"You're a dunce," his brother said again. "You're never at a loss for words, but now, when it counts, you act as if you're dumb. And you pull tricks behind your father's back that'll ruin his good name. What were you getting educated for all this time?"

His brother took the letter from the table and began rolling it himself. The stationery rustled in the quiet room. Seigo put it back in the envelope and put it away in his kimono.

"I'm going," he said, this time in his normal tone. Daisuke bowed politely. His brother said briefly, "I won't see you any more either," and went to the entranceway.

After his brother had left, Daisuke sat without moving for some time. When Kadono came to clear the tea service, Daisuke suddenly stood and said, "Mr. Kadono, I'm going out to look for a job." Then he immediately put on his cap and flew out into the heat of the day without even taking a parasol.

Daisuke hurried in the heat, almost breaking into a run. The sun shone straight down upon his head. The dry dust covered his bare feet like powdered fire. He felt as if he were being scorched.

As he walked, he repeated to himself, "I'm burning, I'm burning."

When he came to Iidabashi he got on a streetcar. The streetcar began to move straight ahead. Inside the car, Daisuke said, "Oh, it's moving, the world's moving," loudly enough to be heard by those around him. His head began to spin at the same speed as the train. The more it spun, the more flushed it became from the heat. If he could ride like this for half a day, he thought he could be burnt to ashes.

Suddenly, a red mailbox caught his eye. The red color immediately leaped into Daisuke's head and began to spin around and around. An umbrella shop sign had four red umbrellas hanging one on top of the other. The color of these umbrellas also leaped into Daisuke's head and whirled around. At an intersection someone was selling bright red balloons. As the streetcar sharply turned the corner, the balloons followed and leaped into Daisuke's head. A red car carrying parcel post passed close by the streetcar in the opposite direction, and its color was also sucked into Daisuke's head. The tobacco shop curtain was red. A banner announcing a sale was also red. The telephone pole was red. One after another, there were signs painted in red. Finally, the whole world turned red. And with Daisuke's head at the center, it began to spin around and around, breathing tongues of fire. Daisuke decided to go on riding until his head was completely burnt away.

Afterword

BY NORMA MOORE FIELD

SIXTY YEARS HAVE ELAPSED
since the death of Natsume Sōseki. In Japan he continues to be the
towering figure of modern literature, overshadowing such writers
as Kawabata Yasunari, Tanizaki Jun'ichirō, and Mishima Yukio
who have attracted a more enthusiastic following in the West. In
1976, Iwanami Shoten, the distinguished publishing house, came
out with yet another complete edition of Sōseki's works, in seventeen volumes. New Sōseki items continue to turn up, and the discovery of a letter warrants television coverage. A Tokyo department
store is in the process of issuing facsimiles of the first editions, with
original paper and bindings. When the critic Etō Jun announced
that the secret woman in Sōseki's life was his sister-in-law Tose,
the response was sensational and even led to a heated exchange in
the *Asahi Shimbun*, the mass circulation daily for which Sōseki began to write seventy years ago.

Sōseki is one of those rare writers loved and revered in their
own lifetime. Now, six decades after his death, the Japanese public
continues to bestow its affection and esteem upon him. Obviously,
there are important extra-literary dimensions to his stature; he was,
and continues to be, a public figure as much as an artist. How are
we to account for his distinctive status?

Sōseki's life coincided with one of the most dramatic periods in
Japanese history. He was born in 1867, the year before the Meiji
Restoration that marked the downfall of the Tokugawa shogunate.
The Tokugawas had ordered Japanese life for nearly three centu-
ries, primarily through the imposition of a rigid social hierarchy
supported by the twin pillars of neo-Confucianism—loyalty to the
nation and filial piety to the family. It was into this world that Dai-

suke's father, for example, was born, and these are the ideals he professes to have maintained even after the old order had collapsed.

By the middle of the nineteenth century, the image of static harmony which had long characterized the Tokugawa regime hardly fit the reality. The stability and prosperity that the regime had made possible contained the seeds of its own destruction. For instance, the merchants, who by decree were at the bottom of the social order, had been able to acquire power over the decaying warrior class and to lay the foundations for a modern economy. For this and a variety of other reasons, the stage was set for a change of players when Perry arrived with his black ships in 1853. In one of those characteristic twists of Japanese history, the shogun was overthrown for his failure to "expel the barbarians" and the emperor was restored to his ancient position of authority, whereupon his advisers embarked upon a breathtaking course of modernization—that is, Westernization.

On the eve of these events Natsume Kinnosuke (Sōseki was a pen name adopted in his student days) was born as the eighth and last child in a family of well-to-do townsfolk. Although Sōseki's father was a commoner, the family had held for some time a hereditary administrative position that had brought them material comfort and local prestige. With the change in government, however, the Natsume fortunes began to decline steadily. When Sōseki was born, his father was fifty and his mother forty-one. Whether for reasons of economy or of shame at having a child at such advanced ages, Sōseki's parents quickly sent him to nurse with a family that owned and operated a secondhand store. Night after night he lay in a basket in a streetside stall, until one night an older sister spotted him among the dusty household goods and took him home out of pity. Their father was not pleased, and Sōseki was adopted by another couple. The miserable childhood he spent with this pair, who spoiled him materially and tormented him with demands for affection, is vividly recreated in his one explicitly autobiographical novel, *Grass on the Wayside* (*Michikusa*, 1915).

The divorce of his adoptive parents resulted in his return to his own family at the age of nine. For some time he did not know that he had come home to his parents, for they continued to let him believe that they were his grandparents. It was only through the whispered kindness of a maid that Sōseki learned his true parenthood. Despite this unpromising beginning, Sōseki developed a deep and abiding affection for his mother. She died when he was fourteen, however, and over the next few years Sōseki also witnessed the death of several of his siblings. Indeed, he, the unwanted son, soon turned out to be the only source of hope for the family; his brothers were too sickly or too dissipated.

The promising son had no easy time settling upon a course for his future. Sōseki's struggles to find a direction for his life afford a microcosmic view of the conflicting strains in recent Japanese history. The Tokyo of his youth was still rich with the legacy of Edo culture, and Sōseki became a devotee of the vaudeville raconteurs whose language and humor would later enhance his writing. He had access to an even older world in the Chinese art and literature that he came to love in childhood. In the course of his formal schooling, he even entered a private academy where only the Chinese classics were studied. We should bear in mind that this choice was made in a society witnessing the introduction of telephones, trains, baseball, Western-style architecture, milkshakes, and beef-serving restaurants.

By the time he was sixteen, however, Sōseki decided that a training in the Chinese classics would hardly prepare him for the world of the future. He thereupon embarked upon a course designed to lead to the Imperial University. This entailed the serious study of English which, then, as now, was a prerequisite for a successful career. Sōseki even found himself conducting a geometry class in English at a private school where he taught to support himself. After a brief flirtation with the possibility of becoming an architect, he decided to commit himself to English studies, a decision that was to govern his career until his fortieth year, when he became a professional writer.

Two observations should be made about the final stage of Sōseki's formal education. The first is that he was surrounded by young men who were to constitute the next generation of Japanese leaders. Of his many important friendships, the one with Masaoka Shiki should be singled out for its influence on his literary development. It was the consumptive Shiki who was to single-handedly revitalize interest in haiku poetry in an age that had eyes only for the new and Western. Sōseki himself became a gifted practitioner of this verse form, which was to have an important influence on his prose style.

The second observation is that Sōseki was an excellent English student. His studies were far-ranging, and his command of written English, at least, would be the envy of students in English literature departments today, nearly one hundred years later. Nevertheless, when he left the university armed with one of the first bachelor's degrees in English granted in the country, he had serious misgivings about his vocation.

Upon graduation, Sōseki began teaching at the Tokyo Higher Normal School in 1893, the year before the Sino-Japanese War. Unlike his friend Shiki—and almost all his compatriots, for that matter—he was never caught up by the wave of nationalism that swept through the country. He was by temperament disinclined to such emotions and, in any case, was much too preoccupied with his own inner turmoil. This took expression in his resignation from the Tokyo position to become a middle school English teacher in a provincial town far, far from Tokyo, on the island of Shikoku. It was a curious move for a promising young man to make, and it continues to puzzle scholars. He soon left this school for one even further west, the Fifth Higher School in Kumamoto.

His stay at these hinterland schools was, like any other period in Sōseki's life, characterized by multiple activities. First, he became so accomplished a haiku poet that he made a name for himself and began to have his own pupils, some of whom were to become disciples for life. In Kumamoto he began the serious composition of Chinese verse; his poems are considered the finest in modern Japan. He also continued to write and publish such scholarly pieces as a major study of *Tristram Shandy*. From time to time he contributed essays to the school paper on various topics of personal concern, on the duties of a teacher, for example, or the painfulness of decision-making in life. These are formally intimate pieces, serious without being priggish.

During the Kumamoto years Sōseki married Nakane Kyōko, the daughter of a high government official. Although domestic life had its consolations, it added new strains, material as well as emotional, to an already sensitive and tense spirit. Kyōko has not had a good press in Japan, perhaps because her husband's disciples found her insensitive to his needs; but one can readily imagine that the serious, brooding Sōseki, uncertain of his vocation and every other facet of his existence, who still persisted in working himself to the breaking point, was a difficult person to live with. Kyōko was high-strung in her own way and subject to breakdowns, particularly during her many pregnancies (the couple eventually had seven children). After her first pregnancy miscarried, she attempted to commit suicide by plunging into a river near their house in Kumamoto. The incident was hushed up, but an anxious period followed for Sōseki, who never slept without tying his body to Kyōko's with a long cord. The ordeals to which this pair subjected each other and their endurance are something of a marvel to contemplate today.

While Sōseki was still considering giving up teaching altogether, the government ordered him to England for two years to further his English studies. The year was 1900. Sōseki was thirty-three years old, the father of one child with another on the way. Kyōko and her daughter were sent to stay with her family in Tokyo, and Sōseki set sail across the Indian Ocean. The government scholarship, which was a second chance for a man who had deliberately veered from a successful career course, became the occasion of a severe and protracted crisis, one of the milestones of Sōseki's life. When Sōseki left, he did not know where he was to study, or, for that matter, whether he could study literature rather than language. Shortly after his arrival he settled upon the University of London but soon gave up attending classes and began private lessons with W. J. Craig, editor of the *Arden Shakespeare*. These lessons, too, proved unsatisfying and came to an end. Sōseki's life was more solitary than ever.

It is heartrending to picture Sōseki's life in London. He was acutely conscious of being short and pockmarked in a land of tall, handsome men. (His novels consistently contain references to height.) Poor and friendless, though as much by choice as by necessity, he lived in shabby rooms among dreary people. His stipend was such that he frequently skipped meals in order to buy books. Letters from his wife became infrequent and he was left long in suspense about the birth of their second child. (Kyōko was also having a difficult time. The government allowance for dependents was laughably meager, and with her own family on the brink of economic collapse, she could barely keep herself and the children clothed.) Sōseki despaired of achieving anything "for the country"—he was, after all, on a government scholarship—by pursuing English literature. His old doubts that he, a Japanese, could ever truly understand English literature, let alone contribute to its study, came to a head. After a rare visit from a Japanese friend, a chemist, Sōseki decided that only the scientific method, with universally verifiable results, had any validity. He thereupon tried to develop a scientific approach to literature. Deciding that literature books were useless in this endeavor, he packed them in his trunk and began instead to devour works on philosophy, psychology, and the various natural sciences, accumulating notebooks filled with microscopic writing. Not surprisingly, rumors of his madness circulated.

Sōseki returned to Japan in 1903, driven by the need to complete his monumental work on literature and fearful of not having the necessary time and money. He did manage to produce three works to show for his efforts, of which the middle one, the *Theory of Literature* (*Bungakuron*, 1907), is the most significant. These studies are of historical interest, but they will probably be remembered for the confessional quality of the preface to the *Theory*, in which Sōseki reveals the painfulness of his encounter with English literature.

The years following his return were extremely trying. He had two positions, one as a teacher at the First Higher School, one as a lecturer at the Imperial University. He found his teaching duties oppressive and the lectureship particularly troublesome, for he was replacing the popular Lafcadio Hearn. It was a significant appointment, of course: Japan was coming of age when it felt that its own students could teach a foreign literature. Sōseki acquitted himself with distinction and won his own enthusiastic following, especially after a series of Shakespeare lectures. He was still an unhappy, driven man, however, continually harassed by lack of time and money. Perhaps the experiences of this period are sufficient to account for the persistent money concerns in his novels.

During this difficult period Sōseki began to write what was to be his first novel, *I Am a Cat* (*Wagahai wa neko de aru*, 1905), together with smaller pieces drawing upon his London experiences. *Cat* was immensely popular and initiated a flurry of literary activity that culminated in his leaving the university in 1907 to join the staff of the *Asahi Shimbun*, the nation's largest daily. In those days newspapermen occupied a low rung on the social ladder and could hardly be compared with professors at the Imperial University (Sōseki at this time was being considered for a chair). It was, in short, a sensational step.

Sōseki was forty years old at the time, with nine years left to his life. They were a crowded nine years. He completed eight novels and was in the middle of writing his ninth and longest work at the time of his death. He wrote a considerable number of essays, which contain some of the most beautiful prose in Japanese literature. He lectured extensively, offering acute critiques of Japanese civilization as it entered the twentieth century. Some of these lectures, particularly "My Individualism" ("Watakushi no kojin shugi," 1914), continue to be widely anthologized. Although he had retired from formal teaching, he had an ever-growing number of "disciples" about him. He was an active figure on the literary scene and extended generous support to young writers from whom, in turn, he received important stimulation. On Thursdays, which were set aside for his young followers, his house became a major artistic salon.

All these activities—and one must keep in mind the particular pressures of serial writing—took place against a background of deteriorating mental and physical health. Fortunately, his money worries were largely over despite the size of his household, for Sōseki was an immensely popular writer by the time he joined the newspaper. In fact, when *Wild Poppy* (*Gubijinsō*, 1907), was announced as his first serial novel, stores began to sell "Gubijinsō yukata" (cotton summer kimonos) and "Gubijinsō rings." Still, his life continued to be troubled. His constant depressions occasionally brought on severe breakdowns, in one instance forcing him to interrupt his serial writing for months. He also suffered from chronic gastric ulcers. He nearly died of an acute attack in 1910, but miraculously recovered to write his most critically acclaimed novels. He continued to suffer a series of attacks until the final one caused his death in 1916. He was forty-nine years old.

Because Sōseki was such an important public figure—the Meiji intellectual par excellence—whose private torments have become symbols of an entire age, discussions of his works have all too often been reduced to the facts of his life. There is, however, very little raw autobiography in Sōseki's novels; in fact, this is one of the most important distinctions between him and almost all his contemporaries as well as many of his successors. Still, his life undeniably furnished some of the major themes of his art, and a brief glance at this connection may add perspective to a discussion of the novels.

The first, most obvious theme taken from his life is that of abandonment. Many Sōseki characters are literally or figuratively abandoned children, who must therefore grapple with basic questions of identity.

Another important theme is ambivalence, if not outright skepticism, toward modernity and Westernization. Sōseki witnessed the melancholy effect the disruptions of the Restoration had on his family. He was also pulled backward in time by his love for Chinese art and literature. His anguish when it came to choosing a career was really an anguish over whether to cast his lot with the future or to desist from taking part in the "struggle for survival" (a phrase which recurs throughout his writings) altogether. This ambivalence about modernity is also a dimension of the abandonment theme. As Etō suggests in his study, *Sōseki and His Age* (*Sōseki to sono jidai*, Tokyo: Shinchōsha, 1970), his decision to embrace English no doubt reflected Sōseki's fears of being left behind by the future.

Finally, and most importantly, all these concerns are part of the theme of alienation. If there is one characteristic that all Sōseki heroes share, it is a sense of discomfort in the world. They are all anxious outsiders.

In reviewing Natsume Sōseki's career as a novelist, one is impressed by the rapidity with which he made the shift from academic to novelist and by his subsequent progress as a novelist. The first novels and stories, from *I Am a Cat* through *The Miner* (*Kōfu*, 1908), quite naturally show Sōseki experimenting with various styles, structures, and subject matter. There are samples of near-burlesque satire and comedy, Gothic romance, Kafkaesque documentary, haiku, Chinese verse, and prose-paintings. It is in the first trilogy, consisting of *Sanshirō* (1908), *And Then* (*Sorekara*, 1909), and *The Gate* (*Mon*, 1910), that we see the emergence of the mature novelist. In these works his style solidifies; he identifies the questions he wishes to investigate; he chooses the characters he will employ for that investigation.

Before discussing these three works, it may be wise to consider the basis for calling them a trilogy. After *Sanshirō* had appeared in the newspaper, Sōseki explained in an advance notice that he was titling the next work "And Then," first, because *Sanshirō* was about a university student, and the new work would be about what "then" happened; second, because Sanshirō was a simple man, but the new main character would be in a more advanced stage; and finally, because a strange fate was to befall this character, but what "then" followed would not be described. *The Gate*, the last novel in the trilogy, is about what "then" might have followed. Obviously, these are only the most schematic links between the novels. The progression of age and situation of the central characters provides a framework for the complex interaction of Sōseki's lifelong themes. The three novels anticipate and harken back to each other in such a way that a consideration of them as a group becomes valuable.

Sanshirō is the story of a youth, Ogawa Sanshirō, who comes to Tokyo from the provinces to enter the Imperial University. He is a timid, unsophisticated though not insensitive young man, and the new world he encounters is at once exhilarating and frightening. This world becomes populated by characters unknown in his Kumamoto village. There is Hirota, a higher school English teacher who pronounces on everything from art to ethics to the perilous state of Japanese society. Yojirō, a student who lives with Hirota and takes Sanshirō under his wing, is a well-meaning, wheeling-dealing maneuverer. His campaign to win a university appointment for Hirota, whom he has nicknamed the "Great Darkness," constitutes the novel's subplot. Nonomiya is a scientist whose research on the pressure of light has won him a name abroad; in order to continue his successes, he must spend much of his life in his underground "cave." Nonomiya's sister Yoshiko and her beautiful, elusive friend Mineko complete Sanshirō's circle. Sanshirō is bewitched the first time he sees Mineko, and his shadowy, inarticulate pursuit of her provides the principal narrative interest.

Sanshirō is Sōseki's sweetest novel, the culmination of one level of his art before he attempts to climb to another. Here, the bald comedy of his earlier works has been refined into a more subtle humor that adds just the necessary touch of irony to his compassionate treatment of Sanshirō. Because Sanshirō is young and lacking in both internal and external experience, the novel does not have the dark staying power of the later works. Perhaps it will finally be remembered for its series of beautifully wrought scenes which are as eloquent a testimony to Sōseki's artistry as anything else in his work. How can any reader forget Sanshirō's night with a strange woman on his way to Tokyo, when he rolls up the sheet from his half of the bed to make a boundary in the center? Or his hopeless ventures into the library, where he checks out book after book, hoping to find one that no one else has read? The encounters with Mineko ache with suppressed longing, fulfilled only by a brush of the sleeves here, a glance there. Is it not a quintessentially Japanese passion—wordless and almost gestureless—that Sōseki has described in the scene in which a beautifully dressed Mineko appears to Sanshirō in a mirror while his back is turned to her? Or when the two of them, seeking refuge from the rain under a cedar tree, inch closer and closer as the rain falls harder and harder, until they are almost standing shoulder to shoulder?

These are among the scenes that make *Sanshirō* memorable, but there are other dimensions that help lead us to the subsequent works. I have characterized *Sanshirō* as a "sweet" novel, but its sweetness does not preclude shadows. Despite its being a story about youth, the novel begins in late summer and ends with the onset of winter; the recurrent death images are delicate and beautiful, but nonetheless ominous. As his later works will show, for Sōseki, love and death are never far apart.

We must look to the characters of Mineko and Hirota to anticipate the concerns of the next two works and, in addition, to clarify Sanshirō's plight. Mineko is important first of all for the elegiac note she lends to the narrative. If *Sanshirō* is a tale about youth, Mineko represents the dying of youth. The portrait for which she chooses to pose in the attire in which Sanshirō first sees her is the death mask of her youth.

There is a second, more significant function for Mineko. It is she who articulates a central Sōseki theme when she describes herself and Sanshirō as "stray sheep." Mineko is clearly a new type of woman, and this is reason enough to make her stray. In her reaching out to Sanshirō, she is seeking something—something that she had apparently sought in the scientist Nonomiya and failed to find. Her portrayal is incomplete and ambiguous, thus we cannot specify what she is seeking—perhaps simply some form of meaningful communion, some sympathetic understanding of what it means to be an intelligent young woman in a society that tantalizes her with new horizons but will not permit her to explore them. In any case, we cannot miss the punitive quality of her fate, for she is quickly married off to a man whom her less independent, less attractive friend Yoshiko had refused. In Mineko's last words to Sanshirō, she quotes from Psalm 51: "For I acknowledge my transgressions: and my sin is ever before me." Mineko's fate dimly prefigures the sanctions society will impose on the aberrant lovers of *And Then* and *The Gate*.

Hirota, perhaps a more important "stray sheep" in the Sōskei genealogy, will find his way into almost all the subsequent Sōseki novels. Here, in keeping with the overall tone of the novel, he is a bemused, benign spectator-critic, not yet driven by the vanity and hypocrisy surrounding him to the obsessive bitterness of his heirs.

There is a small but important exchange between him and San-shiro toward the end of the novel that sheds light on the origins of the stray sheep as spectator. Hirota recounts a dream of a forest re-union with a beautiful young girl whom he had seen in a funeral procession twenty years before. He has never seen her since; he has also never married. When Sanshiro suggests that he never married because of love for that girl, Hirota laughs at the idea. He then tells an anecdote to explain his skepticism about marriage. The year af-ter he saw the girl, his mother told him on her deathbed that his true father was someone other than the man whom he had always believed was his father. Hirota implies that he was hurt both by his mother's infidelity and by her duplicity.

These two brief sketches are rich in suggestions about the na-ture of the relationship between love and society. One such thought is that an ideal love cannot exist within society; at the same time, it leaves its subject unfit for more mundane attachments. Another is that a deep disillusionment in love, whether filial or romantic, may leave one permanently incapable of serious intercourse with soci-ety. In both cases, the result is alienation.

In contrast to Mineko and Hirota, Sanshiro has little under-standing of himself as a stray sheep. Early in his Tokyo life, he identifies three worlds at his disposal: the world of his mother, which he has left behind but will not jettison altogether because of its comfortable familiarity; the world of learning, represented by Hirota and Nonomiya and the library; and, most exciting of all, the world of action and beautiful women. He thinks that he was meant to play a central role in the last, yet somehow, he cannot find his way in. In fact, he belongs to none of these worlds. He will never be able to go home again, and he is not dedicated enough to occupy the scholar's world. His timidity, if nothing else, bars him forever from the third world. At the end of the novel, we sense that Sanshiro has been touched in some fundamental, unalterable way by his experi-ence with Mineko. We also sense that he is one of those destined to stand wistfully between worlds, never able to step in. What we cannot tell is how much of this he will ever understand. This is what keeps him from being a great Soseki character, and this is why

Mineko and Hirota make better guides to the world of *And Then*, whose hero Daisuke is an acutely self-conscious stray sheep.

And Then opens ominously with a red double camellia falling on the floor. The camellia flower, which drops as a whole rather than petal by petal, was distasteful to samurai because it reminded them of falling heads. Daisuke is introduced to us as a healthy young man neurotically concerned with his physical well-being—so much so, in fact, that he cannot take for granted the life that flows through his body day after day.

It is not just his body, of course, that Daisuke views with detachment; he stands outside every aspect of his life—his family, society at large, and most importantly, his own heart and mind. What is responsible for this state of affairs?

Daisuke himself would probably point to the state of Japan and the world as the principal cause. The novel is set four or five years after the Russo-Japanese War (1904–1905), perhaps the Meiji government's proudest international moment. The Japanese victory was widely taken to mean Japan's coming of age, its right to stand shoulder-to-shoulder with the nations of the West for the first time since the humiliating years of the forced opening. The postwar years were a bombastic, ostentatious period for the nation as a whole, and Daisuke's skepticism and disaffection may be taken as an accurate reflection of his creator's views.

It is not so much the question of Japan's standing in the world that troubles Daisuke and Sōseki but rather the dislocation of values brought on by the breathtaking changes since 1868. Unlike his father, Daisuke recognizes that the hierarchical, well-ordered world of feudal Japan, in which loyalty to one's superiors was the supreme value, fostered tremendous hypocrisy. Modernization swept away the old value structure without creating anything in its stead. Daisuke cannot identify any ideals on which to base his conduct with others, though of course, by the time we meet him, he is probably too sophisticated and too jaded to admit to a desire for such ideals. Still, there is a perceptible vacuum in him, and this vacuum is dangerous, not only for Daisuke but for all Japanese, because industrialization—that is, Westernization—has dazzled the eye with the possibility of hitherto undreamed of material comfort. This is the content of what Daisuke refers to as the conflict between the life appetites and the moral appetites.

These passages of social commentary, pedantically written and awkwardly interpolated, are part of what sustains Sōseki's reputation as a social critic. They are convincing as a partial explanation for Daisuke's disaffection; but in order to truly understand his malaise—and Sōseki's wisdom as an artist—we must go further. Sōseki himself encourages us to do so by saying to Daisuke through Michiyo, "I think you're cheating a little."

Let us look first at Daisuke's relationships with his father, Hiraoka, and Michiyo. In his study, *The Psychological World of Natsume Sōseki* (*Sōseki no shinteki sekai*, Tokyo: Shibundō, 1969) Doi Takeo, the well-known psychoanalyst, emphasizes the gravity of Daisuke's disillusionment with his father. His point is well taken. We are told that Daisuke ceased to have temper outbursts at his father from about the time he graduated from the university. Perhaps this marks the beginning of Daisuke's alienation. Recognizing and accepting one's parent's shabbiness of character is a serious business. Moreover, Daisuke can easily generalize from his father to the society around him, for his father is more the rule than the exception. His brother Seigo differs from him only in being less hypocritical, in claiming no values whatsoever. Such a realization understandably both dampens the desire and impairs the ability to deal earnestly with other human beings, let alone form attachments. Daisuke's case is exacerbated by the position of dependence on his father in which he chooses to remain. Daisuke thinks he is too worldly to be disturbed by the contradiction of allowing himself to be supported by a man whom he respects not at all, and yet, he finds himself disturbed by the contempt he feels for his father.

These circumstances constitute part of the answer to Michiyo's poignant question, "But why did you let me go?" when Daisuke at last declares his love. It is something of a vogue nowadays to posit a homoerotic relationship between Sōseki's characters, perhaps supported by such overtones in the relationships between Sōseki and his disciples. Dr. Doi, in the above work, suggests such an undercurrent between Daisuke and Hiraoka and, as a corollary, reasons that Daisuke could not have truly loved Michiyo; he would never have given her up in that case, not even for the exalted ideal of friendship. The homosexual theory is debatable on two grounds. First, it is hard to imagine that Hiraoka, even before the changes brought on by his downfall, had any deep, enduring appeal for Daisuke. He is too much of a philistine, a member of Daisuke's father's and brother's camp. Secondly, there are many specific suggestions of Daisuke's longing for Michiyo. One example is the quality of his memories of her—the attentiveness with which he has observed and remembered her eyes, her clothing, her hair. We must also remember the subversive gold ring he gave her as a wedding gift. No, Daisuke did love Michiyo at the time he gave her up, but only within the limits of his ability to love. He let Michiyo go because he simply did not have it in him to take the initiative to marry her; moreover, he threw himself into arranging the match with Hiraoka in order to avoid having to confront that vacuum in himself.

In the three years following Hiraoka's and Michiyo's wedding, these circumstances—his ambiguous position with his father, and his (unacknowledged) inability to admit his love for Michiyo—have had a cumulatively debilitating effect. Add to this the more concrete reasons for which society at that time should appear repugnant to a thoughtful, sensitive individual like Daisuke, and it becomes only too natural that he should be neurotically incapable of action.

Yet, having said this, I am still unconvinced that we have truly understood Daisuke. Is it not possible that Daisuke would have been much the same even had he lived in a more sympathetic age and even had his father been warm and admirable? Has Sōseki given us in Daisuke a portrait of the most irredeemable stray sheep, the most radical form of alienation of all—that is, the individual who is burdened with an acute awareness of the impossibility of existence such that nonexistence appears more real and more natural? And, finally, what of the possibility that Daisuke is, after all, just a decadent coward? Let us examine what happens with Michiyo.

Daisuke's declaration of love to Michiyo, with its implications of ostracism by family and society and consequent financial disaster, has usually been read as a redemptive, regenerative act. For one thing, it is beautifully written; the image of the lovers sitting opposite each other, motionless and wordless, has a secure place in the collection of memorable Sōseki scenes. Daisuke himself says that he is in heaven. Michiyo is undeniably a revitalizing force. This is emphasized by the recurrent water imagery, such as the water she drinks from the flower bowl or the rain that brings her to Daisuke's and then shields and isolates the lovers. It is also unquestionable that acknowledging his love has a restorative effect on Daisuke. Still, in what way is Michiyo revitalizing, and to what is Daisuke restored?

Once the blissfulness of declaring himself to Michiyo is past, Daisuke is beset with anxiety over the future. He is worried about money. In his mind he casts an eye over that region of life called work but finds nothing until he comes upon the domain of beggars. Indeed, it is virtually impossible to imagine Daisuke working to stave off starvation. Here the question of cowardice presents itself. Is Daisuke losing his recently earned redemption when he discloses his financial worries to Michiyo, or when he cancels his arrangements with the secondhand bookseller after receiving Umeko's check? It is possible, of course, that Sōseki has taken such pains to present us with an interesting moral coward; still, the work suggests greater richness.

It can be no accident that Daisuke is able to commit himself to a woman with a heart problem, a woman from whom no children will issue, a woman who repeatedly states her readiness to die. In the very act of returning to his original self, Daisuke is embracing death. In fact, he was never seriously interested in existence; that is why he cannot fight for it, unlike his university friend Terao, or Hiraoka, or, for that matter, his father and brother. There are a number of indications (e.g., the flower-scented sleep in which he drowns himself when the "stimuli of the universe" become too much for him) that nonbeing was always attractive to him. Even his obsession with health is the other side of the coin of a fascination with death (evident, for example, in the delicious horror with which he contemplates the execution scene from Andreev). For Daisuke, to be consumed with Michiyo in the flames of society's wrath is indeed an act faithful to his original being.

The end of the novel is unclear; it is unnecessary to specify whether Daisuke goes insane, commits suicide, or is destroyed passively. In any case, it is difficult to postulate a reunion with Michiyo. The ominous signs throughout the book—the surrealistic train rides at night, the earthquake, the motionless gecko above Hiraoka's door—reach a climax in the brutal red imagery of summer, which blindingly reflects the red camellia at the opening.

The contrast between the burning sun with which we leave *And Then* and the lingering warmth of the autumn sun with which *The Gate* begins accurately indicates the distance between the worlds of the two novels. *The Gate* is a quiet tale about Sōsuke and his wife Oyone, who live in a house beneath a cliff. During their student days, Oyone had been with Sōsuke's friend Yasui (as his wife? the novel does not say), but a moment of indescretion drives her and Sōsuke to the edge of society. Rather than support the possibility that Daisuke and Michiyo take up life together after his declaration of love, *The Gate* graphically illustrates the implausibility of that idea. Daisuke could not have endured for one minute Sōsuke and Oyone's existence.

If *Sanshirō* was a novel about youth and *And Then* a novel about troubled adulthood, *The Gate* is a novel about middle age. Sōsuke and Oyone live without any dreams for the future in a shabby house on which the sun rarely shines. To get anywhere from the house, Sōsuke must go through mud. His shoes are old and leaky, just like the roof. He has a loose tooth for which the dentist can do nothing; it will simply fall out one day. He goes each morning to a lowly civil service job that barely pays enough to maintain the couple's patchwork existence. When he comes home at night, he and Oyone share a modest meal and then, if it is warm enough, sit on the dark verandah and talk while watching the stars come out. They are Sōseki's happiest couple, and it is with good reason that this work has often been characterized as idyllic.

The pair have few contacts with the outside world. They feel that they have no claims on anyone, not even the occasional strangers with whom they have impersonal dealings. It is not that they are guilt-ridden by their misdeed, for in fact, they do not feel responsible: fate took them unawares, and they found themselves at the edge of society before they knew it. Although they do not understand very well what happened, they accept their punishment and ask merely to be left alone.

There are two crises in the book. The first comes when Oyone falls acutely ill. She has never been healthy; the strain of trying to deal graciously with Koroku, her husband's brother, who clearly blames her for her brother's and therefore his own downfall, proves to be too much. After this seizure has passed, Oyone discloses to Sōsuke that she visited a fortuneteller after her last unsuccessful pregnancy. He confirmed her suspicion that she would never give birth to a healthy child and attributed it to her having wronged someone.

The second crisis comes when Sōsuke discovers, almost by accident, that Yasui, the friend whom he had betrayed, is to visit Sōsuke's landlord's home. The news is so shaking that he takes ten days off from work to go to a Zen temple. He knows nothing about Zen and has no idea what to expect, but he goes with desperate hopes for a miraculous reordering of his life. Needless to say, the venture is unsuccessful. He is told to consider the nature of his soul before the birth of his parents, but he fails to come up with any thoughts.

Sōsuke returns home looking more spent than when he left. On the surface, however, things are not bad. He manages to hold on to his job through a personnel review and even gets a raise. Still, when his wife happily remarks on the coming spring, he can only think about the next fall.

Sōsuke's and Oyone's flaw is, essentially, lack of self-knowledge. Each is driven to a crisis, each seeks help, and each returns unenlightened. When Sōsuke hears about the fortuneteller episode, he tells Oyone never to go again, that it is foolish to pay money to hear such things. Oyone agrees that she never will, for it is too frightening. When Sōsuke returns from the Zen temple, he wishes he could change his name to lessen the chances of accidental encounter with Yasui. Both he and Oyone want to escape from their past, and, by extension, from themselves. They are stray sheep lost not only to society but to their own souls. The Zen temple episode is crucial in clarifying this theme. The seemingly irrelevant kōan assigned to Sōsuke was in fact directing him to think about a most urgent issue—the essence of his being, indeed, of life; but Sōsuke's unexamined fear blinds him and he does not know that he must look into himself to right his skewed universe.

The question of self-knowledge raised here adds a new dimension to the trilogy as a whole. At the end of *The Gate*, as Sōsuke prepares to leave the temple, he is described as a man fated to stand at the gate, knock, and receive no answer. At the same time, he is not one of those permitted to go through life without seeking the gate. Might this not describe Sanshirō as well? Daisuke, on the other hand, is one who chooses not to seek the gate. Being far more introspective and analytically acute than the other two, he consciously shuns self-knowledge in order to make life tolerable. Yet, in the end, he, too, finds himself at the gate—with the door flying open in his face.

Sōseki is not severe with the patiently cowardly Sōsuke. His compassion is evident in the quiet love, the enduring devotion of the couple that permeates the novel. It is not a love to have satisfied the young Sanshirō, much less Daisuke. It is a love granted to a pair who have lost everything else. Sōsuke and Oyone are, in a sense, dead to society. We might think of this as Sōseki's final comment on love in this trilogy.

In retrospect the trilogy can be seen as a web spun around the points of love, death, self-knowledge, and society. These points are linked to one another in a complex series of relationships that are examined from a different angle in each novel. Sōseki continued to examine these same ideas in his later works—what else is there for the novelist to explore?—but from a darker and darker perspective. His spectator-heroes become increasingly bitter and obsessed with the impossibility of existence until Sensei, the hero of *Kokoro* (the last novel of the second trilogy) has no choice but to commit suicide.

Having let his hero die (and also having reached a technical impasse —the novels of the second trilogy are structurally awkward, as if the framework can no longer bear the weight of the content), Sōseki shifted gears in his next novel, the autobiographical *Grass on the Wayside*. By the time he died, while working on *Light and Darkness* (*Meian*, 1916), he was clearly headed in a new direction. It is regrettable that we cannot know where it pointed.

Even this brief examination of his works should indicate Sōseki's complexity as a writer. Yet, one wonders how much of this complexity is appreciated today. As stated at the beginning of this discussion, Sōseki remains the great master of modern literature in Japan. He is different from other masters of modern literature in that he was a popular writer who touched upon popular concerns in an accessible manner. There are several Sōsekis whom posterity can choose to remember. No doubt, many, perhaps most Japanese readers today read him for his humorous early works, *I Am a Cat* and *Little Master* (*Botchan*, 1906). Others read him for the so-called ethical messages in such works as *Kokoro*. Students of English literature must still find comfort in his struggles to make his English studies meaningful at the same time that they may envy his attainments. Finally, for anyone interested in the development of Japanese culture and society in the modern world, Sōseki will continue to be for some time to come an accurate and penetrating critic. Things have not changed that much between Japan and the West since he wrote, particularly from the Japanese viewpoint.

All of these facets, attesting to the multiplicity of Sōseki's talents and energies, tend to obscure the novelist. Etō Jun's *Natsume Sōseki* (Rev. ed.; Tokyo: Keisō Shobō, 1965) is a milestone in Japanese Sōseki studies in its effort to retrieve the complex human being from the sanctified master and in its sensitivity to the artist. Yet even Etō says that it is Sōseki the representative Meiji intellectual who commands more interest than his works. He finds it regrettable that this is the case with so great a writer but argues that it is inevitable because of the unhappy relationship still existing between the Japanese and the arts. This observation, which reveals more about Etō and the cultural-intellectual state of Japan today than it does about Sōseki, is yet another ironic testimony to the continued validity of Sōseki's socio-cultural concerns. The Japanese are still asking what art is, and if true art is possible in Japan, perhaps in a way similar to the American posing of these questions earlier in the history of the United States. The more Sōseki the "critic of civilization" (Etō's phrase) prospers, the more the artist suffers. One hundred years from now, will the struggling artist who grappled with the perennial questions of the universe, whose answers can be reduced neither to ethical values nor to socio-historical concerns—will that artist be remembered? Will he ever be known abroad?

Selected Bibliography

The following is a list of current translations in English of Natsume Sōseki's works:

Botchan. Translated by Umeji Sasaki. Rutland, Vt.: Charles E. Tuttle, 1967.

————. Translated by Alan Turney. Palo Alto: Kodansha International, 1967.

Grass on the Wayside (Michikusa). Translated by Edwin McClellan. Chicago: University of Chicago Press, 1969.

I Am a Cat (Wagahai wa neko de aru). Translated by Katsue Shibata and Motonari Kai. London: Peter Owen, 1971.

————. Translated by Aiko Itō and Graeme Wilson. Rutland, Vt.: Charles E. Tuttle, 1972. (This is an incomplete translation.)

Kokoro. Translated by Edwin McClellan. Chicago: Henry Regnery Company, 1957.

Light and Darkness (Meian). Translated by V. H. Viglielmo. Honolulu: University of Hawaii Press, 1971.

Mon. Translated by Francis Mathy. London: Peter Owen, 1972.

Sanshirō. Translated by Jay Rubin. Seattle: University of Washington Press, 1977.

Ten Nights of Dream, Hearing Things, the Heredity of Taste (Yume jūya, Koto no sorane, Shumi no iden). Translated by Aiko Itō and Graeme Wilson. Rutland, Vt.: Charles E. Tuttle, 1974.

The Three-Cornered World (Kusamakura). Translated by Alan Turney. London: Peter Owen, 1965.

The Wayfarer (Kōjin). Translated by Beongcheon Yu. Detroit: Wayne State University Press, 1967.

SELECTED BIBLIOGRAPHY }

The following is a small selection of books and articles that may be helpful to the general reader:

Doi, Takeo. *The Psychological World of Natsume Sōseki* (*Sōseki no shinteki sekai*). Translated by William Jefferson Tyler. Cambridge: East Asia Research Center, Harvard University, 1976.

Etō, Jun. "Natsume Sōseki: A Japanese Meiji Intellectual." *American Scholar*, XXXIV (1965), 603–19.

Hibbett, Howard S. "Natsume Sōseki and the Psychological Novel." *Tradition and Modernization in Japanese Culture*. Edited by Donald S. Shively. Princeton: Princeton University Press, 1971.

McClellan, Edwin. *Two Japanese Novelists: Sōseki and Tōson*. Chicago: University of Chicago Press, 1969.

Miyoshi, Masao. *Accomplices of Silence: The Modern Japanese Novel*. Berkeley: University of California Press, 1974.

Ueda, Makoto. *Modern Japanese Literature and the Nature of Literature*. Palo Alto: Stanford University Press, 1976.

Yu, Beongcheon. *Natsume Sōseki*. New York: Twayne Publishers, 1969.